AMONG

IMMORTALS

AMONG THE

IMMORTALS

A NOVEL BY

Paul Lake

STORY LINE PRESS
1994

Published by Story Line Press, Inc., Three Oaks Farm, Brownsville, OR 97327

This publication was made possible thanks in part to the generous support of the Nicholas Roerich Museum, the National Endowment for the Arts, the Andrew W. Mellon Foundation, and our individual contributors.

Lake, Paul, 1951–
    Among the immortals : a novel / by Paul Lake.
        p.   cm.
    ISBN 0-934257-73-6
    1. Shelley, Percy Bysshe, 1792–1822—Manuscripts—Fiction.
2. Authorship—Fiction. 3. Vampires—Fiction. 4. Magic—Fiction.
I. Title.
PS3562.A379A7   1994
813'.54—dc20   94-7686
                                                                          CIP

1

Except for the black leather shaving kit on the sink beside him and the razor in his right hand, everything Derek Hill owned was already loaded in the small panelled van parked thirteen floors below. He'd been so busy packing last night and cleaning the apartment this morning that he'd forgotten to shave and now did it hastily, his hand guiding the blade across patches of white foam, his nerves brittle from lack of sleep.

It was Thursday morning, four days after the murder, and still his throat tightened whenever he thought of it. He'd heard the news on the radio, rising late for a Monday morning class, sunlight pouring through the window beside him, the voice on the radio all the more unnerving for its tone of distant unconcern.

A national broadcast, ironically. The murder had taken place in Professor Watson's office on Sunday night among the sandstone buildings of the quad. Some wire service in San Francisco must have picked up the story overnight from the Palo Alto police, alerted by a local news editor, Derek guessed, after a passing student stumbled onto the scene in Professor Watson's office. By rush hour the next morning the facts made a chilling tableau. Renowned professor of English literature bludgeoned to death in his Stanford office by student; killer apprehended at three a.m. on a street corner in San Jose; murder weapon, an iron jack handle, found bloodied on the campus green.

Derek wiped off the remaining patches of foam with a damp paper towel and studied the strained lines of his face. Brown hair brushed back off his forehead, he could see thin cracks in the glaze of skin over his brow. A single filament of gray hair at the right temple. In two months he'd be thirty. Grief and sleeplessness gave him a new premonition of his faded youth.

Outside, the air was clear and dry, the grass still golden on the surrounding hills in mid-October before the coming of the winter rains. Sunlight glinted cheerily off the windshield of a passing green sedan as he crossed the parking lot and tossed his kit across the van's vinyl front seat, then locked the door, turning toward Hoover Tower and the center of campus. His bike was crammed into the front of the van behind boxes of books, so he had no choice but to walk. With some luck, he thought he might run into some of the usual crowd at lunch at the campus pub. Classes resumed today. He could have one last face-to-face this afternoon and then drive into San Francisco later tonight. Lisa wouldn't be back to her apartment till after supper. There were still things he needed to get straight before he could go.

A week ago—it seemed much longer—Derek sat in Watson's graduate seminar in Gothic literature, exploring the dark side of the Romantic imagination with the cagey old man. With his clipped British baritone and white hair, Watson epitomized the English scholar, sitting among them in his khaki slacks and short-sleeved cotton shirt, his brown weathered face smiling often as he teased out the implications of a difficult passage. Twice, after Watson sprained his ankle, they'd met at his house. His Irish wife, Eileen, served them tea as they sat on the overstuffed chairs of his living room, arguing over books full of dungeons and secret passageways and dark family secrets, books that no one but specialists ever read. The other students began to call him by his first name, Sean, with an ease that eluded Derek, who preferred the more formal mode of address even after they'd warmed to each other. He'd paid for this fall's course out of his own dwindling savings just to spend ten more weeks with the old man. His fellowship had ended in June. He hadn't planned on moving in with Lisa until after Christmas.

It chilled him now to think how often he'd sat at the long mahogany table in the little seminar room in the quad, like Simon or James next to Judas at the Last Supper, unsuspecting. Ron Pruitt, Watson's research assistant, still seemed too bloodless a thing to have housed such a murderous passion.

None of the newspaper accounts Derek had studied since Monday had hinted at a motive. When the police found the body, its skull had been hammered to bloody fragments. Blood stained the books and papers that the two men had read and studied together for two years. Shelves had collapsed, books avalanching in the fury of Pruitt's assault. Maybe additional facts would come out later in the trial. Maybe they'd never come out. Now Derek wanted to talk to someone and hope for . . . what?

Insight, maybe. Or sympathy, if not understanding.

Dodging a whirring bike, Derek stepped across the crowded plaza at Tressider Union. In the outdoor dining area abutting the pub, he spotted a familiar face. He raised his hand, started to open his mouth, but Esther hadn't seen him. He elbowed his way to her table, keeping her profile in view.

The mood of the group was somber. Like earthquake survivors, Derek, Esther, and Kevin waited for the next aftershock to bring down the rubble on their heads. Esther had just dried her eyes with a wadded tissue and looked up now, in a bitterer mood, as Jeff Paxon speculated about the killer's motive.

"Maybe Watson said something to Ron about his dissertation, and he just snapped. You've all heard the horror stories. All that work, then the gentle letdown, the helpful suggestions. Maybe it got to be too much."

Jeff Paxon sat across the wooden picnic table in a patch of shade. He spoke just loud enough to be heard over the lunch-time babble in the outdoor dining area.

"Ron told me it was almost finished," Esther replied. "I heard Sean tell him fine job or something to that effect when he returned his last couple of chapters in June. Ron was downright smug about it. The little bastard."

Esther was in no mood today to be reasonable. Her narrow face was pinched; her nose and small chin, hawk-like, fierce.

"There's just no rhyme or reason. I don't care why he did it. I hope they fry the little prick."

Kevin Grace, sitting next to Derek, exhaled cigarette smoke, waved his hand at a fallen lock of blond hair, affecting disinterest. He was the only one of them who hadn't been taking Watson's course when he was killed.

"Maybe it was a sexual thing," he suggested.

"You think everything is a sexual thing," Esther snorted. "Be serious, for once. Sean had kids older than Ron. The man was a straight arrow, strictly old school."

"I didn't say it was requited. Maybe Ron loved him from afar. We all know he thought Sean was God. Maybe he tipped his hand, Watson freaked, and things got out of hand."

"He used a tire iron," Derek said. "He must have carried it to Watson's office from his car. It was cold blooded. Nothing spontaneous about it.

"It doesn't make sense. What did Ron have to gain? With Watson's recommendation, he could write his own ticket in another few months."

"So when was murder supposed to make sense?" Kevin asked. "Maybe Ron just flipped."

"Right," Esther interjected, "temporary insanity. Maybe they should just expel him from school. Mustn't kill professor, naughty, naughty. Now bring a note from your parents or we'll cancel your library privileges. Ron was as sane as you or me. I hope they hang him by the balls."

Kevin took a long drag on his cigarette and exhaled.

"Don't tell me you didn't notice a change in our little friend this fall. A certain looseness of dress, a certain laxness in matters of personal hygiene? Was that like our anal-retentive friend, Ronald Pruitt, research assistant extraordinaire?"

Kevin narrowed his blue eyes confidentially.

"My sources in San Francisco told me a few weeks ago that Ron was getting into some very strange stuff this summer. I wouldn't normally have said anything—different strokes for different folks, as they say—but under the circumstances . . . ." He waved his cigarette, shrugged.

"So maybe he just went too deep and couldn't come back up for air."

In the silence that followed Kevin's remark, Derek remembered the change that came over Ron in the final days before the murder. At their last class together, Ron had arrived late, wearing a red Stanford sweatshirt and ripped jeans instead of his usual sweater vest and white shirt. The lettering on the sweatshirt had been cut out and restitched so that it made a new word: SNODFART.

"Kevin's right," Derek said. "Ron didn't seem quite himself this fall. Especially toward the end, remember? He was late a couple of times that last week. The guy was a stickler, a nitpicker over details, a—"

"Royal pain in the ass."

"—a pain in the ass, but a good scholar. He got the job done. He was thorough. Prompt. Punctilious."

"A brown-nosing creep. Admit it," Esther challenged, "you couldn't stand him. It was obvious to everybody. You thought he was a suck-up. A toady. A glorified gofer—not like you, a writer and a poet. Ron knew it, too. Maybe it's a good thing you weren't around when he went over the edge."

Derek hid his surprise. "It was that obvious, that I didn't like him?" He wondered if the others had noticed a similar attitude and resented it. He couldn't help it. He wrote poems, they studied them—not quite the same thing.

"Don't worry about it," Esther replied. "You have your endearing qualities, too. Yeah, we noticed." Esther smiled. "I wouldn't worry about Ron, though. He's got bigger fish to fry now. No pun intended."

A breeze drew across their table, rattling the tiny bright leaves in the tree overhead. The scent of eucalyptus mingled with an odor of grease and cooked hamburger meat. Most of the other tables had cleared and Derek could hear the clank of bus carts as student workers and cafeteria employees began their afternoon cleanup. He thought about his rented van in the parking lot across campus.

"What was Watson doing in England?" he asked finally to break the silence.

"The late Romantics, mostly," Kevin replied. "He was at the Bodleian Library, looking at manuscripts for a new book on Byron and Shelley. Ron hinted he'd made some big breakthrough. Then he went somewhere in Italy for some follow-up research. Ron told me last month, before he started going downhill."

"Ron told you that?" Derek was curious again.

"Yeah. That was the last time we talked. If you'll remember, Ron and I were both at Columbia together. We used to be on pretty good terms. Who ever expected this?" Kevin shrugged again, palm up.

"I wonder how much of this the police know?" Derek had a naive faith in the power and wisdom of authorities. The news accounts were vague. Maybe they'd missed key information, leaving questions unanswered, motives unexplored.

"What difference does it make?" Kevin replied. "He confessed. Why all this morbid curiosity?"

Jeff Paxon gave up on his lunch and leaned forward over the table, talking softly as if afraid of being overheard. "I heard a rumor yesterday. I heard Ron's going to plead insanity. They're going to have him evaluated by a psychiatrist. Maybe the guy really is crackers."

"I knew it," Esther snorted. "The fucker'll probably get off easy. What did I tell you?" She sat back, uncrossed her arms. "I'm going home. See you guys tomorrow." She picked up her purse, arranged her books, but didn't get up.

For a moment, they were silent again. Derek told them about his move.

"What about the convention?" Esther asked, still sitting on the edge of the bench.

"I guess I'll see you all there. I've got to read my Keats paper, remember?"

"As if you'd let us forget." Esther grinned. "Seriously, though, what are you going to do next year? Teach?"

"Starve, more likely. I've applied to Berkeley, but I doubt I'll get an assistantship this late for the winter quarter."

"I thought you didn't want a doctorate."

"I don't, especially. But what are the alternatives? I suppose I can play at being a student a little longer, if they'll have me."

Derek hoped he sounded wistful, then indulged in a moment of genuine self-pity. Esther, Jeff, Kevin all had clear paths ahead at Stanford, solid academic jobs a few years down the line. He alone was exiled from Eden, his future uncertain. They were probably already looking at him through drifts of fog.

Still, Derek thought, for a working-class kid from Baltimore, it had been a lovely ride. He remembered his excitement the first time he drove onto campus in his battered green Pinto after a four-day trek across the country. Weary as he was, he felt exhilarated driving down palm-lined University Avenue as the Stanford chapel rose into view like a vision out of *The Arabian Nights*.

Two years ago, he reminded himself, he was teaching tenth-grade English in Dunbar High School, longing for escape.

"Look, I've really gotta go," Esther said. "Good luck, Derek."

Jeff Paxon followed after Esther. Derek stood to go, feet squelching pebbles, but Kevin held his arm with a delicate touch of his hand.

"Wait. I wanted to ask you something. It'll only take a minute.

"It's about Ron," he said. "If you're going to be at Berkeley, I thought you might do something for me."

Kevin lit another cigarette, looked away. A small diamond glittered on his earlobe. His head looked small and fragile under the blond hair.

"I have friends in San Francisco. I hear things. And lately I've been hearing some very disturbing talk on the grapevine. I worry. For my friends, I mean—and for that matter, a little for myself. I've been known to frequent the city night spots on occasion. Not often, but when the spirit moves.

"While you're living there, I thought you might keep an ear to the ground for me. There's a man . . . not an acquaintance of mine . . . I'm not asking you to do anything that would disturb your middle-class sensibility . . . a total stranger. An English-man—or maybe Italian. I only have a first name. Am I being mysterious? It's tied in to our mystery. Because I feel Ron's a victim in this thing, too, whatever the rest of you think. He was not a bad person once. But that's not the point I'm getting at." He drew on his cigarette nervously.

"It's this other man, the Englishman, if that's what he is. Julian. I think he might have inspired some sort of bizarre passion in our friend Ron this summer. Maybe it's all tied in." An embarrassed grin.

"That's all. I hear he lives in Berkeley. That he knows some university types you might bump into while you're there."

"Why don't you tell the police? If you think it's tied in, maybe they'd like to know about it."

"Why?" Kevin asked, "they've got their man. The case is cut and dried. Everybody's happy. Except Ron, of course."

And Mrs. Watson, Derek felt tempted to add, and half of Stanford. Kevin's compassion for Ron Pruitt struck him as a little misplaced.

"He's some sort of Svengali type, this Julian," Kevin added. "If you happen to cross paths, keep your wits about you. Artistic types seem particularly prone to his seductions. I know that beneath that stodgy persona lies a stodgy middle-class soul." Kevin smiled. "Nevertheless, you lucky bastard, you're a poet. I've read your stuff. You're a sort of Middle American Keats. Over-aged, of course. Who can explain it?" Kevin tossed his cigarette, half smoked, into the gravel beneath them.

"So please stop giving me that look. There are more things on heaven and earth, Horatio, than are dreamt of in your philosophy. Just allow me to give you a bit of parting advice. Stop fancying yourself such a rationalist. Whenever you put on that air I feel as if I'm watching a bad actor in a Noel Coward play. Really, Derek, I see you as a sort of noble savage, dancing around a fire in your witch doctor hat and face paint, chanting your poetic nonsense to the moon, all the while thinking you're an anthropologist doing field work for *The National Geographic*. You're a shaman, not a thinker, and the sooner you realize that, the sooner you'll write the great works you're destined for."

Kevin smiled again. "But seriously, take care. And stay in touch. You'll only be forty miles away, even though you're moving to a cooler climate. And don't envy us here. Think of all the boring papers we'll be writing while you're off cavorting with the muse."

2

Even at nine-thirty on a Saturday morning, Washington Square Park was already filled with picnickers, tourists, and street people basking in the early morning sun. Huddled on benches, elderly Chinese and Italian women gabbled loudly in foreign tongues.

Like walking through a picture postcard, Derek thought, entering its football-field length of green. His tennis shoes, wet from the dewy grass, squelched on the macadam footpath. The cool, damp air was laced with the last wisps of morning fog and smelled of coffee from one of the nearby shops. In the shadow of Peter and Paul Cathedral, straight ahead, a white-haired Chinese man in a black robe led a row of elderly women in the slow motion dance of t'ai chi.

Derek steered out of their line of sight and cut the corner of the park to Filbert Street. A block up the hill, past the cable car rails embedded in the street, he reached the apartment. He closed the wrought-iron gate behind him as shouts from upstairs echoed down the stone hollow of their shared entryway. Mrs. Fong was dressing down her youngest daughter again in interspersed phrases of English and Cantonese.

"I don't care what other girl in school do," she shrieked, "you Chinese!" A burst of consonants and clanging vowels. "No, no, no, I tell you one more time, you gonna . . . ." Loud wails, tears. A final sentence in which every other word was English, " . . . respect . . . you listen . . . back home . . . no more . . . I teach you . . . ."

Derek shut the front door, but could still hear it going on through the floor overhead.

Lisa sat at the kitchen table sipping coffee, dressed now in slacks and tennis shoes, almost ready. Her long auburn hair was tousled about her face, her pale skin glowed after the long night's sleep. Derek's heart lifted as she smiled sleepily, bright and cool as a spring dawn.

"Drink, drink," he said. "It's a perfect morning."

"Espresso's not a drink, it's a drug. Give me a minute to let it kick in."

Derek busied himself with straightening a pile of books on the counter that divided the kitchen from their tiny living room, watching Lisa from the corner of his eye. It was more than a night of love-making and ten hours' sleep that had left her so groggy and pale. Two months of law school had taken a toll; the relentless pace, the mindless preoccupation with precedent, the endless recitations of facts, had subtly undermined her self-esteem and dulled her lively intelligence. In the few days since he'd moved in, he found her normal reserves of good humor lower than he'd ever seen them. He was beginning to worry about the way she was driving herself.

Lisa yawned and set down her cup, then pointed to an open carton of books on the table beside her.

"So, what are all these lovelies in the little box?" she asked. "Frankenstein, The Monk, The Mysteries of Udolpho, The Dracula Book of Great Vampire Stories. A regular dirty dozen." She held up the cover of Dracula, a garish print of the famous count in full regalia, black on red.

"Don't mock. They were for the class I was taking with Watson. I thought I'd go ahead and give myself the course. I could use the library while you're in school on days when I'm not writing. We could ride together. Sorry. I haven't finished unpacking yet."

"What about Berkeley?"

"Still no word."

Derek tried to catch a glimpse of her face out of the corner of his eye as he balanced a pile of paperbacks.

"When will you hear about the grant?" Lisa asked.

"Not till January. And anyway, I wouldn't hold my breath on that." Derek slid a handful of books into place as Lisa rose to put her coffee cup in the sink.

"I thought you liked your manuscript this year."

"I do. But the NEA still prefers safe, predictable mediocrity."

"To your aspiring genius."

"Exactly."

They smiled together, but Derek wondered if her interest in his prospects hadn't become a little more solicitous now that he was sharing rent.

"I've still got a little money in the bank," he assured her. "I think I can hold out till the new year. I'll get my money back for the course in a few weeks."

"I wasn't worrying about the money." Lisa's voice was consoling. "I just didn't want you to feel adrift. It must have been an awful shock having Watson killed like that." Slight pause. "Have you applied for any teaching jobs?"

Derek wouldn't blame Lisa if she was a little nervous about his moving in. Though they were practically living together in his apartment at Stanford, Lisa kept up the pretense of staying in her dorm room for the sake of her parents. Still only twenty-three, she had all the rigors of law school ahead of her. Her father, a retired Air Force colonel, liked Derek well enough, but how would he feel about a poet in his daughter's future, Derek wondered. It wouldn't go over real well with the boys at the officers club.

Derek walked to the door. A minute later Lisa was bouncing beside him, swinging her oversized denim purse as they descended the hill toward the park.

With a toss of her head, Lisa shook her hair over her shoulders and gave Derek a glance charged with excitement.

"It feels good to be doing something for myself for a change. I've been living in the city for over two months and the only thing I've done so far is go to supper at the Mexican restaurant around the corner a couple of times. Last time I did anything but school work was when you were up."

"See what a good influence I am." Derek squeezed her shoulder.

The bus stop on Stockton was packed with tourists and Chinese women hauling plastic shopping bags. Buses were supposed to run every seven minutes, but they often came around the corner bunched in groups of three, brakes hissing, after twenty minutes or more.

"Let's walk," Derek suggested. "We'll go through Chinatown, hit Market, then circle back on the cable car and do a little bookstore hopping on Polk."

"You've been studying your map."

"I did a little exploring yesterday while you were in school. Just bull your way through." They shouldered their way past the crowd at the bus stop, then started south through the heart of Chinatown.

Every few feet on the narrow pavement, they stalled where Chinese entrepreneurs had stacked wooden crates on the pavement.

"See what you miss by driving everywhere?" As Derek spoke, an elderly Chinese woman elbowed him in the ribs, jostling toward a shop door. He planted his feet and stood his ground while Lisa drew beside him. "The Chinese don't share our quaint American custom of queuing up. Wait till you try getting on a bus. It's every man for himself."

They walked past a restaurant with ducks hanging upside down in its window; a truck was unloading in the street outside. In the open back of the truck, eviscerated pigs hung upside down from hooks, gaping red between stiff legs.

"Look," Derek said, "America's sweethearts." He pointed to their reflection in a shop window, then stood beside Lisa, posing as if for a catalog. "Think what beautiful children they'll make."

Lisa leaned her weight against Derek's shoulder. At five ten, Derek stood six inches taller. Though he'd gained twenty pounds since the days when he ran track in college, he still looked trim and athletic. The extra weight only gave him some added bulk in the chest, shoulders, and thighs. Lisa's curves set off his sharp angles. She was short-waisted, with large breasts and broad rounded hips, the hourglass look of a fifties' pinup, even disguised by her blouse and loose slacks. His face was sharply angled, the face of a long-distance runner or outfielder. Beside him, Lisa's face was a pale oval.

"See," Derek said. "Joe DiMaggio and Marilyn Monroe."

Lisa elbowed him gently in the ribs, but smiled.

A bus caught up to them from behind, passed, then stopped, hissing. Passengers poured out onto the pavement, bringing sidewalk traffic to a halt.

"Let's go in here," Lisa said, nodding toward a shop with painted dragons on its window. She held Derek's hand tightly while he pressed toward the door, towing her in his wake.

The next shop wasn't for tourists, but a Chinese apothecary, its shelves full of exotic-looking items in bottles and plastic bags. Clusters of black mushrooms, dessicated fish, twiggy looking things. "Bird nests and pickled fetuses," Lisa joked, emerging from the spice-scented interior. "Let's get to the cable car."

At its downtown terminal on Market, they boarded the cable car, then rode it back toward North Beach. Once within a short walk of the string of paperback bookstores on Polk, they hopped to the pavement again.

"I'm starving," Lisa said, enthusiasm dimming. "Let's find a place to eat. My feet hurt."

The sun had passed behind a bank of clouds and the air was cooling quickly, gusting between buildings and down the street. The short-sleeved shirts they'd started out in this morning suddenly felt inadequate. They scuffled down the street arm in arm toward a promising sign at the end of the block.

Bob's Cafe.

"I don't know," Lisa said, "fancy name."

Inside, it was nearly empty. Two middle-aged men in sport shirts sat on stools at the counter. The rest of the restaurant was empty: red vinyl chairs, padded booths, wooden tables. They chose a booth in the middle and signalled the waiter.

"I sent off my manuscript this morning," Derek announced over the menu, "about sixty pages of the stuff I did last year. Didn't realize I'd written so much. I've got enough left over for another book."

"So that's what got you up so early. Where'd you send it?"

"Yale, Wesleyan, Knopf, a couple of other places." Derek tried not to sound hopeful. Sending off poetry to publishers was a pig-in-the-poke, the odds against publication were astronomical.

"Well, good luck."

"Luck's about what it comes down to."

The waiter, a tall black man, arrived at last at their table. He read back their order in a high-pitched, breathy voice. When he returned several minutes later with their sandwiches and coffee, he smiled mysteriously.

"I don't know if I told you already, but *Southwest Review* took three poems right before I moved. A few more publications like that and—" Derek paused. Lisa was looking over his shoulder at someone coming in the door.

Derek turned and saw a young man in his early twenties, wearing a strategically torn tee shirt. His exposed nipples were pierced by small gold-loop earrings that bobbed against his hairless chest.

"Ouch," Lisa whispered, cringing.

Things were beginning to pick up in the little cafe. A minute later, another customer entered. Dressed in black leather from shoes to shiny black cap, he swaggered toward the counter, sat down. When he turned on his stool, silver handcuffs flashed from his belt.

"Joe Friday under cover," Derek whispered. "Just the facts, m'am." Lisa shushed him, stifling a giggle.

The sun shone brightly through the large picture window. A third man entered the cafe, frizzy red hair sticking out from under a blue denim cap. What struck Derek's eye, though, was the man's outfit: denim shirt, pants, vest, and cap were all peppered with gleaming metal studs. The blunt silver heads glistened menacingly. A cat-o'-nine-tails hung from the man's belt, sweeping down to the floor. Each leather strand was studded and tipped by a sharp silver point.

"I thought we were too far up Polk for this sort of thing," Derek muttered.

"Apparently, this is some sort of outpost." Lisa smiled nervously.

"The place looks so innocuous on the outside." Derek glanced at his watch. "It's three-thirty in the afternoon."

They hastily finished their sandwiches and downed their coffee as three more men walked in together. Shaven heads. Muscles bulging under black leather vests. Silver chains dangling from their shoulders like enormous epaulettes.

"Don't worry," Lisa whispered. "To them, we probably look like weirdos."

"Let's go," Derek said.

They gathered their bags, paid their check at the counter, and left through the swinging glass door.

"Welcome to San Francisco, gringo," Lisa said once they reached the sidewalk. "Let's get home."

They hurried through the chilly air toward the bus stop up the hill, clutching each other to stay warm.

3

Seven weeks after that first carefree ramble through the city, Derek sat on the sunny veranda of the Savoy Tivoli, sipping a lukewarm cup of cappuccino and remembering somewhat bitterly their early weeks together in the new apartment, the giddy excitement of discovery on weekend trips. These days, Lisa was rarely home till late. Most weekends found her buried in the University of San Francisco law library while he sat home, reading or watching late movies on television. Last night, she stayed over again at her friend Jo Waniak's apartment a few blocks away from campus, halfway across the city. The two women were in the same study group, shared notes, and grilled each other on legal details before tests and briefs. Spending the night there, Lisa explained, saved the time and trouble of the two-way commute.

Derek squinted through the reflective lenses of his sunglasses as he watched the foot traffic on Grant Street. He'd spent all morning and afternoon finishing a long lyric at his desk. His euphoria had dimmed now to a relaxed concentration on the street before him, the hum of conversation nearby, the tinny clatter of cups and spoons. As he lifted his cup to his mouth, he watched a paunchy white-haired man in baggy gray pants stroll down the block toward the cafe's entrance.

Henry Lombardi.

Derek recognized his face from the cover of his poetry collection at City Lights Books. A holdover from the days of the Beats, Lombardi was something of a minor celebrity among the street people and literary bohemians of North Beach. A self-proclaimed street poet, the old chiseler had no permanent address, Derek gathered, crashing instead with friends and acquaintances until his welcome wore out. No doubt he spent many nights outdoors. The poetry Derek had read, thumbing through the man's book, was raw, predictable stuff, vulgar and mawkish by turns.

A week ago Derek found himself walking behind Lombardi at the edge of Washington Square Park. The man strutted down the pavement like a ham Italian actor, suddenly stopping at an open trash bin when something caught his eye; then he reached in, lifted out a bit of refuse from the top, and tore off the loose white paper in which it was partly wrapped. After inspecting it, he gave a discerning sniff with widened nostrils, took a hearty bite, then swaggered up the slight incline toward the Powell Street Bar with his meal clutched like a prize in his dangling mitt.

Derek watched uncomfortably now as Lombardi selected a chair at the empty table next to his. A stub of cigarette jutted from the poet's mouth as he leaned back to savor the late afternoon sun, waiting for service.

Derek looked away.

Loafing mid-afternoon here on the Savoy veranda in his own green army pants, he might look like a slimmer, younger version of Lombardi. A writing fellow at Stanford yesterday, today unemployed, he thought: a day in the life of an American poet.

Derek rose from his chair, took off his sunglasses, and zipped up his jacket. The air was cooler now in December, damper. He walked back to the apartment into the wind.

At his entrance, he saw that the mail had come while he was out, a thick wad of it, some promising looking.

At the kitchen table, he took a tally of the damage. Three rejection slips, two bills, a short letter from his parents in Maryland, and—almost lost in the clutter near the bottom of the pile— official letterhead stationery: his answer from UC Berkeley.

He read the two short paragraphs with unsteady hands.

Bad news. They'd turned him down for the teaching assistantship, accepted him into the Ph.D. program only provisionally, in a rare bureaucratic move. He'd have to make up deficiencies in his literary studies, the letter said, and pay for his own tuition—an impossibility.

His stomach sank.

He took a deep breath and tossed the letter aside. For a moment he had a vision of himself stalking the streets of San Francisco in baggy pants, Henry Lombardi *redivivus*, sleeves frayed, begging for loose change. Or nearly as horrifying a thought: teaching high school English again to the constant clang of the bell, burnt-out from the daily mismatch between paunchy age and lean-limbed adolescence.

"Christ," he said out loud.

He noticed the small red light flashing on his answering machine. More good news, no doubt.

Derek rewound the tape, played back its message. Lisa's voice. She was staying over again at Jo's, she'd see him tomorrow. Sorry.

Another night alone.

The thought stupefied him. Derek's eyes still hurt from reading most of yesterday and writing all day today. Since moving to the city, he'd finished all of the books for Watson's course and had begun a biography of Byron in anticipation of a winter seminar at Berkeley. He didn't feel like finishing the biography now. To hell with poets and poetry, to hell with school. He'd snack his way through another old movie tonight.

The following evening after Lisa returned from Jo's, Derek waited for a chance to mention his idea. Lisa was in a receptive mood after acing a test in property law that afternoon, so he pushed back from the table and spilled it casually.

"I thought I might drive up to Vacaville tomorrow," he said. "To visit Ron."

He let the thought sink in. Lisa leveled her gaze at him across the table.

"*The* Ron?" A long pause. "You're kidding."

Derek was careful not to betray his enthusiasm.

"I talked to Esther today. They're holding Ron in Vacaville for psychiatric evaluation. I thought I'd borrow your car tomorrow—if you don't mind—and drive up there in the morning after I drop you off at school. I called. They have visiting hours from ten till noon."

Lisa forgot her coffee now. "What makes you think he'll even see you? What's the point?"

"I'm just curious. I want to see if he's crazy or just a devious little murdering bastard."

"Oh, that's all," Lisa said with a derisive grin. "You just want to hear the killer's confession, personally. Seriously, Derek, do you really think he'd want to see you under the circumstances? Have you contacted his lawyer? The guy's still a defendant in a murder case; anything he says to you could be used in his trial. He'd have to be crazy to talk to you. His lawyer would be derelict to even let him think about it. Forget it, it's just not gonna fly."

"So maybe he's crazy enough to see me. I could tell them I'm a friend of his from school. I'll bet no one but his mother has gone to see him. Maybe he's lonely enough to take the chance. I thought I'd just go up there and make myself available. With some luck, he won't even ask his lawyer. I've got nothing better to do." The last sentence was an afterthought; Derek could see now it was a mistake.

"What about job hunting? After all, Berkeley's turned you down. I don't mean to be pushy, but is that really all you've got to do with your time, chase butterflies? And don't give me your line about being a writer and a student of life. It's just morbid curiosity and you know it."

Derek decided to play dirty. "So can I use your car? I'll be back in time to pick you up. That is, if you're coming home tomorrow night."

"Why don't you wait till we go up to Sacramento for Christmas?" Lisa was softening. The ploy had worked.

"I want to go tomorrow. I've got this feeling that he'll see me. In a couple of weeks, everything could be different. Maybe he'll be moved to another facility, who knows?

"Oh, and another thing," Derek added as if the idea had suddenly occurred, "I'd like to borrow that little pocket tape recorder of yours. If you don't need it, of course." He'd already stowed the recorder in his satchel—Lisa hadn't used it since her first week of class.

Lisa's eyes narrowed, the corners of her mouth turned down. "I don't imagine you were planning on informing Ron. You're really getting flaky about this. Nothing he said on the tape would be admitted in court, naturally, so what earthly purpose would it serve?"

"I wasn't planning on letting anyone hear it. I'm not that stupid. I wanted it for myself, in case I want to listen to it again. All right," Derek admitted, "I don't know why the hell I'm doing it. But that son of a bitch beat Professor Watson to death. To *death*—" Derek rode the sudden surge of feeling, tears pooling in his eyes, throat tightening. "I've got to have some idea why it happened."

Lisa eyed him coldly for another second, then smiled conciliation.

"Just don't get caught," she said. "Odds are, you'll just be wasting gas."

Derek walked over to stand behind Lisa's chair.

"Thanks. I won't get loony over this, I promise." Derek gripped Lisa's shoulders and gently began to massage them. He could feel her resistance weaken as her muscles relaxed.

He'd call Vacaville in the morning before they left for school to let them know he was on his way.

4

A fine mist smeared the windshield most of the way from the city to the outskirts of Vallejo, but at the bridge that spanned the little bay there, it thinned and disappeared. The sky brightened, but remained low and ominous. Derek turned off the windshield wipers and the headlights. It felt good to be back in the driver's seat again on open highway, the little red Toyota's speedometer sitting steady at sixty-five. As he hit the mountainous stretch of Interstate 80 that wound toward Vacaville, the hiss of his tires turned to a high-pitched drone on the dry pavement. It wouldn't be long now till he was there.

He left the radio off and drove in silence, thinking ahead to his interview. He wasn't sure what he would say to Ron, even if they gave him the chance. He tried to picture his former classmate's face as he meandered among the green felt-covered hills, but the details in memory leached away.

A little later, Derek began his descent from the foothills. The smell of onions brought him out of his reverie.

Vacaville.

The whole town reeked with the scent for several miles out.

Derek sat up now, alert. In another mile, he spotted the white lettering of his exit sign. State Correctional Facility for the Criminally Insane.

He had a sudden impulse to swerve back into the left-hand lane and drive north to Oregon, Canada, Alaska—or to turn the car around and go back home. He couldn't remember exactly why he was doing this; wondered if he'd have the nerve to brazen his way in. As he drifted toward the exit, right foot poised over the brake pedal, the words from the sign echoed nonsensically in his head: Criminally Insane, Insane, Insane. Such strange words, they seemed, to paint on a road sign, like the name of a town or college or historic site.

Three minutes later, Derek nosed into the lot marked Visitors Parking and climbed stiffly out of the little car, filled again with a sense of the strangeness of what he was doing. He stood on the sidewalk, looking down the prison's uninviting length. Behind those tiny second story windows, psychotics and maniacs dreamed of mayhem and escape. Iron bars or mesh covered every window, the glass of every door. Even the tiny window in the door of the visitor center was reinforced by sturdy iron mesh.

Beyond the door, Derek passed a blue uniformed guard, crossed a short expanse of gray and white tile, and approached the grilled window of the receptionist's counter. The bleached blond behind it asked him what his business was, then slid him a short form through the slot before he answered. Derek ignored her brusque manner and smiled.

"I called earlier this morning, requesting a visit. I'm here to see Ronald Pruitt." The name tripped off his tongue with surprising ease.

"All right," the receptionist said, "but you're still gonna need a pass."

Derek filled out the blanks with a ballpoint pen and handed it back. Then he sat in the front row of the waiting area where the woman had to look at him. Less than ten minutes later, a muscular blond guard with a ring of keys at his belt read Derek's name from a clipboard. When Derek stood, the guard sidled up to his chair and pinned a blue identification tag to the lapel of his corduroy jacket.

"Follow me," the guard said, abruptly turning away.

Without a glance behind, the guard marched out of the waiting area past another guard armed with a holstered .45 into a maze of gray-painted corridors. The hallways were unusually quiet for a prison and smelled of Lysol and disinfectant. Derek could hear the squelching of their shoes on the bare pavement as they passed rows of thick iron doors. After several turns, they stopped at a door labelled simply Room 200. Still silent, the guard unlocked the bolt and stood back. "Here you go," he said, leaning away to let Derek pass.

The room Derek stepped into was long, high-ceilinged, occupied only by a long steel-topped table and an even dozen metal chairs.

From the opposite side of the table, midway down its twenty foot length, Ron Pruitt sat stiffly, looking at him over a low glass partition.

Over his shoulder, Derek heard the guard shuffle from the room and a bolt clank into place.

"I told them you were my new lawyer," said the familiar ghost. A short staccato laugh like a dry cough. "You don't look like a lawyer. It's a good thing you brought the satchel. Did they search you?" Ron laughed again, lungs barking, but Derek didn't feel like joining in.

Derek looked at the face across the table and forced a smile. Ron looked pale and shrunken and sported a week's worth of scraggly beard. A washed-out gray shirt, several sizes too large, hung on his rounded shoulders, and the frames of his round-rimmed glasses were held together at the corner by a strip of black electrical tape. Ron's brown hair was short and stiff with grease. It looked as if it had been plastered back off his forehead with a spatula. A faint odor of paint thinner and rancid meat emanated from his clothes.

"My lawyer would kill me if he knew what I was doing." The prisoner looked across the table as Derek pulled up a chair. Anxiety flickered across his carefully composed mask; for an instant, he looked as if he was afraid Derek might disappear. Then the old arrogance returned.

"You know, I really shouldn't be indulging you like this."

Derek forgot the openings he'd practiced in the car.

"I thought you might want a little company," he began, then corrected himself when he saw the contemptuous sneer to, "I don't know why I'm here, really. Guess I had nothing better to do."

Ron narrowed his eyes. "All right," he answered, "that was only slightly less than honest. But you'll have to be amusing if you want to stay and chat. I'm not just anybody's fool."

Ron looked Derek over, obviously savoring his power to control the interview. When he spoke again, his manner was almost a parody of his classroom demeanor at Stanford.

"So, tell me, Derek, have you read any good books lately? The library here is pathetic. You couldn't imagine."

Derek held his eye, silent, watching.

"Seriously," Ron added more softly with a nervous bodily twitch, "what have you been reading these days?"

Ron tapped his finger on the table. He was clearly starved for talk. Derek decided to play along.

"The books for the course, mostly. All but that godawful thing by Ann Radcliffe, *The Mysteries of Udolpho*. I only made it halfway through. Couldn't stomach the prose."

"Try *The Italian*, it's much better . . . if you're into that Gothic thing. I always preferred the straight Romantic stuff, myself.

Have you got a cigarette? Of course not," Ron shrugged, "you don't smoke." The prisoner looked bored now, eyes glancing over Derek's shoulder to the blank wall. "So what's new at Stanford these days?"

"Jeff Paxon dropped out of the program and went back to Iowa."

Ron gave a contemptuous sniff. "That's no great loss to scholarship. What about that blond fairy friend of yours?"

"Kevin?"

Derek studied his former classmate's face, decided to risk it.

"It's funny you should put it that way. Kevin's theory was that coming out of the closet was what flipped you over the edge."

Ron shifted nervously in his chair, his hand went to his glasses. "If that's your idea of being amusing, this is going to be a very short conversation." He pushed his glasses back on the bridge of his nose with a stiff finger, then the hand fluttered to his shirt pocket and pulled out a half-smoked cigarette and a book of matches. His hands trembled as he lit up and sucked hungrily on the butt.

Watching the smoke curl into the air around him, Ron became less agitated.

Finally, he asked, "What about your Keats paper? Aren't you just giddy with excitement about being on a panel with the big boys at the MLA! Your heart must be fairly aquiver."

A thin whine of envy filtered through the sarcasm and for an instant Derek felt almost sorry for the wreck sitting across from him in his absurd prison uniform. Ron's future had been dashed, too, in those few frenzied minutes in Watson's office.

"I'm afraid it'll be my swan song as a scholar. I'll be glad to get it over with, actually."

"As if you really cared. After all, you're a poet. You shouldn't sully yourself with mere criticism. God, how I envy your all-consuming egotism."

Ron took another long drag on the cigarette. The smoke seemed to mollify him again as he leaned back in his chair.

"It's a hell of a fine piece of criticism, though. I'm glad I showed it to Sean."

Somewhere overhead an iron door clanged into place. For an instant, staring across the long table, Derek felt as if he were back in the seminar room at Stanford. He half expected to turn and see Professor Watson sitting at the end of the table; hear him cut in with a short laugh and a carefully aimed *bon mot*. The clang of the door brought Derek back to the present and the terrible absence that hovered about that casually uttered name.

A milder shock was the news that Ron had read his "Lamia" paper first. Derek still remembered the afternoon when Watson handed back the essay after class, saying simply, "You should do something with this." Meaning publish it. Watson suggested submitting it to the special session at the upcoming convention, congratulating Derek later with a proprietary nod on being told the news of its acceptance.

"Well, look at you. You're actually surprised!" Ron seized on Derek's discomposure. "What did you think—that Sean spent time pouring over the eager critical efforts of every semi-literate that stumbled into his classroom? The man taught at Oxford once.

"I graded his student papers," Ron finished with a note of pride. "Jesus, you're naive."

He grew more animated now that he was talking of classroom politics. A bit of color returned to his cheeks.

"That essay of yours was really first-rate work, though. Well written, too. Not many people understand how that over-rated little schoolboy poet had it in him to write such a nasty attack on normal sexual relations between men and women. But I suppose being a poet yourself gave you an advantage."

Ron snuffled to himself. "You displayed real insight there. But you stopped short of identifying the essential vampirism of the man's work. Did you know that one definition of lamia is vampire?

"Of course you wouldn't," Ron continued. "Too close to home.

Look it up when you get home."

Ron was warming up now. His voice grew more distant as he fell into his classroom manner of old.

"The lamia in Keats's poem was a composite figure, of course, as you so tellingly remarked in your essay: half the inaccessible Miss Fanny Brawne and half dear old Mum, wasting away with consumption. But did you ever wonder that those beloved family members tended by little Johnny Keats so self-effacingly wasted into pale gray corpses, every one? We naturally assume it was consumption." Ron took a quick drag and grinned.

"There's an interesting book by a scholar named Montague Summers on the subject of vampirism you might want to take a look at. Very revealing. You'll be amused to know that Summers was also quite a serious scholar, when he wasn't documenting cases of vampires and witches with his usual pedantic thoroughness. He wrote one of the classic studies of the Romantic novel, in fact, *The Gothic Quest.* Anyway, in that little vampire book I've forgotten the title of, he records instances of what he calls 'the psychic sponge,' a mild sort of vampire that absorbs the spiritual and mental energy of those around him till they're quite wrung dry. Sucks the life-force right out of them.

"That's Keats, exactly," he said with a decisive wave of the hand. "It was all that negative capability knocking around inside him, sucking the juice out of everyone near him like a little black hole. There's your poet for you: a psychic sponge. When I think how I almost spent my whole career breathing life into their pathetic little scrawlings, I feel a bit sick.

"But of course none of this is news to you," Ron continued, eyeing Derek with a contemptuous curl of his lip. "You're probably converting me into subject matter even as we speak. You'll probably get a sonnet out of it—isn't that what you say?—when you get home tonight. I'll be embalmed in iambic pentameter for future ages." He eyed Derek fiercely.

"Why don't you just get the fuck out of here now? I've had enough of you blood-sucking prima donnas to last me a lifetime."

Ron's voice quivered. He clenched his jaws and took a deep breath through his nose. Then he continued, though a small quaver disturbed the even timbre of his voice. He wasn't quite ready to let Derek go.

"Keats wasn't the worst of them, either. Fuck no. He was only a schoolboy compared to the others. It takes real ambition to make the final grade, and the little five foot wonder never even got the chance. Why? He was too busy pimping his talent trying to write a commercially successful play. His admirers like to forget that little *Otho* episode. Little John Boy was no ethereal spirit, too refined and selfless for this ugly world, as the vulgar believe. Take a look at that nasty little passage he wrote to Fanny Brawne, his own true love—in a letter, as I recall.

"Here, I think I've got it by heart now." Pruitt looked over Derek's head into nothingness, then recited the lines tonelessly, like an old recording.

> This living hand, now warm and capable
> Of earnest grasping, would, if it were cold
> And in the icy silence of the tomb,
> So haunt thy days and chill thy dreaming nights
> That thou wouldst wish thine own heart dry of blood
> So in my veins red life might stream again,
> And thou be conscience-calm'd—see here it is—
> I hold it toward you.

"Now there," Ron finished, leaning back in his chair, "isn't that a charming sentiment to include in a love letter?"

It was obvious what Ron was up to: He was trying out his insanity defense. There was no forgiving such cynical wickedness.

"You don't expect me to believe in vampires, do you, Ron? Come on, I had that stuff figured out when I was ten years old. I was a horror movie fan when I was a kid. If vampires could do what the legends said, there wouldn't be a living soul left on earth in five years. They'd increase exponentially till there was nobody left to feed on."

Derek saw Ron rise to the bait. Placing his skinny elbows on the edge of the table, the prisoner eyed him wickedly.

"You're such a petty little vulgarian. Movies, Hollywood. And you're supposed to be a poet. Use your fucking imagination. Who do you think was the father of them all—Count Dracula's daddy?" Ron glared across the table, waiting for a reply. With those eyes magnified to bull's-eyes, he did look a little deranged.

"I give up," Derek said. "Who?"

"Lord Byron. If you were even half the student of literature you think you are, you'd have figured that out."

Suddenly Ron faltered, eyes dropping to the table top. "Well, maybe not. It took me a while to get it right. It's all there in the standard biographies, though.

"I guess we just can't fathom what a mind like that is capable of. The pity is—or maybe the justice of it is—that the poor bastard never even pulled it off. He waited too long. That was Sean's theory."

Ron looked up, his gray eyes beaming malice.

"You know, Derek, you should really give some thought to your own future. I've seen a little of your work. Very impressive. I mean that sincerely. You're good. Your reputation will eventually catch up. Think of the advantages you'd have being one of the undead—later, of course, when your talent and life-force were all used up in pursuit of the muse.

"True poets, the really great ones, have the souls of world conquerors—that's the source of their strength. The purest, most complete egotism humanly imaginable. It's no coincidence that the only living vampire is one of our immortal bards. You might have the luck to cross paths with him. Who knows, he might give you the chance to become one of the immortals of literature. Literally."

Ron laughed again. Then he saw that he was being studied and drew back.

"So just what the fuck do you think you're doing here, anyway, feeding off my misery, you bloodsucking bastard. I ought to turn you in for impersonating an attorney."

Derek took a slow breath and eyed the prisoner coldly.

"I thought you might tell me why you did it," he said softly. "Why'd you kill him, Ron?"

Ron's face went pale. He looked as if he'd just been dashed by a bucket of ice water. It took him several seconds to gain enough self-control to speak.

"All right," he said finally, eyebrow twitching. "You're a slick one. What did you think—that I'd break down? I've already done my mourning." Ron pushed his glasses back with a quick jab.

"What the hell would you understand, with your pious little poet's soul? I was overmastered. And now the bastard's letting me rot away in here. Maybe he thinks that's punishment enough. It'd be just like him. But that's where the son of a bitch miscalculated. Because the spell's had time to wear off. So you see, he's not invincible, after all." A tormented smile broke across Ron's face, like a winter dawn. "He assumes I burned the letters."

A dry coughing laugh. "Can you believe it—the son of a bitch wants to keep his precious reputation intact. He wants future ages to look into that Caliban face of his and see Ariel, the blithe spirit of his own self-created legend.

"It's funny, isn't it," he continued more soberly. "I could murder Sean, but I couldn't burn those goddamn precious letters. As far gone as I was, I kept them out of harm's way. So maybe I've got no right to criticize you."

The prisoner looked across the little partition, his face bloodless and soft now, like the skin under a bandage. The effort of speech seemed to have wrung him dry.

"Goodbye, Derek," he said in a voice drained of human concern. "The show's over. Now go on home."

Ron leaned forward, put his head down on the table, and covered it quietly with his arms. The hiss of his breathing deepened, then continued mechanically, like a small bellows. Derek concluded that their conversation was over.

He summoned the guard with a loud knock; then when the door opened, he padded quietly from the room.

The instant before it slammed shut, he thought he heard a muffled sob behind him.

5

"Ron may be mad as a hatter," Derek said, "but there's at least a little method in his madness. I've been doing some reading the last few days."

He was walking next to Lisa up Filbert toward the Art Institute, leaning into the steep incline, breathing heavily. She was a half step back, arms folded to conserve body heat. Wearing only a nylon windbreaker over her blouse, she was underdressed now that the wind had picked up, blowing damp and cold off the bay. They were high enough up the hill to see the light flashing from its tower on Alcatraz through the evening mist.

"This poetry reading better be good."

"I didn't say the guy was good." Derek grinned. "I said he was more interesting than most."

"High praise from you. I expect to be transported on the wings of poesy."

They were on their way to hear Simon Macbeth, a sixtyish survivor of Black Mountain College, reading poems from his recently published book in the Institute's little theater. It was Macbeth's first volume in seventeen years and perhaps his last. The poet gave few readings even here in the Bay Area, where he'd lived for thirty years, and was rumored now to be in ill health.

"So what was the method in his madness?" Lisa asked. "You were talking about Ron Pruitt."

"The stuff about Byron. Ron called him Dracula's daddy. I thought he was being literal at the time, just crazy.

"Turns out, Lord Byron really was the father of all vampires—in English literature, at least. That night when he and Percy and Mary Shelley were at Lake Geneva telling ghost stories to each other—the night Mary dreamed up *Frankenstein*—Byron started to tell a story about a vampire, but never finished it. A guy named Polidori, who was Byron's doctor and travelling companion of the moment, later finished the story and published it anonymously in England under the title *The Vampyre*. The funny thing was, everybody thought the story was written by Byron. In effect, it was the first real vampire story in English."

Derek flashed a suggestive smile.

"Other writers imitated the book until a guy named Le Fanu wrote a story called *Camilla*, about a woman vampire—with very heavy lesbian overtones. Very sexy. Bram Stoker read it and loved it. Stoker was the author of *Dracula*; so you can trace the literary lineage of the blood-sucking Count right back to Lord Byron himself. Polidori even modelled his vampire after Byron, so all the sexy, melancholic vampires that followed were drawn from him, right down to George Hamilton in *Love at First Bite*."

"The Vampire as Byronic Hero," Lisa said. "Makes me almost nostalgic for writing term papers again."

"It's never too late to switch back."

"I said almost."

They were higher up now, walking past Lombard, "the crookedest street in the world." Even at this hour, a blond woman stood at the bottom of the hill, aiming a video camera at the blue Oldsmobile snaking down its preposterous curves with her husband and two children whooping inside.

"I can see where Ron got the idea," Derek added. "If you get yourself in a certain frame of mind, some things in Byron's life make a strange kind of sense when you look at them that way."

"Like what, for instance?" Lisa grinned. "You're getting weird. I think it's time you did something on your extended vacation besides read and write. It's not healthy."

"As if you were some kind of social butterfly. You haven't done anything but school work in months."

"Yes, but I'm in class. With other people. Humans."

"All right, counselor. May I proceed?" Derek caught his wind. Talking while marching along Russian Hill counted as vigorous aerobic exercise.

"In an appendix to one of the Byron biographies I've been looking at, there was an account by an English guy named Houldsworth called, 'The Opening of Lord Byron's Vault.' Apparently, a bunch of people decided they wanted to see the body of the great poet. There were about forty people present when they opened it, but only two or three actually went down into the vault.

"When they opened Byron's coffin, they discovered that his body was extremely well preserved. No decomposition had taken place: that's an exact quote. Byron died in 1824. I thought it was pretty remarkable that fourteen years later, in 1838, they could still comment on how well the old boy's body had been preserved. And then I looked again at the date when they re-opened the coffin. Not 1838, 1938! A hundred and fourteen years later and they were still commenting on how well his famous pecker had held up.

"And his heart and brains," Derek added with an insinuating leer, "were kept in a separate casket. Two ways to put a vampire's soul to rest, according to legend, are to decapitate him and cut out his heart."

Lisa eyed him skeptically.

"They'd performed some kind of crude autopsy on his body back in Greece after he died.

"Still," Derek added, putting on a Boris Karloff accent, "it's all raaaather ghoulish the way they butchered Europe's most famous poet, wouldn't you say?"

"Clearly, the guy was a vampire," Lisa deadpanned. "Excellent work, Holmes."

"Elementary, my dear.

"We're almost there," Derek added, pulling Lisa along now.

"This is Chestnut."

They walked a half block down the hill to the large door of the Institute, entered, then passed through an inner courtyard with a small decorative pool full of lily pads and goldfish. They continued up a ramp to the top floor, where the auditorium was located. Inside, they found a seat halfway up the incline that circled the little stage and its wooden podium. The auditorium was filling quickly: art students, literary bohemians of various stripes, and a few intrepid professors of modern poetry from the local colleges settled into noisy, competing factions. Spectators craned their necks to see who else was there. In the insular world of American poetry, the night was beginning to shape up as an event of some proportions.

The feeling of excited expectancy increased when Edward Houston, a professor of modern literature at Berkeley, rose to introduce the poet. Houston was himself imposing at six feet seven inches in height. Nearly 300 pounds hung on his large, stooped frame. His medium-length gray beard gaped as he rolled off superlatives about Macbeth's poetry in a rumbling voice-of-God bass. The professor drew parallels between his friend's work and that of Dante, Shelley, Wordsworth. At one point, he suggested that Macbeth's achievement might fittingly be compared to that of William Butler Yeats.

After finishing his introduction, the professor slouched toward his chair and was replaced behind the podium by the slight, gray-haired poet. Enthusiastic applause rocked the auditorium as Macbeth nodded toward the audience.

"I'm going to read this first poem from my new book, *In Apollo's Gym*," the poet announced, gazing over the heads of the crowd, "for my dear companion Linden. Lindy is designing the stage set for the San Francisco Ballet's production of this poem-in-progress I've been composing now for thirty-five years, using all organic fabrics and dyes, and Michael Plover has written a score for zither and xylophone which captures the ethereal spirituality of the work, I think, beautifully."

He continued in the same vein for five more minutes before

reading his first poem, "Minerva's Slippers." Then he introduced his next poem with five more minutes of chat. The topics ranged from Lindy's latest recurring dream to Egyptian cat mythology, from Celtic body painting to the etymology of the Greek word for harmony. The talk served as a bridge between poems, which explored the same subjects, but at greater length, with some additional references to Greek and early Christian mythology added to provide the mythic force noted so often by Houston and other critics. The savior-hero that emerged from the poet's delving into the Christological myth, Derek concluded after hearing several more poems, resembled Jesus of Nazareth rather less than he did Simon Macbeth himself.

After the warm reception of the first poems, Macbeth then read several pages from his diary, told anecdotes about his childhood in Indiana, and gave a brief review of the movie *Gone with the Wind,* describing the apocalyptic dimensions of several of its scenes from a Jungian perspective before reading his famous anti-war poem, "Nixon's Sin Against the Holy Spirit, or, Parzival's Fear of the Yellow Knight." He finished his reading with a recently composed song cycle, which he sang a cappella to tunes of the moment's inspiration in a quavering, bird-like falsetto. When he finished, bowing shyly at the crowd, he received a standing ovation.

"Let's get out of here," Derek growled. "I need some air."

Back outside, they maneuvered through the departing crowd on the sidewalk then descended the steep hill to the park. Crossing the park, they stopped at the Cigar Store, a coffee shop dating back to the days of the Beats.

The little room was crowded and dense with smoke. They selected a table next to the wall beneath a large black and white photograph. The picture dated from over thirty years ago; Derek recognized the faces of Gregory Corso and Lawrence Ferlinghetti among the dozen long-haired men and women captured laughing over drinks.

The coffee was lukewarm when it finally arrived at their table.

"That was the worst reading we've been to since hearing Merwin at that church in the Heights. You've really been picking them lately."

"Come on, now, Ginsberg was fun."

"Macbeth's book jacket compared him to Dante; so did that professor. I feel as if I've been through purgatory." Lisa sighed into her cup.

"They must have meant Dante Gabriel Rossetti. The guy's a latter-day Pre-Raphaelite. All that Romantic horseshit—angels and noble savages and Greek mythology—it's as if the twentieth century never happened. The only times he mentioned anything more recent than horse and buggy days was when he was comparing some president to Hitler or Attila the Hun. Nixon was no saint, but he wasn't Hitler, either. Sometimes I hate admitting I write the stuff."

Derek looked past Lisa and spied a man from the reading at a nearby table. He was easy to spot: tall and lean, with a day's growth of beard, he was dressed entirely in brown leather and sported a matching leather cap. His vacant gray eyes appeared to be fixed on Derek.

Derek had seen the stranger on a bus the day before on his way home from the USF library and again later at a coffee shop when he stopped for lunch. In a city of over a half million, it seemed more than a coincidence. Derek decided to keep an eye on the stranger.

"Why don't you give a reading?" Lisa suggested. "You've got more than enough work."

"I've tried, actually," Derek replied. "I'm afraid I don't belong to the right circles." He leaned back in his chair.

"You wouldn't believe the stuff that goes on here. I went to a reading at Cody's Bookstore in Berkeley a while back, and this guy was standing in front of the audience pulling the string of a children's toy—the kind that talks when you let go of the cord. The toy was saying stuff like, 'Bee, buzz buzz; Cricket, chireep, chireep' in this eerie little mechanical voice.

"After about a half dozen noises, the guy put the toy down and started saying them himself—buzz buzz chireep chireep click

click—for like five minutes. When he finished, everybody clapped like he'd just done the cleverest thing in the world."

Derek spied the stranger watching them again over the rim of his cup. The man wasn't even being subtle about it, barely shifting his gaze when Derek looked his way. The eyes looked hard and cold as ball bearings.

As soon as Derek turned, he could feel their cold scrutiny bearing down again.

"There's a house around the corner from us that sponsors a weekly reading series. I left my chapbook with the woman who runs the place right after I moved up here. I went back two days ago to see why they hadn't gotten in touch with me and caught them in the middle of a meeting. The woman was polite but said the committee hadn't responded well enough to my poetry to give me a date. I could hear them arguing in the other room over future readers. This affected little twerp was saying, 'We have to have a lesbian feminist, does anybody know a good lesbian feminist?'

"They were starting with the goddamn categories—lesbian feminist, neo-Beat, save-the-ozone layer, Hispanic surrealist—then filling in the blanks with names. The actual poetry was the last thing they cared about. They had quotas to fill. If I want to read in this city, I'm going to have to join the street poets down at the Gold Rush Bar on open reading night. Maybe I can share a sandwich with Henry Lombardi."

Derek pushed back from the table.

"Why don't we get the hell out of here? There's a guy behind you that's been staring at us ever since we walked in. Don't turn around. Let's just pay our bill and leave before I get too wound up to get to sleep."

Back in the apartment, Lisa shed her windbreaker and blouse and, now barefoot, was standing in the kitchen in bra and slacks with a glass of milk in one hand, a large chocolate cookie in the other.

"What's with all of this leather?" Derek asked. "Everywhere I go, I see these weird little secret signs: colored handkerchiefs sticking out of back pockets, earrings, leather clothes, whips and handcuffs, strange hats—like some kind of private code. Is there a handbook or something that tells what they all mean? Everybody seems to know the language but me."

"You'll get used to it," Lisa counselled. "I think they call those leather hats Master Caps, but I'm not sure. It's some kind of S&M thing, I suppose."

"And what was that guy staring at?" Derek hesitated for a second, then added, "I think he's been following me for the last couple of days."

"Maybe he likes you."

"Very funny. I'm being serious."

"You sound just a wee bit paranoid, wouldn't you say? Why would he want to follow you?"

Derek decided to drop the subject. He walked to the couch when Lisa vanished into the bedroom to finish undressing. He flipped on the television to the local news and settled down to watch but didn't really pay attention until a continuing story he'd been following caught his interest.

A TV reporter was interviewing a slender young man in a sports shirt. The ostensible subject of the interview was property rights and invasion of privacy. Three days ago, a fire had burned down a whole block of the Castro district, the gay city within a city. The young man was complaining now of teen-aged looters who were invading the block.

By news standards, the fire was already ancient history. The invasion of teenagers wouldn't normally have warranted such extended coverage, but the booty turned up by the vandals had a salacious quality irresistible to any news director. In the rubble of homes and nightclubs, the looters were discovering all sorts of sexual paraphernalia: chains, whips, leather restraints and masks, pornographic photographs and video-tapes, sexual aids, medieval instruments of torture. All the stock and trade of a sexual underground.

The young man denounced the looters' depredations. The reporter nodded sympathetically while milking the interview for all it was worth.

Derek grinned at this latest sign of hypocrisy. Like everyone else who moved to the city, he'd grown used to the disproportionately large number of homosexuals living here, the electric air of sexuality which hung over the city like morning fog. Sometimes, though, when he read of such excesses as the Glory Holes, he still felt a twinge of unease. Once by mistake, he'd gotten off the bus in the Castro by himself. He joked about it afterward with Lisa, mimicking imaginary tourists ogling him, but his reaction to the experience still provoked a small pang of guilt.

"I'm finished. You can jump in the shower now." Lisa was beside him, wrapped in a damp towel, hair swathed by a turban.

Derek turned from the set and walked to the bathroom. Once under the shower's pummelling stream, he forgot the poetry reading, the intrusive stare of the stranger, lost in the soothing sensations of water and heat. As he soaped up his chest, he saw Lisa's blurred silhouette through the stall's rippled glass door.

He smiled to himself. The coffee had jangled his nerves. A little friendly slap and tickle would be just the thing.

The door rolled back on its track with a rumble.

Through the swirling steam, Derek saw he was wrong about Lisa's motive. She was still wrapped in towels; her face looked pale and grave.

"Something on the news," she said. "I thought you'd better hear. Ron Pruitt killed himself in his cell in Vacaville. They just announced it."

Her words failed to register for a minute, then their dark weight descended on him. Derek felt sick. He could still see his former classmate's face contorted by guilt and contrition as he spoke of Watson's murder.

"How did he do it? He wasn't even wearing a belt when I saw him."

Lisa hesitated. Her eyes darted nervously away.

"He bled to death. He . . . they said he must have chewed through his wrist. God, it's so horrible."

Later, in bed trying to fall asleep, Derek couldn't stop thinking about it. Gas, a bullet through the head, were horrible enough. But what could make a man chew through the flesh and rubbery arteries of his own wrist to find the solace of oblivion?

And then to lie there bleeding afterward, not calling for help as the life leaked out of him . . .

Exhaustion finally made Derek roll over on his side and think of something else. Lines from a poem he was working on sounded in his head. He repeated them like a mantra till their rhythms and pounding rhymes lulled him finally to sleep.

6

Derek was awakened by a quiet rhythmic tapping like the striking of a small hammer or the thump of a tiny mechanical heart. As he rose slowly from sleep to consciousness, he groped the bed beside him with his left hand for Lisa's body but touched nothing but empty bedclothes. He swept the hand further up to find her hair, but met only the cool empty pillow where her head should have been. Before he had the chance to wonder where she was, he realized that the tapping was coming from above his right shoulder, from the room's single square window, a drumming of knuckle on glass. The window looked out onto the empty courtyard behind their apartment, a space enclosed on four sides by houses, with no access to the street—so, Derek reasoned groggily, whoever was tapping must be someone from this end of the block, a neighbor or one of the Fongs, or maybe Lisa outside trying to get his attention. He started awake, then climbed out of bed to his bare feet.

He turned toward the window and focused his eyes. A full moon and a couple of porch lights from neighboring houses provided the only light, so the figure in the window was at first only a silhouette against the dim glow. The bedroom itself was nearly black.

"Open the window," said a man's voice. "It's me."

Derek squinted as his eyes adjusted to the light. When he recognized the face pressed forward for his inspection, his heart nearly stopped cold.

"Open the goddamn window, Derek," the familiar voice repeated. "I want to come in for a minute. It's important."

Derek was paralyzed. He couldn't remember where the door was even if he were suddenly able to unlock his frozen muscles and bolt.

"Look, I don't have long, so open up, will you?" The face smiled. "Come on, don't just stand there."

"You're dead," was all Derek could answer through clenched teeth. "Go away."

"The fuck I am. Now let me in. It's important."

You chewed through your wrist, Derek thought, you're dead, this is impossible. But still he stood frozen in place, hypnotized by terror, facing the awful thing.

"The newscast was wrong, you moron. I'm out on bail. The story was a plant. Now let me in the goddamn apartment before it's too late.

"Look, Derek," said the face in a more conciliatory tone; he held up his left wrist for inspection and pressed it to the glass. "See?" The flesh was unmarred, pale, over invisible veins and tendons.

"Didn't you read Summers like I told you? I know what you think, that I'm one of the undead now, right? If I were, I could only harm you if you let me in the first time I asked. I've been pounding on this goddamn window for ten minutes out here and you've turned me away, so it's all right, you can let me in now. Even if I were a goddamn vampire I couldn't hurt you. Do your research like I told you. Look, I'll come to your back door, just hurry the hell up. I haven't got all night."

"Let me see your other wrist first," Derek heard himself say.

"Have it your way," the voice replied through the glass. "Look, not a bad job, eh?" He held his right wrist up to the window obligingly. "There now, open up."

Derek squinted. There must have been another light turned on outside because he could see more clearly now. The right wrist was stitched together with two thick ribbons, one red, one blue; a foot of extra ribbon hung from the stitches in a neat braid, ending in a decorative little tassel that swept back and forth in the air. The flesh was pulled tight around the stitches and looked raw and ragged even where held tightly by the interwoven strings.

Derek tried to scream but nothing came out of his mouth. His heart was pounding so hard he couldn't breathe. He wanted to move, to run, but stood locked in place, suffocating from fear. His eyes went black as he tried to force his lungs to suck in air.

Then his chest loosened; he opened his eyes again.

It took fifteen seconds before he realized where he was. He heard Lisa breathing beside him and let the slow rhythmic rush of air quiet his heart and gasping lungs. The room was dark, so memory took the extra time to pinpoint his location.

He was lying in the bed of the Seiferts' guest room on the second floor of their tract home in suburban Sacramento. Lisa's parents had let them sleep together during their Christmas visit, seeing that they were already house mates and lovers back home. It was the day after Christmas, a Monday, the third day of their stay, and today Derek would be returning to the city by himself to attend the convention. Lisa was going to stay here till after New Year's Day for an extended family visit. He was secretly glad to cut his own visit short.

Between slats in the blind, a street lamp cast pale slivers of light into the room, so Derek could now make out the dark bulk of the dresser on which his wallet and watch reposed, the dim mass of an easy chair next to the bed. Reassured, he thought again about his dream, piecing together its sources in real life, speculating about its meaning.

It must have been the photography exhibit, he decided. The day before driving north, he and Lisa had visited an art gallery downtown near Union Square. The bare white walls in the spare little room featured a group of photographs documenting the performances of Eastern European artists. He and Lisa had looked at them, puzzling over their strangeness in silence until they left the gallery and began to walk back home.

The performances involved various types of self-mutilation. It's no wonder his mind conflated their images with those of Ron Pruitt's suicide. In one picture, an attractive, dark-haired Czech had pierced both of her cheeks with long knitting needles while staring expressionlessly at the camera. In another, a blond Hungarian woman with pale eyes and skin sat on a stool, offering the sight of her forearms to the camera's lens. Each arm had been stitched from wrist to elbow with colored ribbons; the needle still pierced the skin where the process had stopped right below the joint in the tender skin above her bulging veins.

The most startling picture was of a Rumanian woman, dark-haired and seductive, with long braided hair falling down to a white cotton gown. She was photographed with her mouth open and her tongue protruding toward the viewer. In her right hand, which was posed at eye level, she held a razor. The front of her gown was stained dark red where blood had dripped from two self-inflicted razor cuts on the tip of her tongue. The woman's eyes stared absently at the viewer as her blood soaked the front of her bodice, embroidering the edges of the stain with fine delicate droplets. The effect of her performance was disquieting. One imagined the seconds before the shutter clicked, the tongue's sensitivity to touch and taste, the delayed sting of the blade.

Derek had heard of other performance artists, Americans mostly, who had performed more violent feats: shooting themselves with small caliber weapons or having themselves crucified to the hoods of cars. But the sheer absurdity of their violence made their acts less disturbing than the acts of those European women frozen on celluloid. Whether or not any of it deserved the name of art was another matter. Derek doubted it.

Derek rolled over and touched the warm shape beside him under the covers; slid his hand up Lisa's thigh and over the cello curve of her hip, barely touching the bare skin. Her breathing was still deep and regular, but Derek's began to quicken now as he felt the heat of woman-flesh on his gently gliding hand.

Lisa was lying on her side, facing the wall. With a gentle pull, Derek rolled her toward him so that she lay sleeping on her back, still breathing softly.

He loosened her thighs, wetted his hand at his mouth and began to massage between her legs.

When he entered her, Lisa's arms encircled his back, her thighs widened; he felt the touch of her hand on the nape of his neck.

After a few minutes, he climaxed with a silent moan into the pillow beside her head. Within seconds, Lisa's hold slackened as she fell almost instantly back to sleep. Derek dismounted carefully and lay on his side next to her. In a minute he was on his back again, matching her breath for breath, sliding toward darkness. The last thing he remembered was a sigh, his own, echoing in the dark room before surrendering himself to sleep.

7

Derek walked to the convention through Chinatown—it was too fine a day to take the bus—until he reached the hotels on Union Square, where the Modern Language Association's national convention was being held. It was just good luck that the winter rite was taking place in his own back yard this year. He had only to pay a small registration fee at a table inside the Hilton to have access to the entire affair. As he climbed the steps to the hotel's front entrance, he spotted the yellow identification tags on the other conventioneers and thought with irony of the three days that lay ahead. Tomorrow he'd be serving on a panel in one of the hotel's beautifully appointed conference rooms, the lone poet among the high-priced scholars beside him on the dais. As he pushed through the revolving glass door and entered the hotel's impressive lobby, he observed the smug confidence of the other conventioneers, smiling: his own future in teaching was rather less assured.

The morning passed quickly. After attending two sessions on twentieth-century American poetry, he had lunch in the hotel dining room. He'd arranged by phone to meet Esther Klein later in the afternoon at the open bar that followed the annual meeting of the Byron Society, so after lunch he walked across the little square to the Saint Francis and took the elevator to the seventh floor.

He arrived just as the meeting was breaking up. As he waited for the bar to open, he drifted across the large ballroom, reading the name tags of participants. In five minutes he spotted a half dozen academic stars. Harold Bloom stood in a corner talking to one of his Yale colleagues. Edward Houston of Berkeley towered over a clutch of West Coast academics across the room, filling his quadrant of the ballroom with sporadic peals of his own deep rumbling laughter. Lesser lights mingled desperately, eyeing each other in a ritual display of plumage and body language.

At last the bar opened and Derek picked up a plastic cup of white wine. Halfway through his drink, he spotted Esther and another Stanford grad student, Debbie Witherspoon, coming through the wide doors. He returned to the bar, picked up two more cups, and threaded his way toward them, meeting them about midroom.

Esther embraced him. Debbie hung back, complaining when he handed them their drinks, "Is that all they've got, wine?"

Derek noticed her expensive outfit: brown wool skirt and matching jacket, Gucci handbag and shoes, real pearls swinging in a loop from her neck. She was paying full tuition at Stanford and still had the money for rich clothes and weekend ski trips to Tahoe.

"I thought Kevin was coming with you," Derek said, addressing Esther.

"I thought I told you. Kevin dropped out of school."

Esther seemed to relish the chance to share gossip again; her gray eyes brightened as she sipped her wine.

"Apparently, Kevin's got a lover," she said over the rim of her cup. "He moved to the city last month. I thought you might have heard from him, actually. He's got a place somewhere in the Heights." Esther smiled. "I guess you travel in different circles."

"He just up and left without telling anyone," Debbie added, eyes scanning the room behind Derek through wide glasses. "The only ones left from Sean's seminar are me and Esther now, and she's leaving for Norway in the spring."

"Why Norway?" Derek tried to catch Esther's eye.

"To study Old Norse. I think I'm going to specialize in Old English and Scandinavian epic."

"I thought you were strictly nineteenth century, the last great Romantic." Derek noticed she was avoiding his stare.

"Yeah, well, things change," Esther said, no longer smiling. Now she was scanning the room, too, over her drink. This wasn't the warm reunion Derek had envisioned when planning their meeting over the phone. Maybe Esther was right. Things change.

Derek sipped the cheap California chablis and began to survey the room himself. Latecomers were still arriving through the wide double doors. The din in the hall increased as old friends and former colleagues exchanged backslaps and loud greetings. Everyone in the brightly lit ballroom looked orderly, prosperous, dull. Derek suddenly wondered what he was doing here.

As he brooded, a breeze seemed to stir the air. He looked up just as a tall, slender blond stepped past a knot of young assistant professors and entered his section of the ballroom. In her simple calf-length silk dress, she looked more like a movie actress than a professor of English. Her unbound breasts plumped the sheer fabric in gravity-defying magnificence; her nipples dimpled the sheen of the yellow silk like thumbs. Derek was taken by the woman's audacity. When she turned to talk to a stout red-head in the group she'd joined, Derek felt his blood turn to champagne, bubbles rising to his head.

"Stop drooling, Derek." Debbie had noticed him staring. "If you're nice, I'll introduce you to her."

It seemed too happy a coincidence that Debbie knew the stranger. "Who is she?" he asked, feigning nonchalance. Desire thrummed through his nerves like wind brushing high tension wires.

"La Belle Dame Sans Merci." Debbie grinned wickedly. "Actually, you've probably heard of her. She's a poet, like you. Gretchen Nordhaus. I went to school with her at Bennington. She was a junior my freshman year."

Derek had indeed heard of her. Though a year younger than he, she'd already published her second book with a prestigious New York house and had garnered Guggenheim and NEA grants as fruits of her early fame. Her latest book had won the National Book Critics Circle Award in poetry. That much he'd conned from book jackets. Beyond that lay mystery.

"Tell me about her," he said, watching the stranger's lips move in pantomime across the noisy room.

"Oh," Debbie began gaily, "she created a delicious scandal at Bennington her freshman year. Her Comp instructor—Dick Fairchild— fell in love with her, head over heels. Said she wrote the most brilliant essays he'd seen in all his years of teaching. He and Gretchen carried on secretly for two years until his wife found out and left with their three children. The school fired him; five years later, they had her back to give the commencement address. Did you know she never graduated? But I'm getting ahead of myself."

Debbie took a long sip of her drink, then smiled again, eyeing Derek.

"After the first scandal died down, Gretchen hooked a visiting poet, Robert O'Connor—a very big fish, from what I hear. He was married, too. I think that was part of the attraction. O'Connor wasn't great looking, but he had a kind of sensitivity about him that made him very sexy. I had a crush on him myself. Anyway, after a few months of flaunting their affair all over campus, O'Connor left his wife of nine years and he and Gretchen ran away to Mallorca to work as translators. Apparently she got tired of him there and left him for some Englishman. O'Connor stayed in Mallorca for another year or two and had a major nervous breakdown. Last I heard, she was living somewhere in England. I'm surprised to see her here."

"What was his name," Derek asked, "the Englishman she left him for?"

"I'm not sure," Debbie replied. "It was something classical sounding. Julian something. He's some kind of writer."

Julian. That was the name Kevin had mentioned in connection with Ron Pruitt. It was probably only a coincidence, Derek reasoned, breath quickening. Debbie wasn't even sure if that was the man's name. Still, he had to ask.

"You don't happen to have a last name, do you?"

Debbie wrinkled her freckled brow. "I don't think so." Then brightening, "It might have been Italian. Yes. Gianinni, or Giovanni—something like that. I'm not very good with names." She turned to Esther, who was quickly losing interest in the conversation. "He's supposed to be very sexy. Gretchen always did have good taste in men.

"I wouldn't get my hopes up, Derek," she added, turning back to him. "She's out of your league. My advice is keep a safe distance and admire her from afar. She's supposed to be a good poet, though." She smiled shyly. "I've never actually read her stuff."

Derek was already lost in thought. Kevin had said he wasn't sure if Julian was English or Italian. The Italian surname would account for the confusion. For the first time since the news of Ron Pruitt's suicide, Derek felt his interest in the subject quicken. He had to meet this Julian in the flesh. A meeting with Gretchen Nordhaus would only sweeten the introduction.

"So when can I meet her?"

"Wait till she's free," Debbie replied, grinning. "But don't say I didn't warn you."

After a second glass of wine, Derek drifted with the two women toward the knot in which Gretchen stood sipping wine. Among the newcomers to her circle were Simon Macbeth, whom Derek recognized from the reading, and Professor Houston, looming a head taller than the others.

"Come on," Debbie said, "now's our chance." She took Derek and Esther by the elbows and steamed toward the group with them in tow. At the first lull in the conversation, she jockeyed up and caught her former schoolmate's eye.

"Hi, Gretchen, I'd like you to meet two friends of mine." She leaned toward Gretchen and the two women exchanged quick, perfunctory kisses. "This is Derek," Debbie added suddenly, turning. "He's a poet—and this is Esther, my good friend."

Gretchen sized up Derek with a quick glimpse, turned to the two women. "So glad to meet you," she said to Esther with a cold smile. She sipped her drink then briefly eyed her former classmate. "So good to see you again." There was something regal in her condescension.

"I admire your poetry," Derek began lamely, immediately regretting the mistake.

Gretchen looked at him again more appraisingly.

"I'm Derek Hill."

He realized how ridiculous he sounded, but couldn't correct his course. She'd probably never heard of him—or, if she'd seen a poem or two of his in print, had simply forgotten his name. The gap between an award-winning author of two books and an unpublished poet was an abyss across which his words reached her as faint echoes and whispers.

She stared at Derek vacantly, smiling across the abyss. Her condescension began to get under his skin. He stood, hands in his pockets, looking for an avenue of escape.

Edward Houston tossed him a lifeline. After a glimpse at Derek's name tag, he addressed him in his deep bass. "You're talking about Keats tomorrow, aren't you? I'll be on the panel with you. You were a student of Sean Watson at Stanford, right? Fine man, Sean—a terrible tragedy." He ended with a low grumble in his throat.

"Yeah, I wrote my paper for his class," Derek replied.

A flicker of interest flashed across Gretchen's face and immediately vanished. In her medium length heels, she could look Derek evenly in the eye. Her irises were as depthless and pale as pond ice.

"Where might I have seen some of your work?" she asked coolly, eyeing him between pale lashes.

"You probably haven't. I haven't published a book yet, but I've had work in *Partisan Review*, *Southern Review*, a few places like that."

The group's conversation, which had been suspended during the brief introduction, suddenly resumed. After a final, perfunctory smile, Gretchen turned back to the stout redhead to resume their conversation.

Derek had been dismissed.

Since they remained in close proximity, Houston addressed a final question to him.

"So where did you do your undergraduate work?"

"Baltimore."

"Ah, Johns Hopkins," the tall man boomed.

"No, actually," Derek replied, "I went to a little school you probably never heard of. Towson State."

"Ah." Houston's eyes glazed over. He turned back to a young woman at his side with a feeble smile.

As the circle closed ranks again, Derek addressed Esther.

"Look, I've got to run. I was going to do a little reading tonight, so I think I'll just split early. Maybe I'll run into you later. Will you be at my session?" Assured that she would, he quickly strode out of the ballroom, eager to hit the street outside, to lose himself in the familiar bustle of Chinatown.

Once on the sidewalk, he breathed a sigh of relief. He'd be glad when tomorrow was over. The thought of reading his paper on *Lamia* filled him with repugnance. Walking in the dusk through Chinatown, he tried to dismiss all thoughts of the convention, but one image stuck in his memory like the after-image of a flashbulb: Gretchen Nordhaus, pale, cool, and formidable as an iceberg staring at him for a millisecond with a hint of sexual interest.

He decided not to go straight home. On Broadway, he turned right and walked instead toward the red-light district, searching the distance for the neon glitter of nightclubs and adult bookstores that stretched along the avenue for several blocks.

What was it about conventions? he wondered. He strode down the sidewalk in the cool night air with a growing sense of danger and excitement. What if someone from the convention saw him ogling strippers or thumbing dirty magazines—or simply spied him idling down the street like some conventioning Elk or small-town dentist on the prowl?

Derek laughed uneasily at the thought. Then he spotted the first flash of neon on the misty gray sky ahead and felt its magnetic pull drawing him forward. He slipped his name tag off with a quick dart of his hand, returned it to his jacket pocket, then began to walk more slowly as the sights came into view.

8

The morning after his visit to Broadway, Derek slept late and arrived at the convention a little before noon. He visited only two sessions before walking to the Saint Francis Hotel a half hour early to prepare for his own MLA debut. It was after four o'clock when he finally read his *Lamia* paper in the Sequoia Room before a crowd of nearly a hundred and fifty scholars. He read third, cotton-mouthed and perspiring, after David Milton of Princeton and silver-haired Elizabeth Gleck of Radcliffe.

A minute after he rose to speak, Gretchen Nordhaus entered through the back door and sat down in a rear aisle seat with a sweep of her golden hair. Derek nearly choked on his words. He tried not to look at her while he read, but his eyes kept reverting to that blond aureole and the attentive blue eyes peering up the aisle at him above a faint Mona Lisa grin. Twelve minutes later as he stepped from behind the microphone and sat down again behind the long speakers' table, he was still having trouble swallowing. He took his eyes off Gretchen only for the instant it took to fill his empty glass with ice water and take a quick sip. When he looked up, she was gone.

With two more speakers to go and all eyes fixed in his direction, he couldn't follow her. He abandoned any hope of catching her outside the conference room. By the time the last speaker, Professor Houston, finished his talk on "The Fall of Hyperion," Derek wasn't sure if she'd still be in the hotel.

Finally, the moderator thanked the panelists and the session was over. Before Derek could bolt for an exit, spectators crowded the speakers' table. Derek hadn't even gotten to his feet when an eager grad student from the University of Washington button-holed him. He tried to deflect the young stranger's compliments, but the student was indefatigable. Within seconds he'd launched into his own dissertation on Keats's poem.

At last, Derek shook the young man and made his way out of the room. It was only a little after five o'clock, but hunger already nipped his ribs so he decided to find a cheap place to have supper. He rode the elevator to ground level and strolled out the rear door of the hotel into the street behind it, moving away from Union Square's more posh shops and restaurants in the other direction. He walked two or three blocks in the chill air, noticing the gradual decline in the area's ambience as he progressed.

He didn't want to stray too far from the hotel. It would be dark soon and he looked uncharacteristically prosperous in his jacket and tie. He scouted the street ahead, spotted a cafeteria a few doors down, and steered toward it.

Inside, he went through the line, paid at the register, then selected a small table near the window overlooking the street. Across the narrow avenue stood a laundromat, a news stand, and a disreputable-looking saloon called The Pet Shop. Derek took out the convention schedule to survey the list of remaining activities as he ate. At six, the annual meeting of the Keats and Shelley Society was taking place in the Saint Francis; at seven, the society was sponsoring an open bar. He decided to

attend the latter to bask a little longer in the glow of his reading. He also hoped to encounter Gretchen there. He'd met her
at the meeting of the Byron Society; maybe she'd show up at
this similar affair tonight. This time, though, he'd try to be a
little more engaging.

Last night after leaving the convention and prowling up and
down Broadway, he thought he caught a glimpse of the tall
blond entering a crowded strip joint in the company of a large
group of conventioneers. Her pale face looked radiant in the
neon glow of the sign above the club's entrance. Rising on tiptoes, Derek squinted into the dark door across the street to see
if it was really she.

His first impulse was to cross and follow her into the smoky
den, but he lacked the cash to pay the club's two drink mini-
mum. He'd already spent his money at the Condor Club on the
corner and a small book store a half block south of Broadway
down the hill. So to confirm the sighting, he lingered for a few
moments outside the club's open door in the throbbing waves
of rock music. He wanted to loiter there till she emerged but
lacked the chutzpa to endure the public stare for more than a
few minutes, standing alone in his convention clothes the day
before his MLA debut. He felt awkward enough walking past
the club's barker for the second time after circling back for another look. The barker spotted him peering into the club from
the sidewalk and regaled him with his pitch.

"Take your hands out of your pockets, my man, and come on
in. You'll be feeling yourself again in no time.

"Hey," he mocked as Derek scurried out of range, "what's
the matter with you, don't you like naked girls?"

Not even the lingering image of Gretchen's smile could lure
Derek back for another peek inside.

Now, pushing aside his empty plate, Derek gazed out at the
nearly deserted street. Beyond the window, a pair of men advanced down the block toward The Pet Shop. The older man
was dressed in a dark business suit. The younger one was shirtless
and pale, dressed only in jogging shoes and tight leather shorts.

In the chill evening air, he looked to be freezing. After pushing open the door, the older man steered the young one inside, then pinched him viciously on the rear as they entered the club's dark interior.

Derek pulled out a volume of Byron's letters and journals to read over coffee. He wanted to kill some time before returning to the hotel. After several minutes of reading, he suddenly changed his mind. It was dark now. He wanted to go back to the convention to look for Gretchen. He closed his book, placed a tip next to his plate, and picked up his satchel to leave.

Outside the cafeteria, he swung back toward the hotel. Another couple of men on the opposite side of the street approached the saloon door. As they drew near, Derek noticed something odd in the way they walked. He looked closer and saw that the younger man was wearing a black leather dog's collar around his neck and was being led by the older man at the end of a leather leash. Derek paused for a moment to watch their advance. There was something familiar in the younger man's mannerisms that made Derek curious enough to linger another minute to stare.

The older man hitched the leash to a sign post outside the door, like a cowboy hitching his horse to a rail, then stepped inside. The young fellow on the sidewalk nonchalantly took a cigarette out of his shirt pocket and lit up, waiting for his companion's eventual return. The club's name suddenly took on new significance.

Casually flicking ashes, the blond tossed a lock of hair back from his face with the back of his hand.

The smoker's face was turned away, but Derek suddenly had a premonition of who he was. Without thinking, he crossed the street to take a closer look; he grew surer when the man glanced down the sidewalk, temporarily revealing the side of his face.

"Kevin?"

The blond head turned to face him.

"Jesus, you gave me a start." A wan smile. "Fancy meeting you here."

Derek stopped a few feet short of his friend, unable to approach.

"Observing the natives or just out for a stroll?" Kevin asked. His face was impassive now, almost bored-looking as he turned away. Derek was amazed at his cool composure under the circumstances. Kevin made no effort to extricate himself from the leash.

"I just left the convention." Derek waved toward the cafeteria then toward the distant hotel.

"Ah, yes, the convention. Pretentious little busybodies disturbing the sleep of the great dead with their ridiculous endless talk. If those eager acolytes really wanted to know how their adorable little pet poets lived, they'd leave their gossip societies and live in drunken bliss for their few short days here in Babylon."

Kevin puffed on his cigarette, cocked one eyebrow. "I can never think of the MLA convention without remembering that little epigram by J.V. Cunningham—you know the one I mean—about Homer being poor while his scholars live at ease, making as many Homers as they please. But I've become cynical, as you see." He smiled weakly.

"Please say something, Derek, I feel ridiculous enough as it is. Not that I'm complaining about my chosen lot. Try not to be judgemental. You're a poet, after all. Your nature leads you down these desperate avenues, even if you do it unconsciously, drawn by the devil-knows-what. Don't forget what Blake said about Milton. You're all of the Devil's party without knowing it, you babbling bards, every last one of you. So I hope you'll be polite and stop gawking like a tourist." Kevin fingered his cigarette, ran a hand quickly through his hair.

"Sorry. I don't know what to say." Derek tried to allay his shock and find the right tone. "I didn't expect to run into you. Esther just told me you'd moved to the city yesterday. And now here you are."

"Yes, aren't I, though. I suppose I know how I look, but that's part of the price one pays for satisfaction. Look, Derek, I'll tell you something so you won't think . . . whatever you're bound to think." He turned away again, looking down the block to avoid Derek's eyes.

"We all seek the oblivion of consummated desire," Kevin said quietly, "only some of us are more direct in our approach. Or more extreme, if you will. You have your muse to abandon yourself to. The rest of us have to make our own provisions."

Derek tried not to stare as Kevin talked. The chill air knifed through his jacket and flimsy pant legs as a breeze picked up.

"Plato was right about writing poetry, wasn't he?" Kevin asked. "How it feels to be filled, body, mind, and soul, by the great bitch goddess Inspiration. That's because he was a poet himself. You're all totally unreliable happy delirious fakes. I've told you before what a lucky bastard you are, but you have this very pedestrian desire to succeed in the conventional manner. Listen to your genius. That's my last advice to you, Derek. Take it for what it's worth. It'll probably ruin your life for anything normal, but think what beautiful wreckage you'll leave behind." For the first time Kevin dropped his impassive mask and smiled.

"Now please get out of here. You have no idea how embarrassing this is. Have a bit of compassion. And don't tell Esther you saw me, if she happens to ask."

Derek said goodbye and strode away quickly toward the lighted bulk of the hotel.

After a brisk walk, he arrived there chilly and depressed. He sat on a velvet couch in the first floor lobby and pulled out the volume of Byron letters but was unable to focus his attention on the printed page. A string quartet was just packing up their instruments and taking down music stands as the lobby bustled again with conventioneers heading toward evening sessions on the floors above. Derek abandoned the couch and boarded a crowded elevator then rose toward the seventh floor where the Keats and Shelley Society was due to have their open bar. He planned to loiter among the scholars there in the hope of being taken in for a little conversation. Literary chat would come as a relief after the last twenty-four hours. He looked forward to the bright lights and din of the ballroom, the warm consolation of alcohol.

At the seventh floor, Derek stepped out into a lobby that expanded toward a set of wide double doors. An unaccountable sense of exhilaration filled him as he strode toward the noisy crowd inside the ballroom. Passing the door, he swaggered like a gunfighter.

The first face he saw was Gretchen's. She was standing twenty yards away, head tilted back, laughing with an open red mouth. She caught Derek's eye and smiled; then she raised a shimmering plastic cup of wine to her lips to drink.

Derek walked toward her group, a bevy of University of California professors, Edward Houston looming above the others as usual, like a bear in a man suit. Oddly, the whole group seemed to be watching Derek's approach. The faces looked genial and inviting as he closed the distance and came within speaking range.

It wasn't till he was within a few feet that he realized they were actually looking past him to someone else, someone who must have followed shortly after him through the ballroom doors.

"Ah, there's Julian," Gretchen said, and the others smiled, staring past Derek.

Without turning around to look, Derek walked past them toward a lone man gulping a glass of wine; he recognized him immediately as the student from Seattle who'd cornered him this morning after his talk.

"Hello again," Derek said, forcing a smile. He sidled up after quickly reading the name tag. "Mark Levine, right? It's good to run into you again." Derek held out his hand.

The young man smiled, grateful for the attempt at conversation.

"Yes. I'm glad I bumped into you. I was thinking again about what you said this morning about *Lamia* and had a couple more observations I wanted to share."

Derek looked to his left in time to see Gretchen Nordhaus kiss the cheek of the newcomer, who was welcomed into the midst of the group with much smiling and hand shaking. The man was tall and slim and wore an elegantly tailored tweed suit with a matching cape such as only an Englishman might wear. His light brown hair swept back over his ears and curled above his collar. He reminded Derek of nothing so much as a British rock star.

So that's Julian, Derek thought to himself, with a touch of envy. If only he'd thought to ask Kevin about him again when he had the chance.

"Hey, let me get you a drink," said Mark Levine at his side. Then the student set off for the bar with a tilt of his own empty glass. "I'll be back in a jiffy."

No need to hurry, Derek thought mournfully, observing the levity and high spirits of the others. Everyone seemed to be engaged in loud conversation except him.

"Here you go," said Mark, returning with a glass in each hand. He handed one to Derek. "Here's to Keats and Shelley. Without them, we'd be over in the Hilton listening to some dry-as-dust talk on Dryden or some other eighteenth century geek. Here's looking at you." He downed half a cup of wine at a gulp, then looked up smiling.

"Take a drink," he said more insistently. "Come on, get into the spirit of things."

Derek opened his eyes and saw a room skewed sideways. Sunlight filtered through the large floral drapes on the opposite wall to the Persian carpet below. Something in its pale intensity told him it was morning. He rose to one elbow, head throbbing, to survey the room. There was no one else in sight. He studied the intricate carvings of the legs and clawed feet of the mahogany coffee table beside him as memory fought through the pain behind his eyes. His tongue felt furred and thick, his mouth like pillow stuffing. From behind him in another room came the clatter of breakfast dishes, low conversation.

Derek closed his eyes and eased his head back down to the hard cushion but then decided to face his predicament more bravely. He took a deep breath, sat up stiffly, and stretched.

He remembered the smile on Gretchen Nordhaus's face as she handed him the cool wet glass that sent him down for the count. He must have passed out on the sofa soon after she and Julian arrived at the party. At the rate he was drinking, it was a miracle he'd lasted that long. He barely had time to enjoy the excitement of the unexpected invitation, the buzz of conversation in the Houstons' spacious house before he landed on the couch in mid-party.

He hoped he passed out before embarrassing himself.

"Well, hello there. Would you like a bite of breakfast?" The deep voice of Professor Houston boomed behind him. His host walked to the window and pulled back the drapes, smiling as he turned to face his guest in the wash of morning sunlight.

"I'm awfully sorry. I can't believe I fell asleep on your couch," Derek mumbled, pulling himself together. His tie was off, but he was still wearing his rumpled jacket.

"Have a bite to eat, then we'll give you a lift back to the convention if you're headed that way. You can join the others in the kitchen." Professor Houston was all kindness and solicitude. Derek was mortified, but grateful. He stood up, tucked in his shirt, then ran his fingers through his tangled hair. Houston was already wearing a narrow tie and dark pin-striped suit, ready for the convention's final day, and gave off an acrid scent of aftershave.

"I don't usually crash out on my host's couch," Derek offered by way of apology. He cleared the gravel from his throat and shifted uneasily; his shoes pinched his swollen feet. "I guess I could stand a bite to eat, though."

Standing in the big man's shadow, Derek recalled his surprise last night when the amiable giant crossed the ballroom to issue his invitation. Derek was still downing wine with Mark Levine, a bewildered wallflower, when Houston described the gathering at his house in the Berkeley hills after the convention and invited him to come along. Derek thought at the time that his Keats paper had won him the privilege. But now he remembered the curious way Houston had huddled with Gretchen and the mysterious Julian before his unexpected advance. The next thing Derek knew, he was sharing a ride with three wine-drinking strangers in Houston's BMW as they careered across the bay. Gretchen rode with Julian behind in a black Mercedes, arriving an hour later on the arm of her handsome escort.

Now, as Derek entered the kitchen, he was greeted by Houston's wife. He couldn't recall her name. It might have been Ellen. She was about a dozen years younger than her husband, a trim and sprightly fifty.

"Well, good morning," she said rising from the table to place her empty plate in the sink. She turned and smiled, revealing even white teeth. Derek remembered that she taught French at the university.

Two younger people were finishing breakfast at the long table. For a moment Derek thought they were the Houstons' children; then he remembered being introduced to the man—a protege of Professor Houston—last night at the party. He took comfort in the thought that he wasn't the only one who'd spent the night.

"Thanks for being so kind," he said to his hostess. "I feel terrible about crashing on your couch."

Houston laughed as Derek took his chair.

"Nonsense. Jack Kerouac slept on that couch once for three weeks running. I finally had to throw the bastard out. Bodily. Both him and that drunken friend of his. I was pretty strong in those days—those boys never had much of a chance." Houston chuckled at the recollection.

"A gathering of poets," said his wife, nodding toward the

table. She indicated the redhead across from Derek. "That's Diane Gregor, and that lanky fellow there is David Knight. Diane arrived late, but I believe you met Dave last night."

Derek remembered the brief meeting. He was still on his first drink, not counting the wine he had in the car, so he'd still been fairly lucid. He and the tall classics major talked briefly about Ezra Pound before Derek succumbed to restlessness and gin. He caught the student's eye now and nodded a greeting.

"We're going to try to make the session on John Ashbery," offered Diane Gregor. "You might want to hurry a bit."

"*You* might be seeing Ashbery," said Dave Knight with a grin. "There's a session on Catullus at the same time in the Hyatt for the less trendy."

Derek returned his smile. "I think I'll pass on both, actually. I really have to get back to my apartment to clean up."

The three of them chatted across the pine table as Derek gulped coffee and eggs. After a minute the others rose and left the room, heading for the garage, where Professor Houston was warming up his BMW. Derek followed after tracking down his satchel. He found it against the living room wall then hustled after the others, who were already slamming car doors and calling goodbyes to Mrs. Houston, who would follow later.

In the car on the way back across the bay, Derek searched his memories of the previous night. Blurred impressions of the convention mixed with drunken memories of the party. Whole episodes were muddled or lost in fog. He knew one thing for certain, though: Ron Pruitt had been wrong on one point. It wasn't poets who fed off the labors of scholars, but the other way around.

As he watched the prosperous, well-fed members of the Keats and Shelley Society last night, Derek had to smile, thinking of the two dead men whose work gave them their comfortable livings. Both poets were in their graves at an age when the scholars were still blinking over the footnotes of term papers. Shelley, the senior of the two, reached the grand age of twenty-nine before drowning in the storm-tossed waters of the Gulf of Spezia. Now, close to two hundred years later, middle-aged scholars built fat pensions on those brief tormented careers, poking and prodding the *corpus* of each poet like carrion birds in search of undigested fat.

Later, at the party in the Houstons' house, Derek listened as men and women chatted about their book contracts and lecture fees, compared perks and pensions, salaries and sabbaticals— all in the name of poetry, that dangerous winged thing. Caring little for the poor mortal creatures who wrote the stuff, they preferred their poets safely dead and embalmed in footnotes and commentary. Or if like Professor Houston they cultivated the acquaintance of a few, they did it indiscriminately, one bird pretty much serving for another in the din of competing voices. The whole thing would be funny, if it weren't so predictable and tragic.

"Just drop me at Union Square," Derek called over the seat to Houston, who sat hunched over the wheel. The car was now creeping through thick morning traffic, only a few blocks from the convention site. "I can walk to my apartment from here."

A minute later, Derek said his goodbyes on the curb outside the Hilton and headed up Stockton, walking stiffly on swollen feet.

As he walked through the familiar babble of Chinatown, another memory of last night resurfaced.

He remembered his brief conversation with Julian. He even remembered the Englishman's elusive surname. Ginotti—that was it. He must have overheard it when Julian arrived. Or did the Englishman himself mention it by way of introduction?

Derek couldn't remember. He did, however, recall his surprise when Julian complimented him on his poetry. Drunk as he was, he could hardly believe his ears when the foreigner referred to the poems in his nearly forgotten pamphlet. A small press had brought the thing out five years ago in Baltimore. Most of the two hundred copies still sat piled in his publisher's basement. Julian even remembered the title: *High Spirits in Low Talk*. And the publisher's name: Onion Skin Press.

In the course of their short conversation, Julian made him

dizzy with flattery. When the Englishman excused himself and sauntered away toward the bar to end their talk, Derek's spirits sagged. Not even Gretchen's flirtations a little later wholly restored his happy state of mind. But by then he'd had several more gin and tonics.

Smiling at the thought of Gretchen, Derek arrived at last at his front gate. Mail from yesterday was crammed into the little box. When he unlocked the door and pulled it out, he saw it was only the familiar thick shape of the book manuscript he'd mailed back in October. This one had a New York City postmark, so it must be from Macmillan—his third rejection. Just what he needed to go with his hangover.

When he entered his apartment, he received a more serious shock. The doors of the kitchen cabinets were all hanging open; plates and silverware and cookery were strewn across the kitchen floor. Even the refrigerator and freezer doors were open, drooling frosty air.

Ahead, in the living room, the furniture was overturned and books littered the floor beneath empty shelves. His desk had been emptied and its contents scattered across the room. It looked like a hurricane had blown through.

Or something worse than a hurricane: thieves.

Derek walked through the two rooms surveying the wreckage. After a quick pass through the living room, he dashed into the bedroom. Chaos reigned there, too. Even the bed had been stripped, the mattresses separated and flung across the room. Overturned dresser drawers spewed socks and underwear, tie clips and earrings, bras and nightgowns and belts.

The odd thing was, he could see that Lisa's stereo hadn't been stolen. The television wouldn't have been worth the effort, but why would a thief leave the apartment's most valuable item sitting on its stand unmolested and empty the desk and the freezer? The contents of Lisa's jewelry box were scattered across the bedroom floor. Some of the items were gold and silver. A small ruby ring sat on a white bolt of sheet in the middle of the floor.

Derek felt a surge of relief after a quick inventory of their possessions showed that nothing of value was missing.

An hour later he discovered the bad news.

Whoever had broken into their apartment had taken one thing, it appeared: the tape of his interview with Ron Pruitt. Everything else in the drawer where he'd hidden it was in plain sight in the wreckage around his desk. Searching on hands and knees the length of the living room, he failed to turn up the missing cassette.

The fact that the intruder had taken the time to strip their bed down to the frame after finding the tape suggested that he was after something else as well. Derek didn't even want to speculate right now as to what it might have been.

He crossed the room to telephone the police.

As he reached for the receiver, the phone rang, loud as a fire bell. After a second ring, heart hammering, he picked it up and held it gingerly to his ear.

"Happy birthday, Derek. This is Mom and Dad."

Derek checked his urge to drop the phone; took control of his rapid breathing and assumed a casual tone of voice. No sense alarming his folks about the break-in.

"Hi, Mom. I completely forgot it was my birthday till you called. Lisa's still in Sacramento. It slipped my mind till just now."

"Thirty years old," his father chimed in from another line. "Isn't it about time you settled down and got a job? You can't be a gigolo forever."

A satisfied chortle, then silence, as Derek stifled a reply. The fact that Lisa was a student was a distinction wasted on his dad.

"Did you get your card yet?" asked his mom. "There's a check in it from us."

"No, but I'll look for it."

His eyes wandered over the wrecked apartment as his mother caught him up on family gossip.

"Have you seen your cousin Billy? He left town about two

weeks ago. Said he might drop by to visit if he makes it to California."

The prospect of a visit from his cousin made Derek squirm.

"No," he said, "but I'll give you a buzz if he does."

"Well, you know Billy," his mother sighed. "It'll be a miracle if he makes it past St. Louis. If he does show up, though, make sure you let us know so we can tell Aunt Betty. He'll never call unless he's in trouble or needs money."

Right before signing off, his father got in one last gibe.

"Well, don't forget what they say."

"About what?" Derek asked.

"Don't trust anyone over thirty." With that, his dad hung up.

Derek returned the receiver to its cradle, frowning. His head was ringing like a gong. The sight of the apartment depressed him. He picked up the phone again to call the police. He wouldn't mention anything about the tape, but he wanted to get the break-in on the record.

An hour after his call, the front buzzer rang, signalling the cops' arrival.

When he answered their knock, Derek was surprised to see a plain-clothed cop along with the uniform he'd expected.

"Hi, I'm Lieutenant Graves, and this is Officer Tillson," said the one in street clothes, gliding past Derek into the apartment. "We're here about the break-in." The senior cop was a silver-haired, slouched veteran; the uniform, a tall black man with a neatly trimmed mustache.

Derek gave them a tour of the damage.

"Looks like they used a glass cutter to get in," said the lieutenant, studying the bedroom window. "A little sophisticated for vandals. You say nothing was stolen? They appear to have been looking for something. Any idea what it might have been?" Graves looked at Derek over pad and pencil, head cocked, watching from weary, pouched eyes.

"No. Maybe they got the wrong apartment. I don't know. I first thought they were just out for kicks." The missing tape was beginning to make Derek nervous. He was sorry now he called the cops.

"Aren't you going to take fingerprints or something?" he asked to shift the onus off himself.

The Lieutenant smiled. He left it for the younger cop to reply.

"This ain't exactly a murder case, you know."

"Let us know if you have any further problems," Graves said when he'd finished his inspection. The uniform fell in behind him and then the two of them steered toward the door. Derek followed them outside to their car, which was double-parked in the middle of the street.

"Thanks for coming. I'll call if anything else comes up." He felt a bit foolish now standing beside the police car in broad daylight. Neighbors and pedestrians were watching from across the street.

The uniform hunched behind the wheel, key in the ignition. The lieutenant lingered for another moment on the sidewalk, addressing Derek as he buttoned up his coat.

"Glad to be of help, Professor Hill. Here's my card, if you need to call again." He dipped toward the seat, then rose again beside the door.

"Oh, yes," he added, stepping closer, "there was one unrelated matter I wanted to ask you about while I was here. If you don't mind.

"It's about a visit you made recently to the state facility in Vacaville. It seems you visited one Ronald Pruitt. Correct me if I'm wrong."

Derek was speechless; this was a complete surprise.

"What I was curious about," continued the lieutenant, "was why you visited him in a room set aside for attorneys and their clients. There's some question about abusing the attorney-client relationship involved. They have certain regulations there regarding visitors."

"That was Ron's doing," Derek said, eager to straighten the matter out. "I never claimed to be a lawyer. To tell you the truth, I was shocked when he told me what he'd done."

The lieutenant continued to eye him noncommittally.

"I filled out a form when I was there. I never said anything about being a lawyer. I think Ron was having a little fun at my expense, is all."

"Yeah, that's what the paperwork showed on that." The lieutenant patted Derek's shoulder roughly. "I guess they're just going to have to be a little more careful up there about taking the word of a prisoner. I'm sorry to have had to trouble you about the matter."

The lieutenant didn't look the least bit troubled as he climbed into the passenger side of the car to leave.

When the car drove up the hill and out of sight, Derek stood for some minutes on the sidewalk. It suddenly struck him as odd that the lieutenant had addressed him as Professor Hill. He was sure he hadn't mentioned anything about himself other than the simple facts of the break-in, either over the phone or when the two cops arrived. That and the question about his visit with Ron Pruitt gave him a sense of vertigo.

He walked back inside to his apartment with a vague sense of unease. He didn't know what it was exactly, but there was something terribly important now he had to do.

10

Menlo Park, Palo Alto, Mountain View, Sunnyvale, Santa Clara— the highway signs went past like flash cards, now that Derek was in the South Bay only a few miles from his destination. After the morning's fog and confusion, the unaccustomed power of the rented Oldsmobile filled him with a sense of mastery as he cruised toward San Jose down the interstate in bright sunshine. Even his headache had abated somewhat in the excitement of his mission.

After the cops had left his apartment, Derek reviewed his memories of his conversation with Ron Pruitt—he'd listened to the tape a dozen times in the previous weeks and retained almost the whole interview verbatim. He decided that though Ron might indeed have been crazy, he hadn't killed Professor Watson for nothing. Derek was convinced that Watson had turned up some kind of letters over the summer in England or in Italy, just as Ron had suggested, and that Ron had murdered him to take possession of them himself. He'd told Derek as much in their talk. That the police hadn't come up yet with Ron's motive was no surprise. He certainly wouldn't have told them about the letters, and even if they'd searched his possessions, there was little chance they'd recognize what the letters were, even if they stumbled across them. Without Ron's hints, Derek wouldn't have thought of looking for letters, either, and he'd have some idea of what they were if he came across them. He doubted the police academy included a course on the interpretation of literary manuscripts.

Standing amidst the wreckage in his apartment, it occurred to Derek this morning that whoever stole the tape might soon reach the same conclusion and try to track down the missing manuscripts himself. He hoped he wasn't already too late to beat the thief to the prize.

Once he realized what he was after, he put his plan quickly into action. He called up friends at Stanford till he'd tracked down the phone number of Ron's former roommate, an obliging grad student named James Chin. From him, Derek learned that all of Ron's possessions, mostly books and file cabinets, were now stored in his mother's garage in San Jose. Chin had helped Ron's mother pack and store the stuff himself. He even gave Derek the woman's name and San Jose address. Since Ron was picked up in San Jose on the night of the murder, the odds were good that the missing manuscripts were there. It was the only place Ron would have felt they were safe. At least that's what Derek hoped.

He still had the slip of paper in his pocket with the name and address: Emma Pruitt, 1121 San Jacinto St. At the car rental place on Van Ness, he'd picked up a San Jose street map then circled his destination with blue ink.

He found the house in a northern suburb a mile off the interstate. It sat in the middle of a block in a lower-class neighborhood of stucco duplexes and green-roofed bungalows that had seen better days. Derek parked at the curb and eyed Pruitt's ramshackle bungalow. A bedraggled palm tree stood in the middle of the front yard, badly in need of water. As he walked to the front door, Derek rehearsed the story he'd told Emma Pruitt on the phone, arranging his visit.

On the front porch, he rapped three times with a tarnished brass knocker.

After his fifth series of knocks, there was still no answer.

Derek remembered the way Ron's mother had slurred her words on the phone. Maybe she was too drunk to answer.

Derek peered through the picture window beside the front door, but the gauzy curtains inside were just thick enough to completely obscure his vision.

He drifted along the front of the house. At the side of the building between the house and a tall redwood fence, he found a flagstone path covered by a low arbor. He followed the path to the back, unhooked the gate's stiff latch, then entered the dusty little yard.

Not a sound from inside the house. Derek crossed the cracked concrete patio and rapped softly on a sliding glass door. From the kitchen, to the right of the door, a woman's shape suddenly lurched into view.

"Mrs. Pruitt?" Derek spoke loudly enough to be heard through the glass. "Derek Hill. I spoke to you on the phone a little while ago."

The woman pressed her face closer and studied him briefly through heavy-lidded eyes. She did look like she'd had a bit too much to drink. More than a bit, judging from her dazed expression.

At last she opened the door and let him in.

A tattered house coat covered her short lumpish frame. Her hair showed two inches of gray below the carrot-color dye. Her skin was pale and puffy, her green eyes bloodshot. She looked a wreck.

"Sorry," she mumbled. "I haven't been well. It's the medicine I have to take that makes me forget."

Derek looked around at the inside of the house. The place was filthy: dirty laundry piled high on the sofa, coffee cups and bottles on the arms of chairs, an old ironing board erected in the middle of the room amidst a clutter of magazines. Even the walls were smudged and in need of paint.

He suddenly understood Ron's extreme punctiliousness. It must have been in reaction to life with his slovenly widowed mother. Her grief at his death wasn't enough to account for the house's total dereliction. The dirt here had accumulated over years.

"As I mentioned on the phone," Derek said, "I loaned Ron my Wordsworth book in September and, you know, with what happened in the fall, I never had the chance to get it back. It cost nearly forty dollars and I may need it again for a course I'll be taking at Berkeley in the spring."

The woman blinked stupidly. "Are you the one who visited my boy in the hospital?"

At first Derek didn't know what she was talking about. Then he realized that hospital was her euphemism for the Vacaville prison. She probably couldn't bring herself to face the horrors in which her son had been involved.

"Yeah, that was me."

"Well, blesh you then, blesh you." Tongue thickened by drink, she sprayed her S's in Derek's face. "Ron was always a good boy. He never did those terrible things they said. He was a good boy, always. A straight A student, every year since first grade." The effort of speech became too much for her. Ron's mother stared into space, lost in memory.

"What did you say your name was?"

"Derek. I was a friend of Ron's at Stanford."

"Well," she added uncertainly, "I hope you find your book."

"Here, follow me. I'll show you where to go." She stumbled across the den toward a door.

"The garage. You look in there," she said, opening the door to a dark interior. "You go and find it now."

The light revealed an oil-stained concrete slab and rows of wooden shelves, probably dating from the time when Ron lived at home. The shelves were piled high with books; more books sat piled in collapsing cardboard boxes on the floor. Against the opposite wall stood a line of iron-gray file cabinets in a tight row, piled high with litter. There was barely enough room for Derek to weave his way across the floor.

"I'll have to lay down inside for a while. You just look till you find your book." She closed the door behind her, freeing Derek to pursue his search.

He started with the file cabinets—there were five of them—beginning with the names of the six major Romantic poets. He looked up Byron first, then leafed through the manila folders stacked inside. Ron had apparently saved everything since high school, but he was neat and organized, so Derek soon covered all the entries on Byron and began to search the drawer labelled Blake, proceeding alphabetically from there till he'd covered all six poets. Since what he was looking for would be handwritten on old paper, Derek quickly riffled through most of the folders. Photocopied articles from journals, old research papers, and Ron's notes made up the bulk of the stuff.

An hour later, Derek began to doubt the wisdom of making the trip. He'd leafed through most of the cabinets and had turned up nothing. Fortunately, Mrs. Pruitt thought he was looking for a book, so the length of his search wouldn't arouse suspicion. She might even be unconscious by now.

Derek decided to tackle the boxes. Most were falling apart under the weight of their cargo, so he shuffled through them quickly, leaving more chaos than when he'd arrived. Books littered the floor behind him. He doubted Ron's mother would notice the added mess when she looked in next time, or, noticing, care.

Another hour of searching turned up nothing. Derek was ready to quit when he noticed the large metal tool box sitting on top of one of the file cabinets back across the room.

After crossing the garage, he lifted it off the cabinet by the handle and took it down. On top of the box was a masking tape label, with the letters PBS printed neatly in magic marker.

The box was fastened by a metal clasp. Derek quickly unsnapped it and peered inside.

A stack of aging yellow paper—perhaps an inch thick—lay at the bottom of the box. The paper didn't quite fit into the box's slightly narrower dimensions, curling up one side toward the lid.

Derek lifted the first fragile sheet from the pile and studied it in the dim light of the garage's solitary bulb. The crabbed handwriting was almost impossible to read, but he finally deciphered the opening words. The letter was undated.

> Dear M,
>
> I risk putting pen to paper once again to urge you with all possible haste to contact H. about destroying all p.m. letters in his possession. A poet's reputation, like that of a virtuous woman, can stand few . . .

Derek couldn't make out the next several words where the ink had faded. He skipped down to the second paragraph but couldn't make out much there either, so he gave up till he could make the attempt in better light. He skipped to the third and final paragraph and read the letter's conclusion.

> . . . and so my dearest please direct H. to commit these pages to the flames with the others. I continue to think of you as the only true . . . [indecipherable] . . . my soul . . . [indecipherable] . . . than human clay can contain.
>
> Adieu—We shall meet again soon
>
> Your eternally affectionate
>
> S.

Derek started as the door to the den suddenly swung open. He dropped the letter back into the box, then slid both behind a cardboard carton with a quick shove of his knee. Silhouetted by the brighter light from the room behind her, Mrs. Pruitt's plump shape filled the door.

"Did you find your book?"

"Yes," Derek lied. "Thank you, I just found it." He slapped the side of his satchel, which by a stroke of luck was lying next to him.

"Did you say your name was Hill?" she asked. She seemed to have sobered up somewhat in the past two hours. Derek answered nervously, trying to make out her face.

"Just a minute then. I'll be right back," she said, turning back into the house.

Derek hastily stuffed the pile of letters into his satchel and zipped it shut. Then he picked his way among the scattered cartons toward the door, leaving the scene of his theft.

Back in the den, he closed the garage door behind him, anxious to make his escape, but Emma Pruitt was nowhere in sight. Finally, she shuffled around the corner from the living room, slippers flapping, with a short white envelope in her hand. She was almost sober now.

"Ron sent me this from the hospital," she said, handing Derek the envelope. "I should have mailed it sooner, but it slipped my mind till just now when I remembered your name." She eyed the torn flap.

"It wasn't me that did it that way. The doctors read all of his letters while he was in there. I don't know why. It's just a short note."

Derek pulled out a small, nearly blank sheet of white stationery. The message took less than two lines of type and was undated and unsigned.

Derek,

Re our last conversation. Look the word up in the OED. You'll find the entry most enlightening.

That was all it said. Derek thanked Mrs. Pruitt, stuffed the envelope into his pocket, and excused himself. He was afraid she might ask to see the book that served as his pretext for coming and wanted to stow the purloined letters somewhere safe.

"Well, if you have to go," she said. "Are you sure I couldn't fix you a drink of something—some tea or coffee, maybe?" Mrs. Pruitt probably wanted to talk with him about her son. Derek begged off and edged toward the front door.

A minute later, he was back in the driver's seat again, powering his way out of San Jose back toward the city. The next step in his plan called for stashing the letters in a safety deposit box at a downtown bank. Since this was Friday, he still had enough time to find one. Even after the cost of the car, he had enough cash in his wallet to pay for a year's rental. Then he could return safely to his apartment and straighten the mess up there.

The purchase of a safety deposit box at the First National Bank on Market Street proved to be deeply satisfying. The saleswoman explained the whole thing to Derek carefully. It took two keys, his own and the one in possession of the bank, to open the metal box in the bank's thick-armored interior. The keys had to be inserted together and turned at the same time. Then, after the bank employee withdrew from the vault, Derek could transact his business in complete safety. Enacting the procedure for the first time with the bank officer's help filled him with delight. Not only was Derek the only one who knew the whereabouts of the letters, but even if someone discovered their location, he couldn't touch them without Derek's help.

After the saleswoman left, Derek hastily looked through the letters again. Most were signed simply with the initial S, though two or three closed with the puzzling nickname "Elf." One of the letters, in a different hand, was signed with a first name: Mary.

It didn't take a Sean Watson to figure out that the letters were written by Percy and Mary Shelley—in which case they were extremely valuable, whether measured in terms of scholarship or cold hard cash. With a small thrill of delight, Derek weighed the stack of letters in his hand a final time before storing them in their box. Then he left the vault and hurried back outside to where he'd left the rented car parked illegally on a busy side street.

On his way back to the car rental place, his head began to throb again, hammers flailing at the back of his skull.

Still, it had been a good day. The letters for which Professor Watson was murdered were now in Derek's possession. He could sit tight for a while till he decided what to do.

Back in his apartment, tired from the long walk home, Derek's spirits sank again. He'd forgotten how thoroughly the place had been wrecked. He couldn't even lie down and take a nap till he put the bed back together. All his food was ruined, so he'd have to go out later for a meal.

He trudged toward the couch. The red light was flashing on his answering machine. He was half afraid to play back the tape.

The first call was from Lisa, wishing him a happy thirtieth birthday—a fact he'd just as soon forget. She wouldn't be coming home till Tuesday morning, when classes began again after the Christmas break. More great news. That meant four more nights in the ravaged apartment alone on a holiday weekend. He missed Lisa so badly his bones ached.

The second voice made Derek sit up straight.

"Hello, Derek," it said. "This is Gretchen Nordhaus."

He could hardly credit his ears as the rich voice filled the little apartment.

"Julian is having a little get-together on Sunday night to celebrate New Year's Eve. We'd very much like you to come, if you don't have other plans."

Gretchen described how to get to the unfamiliar address in the Berkeley hills. Derek hastily sketched a map on the back of a note pad, forgetting he could play the tape back if he didn't get it all down.

Gretchen's voice sounded warm and musical as she bade him good-bye. She said she looked forward to seeing him again on Sunday night at the party.

Derek stood up after the message ended and paced from the couch to the kitchen. Then he sat at the machine to play the message back, smiling as Gretchen repeated the last words over and over again.

11

After a quick trip to the local public library to pick up a biography of Percy Bysshe Shelley, Derek spent the rest of Saturday putting his apartment back together. It took him till four in the afternoon to finish reshelving books and restoring possessions and furniture to their original places. A few items, such as the glass face on their living room clock, were broken or damaged, but on the whole things were merely scattered about the rooms in random disorder. He didn't want to call Lisa in Sacramento and tell her about the break-in until he could assure her that nothing had been stolen and that everything was back in place. So after a quick final tour of the apartment, he made his call.

His calm assurances finally put her at ease. Nothing of value had been stolen; he'd notified the police. Without having witnessed the devastation herself, she wouldn't share his sense of violation. Hearing her voice on the phone, though, made him realize how much he missed her. Hanging up, he wished she'd come home sooner than planned.

After the call, he started reading the Shelley biography in bed but made little progress before falling asleep, still fully dressed atop the blankets.

He was awakened at dusk by a buzzing at the front gate.

He got out of bed, blinking, and stumbled to the entrance. There, a brown-uniformed man stood waiting at the side of a UPS van, tapping his fingers on the small brown box in his hands.

Derek stepped out to the sidewalk and signed for the box, which was addressed to him. When the van drove away, he peeled away the brown paper in which it was wrapped, then pulled open the two cardboard flaps at the top to see what was inside.

The first thing he encountered was a layer of rust-stained newspaper, which hid whatever was wrapped inside. There was something odd about the newsprint; the paper was yellow, and what had appeared to be black columns of ink were actually lines of hand-drawn cursive. The style of writing reminded Derek of the letters he'd found yesterday in Ron Pruitt's garage. One line of the careful lettering was clearly legible despite the brown rust stains. It read, "The thief must be punished. I write this sentence in blood."

More impatient now to see what was inside, Derek crumpled back the damp paper. Inside, cradled by wilted wrapping paper at the bottom of the box, sat a bloody human heart.

Derek remembered the dream on awakening Sunday morning, still dressed in the same stale clothes. He got up and showered, then walked to the corner newspaper box in the cool morning air to get a Sunday paper.

Tonight was New Year's Eve; he planned to cross the Bay later this evening to attend the party at Julian Ginotti's house. For that, he wanted to be fresh and alert. He started his morning back in the apartment by cranking up the espresso maker and drinking a cup of the thick black concoction over breakfast while he read.

After an hour of browsing through the sports and national news, he still felt weary and depressed. It took him awhile to pinpoint the cause of his ill humor. He was still in mourning for his lost youth. Today was the second day of his thirty-first year. He was officially over the hill.

He remembered Kevin Grace teasing him only a few months ago about his dread of the impending birthday.

"If you'd been born with eight fingers instead of ten," Kevin had joked, "you wouldn't give a damn about turning thirty. It's only the base ten system that gets us all balled up. It's completely arbitrary. If we had eight fingers, maybe we'd get all flaky about turning twenty-four or thirty-two. Don't give it a second thought. Anyway, you've still got a few good months left."

Now, after passing that landmark day, Derek was sure Kevin was wrong. Some metaphysical barrier, some delicate subtle membrane was broken when a man turned thirty. Derek could feel it. Some profound physical change had begun to take place in him, preparing him for the downward slope to death. He kept thinking about Ivan Karamazov in Dostoyevsky's novel proclaiming that his natural vitality would preserve him against life's meaninglessness until he turned thirty, after which he'd blow his brains out in disgust.

Now Derek had crossed that fatal boundary himself; he'd attained a greater age than either Keats or Shelley, two of his literary heroes, and was only six years away from the age when Byron died, a prematurely old man at thirty-six.

Derek turned back to the Sunday paper and read with greater attention. He even gave Ann Landers a quick glance before dawdling through several pages of Bay Area news. He read about people he'd never meet, mused over events in which he had not the slightest spark of interest. For a few minutes, he almost managed to lose himself.

The headline on a little column caught his eye.

> ALLEGED KILLER'S MOTHER DIES IN HOUSE FIRE
>
> Mrs. Emma Pruitt, mother of alleged killer Ronald Pruitt, of 1121 San Jacinto Drive in San Jose, died last night in a fire at her home. Ronald Pruitt, her son, was the suspected killer of Professor Sean Watson of Stanford University. He died by his own hand in his cell in the state facility in Vacaville last month. Neighbors suggest that the fire started in the victim's bedroom, where she was known to smoke after drinking heavily, but Sergeant Jean Rice, spokesperson for the San Jose Police Department, said that arson had not been ruled out. The cause of the fire is still under investigation.

Derek dropped the paper.

Then he picked it up and read the column again. Emma Pruitt's house burned down the day after he'd visited her garage, the day after someone had broken into his own apartment and stolen the tape, with its unmistakable reference to the letters. It was too coincidental. Most likely, whoever stole the tape reached the same conclusions he had and later drove to San Jose to search the house; when they failed to turn up the letters, they must have burned the whole place down to cover their tracks.

No, Derek reasoned, that didn't make sense. Valuable as the letters were, they weren't worth risking a murder charge over. Whoever burned down the Pruitt house with Ron's mother inside was obviously deranged. Derek had a sudden impulse to call the police and tell them everything he knew about the Pruitts. He'd turn over the letters and protest his innocence in the affair. He'd extricate himself from this horrifying mess at once before he was sucked in any deeper.

Then he remembered being questioned by Lieutenant Graves about his visit to Vacaville. Derek didn't feel like being grilled again. True, he had in a technical sense stolen the letters, but his intentions were wholly honorable. He doubted his explanation would sound quite as reasonable in the cool precincts of a police interrogation room.

And then there was the danger. In a very short space of time, all three previous owners of the letters had come to grievous ends. Derek didn't care to emulate them. As of now, no one knew he had the letters. He'd wait for things to quiet down a bit and then turn them over to the authorities. For now, he'd simply keep out of the line of fire and get on with his own life.

He picked up the paper and read the article again. Calmer now, he saw his mistake. Anyone who wanted the letters surely wouldn't burn down the house when he failed to turn them up. What good would that do? He'd have risked a murder charge for nothing. And if he wanted them for their literary content, burning the house down would only insure that their historical import would never be known. No, Derek reasoned, the fire was most likely an accident, an unlucky twist of fate. He'd seen Emma Pruitt himself a day and a half ago: she was drunk as a skunk. If she smoked in bed, as the article suggested, she was a prime candidate for self-immolation. Her timing was just bad luck on Derek's part.

Still, though the facts weren't as chilling as he first feared, the news sobered him up about a lot of things.

For one, he asked himself why he was making such a fool of himself over Gretchen Nordhaus. If she weren't a poet, he'd have noticed her striking good looks, lusted after her in the way men lust after beautiful unattainable women, and let it go at that. His infatuation with the blond was tied to his thirst for recognition as a poet. So far, it had led only to his making a complete ass of himself on two occasions.

He'd go to the party tonight—he still wanted to make contacts and break up the interminable weekend—but he'd keep his distance from Gretchen and moderate his drinking this time.

On second thought, better keep a cool head and not drink at all.

Then there was Julian Ginotti.

Derek would take a little more heed of Kevin Grace's warning about the mysterious stranger. Julian's searching out his chapbook and turning his head with compliments at Houston's party struck Derek now as more than an attempt at polite flattery. The book was damned near unattainable and most of the poems in the little pamphlet weren't all that worthy of praise. Only a handful foreshadowed the much better poems he'd written since then. Julian's attentions made Derek a little queasy in the light of recent events.

Nearly two hours after leaving his apartment, Derek stepped down from the steps of a Berkeley bus at the bottom of a hill in a dark, tree-filled neighborhood. A three-story Tudor mansion peeked out from its shrubbery a half block down the street. Closer at hand, a more modest Victorian illuminated the surrounding woods. Derek stood on the corner under a street lamp, consulting his map and checking street signs. He decided that the house he was looking for sat somewhere higher up the hill. Folding away his map, he started up the hill in the darkness.

As he ascended, the houses got larger and further apart, the landscape steeper and more rugged. As development became more difficult and less profitable, woods and vine-tangled bluffs filled in the spaces between lights. Derek climbed in silence, moonlight shining down on the winding narrow street through patches of leaves. The sidewalk had ended a few paces beyond the bus stop, so he walked now in the middle of the road, looking ahead for house lights.

The house numbers were lost among branches or obscured by darkness, so he finally stopped and scrutinized a mailbox in the beam of his little penlight. The street name was right, so he must be nearly there.

Then Derek saw the glow of lights ahead, the parked cars lined down the side of the narrow street before him, and his mood suddenly brightened.

A sports car rattled up the hill and passed with a soft whoosh, braking suddenly as it pulled in to take its place at the end of the line. Car doors slammed, then echoed, in the surrounding dark. White shirts and pale faces bobbed up the hill, the talk growing higher in pitch as they neared the big house.

The low throb of a bass guitar pounded from giant speakers from somewhere inside: the Rolling Stones' *Sympathy for the Devil.* Mick Jagger's ragged voice growled out the song's familiar refrain as Derek turned off the street onto the long driveway that looped around in front of the house. Beyond the row of parked cars, a half dozen motorcycles were lined up on the grass. A couple of women in long dresses sat on the damp front lawn, sharing a pipe.

The house itself was an architectural monstrosity, more Gothic manse than the Victorian manor it pretended to be. Whoever designed the thing was either deranged or had an odd sense of humor. Its face was all peaked windows and filigree, but the round towers that rose above its overlapping gabled roofs looked like someone's dream of a medieval castle, badly drawn.

Derek entered the large front door and handed his jacket, after a little urging, to a strangely dressed servant inside. The spike-haired young man wore a tailored green jacket and matching bow tie. One ear sported a large gold earring that would have delighted the heart of a pirate.

The guests formed an odd mix. The nearest group was composed of a bearded biker in a Harley Davidson tee shirt, a dark-haired woman in a man's suit and tie, a tall Asian man with a shaven head, and a fat woman with a faint trace of mustache. What they were all talking and laughing about together heaven only knew.

Derek drifted through several downstairs rooms and out onto the back patio, casually eavesdropping. The only person he'd recognized so far was Diane Gregor, who was arguing with a group of strangers back inside.

The patio was surrounded by dense woods. Japanese lanterns illuminated the dark and reflected off the shiny surfaces of leaves. The murmur of voices drifted faintly, pleasantly, in the damp night air.

Behind him, Derek heard a snatch of conversation above the

swish of wind in the tall trees.

"I'm a dream weaver," said a tall gaunt woman in a peasant dress to the woman to whom she'd just been introduced. "Fran told me you were into witchcraft."

"No," replied her companion, "goddess worship, actually."

The goddess worshipper was also quite tall and nearly as thin as the first woman, but wore thick make-up, unlike her dream-weaving sister, who was plain and unadorned, with a wisp of thin gray whiskers trailing from her chin. Swathes of green eye shadow accentuated the goddess worshipper's large eyes, and white powder or make-up gave her face an unnatural sheen. Her voice was low and husky. Derek realized after listening a little longer that she was really a he in drag. He wondered if the goddess in question would invalidate worship on those grounds.

The pungent aroma of marijuana wafted by on the cool breeze. For an instant, Derek experienced a moment of déjà vu, listening to the rustle of leaves, riding the wave of sweet scent. He was fourteen years old again, standing on his front lawn on a cool October afternoon in Maryland.

Mary Rose Keenan, his new next door neighbor, was greeting him for the first time.

"You have a very unusual aura," said the plump, plain girl over the low hedge between their yards. "Come over some time and I'll read your cards for you." She wasn't a bit shy, standing there in her plaid cardigan, her long frizzy hair pulled into two thick braids.

Her face was round; a pair of owlish brown glasses perched on her nose, but her clear skin and bright green eyes almost compensated for her lack of conventional prettiness. A year older than Derek, Mary Rose exuded an otherworldly sophistication that intrigued him instantly.

"Here," she said, "I'll read your palm for you now."

She took his left hand between her two warm palms and instantly Derek fell into a dreamy trance as she brooded over the expanse of open hand.

"You have a very strange life line," she mused, fingering it lightly. "See, it breaks off here and then picks up and runs all the way over here. Either you're going to die young or you're going to live to be a very, very old man. I'm still a novice at palmistry." Mary Rose smiled and gave Derek back his hand. "If you come over tonight, we could hold a seance and see what we can see."

When he arrived at her front door later that night, Derek was surprised to discover that they'd have the house to themselves.

"Mom and Dad are at choir practice," Mary Rose said after greeting him with a shy smile. "Let's go down to the basement, where I've got my stuff."

Derek followed her to a corner of the basement where two battered old chairs and a sagging couch sat on a worn imitation Oriental rug. The little corner looked like a gypsy fortune teller's parlor. Thick curtains covered the tiny basement windows. A shelf full of occult paperback books and a softball-sized crystal ball in a carved wooden hand gave the basement an air of dank other worldliness. Mary Rose read his fortune with Tarot cards, then tried his palm again.

"You're either going to be a poet or a minister," she concluded after gathering her vibrations and consulting a large illustrated book. "I can't tell which."

Derek was impressed by her intuitive grasp of his character. His favorite pastime was reading—he'd often fantasized about becoming a writer—and up until the last few months when he'd begun to question his church's dogma, he'd often considered a career as a Methodist minister. He must have looked impressed because she followed her prediction with a knowing smile. "I'm psychic," she added. "The cards are only a channel. You want to try a seance now?"

Once or twice a week after that, they met to delve into the unknown. Mary Rose was a trance medium—or put on a convincing show. After five minutes of deep breaths and shudders, she'd fall into a trance-like sleep from which she murmured weird, suggestive answers to whatever questions he asked. But that wasn't what brought him back to her basement on nights when her parents were out. After their spook sessions, as he privately called them, she'd sometimes let him fondle her large breasts, curled beside him on the large, dank-smelling couch; afterward, they'd try a second round of questions and answers with the ouija board or another trance. It all depended on her mood.

After several months of breast fondling and kissing, they progressed to nudity and mutual masturbation; they were both too scared to escalate beyond that. Derek was just working himself up to try, when Mary Rose lost interest in him. She'd discovered drugs and older men.

He hardly saw her for a year after they broke off, and when he did it was always in the presence of long-haired, dangerous-looking older boys. She lost weight, exchanged her glasses for contacts, and, except for an unhealthy, drug-induced pallor, began to look sexy in an off-beat way. Derek was surprised one night when, out of the blue, she invited him over to her house again.

But this time there were no trances, no cards or palm reading. After leading him to the basement and stationing him on the familiar old couch, Mary Rose sniffed at some brown powder in a little vial and then handed him a joint. "Smoke this," she said, "it'll make it all more real."

Her paperback books were replaced now by old leather-bound volumes with Latin titles.

"What's that?" Derek asked, pointing to the vial.

"A magic recipe. I need it to do what I'm gonna do. I had a dream about you last night. I'm going to help you with something. It's kind of an assignment." She tipped back the vial and let the powder slide into her mouth, then swallowed. She washed away the aftertaste with a swallow from her can of Coke.

She saw Derek looking at the open book on the stand where the crystal ball used to sit.

"That's the only good thing about being raised a Catholic," she said, grinning. "If you're lucky, you can pick up a little Latin. Here, I'll show you how to read this. You only have to say these parts here where I'm pointing. I'll show you how to pronounce it first."

Derek looked at the Latin. "I've had a year in school," he said. He couldn't read the dense stuff she pointed to with any comprehension, but he thought he could pronounce it if she first gave him a little coaching. "What's it for?"

"First this," she said, passing him the joint. Derek took a hit and choked.

"Strong," he gasped, exhaling thick smoke. He took another hit and began to grow dizzy, fingering the twisted paper. The stuff smelled like grass, but it tasted funny.

"It's treated," she said. "It might give you a little headache later. But don't worry about it. It'll help smooth things out now."

They sat on the couch and she showed him how to read the text while he finished the joint. By the time he was finished smoking it, he could recite his lines from memory.

"I wish I had this last year," he said with a giggle. "I'd be taking Latin XV now."

His remark struck him as hilariously funny. He saw an image of his old Latin teacher dancing in front of the class with her skirt hiked up past her waist and her skinny old legs doing a jig as she led the class in a Latin song. He stood beside her leading a chorus of naked students, understanding every syllable, reeling off Latin riffs like a Roman scat singer.

"What's in this stuff?" he asked, giggling.

He looked on the rug where Mary Rose was crouched over a small wrought-iron crucible.

"You got no clothes on," he said. "Your tits look big like moons. Like big balloons."

Then she was chanting, singing, tossing slips of paper in the pot, swaying and sweating and rolling her eyes.

After chanting a long rhythmical passage, she signalled to Derek to respond. He stuck for a minute, then the words came out, as if on their own. Diabolical, he thought, diabolus, diaboboloobop, song sung song.

"What am I saying?" Song stuff. Song sung strong. His ribs

and throat hurt he was laughing so hard. Mary Rose looked like a pale white fish scaling a falls.

Then she was standing over him beside the couch where he lay flat on his back, legs dangling over the edge of the cushion. He looked down and about a dozen yards away, he saw that his penis was erect and that she was jerking it with her hand, pumping it, tugging.

"What?" was all he could say. What what what. The words stuck in his throat. Then he erupted, bubbling all over. He closed his eyes, falling toward the moon, which was receding below, a great white rimless circle. He was a moon man long long gone. Think this, he thought, think this this this.

"Come on, drink this," a voice said after an eternity of echoes. "It'll help your head. It's all over. I think we pulled it off."

Derek sat up. Pulled it off. He sipped a hot hot liquid and his head hurt.

"That wasn't so bad now, was it?"

"What?" Derek said. "What bad?"

He heard laughter. Opened his eyes. He was sitting erect on the couch, a cup of coffee pressed to his lips; his own arms dangled at his sides like ropes.

"I must have made the stuff a little too strong," Mary Rose said. "You weren't supposed to pass out. I might have a little speed to help you get back up if you'll just stay on your ass a minute and not lay down again."

"No speed," he said. "I'll sit." He focussed his vision and looked into her bright green eyes. "Green," he said. "Your eyes are."

And that was his last memory of Mary Rose Keenan.

A week later she was dead of a drug overdose.

Derek heard the news from a friend at school two days after it happened. She'd been found dead in an abandoned house in downtown Baltimore.

For weeks after the funeral Derek was haunted by nightmares and guilt. Her sudden death and his memories of their last evening together precipitated his last frenzied attempt to believe the Methodist doctrines of his youth. He read the Bible, attended church every week, meditated, prayed. Still, the nightmares persisted. In fact, they grew more frequent and intense. He was afraid to go to bed at night. After several more weeks of trying to fight off sleep, his grades started slipping, his deteriorating appearance signalled trouble.

Immediately his parents intervened. They took him to a child psychologist, a smiling crewcut man with a brisk manner. Derek hated him on sight. In several sessions, Derek hardly uttered a dozen sentences.

After three weeks of analysis, the doctor pronounced that Derek was an incipient schizophrenic in need of treatment. His parents told him the news. Derek begged and pleaded till they agreed to let him see another doctor to get a second opinion. The new doctor rejected the original diagnosis and said that Derek was suffering from manic-depressive syndrome. By then, Derek had decided to take things into his own hands.

He read Bertrand Russell's *Why I Am Not a Christian* and decided he was now an unbeliever. He would imitate Russell's Olympian indifference to the demands of faith and in the future maintain a strict rationalism.

After a few weeks of analyzing his nightmares and guilt, the bad dreams stopped. He began to write poetry, inspired by the collected poems of Dylan Thomas, a Christmas present from the Keenans next door. To college friends who later accused him of being an unnatural hybrid creature, half rationalist and half daimon-possessed bard, he quoted Thomas's statement that a poet was just a man like other men who happened to be good with words. Later experience confirmed that judgement. Being a poet required only sanity, insight, and a gift for language. Derek had only scorn now for the dreamweavers and holy fakes of the world.

Turning away from the pair of weird sisters chatting beside him, Derek left the patio and went back inside Julian's house. He looked for familiar faces but could no longer find even Diane Gregor. His host was nowhere in sight. He was beginning to wonder if either Julian or Gretchen was in attendance at their own party when a soft touch on his arm made him turn around.

"Hello again. I'm glad you made it."

Derek returned Gretchen's smile and took in her appearance at a glance. A simple black pant suit set off her pale face and golden hair. Though fashionably loose, it also managed to show off her lithe figure.

"I hope you didn't have much trouble finding the place."

"No. Your map was perfect." Derek swept his eyes over the large room. "This is quite a house."

Gretchen turned up the wattage of her smile another notch.

"Julian calls this Nightmare Abbey. Don't be too impressed with this Gothic horror. It's rented. We only moved in last August. Most of the furniture's rented, too. All the good stuff is upstairs.

"Come on," she said with another light touch of his arm. "I'll take you to the real party. Poets and special guests only."

She led him through two more crowded rooms, then turned down a narrow hallway. At the hall's end, they climbed a flight of stairs and passed through another corridor, then turned at last into a little uncarpeted room furnished only with a cupboard and a pair of matching chairs. Set in the opposite wall was a narrow wooden door with an old-fashioned keyhole below the handle. As he approached it a step behind Gretchen, Derek realized the door was little more than five feet high, like something out of *Alice in Wonderland*. To step through it, they'd have to duck.

Gretchen put the key in the little lock and turned, but nothing happened. She then walked back to close the door through which they'd entered, grinned, and said, "This is kind of cute. Watch now."

She closed the door to the hall. As she did, the entire wall across the room (the key was still sticking out of the lock in the little door) began moving with a quiet rumble. A gap appeared along the left side of the door's frame, then widened as both walls rolled back into a much larger room beyond.

As the gap widened, Derek spotted Dave Knight and Diane Gregor among the guests mingling on the flowered carpet inside. They must have been recruited earlier while he was outside on the patio. He quickly surveyed this new looking-glass world and spotted some other familiar faces. Simon Macbeth and Professor Houston were talking to a student he recognized— Mona something; Julian Ginotti was conducting another guest down the opposite hall. Derek recognized his host's gliding gait and the long hair curling over the back of his collar.

Derek hesitated for a moment before stepping onto the carpet. Gretchen was already two paces inside.

"Well, come on," she urged, turning back to smile at him. "Haven't you ever been to a haunted house before?"

12

"Where did Julian go?" asked Derek as his host disappeared down the hall.

"Back downstairs for a bit, I'd say." Gretchen was guiding him around the room, searching out a group for him to join.

"Julian has an insatiable appetite for people. If you spent much time downstairs, you saw how eclectic his tastes are."

Derek noticed that Gretchen's speech had a trace of English accent overlaying a soft New England twang. The combination proved agreeable, giving her voice a soft musical lilt.

"Do you read Greek?" Gretchen was eyeing a knot of guests that included Dave Knight.

"No, afraid not. All I've had is a little high school Latin."

"Not to worry. We'll fix you up."

Now she was eyeing another group standing next to an antique walnut table. Julian's taste in furniture was as eclectic as his taste in people. Antiques—mostly nineteenth century English and American—were scattered sparsely about the room and down the corridor in an agreeable mix of styles.

"Here we go," Gretchen whispered as they approached another set of guests. "Have you ever met Robert Best?" She indicated a short, stocky man with a shaven head standing in the group they were nearing. "He's a charming wild man. I believe you already know Diane Gregor." Derek spotted the redhead standing next to the famous performance artist. There were two others in the group he didn't recognize.

"Come on, I'll make the introductions." Gretchen steered Derek toward them with a light squeeze on his elbow.

"Can I get you a drink?" They reached the outer edge of the little circle and Derek edged in.

"Just coffee, thanks."

The two strangers in the group were Sidney Frieze—Gretchen introduced him as a language poet—and Dorothy Lanier, a freelance journalist. Gretchen introduced Derek then left to fetch his drink.

Derek sized up Robert Best, who faced him across the circle. In addition to his shaven head, the artist displayed other eccentricities of dress and manner. He stood on the plush carpet in calloused bare feet and wore a car key dangling from a ring in his right ear. His short-sleeved shirt showed hairy muscular arms and a thick mat of dark curly hair erupted from his open collar. He was shorter than Derek by two or three inches, but looked vigorous and powerful. From what Derek knew of him, he had to be. Some of his exploits required considerable physical strength—not to say a foolhardy courage. In his most famous performance he'd walked a tightrope over a vat of liquid nitrogen, while holding a pole for balance. In another Derek had seen only in still photos, the artist had plunged his left arm into a tank of water and held it there for thirty seconds while a video camera filmed a half dozen hungry piranhas feeding frenziedly on his flesh.

His most controversial piece, though, was produced in an earlier phase of his career. Entitled *Poisoned Fountain*, the sculpture looked like an ordinary public water fountain. Derek saw the work on an early visit to the San Francisco Museum of Art, where it was now permanently installed. The fountain, set on top of a free-standing pedestal next to a wall, spewed a steady arc of clear water above its stainless steel basin. A sign above the fountain displayed the work's title and explained that inside its pedestal was a device through which the water passed to the nozzle above. A timer installed in the device was set to release a powerful dose of cyanide into the stream of drinking water at a random day and time sometime within a hundred years of the fountain's installation. Visitors were encouraged to drink, if they so desired.

The conversation, which had stopped when Derek was introduced, now resumed. Sidney Frieze was addressing the journalist.

"You don't understand," he said in a petulant, high-pitched voice. "I don't want readers. For me, the poem is merely a text. It doesn't address an audience about something out there in the real world. The language is entirely self-referential; the idea of meaning is irrelevant. Any attempt to regard it as a communication from writer to reader misconstrues the act of writing."

Robert Best suddenly interrupted. "But what about Gretchen's work. I've read her stuff and I think it's terrific. You can't tell me that poem about watching her sister die of cancer didn't have subject matter."

"Look," explained the bespectacled poet as if lecturing a child, "Gretchen Nordhaus is very successful at producing conventionally beautiful objects. Just the sort of commodity the publishing industry can sell to the bourgeois public. Language poetry resists the notion that a poem is something a reader possesses like a house or a car. To us, a poem is not a way to manipulate an audience; it asks the reader to participate with the writer in the construction of the poem's meaning."

"I thought you said poems didn't have meanings," objected the artist with a wink at Diane.

Frieze looked at the artist with disgust.

"Look, Bob," he entreated, his voice rising still higher, "performance art is just like language poetry. We're both against the idea that art is some object you put in your library or over your sofa. I would think you of all people would understand that."

Gretchen had returned to the group with a tall opaque drink and a cup of coffee for Derek. Gliding up to the circle, she jockeyed next to Derek and handed him the warm mug.

Either to impress her or because he was full of the spirit of opposition tonight, Derek decided to egg Frieze on a bit. He savored the thought of a little genteel combat. Besides, he was fed up with all of the pretension and bullshit he'd seen in the arts lately.

"That's something that always baffles me," Derek said, watching Gretchen from the corner of his eye. "Performance artists are always saying their art is pure because they don't produce a saleable object to hang in a gallery or museum. But they always make damned sure someone's there with a camera to get it all down for posterity. So instead of a well made object—say, a painting or a piece of sculpture—you get a grainy videotape or a black and white photograph to document the performance. I don't see how bad writing, bad acting, bad filming, and half-assed thinking add up to a revolutionary new art form. The performances I've seen look like something out of a high school variety show."

"You're wrong there, fella." Robert Best swung toward him, smiling up aggressively into Derek's face. The wrinkles around his eyes branched into lightning. "Sometimes," he said, "I think the idea of high art in the old sense is a complete sham."

Still grinning, Best looked like a pit bull that someone had mistakenly let off his chain.

"I'll tell you about something that not only changed my ideas about art, but changed my whole life. You tell me if there's ever been a poem that did to you what this number did on me."

The artist's eyes swept the circle as he spoke, hands on his hips, weight shifting from leg to leg.

"I used to be a fairly normal guy, believe it or not." The artist chuckled. "There I was knocking out my little avant-garde masterpieces in my studio down in the Mission District. Everybody loved my stuff, especially my dealer, who was selling it faster than I was knocking it out.

"I was starting to feel like a big success, in the conventional sense. My work was getting reviewed in *Artnews*; I was starting to make a name for myself. But the whole time I'm making my little fiberglass constructions, I feel like a phony, getting all this attention for doing the expected thing.

"About that time, I had this friend named Jerry Wade, who was always dragging me around to see this new thing called performance art—but I wasn't buying. It looked like a lot of phony-assed shit to me. I quit hanging out with Jerry—who I heard quit doing art to join a punk rock band—and started making these big free-standing sculptures. I had a commission from the state of California to do a series of pieces on saving the environment for a state office building downtown.

"So everything's going great, right? I'm treated like a rock star or some big fucking VIP. Then one day I'm working in my studio running some electric sander or something and I turn around and there are these two Iranian-looking guys pointing rifles at me. They order me to lie face down on the floor and then tie my wrists together behind my back with duct tape. Then they put a black hood over my head so I can't see shit and drag me out of there and stick me in the trunk of a car like some big goddamn suitcase or something.

"The next thing I know I'm bouncing around in the back of this car trunk with my knees in my face thinking, What the fuck is going on here? There was a lot of terrorism going on at the time and I figured my number had just come up. Then I figured they were after me for my money. I was raking it in pretty steadily at the time, and to some people I might have looked like I was good for a pretty big payoff.

"Anyway, after about two hours of bouncing around back there, I finally feel the car stop. They open the trunk babbling a lot of foreign crap at me, then drag me stumbling and tripping all over the place up this very bumpy dirt road. I can smell sage and hear bird songs, so I'm thinking, Great, they're gonna bury me up here in the fucking wilderness where nobody's ever going to find me again. I can hear and smell everything—the scent of old pine when they drag me up some steps into a house, the way the tap of our shoes echoes off the walls, the smell of coffee coming from a stove nearby, the feel of the hood's rough cloth against my face.

"Well, they drag me across the floor into another room, I hear a door open, and the next thing I know I'm bouncing off the wall of a closet onto the floor, still wearing that goddamn hood over my face.

"For days, that's where I sit. Every now and then I hear the bastards talking out there beyond the door, but can't understand a word they're saying. They pass me meals through the door, and about twice a day hand me a bucket to do my business in. These are like the highlights of my day.

"Finally, one day they take the tape off my hands, like I'd been begging them to do since they picked me up. When they shut the door, I take the hood off my face to breathe better and to get that rough cloth off my skin, which has taken a hell of a beating. That's the good news. The bad news is that some guy is now shouting at me in broken English through the door that I'm going to be executed the next day for my wicked imperialist crimes—whatever the hell they were supposed to be.

"Then a funny thing happens. I hear them leave the house and then a few minutes later a car engine cranking up outside. I hear the car drive down the road and then—nothing. Silence. I figure they had to go out for supplies or something.

"I suddenly remember something funny. When they closed the door to take off my tape, I didn't hear the lock when they shut the door. So now I'm dying to reach up and touch the knob to see if it's unlocked, but I'm afraid there's still somebody in the house. I listen. I don't hear anything but the blood pumping in my ears. I think about trying the door. This goes on for what seems like hours. Then I finally reach up and touch the knob.

"I feel the thing turn in my hand. The door's unlocked! As I hear the bolt click free, the feeling is electrifying.

"I wait like another hour to make sure the coast is clear, then I quietly open the door. I listen, but the house is completely empty and still.

"Now my heart's in my throat. I run outside and tear down the road like my clothes are on fire. After a couple hundred yards, the trees open into a wide meadow and I can see I'm near the top of a huge hill. The sun is shining and I'm thanking God and the wind and the clouds for letting me get away from that hell-hole when I hear hoof-beats pounding toward me from behind a grove of trees.

"I look to where the sound is coming from, ready to run if it turns out to be the two Iranian guys, and just about the time I do, I see the horse and rider break into the open across the meadow.

"The horse looks gigantic, a huge black stallion with a shining coat, and on top of it is this woman with her hair fanning out behind her in the wind. I realize in a flash that she's not with the kidnappers and start waving my arms and shouting for help.

"She finally notices me and starts in my direction. As she starts to get close, I can see that she's completely naked. Her breasts are flying around in these tiny little circles as the horse runs, and she looks white as a cloud.

"She pulls the horse up in front of me and looks down. The most beautiful woman I've ever seen in my life. Stunning figure, long waves of auburn hair, huge almond eyes. And sitting there in her birthday suit like it's the most natural thing in the world.

"I'm shouting at the top of my lungs about being kidnapped and begging her to get me the hell out of there, but I can see she doesn't understand a word I'm saying. Either she's deaf or she doesn't speak English. Finally, by waving my arms around and pointing I let her know what I want and she helps me up on the horse behind her. I link my arms around her bare waist and hold on for dear life as the horse takes off again. Her hair is flying back in my face, I can feel her bare round ass bouncing against my crotch, and we're covering ground like a tornado. I've never felt better in my life.

"Then halfway down the other side of this big hill she pulls the horse up and signals that she wants me to get off now.

"I climb down. I thank her by smiling and nodding my head.

"Then she hands me a little scroll she'd tucked away somewhere, kicks the horse, and takes off down the hill like a falling rock. I'm standing there in the middle of nowhere again holding this dippy little scroll, wondering why in hell she gave it to me. I unroll the thing—it's a piece of parchment on two little sticks, about a foot long and ten inches wide—and see this very elegant Gothic script. The letters are hard to make out, but finally I read the message.

"It says, 'I call this piece HAPPY TO BE ALIVE. Love, Jerry.'"

Robert Best broke into a loud belly laugh. When he stopped laughing, he finished the story.

"The next day Jerry calls me up and asks me what I think about the whole thing.

"I mean, I never felt so alive in my life. I thanked the guy, sincerely. Jerry'd given me the heaviest experience of my life. The way I heard and smelled things when they had me in that trunk or locked up in that closet, the feeling that I was *right there* in my body, the feeling I had when I saw that naked girl on that big black horse coming across the field . . ." The artist caught his breath, floundering for words.

"The experience changed my life. From that day on, I decided to live art instead of just making it. I wanted to do for other people what Jerry had done for me. But most of all, I wanted to feel that alive again, pushing the edge to see what I really am when all the bullshit is cut away.

"So," he added, addressing them all but eyeing Derek fiercely, "you tell me what book or painting ever did anything like that to you." He waited with his arms crossed for a reply.

"Yeah," he snorted. "Just like I thought. So don't tell me performance art is bullshit."

Derek finally broke the silence. "If it'd been me, I'd have wanted to kill the guy who set me up like that. Or at least have the whole bunch up for kidnapping."

"Shows how little respect you have for art," Best countered. "I mean, that would be a cowardly thing to do, to spit in the face of a gift like that. Remember, the guy was my friend."

"Well," added Gretchen, "I won't pretend that mere literature can top a story like that. But when Julian comes back up in a few minutes, I can show you some interesting stuff. He's going to open the library to show off his collection a bit."

With that hint of things to come, Gretchen excused herself and drifted away across the room. When the rest of the group began to break up, Derek found himself alone with Diane Gregor.

"I heard Julian has some wonderful stuff," Diane confided in hushed tones. "Unpublished original manuscripts and letters. Gloria Fiedler is angling to see some of it for the critical biography of Mary Shelley she's working on. Do you know Gloria?" When Derek shook his head, she looked pleased.

"I'm sure you've read some of her stuff if you're into the Romantics. She's great. I've asked her to be my dissertation advisor."

Diane's face flushed red. Watching her, Derek saw he could judge her degree of excitement by the various shades of pink and red that flashed across her face. She seemed to be in a continuous state of agitation.

"Gretchen says you're a poet," Diane added, rubbing the back of one hand, "so you must be pretty good. We'll have to exchange manuscripts sometime. I'm into post-modern experimentation, deconstruction—that sort of thing, but I don't go as far as Sidney. I'm a big Ashbery fan. But I'm mostly doing research right now."

"On what?" Derek asked, affecting interest.

"Blake. I'll probably do my dissertation on his prophetic books." Diane's face flushed pink as her eyes suddenly caught something across the room. "There's Gloria now."

Derek followed Diane's eyes and saw a short, bird-like woman in her early fifties, whose cropped gray hair fitted her head like a bowl. Peering out from short, even bangs, the professor was scurrying toward Julian Ginotti, who was apparently ready now to lead his guests to the library.

"There's Julian," Diane whispered, breathy with excitement. "It looks like he's starting to get everyone together. Come on," she added, taking a first step toward the group. "We don't want to miss our chance."

13

Julian Ginotti's library lived up to its billing. Its ceiling arched thirty feet above where Derek stood looking up at the skylights, which in daylight would fill the room with bright California sunshine. At this hour, their panes were black except where they threw back light from the lamps below. Book shelves extended halfway to the ceiling on all four walls. To reach books on the upper shelves, a visitor would have to use a ladder or climb a stairway to the narrow walkway that ran between the upper and lower tiers. Most of the volumes appeared to be leather-bound with gilded lettering on their spines.

On the far side of the room, sixty or seventy feet from the entrance, sat a long rosewood desk. A number of smaller tables and desks were placed in strategic niches around the room, along with ten or twelve high-backed reading chairs. Near the large desk, a half dozen free-standing shelves housed what appeared to be rare editions under locked glass plates, and several illuminated glass display cases glowed near the central desk.

"Gretchen, why don't you give your group a little tour and we'll meet at the far end to bring out some of the rarer items," Julian called. The guests had already begun to form into two groups around their host and hostess.

Derek joined Gretchen's party as she led it down the room's left wall, letting her guests peruse the shelves as they drifted along its length; occasionally she drew out an especially interesting book on which to comment. In the course of their tour, she showed them first editions by Dickens, Thackeray, Trollope, Milton, Gibbons, Johnson, and Pope. By the time they joined Julian's party at the other end of the room, Derek was more than a little impressed.

Guests from the other group were already browsing when he arrived, so Derek joined a cluster of English professors surrounding a brightly-lit display case. As he gazed in, Gloria Fiedler drew back from the glass in astonishment.

"It's a diary by Claire Clairmont, Mary Shelley's stepsister," she exclaimed. "I've never even heard of its existence. Has this been cataloged? Good heavens, where is Julian, I must ask him." She leered into the glass case like a child looking at a new bicycle.

"Here's something hard to come by," said Gretchen, approaching. She pointed to another display case a few feet away. Derek edged close with five or six others and peered in; in an instant he recognized the author, whose electrifying print illuminated the book's cover.

"My God," gasped Professor Houston, who had bulled his way to the front row. "That's Blake's *Jerusalem*. There are only supposed to be . . . what? a half dozen copies in existence."

"Five," corrected Fiedler, who was still reeling from her discovery of the diary. "There are five known copies. This must be a sixth. Why hasn't anybody made a record of this? Where has Julian been hiding these treasures? I'm going to plague that man till I find out."

The guests milled around the other display cases, turning dizzily from one to another with gasps of astonishment. Among those

Derek examined were two containing letters by Mary and Percy Shelley, Edward Trelawny, and Thomas Peacock. Remembering his own recently acquired collection, he saw who shared an interest in his discovery.

"Here's Blake's *Marriage of Heaven and Hell*." Gloria Fiedler looked as if she were going to pass out from lack of oxygen. She was huffing audibly as Derek drew beside her to stare at the rarity.

"Now where has Julian gone?" Fiedler stood on tiptoes and peered out from under her helmet of hair like a turtle, neck straining forward as she searched the room. Derek could tell she was anxious to stake a claim on the material, which contained the stuff on which careers were built.

Diane Gregor silently edged up to the case opposite Derek and whispered to her professor.

"Gretchen just told me they have some unpublished letters by Shelley and Byron." The two women shared a look of furtive discovery. "They're hidden in a safe somewhere here in the house."

Fiedler quickly scanned the walls as if trying to X-ray them with her naked eyes.

"I think we'd better try to talk to Julian tonight," she whispered. "I just don't understand how he could have kept this stuff all to himself for so long. It's mind-boggling."

Before anyone had the chance to corner Julian, the green-suited servant from downstairs entered, pushing a metal cart full of champagne buckets from which the tops of bottles protruded. Inverted champagne glasses glittered in rows on top of the cart on a white linen cloth.

"It's midnight," called the servant. He lifted a bottle out of a bucket and pulled its cork with a loud pop.

Outside, someone was setting off firecrackers. A large grandfather clock in the rear of the room began to chime as the servant poured drinks and everyone gathered around the cart to get a glass of champagne.

"Happy New Year," intoned Professor Houston, raising a sparkling glass toward the black skylights overhead.

Guests toasted the new year as, outside, firecrackers began to explode more fiercely.

"Happy New Year," purred a woman's voice in Derek's ear. He turned and saw Gretchen. Their eyes met for a brief instant, then he felt her warm moist lips on his as she leaned forward and kissed him.

He felt her breath against his cheek as she pulled away. He'd barely had time to return her lips' pressure before they were withdrawn, leaving him giddy with longing. Already she was gliding away through the crowd toward Julian. Too late to return the kiss. Derek stood on the carpet, jostled by other partiers, wondering what, if anything, the gesture meant.

He took a deep drink of champagne by way of consolation, then watched as Gretchen placed her hand on the Englishman's shoulder and leaned her weight against his. Whatever game she was playing, she had Derek's full attention. He looked toward her and for a moment caught her eyes, but their gem-like blue deflected his stare and an instant later she turned away.

Curious now, he downed the rest of his champagne and edged toward her.

After midnight, the crowd began to thin out. Gretchen led several groups of departing guests down a dark little hallway to a hidden exit leading back to the first floor. Returning after each trip to mingle with those who remained, she became gayer as the night progressed. Derek had already given up on the idea of returning her kiss. Now the mood of the other guests was sober. Most of those who remained were from the university. Several were eagerly plying Julian with questions about his collection.

"But what do these new letters reveal about Byron's life?" Gloria Fiedler pleaded, nearly overcome by her host's diffidence. "Don't you think you have an obligation to the intellectual community to make their contents known? All you'd have to do would be to let a few experts examine them for authenticity and then publish transcripts. They might shed new light on Byron's career."

Julian laughed. "Light is just what that poor troubled soul would most likely fear, I'm afraid. Don't you think his privacy has suffered from quite enough scrutiny already? Perhaps his interests would be better served by keeping some things hidden. If you'll remember, he was always hinting at dark crimes." Julian narrowed his eyes suggestively, his mouth betrayed a slight smile.

"Yes," agreed Ed Houston, with a tactful touch of his host's arm, "but we already know about all that—the incest with his half-sister, the pederasty and sodomy during his Eastern tours. That's old hat now. If anything, Byron's benefitted from his reputation for wickedness. He's become a sort of martyr in the cause of liberty and art."

Derek itched to get into the fray. This new line of discussion gave him the opening he'd been waiting for. He wanted to impress Gretchen before this assemblage of scholars. He also wanted to prove to the ones who'd rejected his application to Berkeley that he could beat them at their own game. If he could draw them in, he'd lead them on a merry chase; he'd turn their precious scholarship on its head.

"No, I think Julian's right," Derek interjected, leaning slightly forward on the balls of his feet. Already he could see he'd achieved one of his goals: Gretchen was eyeing him again with apparent interest.

"Byron's friends knew about the sodomy, from his letters, and the rumor of incest with Augusta was pretty widespread throughout England. Byron as much as confirmed it in *Manfred* and some of his other writing. And there are enough surviving references in the letters to sodomy and incest to make it pretty clear that Byron didn't particularly care if people knew about his sexual escapades.

"When Tom Moore burned his letters and Hobhouse destroyed his memoirs, I think they were trying to cover up something worse," Derek concluded. The others were already studying him curiously, waiting to weigh in with their own expertise.

"Such as what?" Gloria Fiedler asked, frowning. Her face became a study of downturned lines.

"Such as the fact that Lord Byron, the most celebrated writer in Europe and one of the permanent stars in the constellation of English poetry, was a vampire," Derek deadpanned. By the looks on their faces, he had his audience hooked. He'd treat them now to some of the facts he'd turned up after talking to Ron.

Ed Houston finally chuckled. A few others snorted or scoffed.

For half a second, though, Derek saw Julian's eyes flare with curiosity and interest. Then the Englishman checked himself. Derek decided to push things a bit further. He described the account he'd read of the opening of Byron's tomb, hinted at its sinister implications.

"Yes," objected Gloria Fiedler, "but the excision of Byron's heart and brain was obviously from the autopsy. To conclude from that that Byron was a vampire is absurd."

"Byron left specific instructions not to have his body hacked after he was dead," Derek explained with mock seriousness. "If they performed an autopsy, it was against his last wishes. The doctors knew what they had to do. Greece was one place where they knew how to deal with vampires. Dying there was just a bit of bad luck on Byron's part.

"Besides," he added, "there's a lot more evidence than the well-preserved corpse. Don't forget how when he was dying of fever Byron asked for a witch to cure him of the evil eye he thought someone had put on him. After his friends found him one, do you remember what he said?"

Ed Houston chipped in with the necessary information as if on cue.

"He said he didn't need the witch after all. He realized his real problem was vampires." Houston laughed at his own recollection. "Vampires. Those were his very words."

"Yes, but the vampires were the doctors," Fiedler exclaimed. "It was just a joke. They were extracting blood from him with leeches to the tune of a pound or two a day. They bloody well were vampires."

Derek continued, undaunted. "There's other evidence, too. Byron's poems are filled with hints on the subject. The famous Byronic pose wasn't just melancholy and world-weariness; it resulted from despair at his inability to die a normal death. He was afraid he'd have to roam the earth forever like the Wandering Jew. Think of Manfred and Cain. Byron described his heroes' predicaments in great detail."

"That's just a literary motif," Fiedler objected, interrupting. "You can't read such things as autobiography. You're making ridiculous leaps from literature to life." She was really getting worked up now. This talk of vampirism was more than she could reasonably be expected to bear.

"Well," Derek asked, "then how would you explain the uncanny powers of attraction Byron possessed? Everybody who came into contact with him felt drawn to him, as if by some supernatural power?"

"Aside from his great beauty and fame," Fiedler countered, "Byron was a Lord, a Peer of the Realm. And then there was his exceptional intelligence and charm. You don't have to invoke vampirism to explain his attractiveness."

"As he was dying," Derek said, "Byron told his servant Fletcher that if he failed to obey his last wishes, he'd come back and haunt him. Fletcher was pretty shaken up by the idea."

"You're grasping at straws now," Fielder complained. "This is all very amusing, but it doesn't speak to the real issue." She turned her attention back to Julian, the little byplay with Derek now over, as she thought. "What exactly is in these new Byron letters you've got? Really, Julian, it's criminal to keep this stuff to yourself."

Julian ignored her appeal and turned instead toward Derek.

"I think our young friend here has a point," he asserted. "Does anyone recall what Byron wrote to his publisher John Murray when asked about the authorship of *The Vampyre*, that little pamphlet published by his doctor?" Julian smiled, waiting for a reply.

"He said he'd known a few vampires himself," Derek answered, "and didn't want to divulge any of their secrets."

Ed Houston broke into peals of laughter. "Touché, Gloria. Ease up a little. It's only a joke."

"No, it's not a joke," Derek replied. "I haven't even touched on the real evidence. Give me a few minutes, and I'll prove Byron was a vampire. There's nothing ridiculous about the idea. Isn't that what the Romantic poets were all about? Defying God and nature and mortality was the name of the game."

He turned to Julian.

"Where do you have your Byron collection?" he asked his host.

Julian extended his arm toward a nearby shelf.

Followed by the others, Derek walked to the shelf, studied its titles for a moment, then extracted several volumes and placed them beside him on a nearby table.

"Here," he said, turning toward the circle of guests who'd gathered behind him. He opened the first fragile pamphlet, unfolding it carefully to keep from damaging its stiff pages. "I'll show you what I mean. The evidence is clear for anybody who has eyes to see it."

14

"Since Julian already mentioned it," Derek began, eyeing the circle of guests, "I'll start with Polidori's story, *The Vampyre*.

"As some of you already know, Polidori finished a tale started by Byron that night when he and the others were scaring themselves with ghost stories in their lodgings on Lake Geneva.

"What is less known," Derek continued, "is how extraordinary his story was when it appeared. The vampire legend was virtually unknown in England at the time. Byron picked up his vampire lore during his travels in the East. It would be decades before Bram Stoker published *Dracula*, so the few people who'd heard about vampires pictured them pretty much the same way they did in Eastern Europe—as ghouls who rose from the dead to prey on the living. Polidori's great invention was to model the vampire after Lord Byron. He named his villain Lord Ruthven, a name Lady Caroline Lamb had used for a character in *Glenarvon*, a fictionalized account of her affair with Byron, and described him in such a way that the British reading public would have no trouble identifying him as the famous poet.

"For those of you who haven't read the story," Derek added, fingering the book in his hands, "I'll briefly summarize the plot. The interesting stuff is the way the story mirrors actual events in Byron's life. But I'll get to that in a minute.

"The gist of the plot is this. Two men, Lord Ruthven and a young protégé named Aubrey, are making the expected Grand Tour of Europe, when Aubrey goes off on a little side trip to Greece. Arriving in Athens, he stays with a Greek couple and their beautiful young daughter, Ianthe, with whom he immediately falls in love. After living with them for a while, Aubrey decides to go on an excursion by himself into the nearby woods, despite the family's warnings about a vampire who roams the district feeding on careless wanderers. Naturally, Aubrey goes anyway. While travelling through the woods, he hears the loud shrieks of a woman followed by peals of sinister laughter." Derek smiled. "Nobody ever accused Polidori of subtlety.

"Anyway," he continued, "Aubrey follows the laughter to a little hut, goes in, and is immediately pounced on in the darkness inside. Just as his attacker crouches over him to work his evil will, men from the village carrying torches conveniently appear and scare the villain off. The next thing Aubrey sees after being brought back outside is the corpse of Ianthe, who shows all of the signs of being the victim of a vampire—blood stains, a bite on the neck, the whole bit. Aubrey goes back into the hut to investigate and discovers a strangely ornamented dagger, which he keeps until later in the story when he makes a very interesting discovery.

"I'll get back to the dagger in a few minutes," Derek promised.

"In the meantime, Aubrey is seized by a violent fever. When he comes back to himself, he sees his old friend Lord Ruthven again, and the two men leave the area to set out on another adventure.

"On this second journey, they're attacked by robbers and Ruthven is fatally wounded. While dying, he makes Aubrey swear never to tell anyone about his death. Ruthven's corpse is then taken away and hidden on top of a nearby mountain, where it's to be exposed to the first rays of the moon. Aubrey climbs to the top of the mountain, but finds no body anywhere in sight. Ruthven has disappeared.

"You can figure out what happened to the corpse," Derek added. "The rest of the story is predictable melodrama. Except for the dagger, which I mentioned earlier. Because while going through Lord Ruthven's effects, Aubrey finds a sheath with the same odd ornamentations as the dagger he found back in the hovel where he encountered the vampire. He slides the dagger into the sheath and discovers it fits: they're a perfect match. Both dagger and sheath are even stained with blood. Later, when Ruthven reappears alive and healthy, it's obvious he's the vampire who killed Ianthe.

"What makes all of this interesting," Derek continued, "are the connections between Polidori's story and certain events in Byron's life, which he fictionalized in his early adventure tale *The Giaour*. Don't forget, Byron himself provided the foundations for Polidori's vampire story. His own tale, *The Giaour*, is interesting because it contains Byron's only other reference to vampires. That alone should make it worth a close look."

"Yes," interjected Gloria Fiedler impatiently, "we're all familiar with *The Giaour*. But you're trying to read literature as biography again. It's the oldest fallacy in the book."

"No, I'll get to Byron's biography in a minute," Derek replied. "It's all tied in. Just give me a few more minutes. But first I have to talk a little more about *The Giaour*.

"You'll remember," he said, lowering his voice again, "that in the tale, the story's hero—who was yet another literary alter-ego of Byron—has an affair with Leila, who belonged previously to the harem of Hassan, a Moslem Turk. As a result of her treachery, Hassan has Leila tied up in a sack and drowned. The Giaour then kills Hassan in a battle, and, filled with guilt over his lover's death, seeks refuge in a Christian monastery.

"Well," Derek continued, "as you probably also know, there was an event in Byron's life on which the poem was based. There are several conflicting versions of the story—which Byron did more to muddle than to straighten out—so let's consider each one briefly.

"First, there's the version we have from a letter to Byron from his friend Lord Sligo. In this account, Byron was simply travelling outside of Athens when he came across a party of Turks carrying a woman tied up in a sack. They were on their way to throw her into the sea as punishment for some crime—probably for being unfaithful to Ali Pacha. Byron was a hero in this version. He held the execution party at gunpoint and threatened and bribed its members till they took the girl to the governor's house, where she was freed. Then Byron supposedly escorted her to a convent, from which she was safely shipped off to Thebes.

"The problem with that version," Derek explained, "is that it doesn't explain Byron's extreme uneasiness over the story. A second version recorded by Edward Williams adds some interesting details. In Williams's account, Byron was having a fling with a young woman whom he believed to be Greek but who was in fact a Turk in the harem of Ali Pacha. When Ali Pacha found out about the affair, he had the girl tied up in a sack and ordered the sack to be thrown into the sea. In this version, too, Byron comes to the girl's rescue and saves her life at great personal risk. But neither of these two versions gets recorded in the poem. In *The Giaour*, the girl is thrown into the sea while the hero watches. He even sees her moving in the sack before it sinks into the waves. The Giaour is haunted by the girl's death—

for which he blames himself. That's why he goes to the monastery at the end of the story—to confess his crime and to escape the guilt associated with her execution. It's important that Byron thought the girl was Greek.

"But the most interesting version of the story," Derek continued, "was told to Tom Moore by Mary Shelley. According to Mary, Byron spoke of her as the girl in *The Giaour*. Those are Mary's exact words." Derek paused to search for a passage in the book he now had in hand.

"I'll paraphrase the rest. In Mary's version, the girl underwent the punishment the poem describes on Byron's account. She doesn't specify what 'on his account' means, and she doesn't suggest a romantic entanglement, either. So it might be for a reason other than sexual infidelity. I think it has something to do with Byron's vampirism. Because Byron never did clear up the actual circumstances of the story. And in his poem, he hints that both the girl and he himself were tainted by vampirism. And remember, in Polidori's story, which also took place outside of Athens, the vampire victimizes a Greek girl.

"So what did Byron himself say about his own encounter with the girl? Only that it contained one aspect more singular than any adventure had by the Giaour in his poem; and—here's another exact quote from his collected letters and journals—'to describe *the feelings* of *that situation* were impossible—it is *icy* even to recollect them.'" Derek put down the book.

"There was nothing icy about recollecting the events recorded by Lord Sligo or Edward Williams, or for that matter by Mary Shelley either—so one can only guess what actually happened that was so awful that even Byron was unwilling to describe it in more detail."

Derek slid the heavy volume back onto the shelf.

"Now let's take a look at the poem."

He picked up a copy of *The Giaour* and flipped to the relevant passage. Fortunately, the lines were numbered in this cheap student's edition, so he found them quickly. No one interrupted him this time.

"Here's the famous vampire passage."

Derek read quietly, listening to the quiet breathing of his audience as he intoned the familiar lines.

> But thou, false Infidel! shall writhe
> Beneath avenging Monkir's scythe;
> And from its torments 'scape alone
> To wander round lost Eblis' throne;
> And fire unquenched, unquenchable,
> Around, within, thy heart shall dwell;
> Nor ear can hear nor tongue can tell
> The tortures of that inward Hell!
> But first, on earth as Vampire sent,
> Thy corse shall from its tomb be rent:
> Then ghastly haunt thy native place,
> And suck the blood of all thy race;
> There from thy daughter, sister, wife,
> At midnight drain the stream of life;
> Yet loathe the banquet which perforce
> Must feed thy livid living corse:
> Thy victims ere they yet expire
> Shall know the demon for their sire,
> As cursing thee, thou cursing them,
> Thy flowers are withered on the stem.
> But one that for thy crime must fall,
> The youngest, most beloved of all,
> Shall bless thee with a *father's* name—
> That word shall wrap thy heart in flame!
> Yet must thou end thy task, and mark
> Her cheek's last tinge, her eye's last spark,
> And the last glassy glance must view
> Which freezes o'er its lifeless blue;
> Then with unhallowed hand shalt tear
> The tresses of her yellow hair,
> Of which in life a lock when shorn
> Affection's fondest pledge was worn,
> But now is borne away by thee,
> Memorial of thine agony!
> Wet with thine own best blood shall drip
> Thy gnashing tooth and haggard lip;

Then stalking to thy sullen grave,
Go—and with Gouls and Afrits rave;
Till these in horror shrink away
From Spectre more accursed than they!

"Pretty gruesome stuff, eh?" Derek looked up from his book to smile.

"According to the curse, the Giaour was supposed to feed on those who were nearest and dearest to him—sister, daughter, wife, in the words of the poem. With that in mind, think of Byron's relationships with his wife, his half-sister Augusta, and his daughter by Claire Claremont, Allegra. He helped to wreck the lives and reputations of the two women, and just as the passage predicted, he buried his youngest child, Allegra, when they were both living in Italy."

"Yes," interrupted Diane Gregor, "but Allegra was safely tucked away in a monastery when she died of fever. Byron was nowhere near her at the time of her death."

"Maybe that's why Byron insisted on confining her to the convent over her mother's vehement protests," Derek retorted. "Maybe he was trying to protect the girl from his own dark impulses. Who's to say he didn't visit her secretly in the convent before she died. Or maybe she was infected by his vampirism before he installed her there—or became infected on one of her visits home. Shelley shows Allegra living with Byron, at least for a time, in his poem *Julian and Maddalo*.

"And then there's the wife Byron left behind in England," Derek added. "The exact reasons for her divorce never did become public. Byron's biographers all record the fact that he terrorized her with litanies of his terrible sins, but there was supposedly one thing which finally frightened her so badly that she couldn't abide life with him any longer. Some people speculate that it was her knowledge of Byron's incest with Augusta that finally drove her to the breaking point; others, that it was because Byron tried to bugger her. But there's evidence against both theories.

"For one thing, her friend Hobhouse drew up a list of all of the worst crimes Byron had ever been accused of, but when she read it, Lady Byron said that her reason for leaving him wasn't on the list. And she never would tell anyone what it was. Naturally, if it were his vampirism, she wouldn't have. Who would have believed her?

"But let's look back at Byron's poem for a minute," Derek added quickly, seeing Gloria Fiedler working herself up to another objection.

"The main thing we have to ask is, What is this curse about turning into a vampire even doing in the tale? All the Giaour did in the poem was fall in love with a girl and kill her murderer in a fair fight. It's true that the affair resulted in the girl's execution. But why would the curse of vampirism have to be called down on his head for that? There's nothing in the poem to justify it. Byron was simply projecting his own predicament with the Greek girl—the recollection of which chilled him years later—onto his hero. Something happened to Byron on that first trip to Greece that made him feel cursed with vampirism." Derek lowered his voice suggestively. "I think he killed the girl with a dagger. Maybe she rose from death afterward and the Turks disposed of her corpse that way as a measure against her return—they might have seen something suspicious in the manner of her death.

"In any case, the dead girl returns to haunt the Giaour. Tell me if this doesn't sound like she's come back as a vampire."

Derek turned to the end of the poem and read again.

> To-morrow's night shall be more dark;
> And I, before its rays appear,
> That lifeless thing the living fear.
> I wander—father! for my soul
> Is fleeting towards the final goal.
> I saw her—friar! and I rose
> Forgetful of our former woes;
> And rushing from my couch, I dart,
> And clasp her to my desperate heart;
> I clasp—what is it that I clasp?

No breathing form within my grasp,
No heart that beats reply to mine—
Yet, Leila! yet the form is thine!
And art thou, dearest, changed so much
As meet my eye, yet mock my touch?
Ah! were thy beauties e're so cold,
I care not—so my arms enfold
The all they ever wished to hold.
Alas! around a shadow prest
They shrink upon my lonely breast;
Yet still 'tis there! In silence stands,
And beckons with beseeching hands!
With braided hair, and bright black eye—
I knew 'twas false—she could not die!
Be *he* is dead! within the dell
I saw him buried where he fell;
He comes not—for he cannot break
From earth;—why then art thou awake?
They told me—'twas a hideous tale!
I'd tell it, but my tongue would fail;
If true, and from thine ocean cave
Thou com'st to claim a calmer grave,
Oh! pass thy dewy fingers o'er
This brow that then will burn no more;
Or place them on my hopeless heart:
But, Shape or Shade! whate'er thou art,
In mercy ne'er again depart!
Or farther with thee bear my soul
Than winds can waft or waters roll!

"It's interesting," Derek noted after finishing, "that the Giaour wonders why Hassan can't rise from the dead, since Leila apparently has. Even though the Giaour's been cursed with vampirism for his part in Leila's death, what in the poem explains why *she* comes back from her watery grave? The Giaour starts to explain, 'They told me ...' but he breaks off with the remark that it's such a hideous tale his tongue would fail him in the telling. He sounds awfully like Byron later recalling the icy memory of his own Greek girl."

Derek paused for a moment and noticed that Julian was studying him with rapt attention.

"I promised to come back to the dagger in Polidori's vampire tale," Derek added,"—the one Aubrey found in the hut where the Greek girl was killed by Ruthven.

"Well, it seems that on his way to Greece—right before he arrived in Athens—Byron was pacing the deck of the ship when he suddenly stopped and picked up a dagger. A Turkish dagger. According to the witness, Byron unsheathed the blade and stood silently looking at it for several minutes. Then he's reported to have said, 'I should like to know how a person feels after committing a murder.'" Derek paused again to let the words sink in.

"The entry appears in Lovell's book *His Very Self and Voice*. The very next entry is Lord Sligo's letter of July 18, 1813, about Byron's supposed rescue of a girl in a sack outside of Athens. You can look it up. Byron's friend Tom Moore reported the incident to an anonymous journalist."

Julian Ginotti broke the silence after Derek finished.

"A most interesting little disquisition. I see you're a scholar as well as a poet.

"However, I do have one further question," Julian added. "You said that Byron was a vampire, yet after his death he was immediately eviscerated and his heart and brains removed during the autopsy. So it would seem he had no post mortem existence. I thought a vampire had to arise from the grave to assume his supernatural powers and longevity."

"Yes, they usually do," Derek explained with less confidence and air of authority. He was winging it now, hoping the answers would come as needed. "I'm still working out the details of how someone actually becomes a vampire. My best guess is that it involves some sort of Faustian bargain with the powers of darkness. Maybe it's necessary to make some sort of blood sacrifice. That would explain the dagger in Polidori's story and Byron's fascination with the Turkish dagger on board ship on his way to Greece. He probably picked up the lore on that first trip through Albania or maybe in Greece itself."

Derek suddenly remembered something said by Ron Pruitt in their last interview and decided to play the card.

"There might be one other factor, too," Derek added. "Age. I have the feeling that a person has to make the conversion while still relatively young. Byron was thirty-six."

"Poppycock," proclaimed Gloria Fiedler. "Byron was as mortal as you or me. Painfully so. Your argument was clever, but that's about all. Now please, can't we all prevail on Julian to tell us more about his collection? I, for one, am positively itching to hear what revelations lie buried in those letters."

Julian once again deflected her inquiries and after another minute of talk signalled the end of the party by yawning. Gretchen then suggested they all return downstairs. Together, she and Julian led the few remaining guests from the library back to the second floor room in which Derek had first encountered them, where the subject of talk shifted to the more pragmatic topic of ride-sharing to the guests' scattered destinations. The only guest crossing the bay to the city was Robert Best, who was already preparing to leave, so Derek quickly arranged to catch a ride home with him. Gretchen then led the two men down a narrow stairway to a hall which emerged, after several turnings, at the front entrance, where she bade them good-bye.

Derek followed the bald pate of the artist across the wet grass to where the nearest cars were parked, surprised at how quickly the little man could move on his feet. He watched as Best skipped deftly between two parked motorcycles, then scurried to close the distance before the artist forgot his promise and left him behind.

15

Derek spent New Year's Day reading and writing and went to bed early, awakening a little after five a.m. Tuesday morning when Lisa returned home early from Sacramento. He heard her key in the lock in the front door and a few seconds later heard a suitcase drop heavily on the living room rug. After a short pause, she padded quietly into the bedroom on bare feet. Through sleep-swollen eyes, he looked up and saw she was naked. Pale in the dim light leaking through the curtain, she tiptoed into the bedroom, lifted a corner of the sheet, and slid into bed beside him.

"I came home early," she explained, husky-voiced. "Thought I'd catch a little extra sleep before I start back to school."

She pulled the sheets up around her neck and scooted her back and buttocks against Derek's chest and groin. He could feel the cool satin of her naked flesh as she edged closer to share his body's warmth.

"What's this?" she asked, hand exploring beneath the sheet.

When the clock radio woke them at seven, they were still tangled in each other's arms.

"Jesus, hit the volume," Lisa muttered into the pillow over her head.

Derek forced himself to get up and turn off the radio, then stumbled into the kitchen to start breakfast while Lisa began the long ritual of preparing herself for law school.

Over coffee and toast, Derek described the New Year's Eve party at Julian's and his harrowing ride home on the back of Robert Best's motorcycle.

"I could see the headlines in the morning paper," he said, grinning. "'Performance Artist and Passenger Killed in Motorcycle Wreck: Art World Loses Rising Star.' You should have seen my face when I climbed onto that big Harley." Derek laughed. "No helmets, naturally. This is a guy who lets piranhas feed on his arm."

Lisa raised her eyebrows in a look of mild distress.

"And you know what the craziest part about the whole thing was? After we made it through Berkeley and were racing across the Bay Bridge at about a hundred miles an hour, I looked out at the stretch of black water and the city lights shining in the distance and actually began to get a kick out of the whole thing. It was exhilarating. By the time Bob let me off at Washington Square, I was glowing like a goddamn comet. I thanked him for the ride, we both had a laugh, and I walked the rest of the way home on this incredible high. I think I was still half high when you walked in the door."

Lisa regarded him skeptically. "It's a miracle you weren't killed. I thought you hated motorcycles."

"I do. This was strictly a one-time affair."

Lisa stood up from the table. "There's a budding Romantic inside of you, yet. The next thing I know, you'll be taking me out dancing."

"Maybe I should buy some shoes, just in case."

Lisa checked a grin then rose from her chair and crossed to the living room to finish preparations for school. After a quick inventory of her things, she muttered, "I forgot my Criminal Procedures notes. I think I left them in the bedroom." Then she paced into the other room, clucking her tongue, to search for the missing notebook.

Derek could see she was already anxious about returning to school and suddenly felt sorry for her. He wished they had more time together. Though they'd lived together for over a year under the constant pressure of tests and papers, something was different now. At Stanford, Lisa had seemed less driven, more self-assured. It was her easy confidence that first impressed him in the early days of their romance.

He remembered the night they met. They were waiting in line outside the Stanford auditorium to see Wertmuller's *Seven Beauties* on a cold November night. The wind whirled round the dark walls of the courtyard in leaf-rattling eddies. Instinctively, they'd sought each other's warmth as the students around them huddled toward the box office.

Once inside, they sat together, laughing at the movie's comic hero, brushing knees and elbows. At every touch, Derek's body grew weightless. By the time the house lights rose, they were holding hands. Within an hour of leaving the theater, they were making love on the floor of his apartment, moonlight washing over their naked bodies. Neither of them slept that night.

Their courtship began in reverse, with sex first. Later they discovered that they were both English majors. They spent long evenings talking over games; gambled over cribbage and backgammon. Sometimes to raise the stakes, they'd play for sexual favors, winner take all. Derek often lost on purpose just to test the depth of her nerve and imagination.

It was during his first quarter at Stanford while taking Watson's course on the Romantic novel that Derek introduced Lisa to Professor Watson at a department party. As they talked, they discovered that Lisa had been born in Watson's home town in England, Bridgnorth, while her father was stationed at a nearby air base. Afterward, whenever Derek ran into him, Watson would smile and ask how their Shropshire lass was doing. That's when Derek really began to like the old man.

As he cleared the breakfast table, Derek mused over the unsettling change. The phone rang just as he started the dishes. Lisa was still rattling around in the bedroom, so he dried his hands and crossed to the stand beside the couch to answer it.

As he hung up, Lisa emerged from the bedroom smiling, notes in hand.

"You won't believe what that phone call was about," Derek said.

"I don't have time to guess, Derek, so please hurry and tell me. It's almost time to go."

He hesitated for another second to heighten the suspense.

"It was UC Berkeley. They just offered me a University Fellowship. I've been accepted into the Ph.D. program, after all. I'm a goddamn University Fellow." He laughed out loud, delighting in the absurdity of the news.

"I thought they turned you down. In fact, didn't they say you could be accepted only on probation?"

"Yeah," he laughed. "They changed their minds. The English Department secretary told me some new funds had become available and that my status had been reviewed and upgraded. A few weeks ago I was persona non grata. Now I'm a goddamn fellow. What a hoot. I'm supposed to go over there this morning to fill out paperwork. Classes start tomorrow morning. I'm a student again."

Once on Berkeley's campus, Derek stopped at the administration building to pick up a batch of admission forms. The brusque and harried secretary there then steered him to the English Department in Wheeler Hall, where he picked up a second batch to fill out and return later in the day. He decided to leave campus to complete the paperwork in a nearby cafe, so after stepping back outside into bright sunlight, he retraced his steps across campus to Bancroft, crossed the busy avenue there, then headed down Telegraph Avenue in search of a quiet, out-of-the-way place.

On Telegraph, he encountered a gauntlet of street merchants and sidewalk stands that slowed pedestrian traffic to a crawl. It was like passing through a Middle-Eastern bazaar. Jade necklaces flashed in the sunlight, crystal wind chimes tinkled in the fanning breeze. Derek edged past a middle-aged couple's table of leather goods, passed a street musician plucking the strings of a zither, then slipped through an opening in the crowd and broke into a stretch of open pavement.

A panhandler, sitting cross-legged on a rug under an awning, thrust an open palm toward him from his spot in the shade. Derek ignored it and pushed toward the knot of pedestrians waiting for the light at the next corner. He'd never seen so many street people crammed into such a small space. Every corner had its resident mumbler or wild-eyed urban hermit. The sunlight and warm air nurtured them like hardy outdoor shrubs.

At the opposite corner, an entire family—bearded father, bangled and beaded mother, and two dirty-faced, blond toddlers—squatted on a frayed blanket in the shade near a busy intersection, like specimens in a scientific exhibit. All of their worldly belongings were packed into a single metal shopping cart parked against the wall behind them.

As he waited for the light to change, Derek overheard the chant of a street crazy droning in the crowd over his shoulder.

"The sky is infected. The air is infected. The trees are infected. The hands are infected. The eyes are infected. The rain is infected. The tears are infected. The rivers are infected. The spit is infected. The grass is infected. The mice are infected. The hands are infected . . ."

The light changed and Derek walked quickly out of earshot, wondering if the litany had an end.

After another half block, the crowd thinned out except for a few knots of students returning to campus. Derek began to look for a suitable cafe. A few doors down he spotted a sunny veranda then left the noisy street for the relative quiet of the shop's interior.

Once settled at a table with coffee and sandwich, he pulled out the two stacks of forms to begin filling in their columned blanks. After forty-five minutes, he pushed the forms aside and ordered a second cup of coffee.

Mechanically, he watched the faces passing on the sidewalk and entering the shop. Most looked like students. As he lifted his pen to return to his paperwork, he spotted a familiar face.

Dave Knight, the classics major he'd met at the Houstons', returned his smile on entering the cafe. The rangy student strode toward the counter to pick up some coffee, then pulled up the chair opposite Derek and sat down.

Behind the thick lenses of his glasses, the student's eyes looked weak and tired.

"What brings you to these precincts?" Dave asked, extending a hand. "I thought you lived in the city."

"Paperwork," Derek answered. "I've just been accepted into the doctoral program. Got the news this morning. Since classes start tomorrow, I thought I'd better get going."

"Nothing like letting you know at the last minute."

Derek explained about his sudden change of status.

"And they gave you a fellowship?" Dave looked surprised. "The deadline was like months ago."

"I know." Derek laughed. "Nobody was more surprised than I was when I got the call. Why, is this kind of thing unusual?"

"It happens exactly never." Dave looked puzzled but impressed. "They must be damned interested in you. Last I heard there was no money for anything. I know two people who lost their t.a.'s last semester."

Dave's comment reminded Derek of his own suspicions earlier. The early morning phone call the day vacation ended was oddly timed, to say the least.

Derek nodded toward Dave's cup. "Double espresso. That ought to get your heart going."

Dave smiled wanly. "I just got out of bed. I work best at night. I never take classes before noon. I'm not *compos mentis* till about eleven-thirty. There are too many distractions in the day."

The student sipped his drink, then leaned back in his chair, eyeing the stack of half-completed forms.

"So what courses are you going to take? I'd recommend Gloria Fiedler's seminar on the Romantic poets this quarter. She's top notch.

"And if you're interested in a writing workshop," he added, "this is Dick Fuller's last quarter at Berkeley. He's going back East in the spring. Can't handle the Berkeley scene, I guess. Boston University's hired him for their graduate writing program."

"Richard Fuller?" Derek asked. "I didn't even know he was at Berkeley."

"Yeah, the university's trying to cash in on the creative writing fad." Dave grinned. "They don't think it's academically respectable, but they've been trying to get their piece of the pie. Dick Fuller gave the experiment respectability. Now they're trying to find a replacement. It should be fun. Over the next two or three weeks, they're bringing in three big-time poets to interview and give readings. It'll be a kind of poetry bake-off. Personally, I think they ought to bring all three on campus at the same time, lock them in a room, and give the job to whoever comes out alive."

Derek smiled at the thought. "Who are the three poets?"

"You don't want to know. Kenneth Galloway, Barbara St. John, and Mark Blotski. The Larry, Moe, and Curly of American poetry."

"It must be a seller's market this year."

Dave smiled. "There's something else you might be interested in. Every winter there's a school-wide poetry contest. The Robinson Jeffers Prize, for the best ten pages of poetry by a Berkeley student. The deadline's tomorrow, if you want to enter. It's worth the hassle. The prize is five thousand bucks." Dave slid back his chair, unfolded his length from beneath the table, and stood up.

As he gathered up his things, he apologized for leaving.

"I've got to do a little reading in the library. Nice bumping into you again. Guess I'll see you around campus." He slung his book bag over his shoulder and gave an off-handed wave as he turned toward the door. "*Ciao.*"

After Dave Knight left the cafe, Derek fetched a third cup of coffee. He was already going over titles of poems for the contest and thanking Dave again for the information.

A rare bird, he thought, knowing how easily Dave might have kept the information to himself for another day or two to lessen the competition.

Through the long window, Derek watched the student's back disappearing down the sidewalk among the crowd of returning students.

A rare bird, indeed.

16

Without a dorm room or apartment to retire to during the long day, Derek found himself living more and more out of the cafes, bars, and restaurants that surrounded campus. He was hiking down Telegraph now to spend a few minutes talking to Dave Knight in a local bar before commuting back across the bay. Since he was ten minutes early, Derek decided to slip into a news stand to browse through the current literary magazines. He hadn't been home to check his mail today and wanted to see if a poem of his, which was scheduled to appear, had in fact been published. It had. His name and the title of his poem jumped out at him from the magazine's contents page. He returned the journal to its place on the stand and stepped back out to the street.

Two blocks later, he found the bar. He entered and stood for a moment to let his eyes adjust to the dim interior. When his vision cleared, he saw that Dave had already arrived and was now occupying a booth against the wall by himself, sipping a beer and jotting sporadically at a page in his ever-present note-book. Derek caught a waitress's eye and signalled to her as she went by, then steered toward the booth, where Dave was still lost in concentration.

Probably revising a poem. Dave reworked his poems obses-sively—between classes, at night in his apartment, at meals, over endless cups of coffee. The stuff he brought to the workshop was always highly polished. This morning he'd submitted two lyrics translated from Horace and Propertius. The other students were so cowed by the stuff that when Dick Fuller finally asked for the group's comments, they were uncharacteristically mild in their complaints. They vented their pent-up fury, instead, on Derek's poems.

Diane Gregor led the attack. Five minutes after her assault, most of the class joined in the feeding frenzy. Dick Fuller's frank praise of the poems only incited the class to greater fury. Luckily, Derek had been in workshops before and knew what to expect.

It came as a relief now to settle at the booth to talk shop with a genuine craftsman. There were things one could only discuss with a fellow initiate. When Dave looked up from his poem, Derek raised his glass and smiled.

"Does Bacchus serve as the spirit of beer or only wine? I feel like communing with a dark god tonight."

Dave closed the notebook and tucked it away in his book bag.

"What, not attending the reading?"

Kenneth Galloway was reading his poetry at a local bookstore tonight. Though not officially part of the selection process, the reading was being attended by some members of the English faculty out of politeness. Derek had no intention of following suit. He'd sat through the earlier reading in Wheeler Hall this afternoon and had heard quite enough of the man's poetry.

"I heard a few other people might be stopping by after the reading," Dave added. "Can you stick around a little tonight? Julian Ginotti might be dropping by."

Derek noted the hint of respect as Dave mentioned the Englishman's name. He decided to pump his friend for a little more information.

"Aside from having a great book collection," he asked, "what's so damned great about Julian Ginotti? The guy can't be much older than you and me."

"For one thing," Dave replied, looking somewhat puzzled by

the question, "the man knows everything. Literally everything. Have you had a chance to talk much with him?"

"Only a few words."

"Well, if you get the chance, do it. In a few hours, I learned more about Greek poetry from him than I did in two semesters with Robert Hutchinson, and Robert's supposed to be top dog in the field. Julian can recite from memory practically any classical poem you name and translate it on the spot. Even Hutchinson has to decode a lot of the stuff we do in class. Julian reads it like it was his native language. A while back, Hutchinson talked with him for an hour at a party and came away dumbfounded. Said he'd never understand Greek like that if he studied it for a hundred years."

"Then why can't I find any of Julian's translations in the library? I've looked," Derek said. "He hasn't published anything that I can see."

"All right, so he hasn't published. The guy's a genius."

"Yes, but what's he done? Have you seen any of his work? I've looked and I can't find a thing, not one blessed thing. Maybe that's all he is—great talk."

Dave looked slightly disgusted at Derek's reasoning. "So when has getting published ever had to do with anything? Julian can talk Dante with Joe Loggia and Goethe with Bill Bennet and when he's done they're both shaking their heads. If he writes poetry, I'll bet it's something to see. Ask Gloria or Diane. I've heard them hinting about his stuff. Diane's practically been living at Julian's since New Year's Eve."

"What's she doing there?"

"She and Gloria are digging through the letters and things he showed us. Gloria's writing a critical book on Shelley."

"I thought she was writing about Mary Shelley," Derek said.

Dave smiled. "That was before she saw Julian's collection."

"And Diane told me she was doing her dissertation on Blake."

"Obviously she changed her mind. Can you blame them? If half of the stuff we saw on New Year's was authentic, they'll be able to put Shelley scholarship on its ear. Any scholar would kill for a chance like that."

Dave took a long drink of beer and sat his mug back down on the glass-topped table.

"Even Ed Houston is getting in on the act," he added. "Ed met Julian back in August when he first came out here. Now he's supposedly working on a book on Shelley, too."

"But Houston's field is American Lit. His big books are on Whitman. Since when did he become a Shelley scholar?"

"Don't be so categorical," Dave replied. "Ed's no fool. He may outdo Gloria before it's all said and done."

Derek sipped his beer. He was getting tired of hearing what a great man Julian was.

"Hey," Dave said, looking toward the bar's entrance, "here comes Dick Fuller. The reading must be over."

Fuller, a small dapper man, wore a pin-striped blue suit and red tie. As he crossed the room, he spotted the two younger men and approached with a friendly nod.

"How'd you pull escort duty tonight?" Dave asked as Fuller joined them. "Get the short straw?"

Fuller didn't comment except to smile. "I see you fellows have the right idea," he said, indicating their glasses. Then he signalled the waitress and ordered two more pitchers. "We can pull up some more chairs when the others get here," he suggested. "Ken Galloway is a beer man. He got a good head start on us down the street on the way over here. They ought to be here any minute. He's taken a fancy to Diane. I gave her strict instructions to get him up here before he gets incoherent."

Fuller's caution proved to have been well-founded. When Galloway entered a minute later in a crowd of escorts, he was leaning heavily on Diane Gregor's arm. The tall craggy-faced poet lurched toward their table, guided by his companion. His cheeks glowed red as he slumped into a chair.

When a second group arrived, the booth proved too small to accommodate the growing party, so after a few minutes they left it for a pair of large tables. Ed Houston and Gloria Fiedler joined the group after everyone else was seated. Julian Ginotti and Gretchen appeared at the table five minutes later and sat down together in a place quitted by two grad students. Julian, in his characteristic open-necked white shirt, sat down stiffly. Gretchen had her hair pulled back tightly and wore a severe smile.

"So you want four more pitchers?" asked the harried young waitress, stepping back from the table. Kenneth Galloway had just patted her on the fanny; a grad student's spilled mug was dripping beer onto her shoes.

"Not me," replied Houston, touching the waitress's arm. "I'll have Scotch on the rocks."

Derek got the impression that the big man was less than happy about escorting this drunken lout of a poet tonight. Gloria Fiedler looked distracted and confused. Julian Ginotti, however, bore himself with his usual aristocratic grace, though a trace of scorn played about the corners of his mouth. Derek wondered what impelled the Englishman to attend such a petty affair. Perhaps his famous appetite for people. Gretchen watched the proceedings as if surveying the party from the top of an adjacent mountain. Galloway, the guest of honor, was too busy trying to grope Diane Gregor to pay attention to anyone else.

Everyone talked about the success of the night's reading. Nearly two hundred people had attended, trailing down a flight of steps to the first floor and out the front door to the sidewalk. If the English Department wanted popularity in their resident poet, they'd clearly found their man. Galloway's drunken enthusiasm suggested he thought he'd pulled off quite a coup. When he thought no one was looking, he slipped his hand over Diane's breast and gave it a quick feel.

"I'm going to be editing a special issue of *Ploughshares*," the tall poet announced suddenly to no one in particular. Then addressing Diane with a cock of his head, he added, "Why don't you let me look at some of your stuff? I'll bet you're one hell of a poet. God, that red hair," he added, running his hand down her back.

Sensing the obvious bribery in his suggestion, she beamed up into his face, then turned triumphantly toward Derek and Dave Knight, two thwarted rivals. Everyone else at the two tables ignored the exchange.

The talk turned from the reading to other topics. Once the subject was no longer his own work, Galloway seemed to lose interest in the conversation. After downing three more mugs in quick succession, the poet rose unsteadily from his chair. "If you don't mind," he said, "I think I'll be getting back to my hotel room now. Diane has kindly offered me a lift."

As he rose, he bumped into the back of a man sitting behind him. "It's been great," he said, steadying himself and lurching toward the door. Diane followed, waving farewell as she overtook her charge; then the pair exited, the tall man leaning on his escort's shoulder as they passed out of sight.

Once the celebrity poet had left, the group at the tables thinned a bit. Those who remained began to talk more excitedly, the mood became lighter, gayer. Somehow, without his noticing when the topic of conversation changed—he was half drunk now— Derek found himself in the middle of another discussion of vampirism. Julian Ginotti was apparently paying him back for his lecture on Byron on New Year's Eve.

"But think of the advantages of becoming a vampire," the Englishman said, laughing. His voice was somewhat high in pitch but was perfectly modulated, like a well-tuned violin. "What is it that every poet ultimately wants, if not immortality—the sense that his work will be read a century, ten centuries hence." He pressed his fingertips together, raised his eyebrows, grinned.

"But as you know, the tides of literary fashion are notoriously fickle. Even at the best of times, the most worthy are not always held in highest esteem—isn't that right?"

Julian's pale blue eyes gazed into Derek's. "What of the poet," he asked, "who's denied the blessing of longevity and fails to see his reputation equal his accomplishment and talent? Worse, what of the poet who lives and dies in complete obscurity— unwept, unhonored and unsung? Think how he might correct the oversights of time and fashion and rescue his works from oblivion if he possessed the power and invincibility of the undead.

"Think, for instance, only of the case of Catullus, to take a very dramatic example. Has there ever been a greater lyric poet in any language?

"Did you know," Julian asked, smiling cannily, "that we owe our knowledge of that poet's work to the survival of a single manuscript? Except for poem number sixty-two, which was happily preserved in a ninth century anthology of Latin verse, all of his poems have come down to us through a single source—a manuscript which didn't surface until the thirteenth century in the Cathedral library in Verona. That manuscript, too, was lost to the depredations of time, but two copies of it survived, and it is to them that we owe our knowledge of Catullus's unparalleled achievement in the lyric. But for that single manuscript, one of the great poets of the ages would be all but lost to us. It's only sheer luck that we know of his work at all.

"Now imagine," Julian continued, "that Catullus had been granted a century or two of post mortem existence—call it vampirism, if you will, though it seems a rather loaded and superstition-ridden term. How would Catullus have employed that supernatural extension of his life—how would any poet?—except to insure that his work and reputation would be passed on to later generations without diminution or loss.

"In practical terms, the poet might see that sufficient copies of his work were placed in strategically secure locations; might place collections of his poems in the way of influential critics and literary historians and anthologists; might, in short, guide and correct the course of his own literary reputation, adapting the spirit of his work to the demands of each new age." Like a virtuoso, Julian paused to allow an instant's appreciation of his artfully arranged clauses, then bent to the strings again for a final cadenza.

"What would you do, my ambitious young friend," he asked, "if given the chance to convey your poems to future ages despite hostile critics, indifferent readers, and the clamor of rival pens?"

Julian addressed his question to Derek, but included the entire group with a graceful wave of one hand. He leaned back and cast a cold smile at Gretchen. As he did, Ed Houston added a coda to the Englishman's remarks. He'd caught the drift of the joke and was apparently having his turn at Derek, too. Looking down at Derek and Dave, he said, "Before you say that no poet would accept such a Faustian bargain, think about this.

"I've read of a study of Olympic weight-lifters, who were asked the following question: If you could take a pill that would enable you to set a new Olympic record in the lift, but, as a side effect, you'd die a year later, would you take the pill or not?" Houston grinned. "What do you suppose the majority of them said?"

"I've heard of that study, too," interjected Gloria Fiedler. "It's no big surprise. The majority said they'd take the pill. Stupid jocks."

"That's right," Houston chuckled. Then turning back to Derek and Dave, he asked, "How about you two young fellows? In my experience, poets have at least as much competitive spirit as Olympic athletes. Sharing your vocation's famous preoccupation with immortality, would you take your chances with posterity or choose the immortality pill—if one existed, of course?"

"Yes," added Julian, smiling. "There's reputed to be only one small side effect. A certain indelicacy in one's evening dining habits."

Everyone at the tables laughed. Derek joined in the general hilarity but felt the first faint stirring of alarm.

"Poets are such curious lovable monsters," Julian added after the laughter died down. "It's a pity the art has fallen into such low esteem that a specimen such as the one we've seen here tonight ranks as a serious practitioner while so many more worthy and ambitious young geniuses surround us on every hand."

Derek accepted the flattery with a nervous smile. Dave Knight simply looked away. It came as a relief when the conversation shifted once again to the qualifications of the two remaining candidates in the department's job search.

Still, Derek thought, listening to the talk, it felt good to be singled out for praise by someone as remarkable as Julian Ginotti. As if reading his thoughts, Gretchen caught Derek's eye and smiled.

Then another idea struck him. Both Julian and Gretchen were beginning to show an inordinate amount of interest in his affairs. Gretchen's smile had barely flickered from her face when Julian turned to Derek and flashed a smile in his direction, too.

Derek put his mug down and tried to clear his head. He suddenly felt as if he were party to a seduction far more subtle and dangerous than the one to which Diane Gregor succumbed earlier with such graceless eagerness. He smiled back at Gretchen, then at Julian. The alcohol, the giddy talk, the beautiful pair's attentions rose in brilliant bubbles to the din inside his head.

17

Derek left home still disappointed and angry over the rejection of his grant application by the National Endowment for the Arts, which he'd received in an official government envelope in yesterday's mail. It was the sixth time in six years he'd applied and been rejected, and this year's frustration and resentment were compounded by the news that both Diane Gregor and Sidney Frieze were among the state's recipients of the award. He read the list of winners that accompanied his form letter and sickened, seeing his two competitors there among the names of the blessed.

Checking this year's judges, he threw down the list in disgust. Kenneth Galloway was on the final panel. Derek remembered the night last week when the tall poet stumbled out of Gordon's Bar on Diane Gregor's arm. Now Diane had twenty thousand bucks of taxpayers' money and the prestige of being one of the winners in this year's literary sweepstakes, while

Derek swallowed the taste of ashes and defeat. The only thing more intolerable was the fact that Sidney Frieze, that near-sighted apostle of meaninglessness, was on the list too. Clearly, there was no justice in the world.

Derek brooded all the way to Berkeley on the train, still sulking as he got off at an early stop to walk to Dave Knight's apartment on the border of Oakland. Dave had invited him by this morning for a visit before they set out from there for class. It surprised Derek now as he turned into the quiet middle class neighborhood to hear music thundering from the direction of Dave's apartment. As he approached the building, he realized the racket was blasting from a side window then echoing off a neighboring house to rock the surrounding neighborhood.

Derek stepped up to the porch and held down the buzzer for a good minute without results, then he hammered on the front door. The music inside modulated into "The Ride of the Valkyries." Derek gave up and waited for a break.

At last, the piece ended. In the brief ensuing silence, he held down the buzzer again. Seconds later, he heard the locks rattling on the other side of the door; then the door swung open and Dave Knight squinted at him into the light of late morning.

"Sorry, about the music. I've got a neighbor who keeps playing heavy-metal when I'm trying to write, so I retaliated with a little Wagner. I think the lesson took." He smiled wanly. "Come on in. I've got some espresso on and I'm almost ready."

Derek climbed the narrow stairs behind him to the second floor. At the landing at the top, he paused to look around as Dave went ahead to the kitchen. Every wall in the apartment was covered by rows of books on crudely made wooden shelves. In the corner of the living room near the bay window, the impressive stereo sat on its perch, giant speakers suspended on either side—heavy artillery in the battle with his rock-blaring neighbor. Dave's classical record collection filled most of the neighboring wall. There must have been days when the guy went without meals to buy new books and recordings; he really was an exotic bird, Derek decided, even for Berkeley.

The kitchen contained exactly two battered chairs, neither of which matched the ancient formica-topped table. An antique refrigerator purred against the wall, little bigger than an up-ended foot locker. When Dave opened it to take out a quart of milk, Derek could see that it was empty except for two eggs inside the door.

Over coffee, Derek complained about the results of the NEA. Dave listened with little apparent interest or sympathy. Not even the news that their fellow students had garnered lucrative grants seemed to disturb his calm. He counseled Derek to put the whole thing out of mind.

"I can't," Derek replied. "It's too grotesque. The only reason Sidney got the grant was that this year Wesley Burnshaw was on the panel of judges. Burnshaw edits the magazine that prints most of the shit Sidney and his friends publish. It's a scandal. Sidney just gave Burnshaw a big review in the *San Francisco Review of Books*. If the amount of money were larger and any-body gave a shit about the arts, there'd be a congressional in-vestigation of half the money they give away."

"In a hundred years, who's going to care who got a grant and who didn't?" Dave asked. "Just keep working to perfect your art. It's the only revenge worth the trouble. Forget about grants. Think about Emily Dickinson," he advised. "She published— what? a half dozen poems during her life?—but left behind over a thousand. Do you think she'd have cared about grants if they'd had them then?"

"Emily Dickinson lived in her father's house till the day she died. If she'd had to teach seventh grade English or wait tables to pay the bills and buy a few extra minutes to write, she'd have crawled to Washington on her hands and knees to get a grant. Jesus! Imagine her typing letters in some big office build-ing downtown, burning to get back to her apartment to finish 'After great pain, a formal feeling comes' or some other mar-vel."

Derek fell back into his chair, arms crossed loosely over his chest. It was fine for Dave to counsel patience. The guy was content to live in genteel poverty for the rest of his life. Emily Dickinson, indeed.

"I get tired of people telling me to stop worrying about money," he added. "It just hit me the other day that of the six poets we're looking at in Fiedler's seminar, five of them didn't have to work for a living. Five. The only one who had to was poor William Blake, and he hated the commercial printing he had to do with a burning passion."

"Well," Dave replied, "you know what Horace said, don't you?"

"Horace's patron gave him a farm. Until somebody gives me one, I reserve the right to bitch about money."

Once outside in the cool morning air, they decided to walk instead of taking the crowded buses. They still had time to make it to class, though just barely. Dave's long legs covered the sidewalk with loping strides while Derek struggled to stay even with him.

After several minutes of silent pacing, Dave opened the conversation again.

"Are you going to Julian's party?"

Derek said he was. Julian had invited them both on the night of Galloway's reading. "Why?" he asked. "Aren't you?"

Dave seemed to weigh the question. "No," he answered finally. "I've seen too many weird changes in people that have gotten near him in the last few months to feel comfortable anymore. If I were you, I'd give him a wide berth. Don't ask me to be more specific."

Derek didn't question him further on the subject. Walking silently, they covered the last few blocks and rounded a corner to turn down the hill toward campus.

In the open space before Wheeler Hall, they paused for a few seconds before heading off to separate buildings.

"See you about four," Dave called. "At the Renaissance. I just finished a new poem I want you to look at." Veering away, he waved over his shoulder. "*Ciao.*"

18

Derek sat alone at a table in the Cafe Mediterranean, waiting for Gretchen Nordhaus to appear. Diane Gregor had told him after their seminar this morning that Gretchen would be in town early this evening and wanted to have a few words with him, though she didn't say what Gretchen wanted to see him about. Derek was supposed to meet the tall blond at six-thirty but had arrived at the cafe an hour early to have a cup of coffee and a light meal while he waited. He wanted to be sure he didn't miss her. Besides, he had nowhere else to go tonight except home, where he'd have nothing to do but read for classes or watch TV until bedtime. Lisa was staying over again at Jo's.

Now, as he sipped at his coffee and watched the door for Gretchen's entrance, Derek thought about this morning's seminar. For over two hours the class had discussed Shelley's *Prometheus Unbound*. Derek defended the minority position, insisting that the drama was seriously flawed, despite the brilliant poetry in the first two acts. He'd never had a very high opinion of Shelley's work, anyway. Most of it seemed vague and generalized, and the play exhibited all the traits he most detested in the poetry of that period. He preferred more hard-edged poets, like Yeats and Donne.

As he thought again of the discussion, Derek began to see more merit in the opposition's view. It was odd. Though he'd always found Shelley a somewhat ethereal and pathetic figure, lately his readings in Shelley biography were beginning to persuade him that the young poet possessed a bolder imagination and fiercer intellect than he'd given him credit for in the past. He'd give the play another close look, he decided, tonight when he got back home.

Derek checked the door again and spotted a familiar face coming toward him: Mark Blotski, a poet who'd read yesterday as part of the department's job search. He was now steering toward Derek's table, evidently with the intention of joining him. Derek was surprised to see that Blotski was still in Berkeley; he thought the poet had been dropped at the airport last night by a faculty member after his day of interviews and readings. Apparently he'd stayed over for an extra day. Now as he crossed the room with precise small steps toward Derek's table, the portly, gray-bearded poet conveyed a sense of self-satisfied dignity.

"Derek Hill, right?" The older man stood hovering over the opposite chair. Derek was surprised that Blotski remembered his name. He asked the poet to join him.

"I heard Barbara St. John preceded me a few days ago," the poet said, once settled. "How'd Saint Barbara do? Still propagandizing for a lesbian state?" He chuckled to himself, then added, "I'll bet she packed them in. The woman should have been a politician. Hasn't written a memorable line since her derivative second book, but her poetry sells by the tens of thousands. A lot of feminists out there. And women read, too—always have. Her last book went into sixteen editions. Sixteen fucking editions. She actually makes money at poetry. One of the lucky few."

The poet suddenly stopped and looked around the room for a waiter, raising his hand to flag one down. Derek was somewhat taken aback by Blotski's bluntness. The man wasn't much for small talk, it appeared.

"Do I sound cynical?" Blotski asked. "I thought from our conversation yesterday at the reception that you were a kindred spirit. We're a funny lot, we poets, aren't we? We don't have money or movie contracts or advances to brag about like fiction writers, so when we get together all we have to chat about is reputations. We're a catty, bitchy bunch, for all our talk of inspiration. I lost friends when I won the Pulitzer years ago. They simply couldn't abide my winning the laurels that go-around. If only they knew what withered and dishonorable weeds they really are."

Blotski sighed, eyeing Derek across the table. "I see it pains you to hear me talking of the Prize Pulitzer in such a derogatory way. Sorry to disillusion you, lad, but listen to the voice of experience. Other than a little extra voltage on the old resumé, it doesn't mean a thing, not a goddamn blessed thing." Blotski chuckled softly seeing Derek's look of mild dismay.

"Who won the Pulitzer in poetry last year?" he asked. "Can you even remember the name? I thought not. Now I'm going to tell you something you probably don't want to hear." He placed his white hands together in front of him on the table and leaned forward. Derek looked into his oddly compelling gray eyes.

"Prizes, fellowships, all that high-sounding meaningless shit is nothing but a trap for a young poet like you. But since you don't believe me, I'll tell you a little story to illustrate my point.

"I had a friend on the Pulitzer committee last year who told me this, so it's more than just the bile of a disillusioned middle-aged poet on the decline. It seems the committee was very excited a couple of seasons ago; they thought they'd found a genuine twenty-four carat treasure: a poetry collection called *Songs of the Medicine Man* from a small press in Oklahoma. Indian country. The author's name was Jim Redfeather. They read the book and the poetry wasn't half bad. Not A material, but a respectable B or B minus.

"My God, the committee members were beside themselves. All that mythological imagery, the chants, the tribal songs. They were going to give the Pulitzer Prize in poetry to an Indian!

"A thing like that . . . Not only would it elevate an unknown poet to national prominence, but it'd give the Pulitzer itself a healthy jolt of credibility in this age of affirmative action. They were all set to give the guy the prize when one of the members did a little research and found out that Jim Redfeather was a *nom de plume*. The author's real name was Jack Bates—some middle-aged hippie living in a commune outside of Tulsa. The committee dropped the book like a hot cow flop and gave the prize to Eliot Witt that year instead.

"I don't need to tell you," Blotski went on, ignoring the waiter hovering at his side, "that that is by no means an unusual case. Have you read Marilyn Lee's work? If you haven't, don't bother. It's typical workshop crap. You could go to the University of

Iowa today and find a half dozen poets just as good writing in the same predictable style. But Lee is an Asian, and a woman. Once I heard she was nominated, I knew the other books that year didn't have a chance. Now that she's got a Pulitzer, she gets five thousand bucks a reading. A cool five grand. And she's in such demand that she turns down a good number of bookings every year. Naturally she's in all the anthologies. Got to have an Asian woman if you want to show the full spectrum of American poetry. The fact that she hasn't written one fully accomplished poem in her life is an irrelevance, I'm afraid.

"Say what you want about the bad old days," Blotski continued, "when a bunch of middle-aged white men decided who had talent and who didn't, but the cream rose to the top back then. As long as you were white and male, or wrote like you were, everything else took a back seat to the poetry. A young fellow like you had a chance to distinguish himself. I've seen a few of your pieces in journals. That poem of yours in the *Threepenny Review* is one of the best things I've seen in a couple of years. But who gives a shit, right? In my day, writing like that, you'd have caught the eye of some elder poet, he'd have given you a push, and the next thing you knew you'd be near the top of the ladder looking down at all the eager wannabes trying to snatch your heels. Now you're lost with all the rest in the general free-for-all. It's nothing but a circus these days. The star system's dead."

Though he suspected he was little more than a foil for Blotski's monologue, Derek nevertheless felt gratified by the poet's praise.

"Have you ever driven through the South?" Blotski asked, lifting a cup gingerly to his mouth. "If you have, you've seen what the American poetry scene's come to. Kudzu. Ever seen it? It's a scrappy little weed that gets a foothold and before you know it it's covering all the other vegetation up, choking it out, eating up its sunlight.

"Well, that's what's happened to poetry in the last twenty years. Kudzu. There's so much crap published every year now that it's choking out the good stuff. Hundreds and hundreds of books rolling off the presses and clogging up shelves in book-stores and libraries so a reader can't see the forest for the leaves.

"And if publication is in a sad state," Blotski added with a smile, "just try getting a job. Or a better job if you already have one. If you're white and male, you'd better have something going for you besides talent and achievement." The poet lifted a hand to stroke his goatee.

"Take Barbara St. John, for instance. If Berkeley doesn't grab her, Stanford sure as hell will; they'd love to have her join their militant feminist ranks down there. The woman is hot, a regular clean-up hitter, with women's studies such a growth industry now.

"So let me give you a little practical advice," Blotski added, leaning forward again. Everyone, it seemed, wanted to offer Derek advice.

"Don't rely on talent, my boy, it's a losing game. Get smart before it's too late. How old are you? Thirty? Okay, thirty. I thought you were a little older. Thirty's old enough, though. Because if you haven't broken through to the big time by then, you're never going to.

"You don't believe that, of course. You believe in persistence and hard work and talent and inspiration. Sorry to disillusion you, lad, but those things count for little these days. There are two kinds of young poets, I've discovered. The ones I call The Chosen Ones, like Gretchen Nordhaus and Bradley Singleton, who went to ritzy Northeastern schools and got singled out early by someone famous, and the also-rans like you and a young woman I know in Boston named Beverly Clive. I've tried to give Bev a push here and there, but I'm afraid my name doesn't carry much weight nowadays.

"Let me give you another example of what I'm talking about," he said, stroking his beard again. "I've got a slightly younger friend named Keith Hamilton, who was once a fine poet. I helped him publish his first book, as a matter of fact. Unless you know someone, you can forget about publishing a first book—unless you're extraordinarily lucky. *Extraordinarily* lucky. But of course you've discovered that.

"Well, I helped Keith get his start. The book was quite good and received largely favorable reviews. Come time to publish his second book, no one is interested. I mean, no one. They've changed editors at his first publisher and now they don't want him. He's not a big enough name to juice up their list. Remember, a poet doesn't make anybody any money, so it all comes down to who's hot and who's not. Forget that Keith's rejected book was better than anything they wound up publishing for the next five years. Six years the guy spent trying to get the damned thing published without results.

"So here he is with thirty rejection slips for a book that took years to write, a part-time job, and a new baby on the way. You know what he finally told me? He said that being a poet today was too degrading; that poetry now was an activity unworthy of a serious adult. Because even if you get lucky and publish a book, who the hell is going to read it, anyway? A poetry collection's lucky to sell a thousand copies. The royalties wouldn't pay one month's mortgage or rent. And since nobody reads the stuff anymore, poetry's no longer a cultural and intellectual force. It's a word game, like cross-words, a nice hobby for the literate.

"So Keith did a very simple and effective thing. He quit sending out the book, gave up writing poetry, and took up fiction instead. Within three years, he sold his first novel, got great reviews, bought a house, and quit his teaching post at Southern Connecticut State. Now he writes full-time, gives readings all over the country, and I occasionally see him on television talk shows, sounding off like an oracle on cultural and political subjects while hawking his latest book.

"So here," concluded the bearded poet, "is my advice. Get yourself an angle. Write fiction; get a Ph.D. and publish scholarly books; or, best of all, become a critic and write articles and reviews. I've known a few young poets who launched their careers by reviewing their more influential elders. A poet by himself is a pitiful thing. He always has a hand out: Publish my poem, publish my book, give me a grant, review me, say kind things. A critic, on the other hand, has power. He can dispense favors and, by cultivating the right people, have other poets courting him.

"A young woman might still be able to make it on her poetry these days," Blotski concluded with a nod of his small round head, "but a young fellow like you had better take up the cudgels and write criticism or he's going to get lost in the shuffle."

With that, the poet sat back in his chair, nodding sagely. Derek was spared further advice when a familiar voice sounded behind him.

"Hello, gentlemen."

Derek saw Blotski's smile disappear as he looked over Derek's head. "Speak of the Devil," the poet said.

Derek turned in his chair to face Gretchen.

"I was just leaving," Blotski said, rising with stately, if somewhat hurried, dignity. His eyes went from Gretchen's face to Derek's, then back again. Then he bowed quickly at the waist and turned. "I have to meet a friend and catch a plane later, so I'll leave you two young folk to yourselves. *Bon appétit.*"

Gretchen smiled at Blotski's back, then sat down opposite Derek in the portly man's abandoned chair.

"Did you have a nice conversation with Mephistopheles?" she asked, once the poet had passed out of range. "What a loathsome little man. I hope you haven't become bosom friends with him already. I feel queasy just sitting in his chair."

"I take it you've met."

"Yes," the blond replied with a smile. "In Cambridge. Massachusetts," she added quickly, "not England."

She placed her elbow on the table, rested her chin in her palm, and studied Derek coolly, blond hair falling past her face. She might have been posing for the cover of *Vogue* in her simple beige suit. Her eyes glittered like ice chips on blue cloth.

"You're probably wondering why I asked Diane to have you meet me here. It's nothing mysterious," she laughed. "It's rather good news, actually. My publisher has asked me to edit an anthology of younger poets, and I thought you might be interested in being included."

Gretchen's words seemed too good to be true. Before Derek could respond to her suggestion with expressions of interest, Gretchen continued.

"You can thank Julian, actually. He's the one who alerted me to your work. He's been tracking down the poems you have in print and passing them my way. He's quite taken by your stuff. I think you're about to be taken up by him; and when Julian takes someone up, things start to happen. He's got the most incredible nose for talent you can imagine."

Gretchen smiled again with devastating charm. "How do you think I got my start?" She laughed. "You don't have to answer that."

"I'm definitely interested," Derek replied. "It's good knowing someone's actually out there reading my stuff."

"Good," Gretchen said, "it's settled then." She suddenly stood up from her chair and clutched her purse.

"I'm sorry to have to dash off like this. I suppose I should have just called you on the phone about the anthology, but I wanted to tell you the good news face to face. I have to meet someone else soon, or I'd stay longer to talk a bit."

"Are you sure you can't stay a few more minutes?" Derek asked, rising to his feet.

"Sorry, no." Gretchen smiled consolation. "There is one other thing I wanted to do before I went, though."

She stepped closer, leaned toward Derek's face, and kissed him on the mouth.

"There," she said, opening her eyes. "I've wanted to do that again since New Year's."

Her face was still so close Derek could feel the warmth of her breath on his cheek. He could still taste her lipstick, smell the rich scent of her perfume.

He cinched her waist with one arm and pulled her to him; then he kissed her again, holding her till she slowly pulled away.

"I've wanted to do that since I saw you standing in the ballroom in the St. Francis," he said. "Can't you stay for another minute or two?"

"Sorry," she breathed. "I really do have to run. I'll see you tomorrow night, though. You are coming to the party."

"Of course," he said. "I wouldn't miss it."

She pecked him on the lips, turned, and strode toward the door. Derek watched her glide across the room and disappear.

He licked his lips, tasted her lipstick again. Peach. The flavor recalled muggy afternoons in his uncle's orchard on the Eastern Shore. As a boy he used to sate himself on the sweet fruit, sitting alone under a tree, till he couldn't take another bite, lips and fingers sticky, glistening around cheeks and mouth. As he walked back to his uncle's farm house, bees would hum round his face, attracted by the scent. He knew now how they felt. Drunk on her fruity nectar, he could still feel the press of her lips.

19

On the night of Julian's party, Derek rode from campus to the house that Gretchen had once referred to as Nightmare Abbey in the front seat of Sidney Frieze's antiquated Chevrolet. Beside him, in the middle of the seat, sat Diane Gregor, who was peering over the dashboard next to Sidney, directing his driving. Three other students from the seminar rode behind them in the wide back seat. After three and a half weeks of school, they were ready to abandon themselves to a little well-earned drunkenness and revelry. Derek was only sorry that Dave Knight had elected not to come.

"Here we are," Diane said as they rounded a bend in the road. "It's the next driveway. Put your signal on."

"I know how to put on my turn signal."

Derek wasn't so sure. Sidney drove like a child. Since leaving campus a short time ago, Diane and Sidney had rubbed each other's nerves to the quick.

Relieved that the ride was over, they pulled into the driveway and parked. Diane led the group to the front door. For her, this was just another homecoming; she'd been living in a guest room since the quarter began. She opened the door without knocking and stepped into the house with a proprietary air. The group was met in the foyer by Julian's spike-haired servant, who took their sweaters and jackets. As Diane handed him her wrap, she addressed him with familiar condescension.

"Thanks, Reggie. Is Julian down yet?"

The servant didn't reply. Diane might be a guest, she wasn't his master.

"Party's in there," he said, nodding toward a large room to their right at the end of a short hall.

A Mozart symphony echoed through the front of the house. The students followed the sound to a large room where a group of students and professors were chatting in small groups. Derek recognized most of the faces from campus. The only strangers appeared in a group surrounding Simon Macbeth, who was giggling loudly and readjusting his large hat.

Derek grinned. Macbeth's outfit looked as if it had been lifted from the prop room of one of his lover's theatrical productions. Along with the wide-rimmed Spanish hat, he wore a black monk's cowl that hung down to his sandaled feet. With his gray skin and bloodshot yellow eyes, he looked like a character out of one of Anne Radcliffe's novels.

Julian sat at the other end of the room, hands gripping the carved rams' heads on the arms of his high-backed wooden chair. Gretchen was nowhere in sight. Derek picked up a drink from a tray when a uniformed servant came by, then sat in a wobbly antique chair to wait for her appearance.

When he finally spotted Gretchen, her entrance took him by surprise. In a strapless white gown, her round shoulders and pale chest glowing, she flashed across the room and sat in a

vacant chair next to Julian. Once settled, she turned to the Englishman and smiled. The sight was almost more than Derek
could bear. He tried to catch her eye when she uncrossed her
legs and absently scanned the room, but she turned back to a
woman on her left without seeing him.

Finally, Gretchen leaned toward Julian and whispered something in his ear. Julian nodded. Then she stood and with a few
swift strides crossed the room and disappeared again. Derek
waited several minutes before following her; when it appeared
Julian wasn't looking, he glided among the other partiers, then
slipped through the open French doors into the next room.

The room was empty. Derek crossed it quickly and passed
through the door on the opposite side.

This room was smaller. An Oriental rug covered most of the
hardwood floor. Vases, urns, and a few small sculptures and
ceramic figurines sat on pedestals about the room. Each of the
four walls had a different-sized door. The gallery itself was nearly
bare of guests. Professor Dupont, the stout pedant from Berkeley's
French Department, stood at the base of the tallest pedestal,
addressing two women loudly and self-consciously in French.
Derek slipped past them to the nearest door and backed out of
the room quietly before they even noticed him. As he ducked
into the adjacent room, he felt a cool hand on his shoulder.

Derek turned and smiled as he faced his host.

"Ah, hello, Julian. This house of yours is a regular labyrinth.
Just when I think I know where I'm going, I find myself again
in some strange room."

Julian's thin lips pressed themselves into the semblance of a
smile. His narrow patrician nose looked long and sleek viewed
from this close; his skin, poreless and white as stationery.

"None of the corners are at right angles," he said. "That's the
secret. The architect was a very subtle and devious man. I've
added a few small refinements to his design, but as we don't
plan on a long occupancy, I've limited myself to minor alter-
ations. I'll certainly regret leaving this house. Did you get a
chance to look at the vases?"

"No. I was looking for a drink."

"You are lost then. The nearest bar is through that door and around the corner. The vases are hardly worth your notice, really. You're a literary man. I would think you'd have eyes only for my book collection. I confess I do take a good deal of pride in that. When I was younger, I wrote poetry; now I collect. It's a very different sort of passion, but one better suited to my current situation. I can no longer endure the ardors of composition, I'm afraid. I leave the field to people like you and dear, irrepressible young Gretchen."

Derek studied his host's face for a hint of hostility or suspicion—Julian's mention of Gretchen's name in conjunction with his own sent a warning tingle of fear down his nerves—but the foreigner wore his look of polite congeniality like a mask.

"I hope you won't be offended," Julian said, "if I suggest to you that I've already detected your fraud."

Derek's hackles rose; he waited for the next blow to fall.

"I mean your charade at scholarship, of course." Julian's eyes sparkled with mirth. "It's very rare that the soul of the scholar and the poet reside in the same breast, and you, my friend, are a poet. I don't believe you have any great passion for literary studies—despite your nominal status as a student of literature." He smiled conspiratorially. "Nevertheless, while I have you alone like this, I'll ask you what I've already asked your teachers and colleagues."

The Englishman paused for an instant and gazed into Derek's eyes. Now his look was an invitation to familiarity—with perhaps something darker and more mysterious implied.

"If in pursuit of your studies you happen to come across any sort of literary artifact—by which I mean original manuscripts, diaries, letters, etc.—I'd very much appreciate it if you would make me aware of your discoveries. As you know, I have an insatiable passion to add to my collection. I have a particular obsession with the personal letters of the great Romantic geniuses of the last century. It's a foible, I know, but an all-consuming one. I'd pay extravagantly for anything of interest.

"I ask this only as a matter of form," Julian added, waving a hand. "One never knows when or where a treasure might turn up. I like to cover all my bases, as you say in this country."

"Sure," Derek replied, trying to keep his voice steady. "As long as you don't tell the others I'm not planning on finishing my degree. I'd hate to have my fellowship cut off just yet."

Julian permitted himself a laugh. "Your secret is safe with me. I see we understand one another."

A stranger observing their conversation would think the two of them were really hitting it off, Derek thought. The actual experience of conversing with his host this way proved, however, to be dizzying. Derek felt as if he were standing at the edge of an abyss.

"Permit me the liberty of offering one small final judgement concerning your own talents and interests," Julian added with a soft touch of Derek's arm. "I've been blessed with intuition about these things to a degree that amounts almost to clairvoyance." He touched the side of his nose with a slender index finger. Then his face grew more serious; his voice dropped to a hush.

"I'd say that over these last few weeks you've begun to experience a surge of creative energy like nothing you've experienced before—am I right? I see by your smile that I am. I told you: it's a sort of clairvoyance I have about these things." He smiled again, this time with apparent warmth.

"I suggest this to you, my friend: that you are on the verge of a very subtle transformation, one that goes right to the well-springs of your talent. One might even say, of your being. With a little guidance, this process might be channeled so that when you emerge from your chrysalis in the full plumage of mature poetic genius, you reach a height few but the most dedicated and gifted achieve. What you might attain with the help of the proper guide, I leave to your imagination."

Julian placed his hand on Derek's shoulder and smiled more warmly. "I hope we'll become friends. As you know, I'm a great admirer of your poetry. I believe Gretchen has already approached you about her projected anthology.

"Well," he added, seeing Derek's nod, "let's say that is the merest prelude to what we might accomplish with a little effort. I have many friends around the English-speaking world who might be of help to a young talent such as yours.

"There," Julian concluded with a sigh. "I've said more than I intended. Let's descend now to pleasantries awhile, shall we? I believe you wanted a drink."

"Yes." Derek was relieved to get a foothold on solid ground again. Julian's talk left him feeling as if he'd been treading quicksand.

"Why don't I go grab one now? I'll keep what you said in mind."

"Yes, please do," his host replied. "And now I'd better spend some time with my other guests. We'll talk again."

Julian turned away. When he passed out of sight around the corner, Derek followed his directions to the bar, but instead of getting a drink there, he continued his search for Gretchen. The other guests had by now spread throughout the first floor. By drifting among them, Derek eventually made his way to the back of the house.

He found Gretchen at last in the kitchen standing next to a stainless steel counter, supervising the last minute preparation of some canapés on a long silver tray. A uniformed young woman stood beside her, a full head shorter.

"I'd forgotten how much students eat," Gretchen said, looking up to meet Derek's face.

"There, Maria, take these to the downstairs reading room, next to the gallery." The girl picked up the tray and glided out of the room. For the first time, Derek was alone with Gretchen.

"I was hoping you'd track me down," she said, stepping close and taking Derek's hand. "I feel rather like Ariadne after Theseus made it through the maze."

"I hope that doesn't mean I'll encounter a minotaur on my next trip through this blasted house."

"Ah, you're reading too much into my words." Gretchen averted her eyes. "I wouldn't put it quite that way."

"I've just had a very interesting talk with a minotaur, as a matter of fact. I'm not sure I understood half of what he was saying, but he somehow made me feel as if I'd just done something terribly clever. I wish I knew what it was."

Gretchen grinned. "Understanding comes with a longer acquaintance. I wouldn't hurry things. There's lots of time."

"Really," Derek said. "Julian hinted you'd be leaving this house before too long. When will you be going? And where to, if I may ask? He didn't say."

"Don't worry, love, I'm not going anytime soon." She released his hand and angled her body closer. "You want to ask me about my relationship to Julian, don't you? Well, go ahead. We're both adults."

"Debbie Witherspoon said you were lovers. It certainly looks that way."

"Actually, that's not the best description of our relationship. Not anymore." Gretchen seemed displeased by the course of their talk. "Julian is my patron. For lack of a better word. He's also been a very kind and patient mentor. You must have realized by now that Julian is an extraordinary man."

She looked across the kitchen, avoiding Derek's eyes. "He's not at all what you think. Julian wants you to know, in fact, that you're not to think of him as standing between us."

Glad as he was to hear the news, Derek found the manner in which she conveyed it a bit disconcerting. It sounded almost as if Julian were giving them permission to be lovers.

"Please, don't be intimidated now," Gretchen added with a shy grin. "That's the first thing I admired about you. Everyone else is so damned fawning and obsequious, it's nauseating sometimes." She sighed. "One gets tired of living with a monument."

She met his eye again.

"I have a confession to make." A crooked smile. "The first time I saw you at the convention, I'm afraid I thought you were just another shlumpy academic, another boring poet-professor on the make. Sorry," she said, "if I wasn't very impressed.

"But later that night, when I saw you at the Houstons' party so young and full of vitality . . . so *fresh* . . . you made me remember how young I still am. All of my lovers have been considerably older and more established. Christ, I feel a hundred years old sometimes."

Gretchen twisted a gold ring on her right hand, mouth set tight as she stared past him. Then her face brightened, she dropped the ring and turned back to Derek, a soft flush suffusing her face.

"When I saw you standing there at that party—so witty and irreverent, like a proud young athlete among all of those tweedy academic drones—something flared up in me, something I'd forgotten I'd even possessed. I felt warm-blooded and alive for the first time in too many years."

Gretchen laughed, teeth flashing. "After you'd had a few drinks, you talked wickedly about the convention. Everyone was laughing, though a little uneasily—and for good reason. You were devastatingly funny. I laughed like I haven't laughed in ages."

Derek turned away with a doleful grin.

"If only I could remember. I must have looked like a perfect ass."

Gretchen stroked his arm. "I couldn't even tell you were drunk till you—"

"Passed out on the couch like a stage lush."

Gretchen smiled. "You're such an innocent. So unspoiled. Sweet. I'd hate to see you wind up another pipe-smoking assistant professor of creative writing. You have real genius. You should try something more adventurous."

"Yes," Derek agreed, "but what?"

Gretchen looked at the floor. She hesitated for a moment, then her voice softened.

"It probably sounds terribly Oedipal to say this, but you remind me sometimes of my father. A lot of people know he was a famous economist, but hardly anyone knows that he put himself through the University of Chicago hustling pool.

"Daddy often said he learned more about money hustling strangers at eight ball than he ever learned in the hallowed halls of his old alma mater. In our family album, there's an old picture of him from those days. He's leaning against the fender of his first car, a big old Mercury, holding a cue stick and trying not to look too smug. God, he was so trim and handsome I almost cried when my mother showed me that picture. You have the same spark in your eyes, the same funny smile, the same look of expectation and surprise at being caught in the act of living."

Gretchen leaned closer and took both of Derek's hands.

"I hope this doesn't shock you, but I want to say it anyway. I want to be with you tonight. Just the two of us, here in this house."

She paused a second to let the thought sink in. "If you're interested, I think we can arrange it."

No longer bold, she looked toward the floor again: a girl's look, embarrassed, shy.

"Of course I'm interested," he said. "How?" His heart was pounding so hard he was sure she could hear it.

Gretchen smiled, a mixture of encouragement and relief.

"Let me leave the kitchen by myself," she whispered. "You wait a minute or two and then go to the southern gallery. You know the room with all the vases? Good. Then go back there and leave through the door at the far end of the room. Through that door is a little hallway. At the end of that hall to the right is a narrow set of stairs. Go up those stairs and go three doors down to the left. I'll meet you in that room and take you to a very private spot where no one will look for us. Can you remember all of that? Wonderful. Then meet me there in twenty minutes. I'll make an appearance back at the party and get there by another route. Julian is going to set off fire balloons outside on the patio in a little while to celebrate Byron's birthday—it's one of his little crotchets—so if we're lucky, we'll have at least an hour together before anyone notices we're gone."

She stepped closer and pecked him on the lips. "You're a sweet." Then she stepped away toward the doorway, blowing a kiss from the palm of her hand like a feather as she passed out of sight.

Derek waited as instructed, though without looking at his watch to time the interval, it might have been only seconds before he followed her from the room.

Going over her instructions again silently, he walked toward the sound of voices echoing from the other room.

20

Derek stood at the top of a narrow flight of stairs in a state of confusion. A hallway did indeed extend from the top of the stairs, as Gretchen had advised, but down the left side of it he could see only two doors instead of the required three of her instructions. On the right side, however, he could clearly see three. He wondered for a moment if Gretchen had transposed the two sides of the hall, envisioning it from the opposite end— or was this simply the wrong stairway? He could only guess. After going through the gallery downstairs, he'd gotten muddled. Through the gallery door Gretchen told him about, there was a small triangular room with two halls leading away from it— she'd only mentioned one and had said nothing about the odd little room. Taking the hall to his right and finding a narrow stairway at the end of it had convinced him he'd chosen correctly. But perhaps both halls led to identical flights of stairs. He thought for a minute of turning back and trying the other way, but then decided to stay where he was and try the third door on the right here first. The party was going on downstairs, so he doubted he'd have to explain his presence in this empty upstairs wing. The mere prospect of doing so, however, made his palms sweat, his heart climb in his throat.

He tiptoed down the carpeted hall past the first two doors. At the third, he paused for a moment before trying the handle. His heart beat faster. Gretchen might already be waiting on the other side.

He twisted the brass knob—it was unlocked—and slowly pushed the door open.

A bathroom.

It seemed an unlikely place in which to rendezvous. He decided to go back to the gallery and try the other way; but first he wanted to take advantage of his mistake: excitement had given his bladder a fierce urgency.

The plumbing in the room was ancient. White porcelain knobs gave hot and cold water in the sink and shower. The toilet was of antique and inefficient design. At the other end of the room, a second door was closed on whatever lay beyond—probably a bedroom.

As he zipped up his pants, Derek heard the shuffle of footsteps on the other side of the door. He froze, hands still on his zipper, hardly daring to breathe.

Then, from just beyond the door, men's voices.

Derek stood before the white porcelain bowl, hands silently locking down his zipper, breath suspended, ears straining. Now he could distinguish two speakers. He recognized the first by his accent. The high-pitched whine of the second man betrayed his identity, too. Simon Macbeth. The old man sounded as if he were crying. In a loud keening voice, he seemed to be repeating some request.

Derek had to hear more. He crossed the tile on the balls of his feet, then crouched behind the door and leaned his ear against its wooden panel.

The sobbing was louder from here. Macbeth was bawling like a child.

At last, the old poet uttered something intelligible. In a hoarse, cracked voice, he cursed his host. "You're nothing but a g-goddamned heartless f-fiend."

Julian laughed.

"Get up, you old fool. You're making yourself ridiculous. Have some dignity. I've told you, there's nothing I can do."

Macbeth collapsed again into wails and shuddering heaves.

Derek listened, ear pressed to the door, heart racing. After a pause in which Macbeth seemed to compose himself, the old poet spoke again, his speech slurred heavily by drink.

"I'll do anything you say; anything. I beg you, please. He's dying. You're my last appeal. I won't lose him, I can't."

Derek dropped to the tile in order to peer through the old-fashioned keyhole in the brass plate under the knob.

Squinting through the little opening, he saw something extraordinary. Simon Macbeth was on his knees, arms upraised, hands clasped in supplication, before Julian Ginotti, whose upper body was blocked from view. Tears ran down the old poet's face without check. His eyes were pressed shut in mute appeal.

In answer, Julian simply turned and walked away. Derek heard his steps cross the room and pass through the door into the hall. Then he thought he heard the Englishman's footsteps shuffling down the stairs.

Derek stood up. His own face in the mirror over the sink startled him. He was shocked by how pale he'd grown.

He tried to recompose himself. He wanted to look normal in case he ran into Julian again. He also had no intention of abandoning his plan of meeting Gretchen. He simply needed a moment or two to pull himself together.

After a little reflection, Derek decided to tiptoe back into the corridor outside and continue his search for the elusive third door further down the hall. Steeling his nerves, he gripped the knob, took a slow breath, and turned.

He peeped through the crack to his left to check the hallway and top of the stairs. The coast was clear. He stepped out into the hall and turned right. As he did, he crashed into someone; he felt his shoulder clip the stranger's chin, saw a black-robed body stumbling backward toward the floor.

Reflexively, Derek grabbed a fistful of clothing to stop his victim's fall. He hauled the man toward him like a netted fish. Simon Macbeth. The old man must have wandered back into the hall after his confrontation with Julian.

Derek tried to steady the old poet but Macbeth was falling-down drunk. It was a wonder he'd walked this far. His eyes were nearly rolling back in his head. His whole body reeked of alcohol.

Derek slipped an arm around the bony waist to guide him back to a bedroom. Macbeth accepted the guiding arm with silent gratitude.

"Here," Derek said, "you'd better lie down for a bit." The old man's cheeks were still streaked with tears as he leaned on Derek's shoulder for support.

Derek led Macbeth to the wide double bed and carefully set him down.

"Just lean back. I'll take your shoes off and put them right here at the foot of the bed." He held up the pair of sandals, then set them down together beneath the fringe of bedspread.

The old man lay on the pillow, nodding gratefully. Derek stood beside him for a moment. "Is there anything else I can do for you? You really need to sleep. Just lie back and rest a bit."

Macbeth raised his head slightly off the pillow as if to speak, then clutched Derek's arm with surprising strength and pulled his face downward toward his own.

"The bastard said Lindy wasn't worthy," the old man whispered thickly. "Said he lacked ambition . . . ambition! Can you believe that?"

Macbeth's hand clutched Derek's shirt sleeve like a claw. His face was flushed and swollen. "He could do it," the poet hissed, "I know he could. Lindy's still a young man." Then the poet burst into tears again; a last strangled sob broke from his chest as he released Derek's arm and fell back to the pillow.

"The son of a bitch," he wailed softly. "Lindy's only thirty-eight years old."

Macbeth turned his face to the pillow, chest heaving. After a minute, he began to breathe more easily. Derek lifted a bony shoulder to see the old man's face and saw that he'd already fallen asleep.

Derek turned from the bed and tiptoed from the room back

into the hall. He walked to the corridor's end, where it termi-
nated against a blind wall.

Another dead end.

He still hadn't found the right hallway and the clock was
already running on overtime. He'd end the night by letting Gretchen
down. He'd go back to the gallery, he decided, and try the other
way.

Then Derek noticed the door.

It wasn't recessed in a door frame, like the others, but was
flush with the wall. Instead of a protruding knob, the door was
fastened with a simple latch. That's why he hadn't noticed it
before.

Most likely only a closet, Derek thought. Still, it was a door.
He fingered the latch and twisted the little oblong knob to open
it.

Not a closet, a small room filled with shelves of linen. A room
behind the third door on the left. Derek glanced down the hall
to the stairway again and stepped inside, pulling the door shut
after him.

Once in the little room, though, with its scent of detergent
and its white stacks of bedclothes, he felt ridiculous. Surely the
twenty minutes were now up and he was waiting in the wrong
place. He pictured Gretchen, blond and desirable, somewhere
in another room, growing exasperated at his ineptitude.

Still, the failure wasn't entirely his fault. Gretchen's instructions weren't as clear as they might have been—and this house
was enough to baffle Theseus himself. He'd make a funny story
out of how he waited for her in a linen closet when he saw her
again. They'd have a good laugh. There'd be other chances to
arrange a meeting, now that they'd committed themselves to
satisfaction. He'd give it ten more minutes then sneak back downstairs to the party. Maybe they could still arrange something
else.

While he waited, Derek reviewed the scene he'd just witnessed
between Julian and Simon Macbeth. A few weeks ago on campus, he'd heard it rumored that Simon's lover, Linden, was suf-

fering from a mysterious wasting illness; but that hardly explained the weird desperation of the poet's appeals. What could
Julian do to help?

Suddenly a sound of creaking and scraping disrupted his musings.

He turned and saw the rear wall of the little room rising like
a garage door into the ceiling overhead. As it ascended, it revealed the feet, legs, hips, waist and shoulders of a woman.
Derek recognized them at once.

"Derek, sweetheart, you found it. I should have warned you
about the linen. Have you been waiting long? I got tied up."

Derek was amazed at the cool aplomb with which Gretchen
pulled off the meeting. Stepping forward, she took his hands
and held them in her cool grip.

"They've already started with the fire balloons outside. We'll
have to move quickly if we want to have some time." She pulled
him gently toward the door and into the darkness behind her.
"I've got a flashlight. Let me close the door again and we'll get
started."

Once the door was closed, they stood in total darkness. Then
Gretchen turned on the flashlight and Derek saw that they were
standing at the foot of a narrow flight of stairs. The walls were
so tight on either side they had to climb them single file, Gretchen
leading. The whole stairway might have been wedged between
the walls of two adjoining rooms, they were so compact and
steep. Derek watched Gretchen's hips swaying ahead of him as
they mounted the stairs, increasing his anticipation and excitement.

At the top of the stairs they turned onto a small landing and
Gretchen pushed open a narrow panelled door. Inside was a
small bedroom, illuminated by a single candle on a round stand
next to the bed.

"Look up," Gretchen whispered as they stepped onto the rug
inside.

Globes of light receded into the blackness overhead.

"The fire balloons," she said, slipping her arm round his waist.
"The ceiling is a skylight." She turned her face to his and smiled
in the candlelight.

"You're amazing," he said. "This is a dream."

Gretchen stepped back and looked him in the eye. "Undress me now."

Derek seized her bright eager face between his hands and kissed her on the mouth, savoring the scent of her hot breath.

Then he obeyed her, reaching round and fingering the zipper at the back of her dress. He slid it down slowly, letting the bodice loosen around her breasts. The loosened fabric slid to her hips, where she wriggled free of it, like a snake shedding its skin.

Naked now, her breasts stood out from her body, round and full and upturned, her nipples teased to erectness. Pink and stiff, they looked as if they could support the weight of Christmas ornaments.

Derek pressed his palm to one and drew her close to kiss those maddeningly ripe red lips.

"Now the panties," she whispered in his ear. She was beginning to breathe harder.

Derek gave in to the weakness in his knees and lowered himself toward the floor. As he descended, he kissed the white expanse above her breasts, then worked his way south, tasting the salty sheen of her skin till he took a nipple in his mouth and slowly, lovingly teased it with his tongue.

Heart pounding, he kissed his way across the flat plain of her belly till he reached her panties. He hooked his thumbs over the elastic waist band, then lowered her white bikini slowly past the golden triangle that filled the cleft between her thighs.

A waft of salty female scent greeted him as he pressed his face against her tangled blond mound. He kissed her through the fur, pressed his lips to the teasing fold underneath.

Gretchen stopped him with a soft touch to the top of his head. "No, it's my turn now. Stand up, please."

When he faced her, Gretchen kneeled before him and loosened his belt and zipper. When his pants circled his ankles, she tugged at his briefs, then lowered them, too, after first feeling the heft of his cock and balls with a cupped hand.

He was half erect, so she tongued him to painful hardness. He closed his eyes and heard soft sucking sounds, the smack of wet lips, muffled moans. He forgot where he was for an instant, lost in the surge of mounting pleasure; then she suddenly stopped. He opened his eyes, recalled the secret room, saw a fire balloon glowing overhead.

"Now the bed," she whispered, standing, one hand still clutching him below.

She led him toward the bed by his shirt; his cuffs were still buttoned around his wrists like handcuffs.

"My prisoner," she said, smiling as they reached the bed. She pushed his chest. "Lie back for a while."

She forced him to his back and fell to his cock again. "Don't come, yet," she said, tongue snaking down its length. "I want you inside me first."

Derek gripped the sheet while she worked on him, with quick, hungry thrusts. Just as he was ready to surrender, she suddenly released him, climbed over his prostrate body, white breasts bobbing, and with a soft moan straddled his cock.

"No, open your eyes," she said. "Watch me."

Gretchen rode him with joyous abandon, piercing herself again and again as she bounced and whirled above, salty, wet, and glowing. Her breasts swelled and glistened, her lips grew ripe and full, her neck tensed, breath quickening to sobs as she ascended the last flight toward consummation.

"Look, look," she gasped, sensing him surrendering again to darkness. "Don't close your eyes."

Derek watched as she bucked and heaved, breasts flailing, till she broke the last frail tendril that bound her to earth and erupted in womanly fire, like the fire balloons exploding overhead.

The sight was too much for him. He closed his eyes and clutched her to him, erupting inside her. With the first wave, she dug her long nails into his flesh and bit him hard on the shoulder.

"God, I'd like to devour you," she hissed.

For an instant he lost consciousness, then the pain of her bite made him push away.

As he settled back on the pillow, she curled against him, face pressed to his chest. She licked the sweat off his skin with a snaking tongue, then nipped his nipple gently with her teeth.

"Ouch."

Her breath blew fast and cool across his sweat-slicked skin.

"That was nice," she purred. She closed her eyes and began to breathe more slowly. "A very nice start. Rest for a minute. I want you again."

Gretchen cuddled into the hollow of his side, eyes closed, a trace of grin at the corners of her swollen mouth. After several minutes of soft cooing and sighs, she lay in his arms, asleep. Derek could feel her chest swelling against his ribs, their bodies' salty moisture evaporating from his hair and flesh as he lay staring up at the dark ceiling overhead.

He closed his eyes to the skylights and saw Gretchen rise white and radiant once again across the night sky, like a constellation. He was just beginning to see her outline dissolve into points of light when a tap at the door startled him awake.

"Gretchen, wake up," he hissed, just as the little door creaked open.

A black figure appeared in the doorway behind the bright beam of a flashlight. Derek gripped Gretchen's shoulder to shake her just as she started awake.

21

Instinctively, Derek feared the intruder was Julian. He wrenched the bedspread over his body and stared toward the door but couldn't make out who it was. The dark shape appeared to be a man.

The shadow stepped closer and called to Gretchen.

"Master says to come down. The party's breaking up now."

Derek recognized the voice and accent before he could make

out the face.

"I heard you, Reginald," Gretchen answered, unabashed by her nakedness. "Now if you don't mind, we'd like to get dressed."

It was Julian's London-born servant, he of the spiked red hair and gaudy gold earring. Derek could clearly make out his face and shape now, though in the dim light, he couldn't see the intruder's expression.

"Goodbye now," Gretchen told the servant, who remained eyeing them. At last she pulled a blanket up to cover herself. "You may go back down. We'll only be a minute."

"All right," the servant said, still lingering in the shadow by the open door. "Only doing my job." Then he strolled from the room, shutting the door behind him, and walked heavily down the stairs.

"Insolent little creep," Gretchen said after the door closed. "He might have tried knocking us up first."

Derek didn't know what to make of this intrusion. Gretchen seemed to be taking things in stride, so their situation must not be too desperate. It was damned unnerving, though. He studied her face as she rose from the bed to find her clothes. She still bore herself like a queen.

"Sorry, love," she consoled. "I didn't think they'd come looking for us. What time is it, anyway?"

Derek looked at his watch. "One-thirty. Jesus, we must have slept for over an hour. I thought I'd just dropped off."

Then, still alarmed by the prospect of going down to face Julian and the others, he added, "I thought you said no one knew about this place but you."

"Well, and Julian, of course," she replied, stepping to the door to search for her dress with the flashlight. "And Reggie, obviously."

She bent to retrieve her clothes. Standing again, she apologized, "Sorry, darling. I really thought we'd have a few moments together; I should have known that was asking too much. I'm afraid I won't be able to see you again like this till Julian takes one of his nights out over in the city. I'll probably be able to tell you sometime later this week." She cast him a smile as she lifted her dress to cover her breasts and wriggle inside. "You will come."

Derek laughed. "I will unless the Big One brings down the Bay Bridge."

He stared at her face, her legs, the soft swell of her hips.

No, he thought: he'd swim across the bay if it came to that. He watched her bend to fit a high-heeled shoe onto a bare white foot.

"We'd better hurry a bit," she said, stepping into the other shoe. "Let me go down first, then go to the front room where you first came in."

She walked through the little door, turned to say a last word before she descended alone.

"I'll try to get down to the campus to meet you somewhere when I can. Don't make yourself hard to find."

"I'll wear a sign," Derek said to her back. "I'll leave markings on walls and billboards telling you where I am."

When Derek reached the front room, he saw that the party was in fact over. The only remaining guests were Sidney and Diane and a young woman with long black hair sitting by herself on the couch. Derek was amazed to see a somewhat steadier Simon Macbeth awake and putting on his wide-brimmed black hat as if making ready to leave by the front door. Julian smiled at Derek on his entrance into the room, all cordiality and solicitude. Derek felt a wave of relief. Julian apparently wasn't jealous. At least he wasn't showing it.

Since neither Sidney nor Diane was getting ready to go, Derek stood uneasily next to a chair trying to decide on his next move. Julian noticed his discomfort and put him at ease.

"Sidney and Diane are staying the night. If you'd like to stay over, we have plenty of room."

Derek looked to Gretchen to see what he should do, but her

eyes deflected his question with a look of studied complacency. He decided he'd better go home.

"No, but thanks for the offer. I've got to get back."

"Well, then," his host replied, "I'll have Reginald take you home in the Mercedes."

Derek had no desire to be driven home by the insolent servant. He told Julian he'd walk to the bus line.

"At least, let him deposit you at the stop. Reginald," Julian added, turning to the servant, "bring round the car and take Mr. Hill downtown to wherever he directs you." Nodding, the thuggish servant turned and left the room.

Reluctantly, Derek accepted his host's offer. He bade the remaining guests goodbye, careful to avoid looking too long at Gretchen. They'd made their arrangements earlier, so he took his leave and stepped outside into the damp night air alone.

As he stepped out to the front porch, he saw that the black Mercedes was already purring on the driveway beside the house.

He opened the back door himself and got in, then slid across the leather seat. Reggie was in front, staring at the driveway ahead. As soon as Derek closed his door, the driver accelerated and sped away from the house, hedging just enough to avoid squealing tires. Then he sped down the driveway, turned onto the main road with an expert jerk of the wheel, and raced down the hill toward town.

Derek sat silently in the back seat, looking out at the empty Berkeley streets as they approached the bus stop. Neither man had yet spoken a word. When he finally spotted the deserted stop, Derek called to the driver, "Just let me off over there on the next corner."

The car slowed to a halt, and Derek climbed out. He thanked the servant for the ride. Three or four paces from the car, he heard Reggie's answer from the open window.

"You aren't afraid to wait in the dark, are you? I'll hold your hand, if you like."

Derek turned around to look. The redhead eyed him, sneering. When Derek failed to react, the driver spat at the ground and looked back to Derek grinning. "Bye," he called from the window as the car shot away. The Mercedes fish-tailed back into the lane and roared down the street, blinking its rear lights in a final taunt.

In his dream, Derek was lost in a large library, looking for a rare book, but not knowing either the author's name or the book's title, he was searching drawers of catalog cards in hopes of recognizing it. He couldn't find it under the letter G, so he began to look under a different heading—but the letters on the cards kept changing as he fingered through the stacks from L to J and then from J to S until he gave up in frustration and decided to comb through the library's shelves instead. He assumed he'd recognize the volume once he saw it.

He planned to start his search on the second floor but then couldn't find the stairs or elevator, so he asked the librarian at the front desk for help. She led him through a series of interconnected offices to a closed wooden door at the end of a narrow hall and gave him directions, admonishing him above all not to go to the top floor, which was under repair. Derek opened the wooden door to an unlighted set of stairs and began to climb. The stairs rose flight after flight without offering an exit, so he climbed till he reached the top and then emerged from the empty stairway into a dimly lit upper floor filled with shelves of books. He wished he had a flashlight. The only light came from a single set of narrow, clouded windows in a wall at the other end of the room. After his eyes adjusted to the darkness, he edged up close to the first dark shelf and peered at the top row of books, squinting at titles and authors' names; then he dropped to the next level and began again, pulling volumes loose and letting them fall behind him. In a matter of a few seconds, he'd emptied an entire ten-foot section and had begun to disarrange the next.

"What are you doing?" demanded a voice behind him. "Pick

them up and put them back on the shelves at once."

Derek turned and saw it was Gretchen. White-fleshed and naked, she looked luminous in the claustral gloom, standing above
him with both fists on her hips and glaring down with fierce
disapproval.

"I'm looking for a book. Only I can't remember its title."

Another voice sounded in the darkness near him, to the left.

"You're not going to find it here, mate. How 'bout getting up
off your knees and giving it a little rest, eh?" Then with a snort,
"Horny fuck."

It was Reggie. Derek stood up and eyed the sneering redhead, thick-tongued as he searched for a reply.

"You really interested in this?" the servant asked Gretchen,
thumbing toward Derek. "Getting a little hard-up, aren't we,
love?"

Another voice, with smoother, more polished tones, from the
dark on Derek's right.

"I believe our friend has made a little mistake, that's all. This
is the wrong floor. Perhaps you mistook it for another," the
voice said, addressing Derek gently. "I believe the book you're
looking for begins with the letter V."

It was Julian. The Englishman walked up behind his two companions and placed his arm around their shoulders, drawing
them to him in a possessive embrace.

"Our young friend here has simply made a small error. He'll
put things right. There's no need to bedevil him with insults.
Let's leave him to his task."

Then they were gone. Derek looked after them, but saw only
a yellow globe of light hovering in the distance across the room.
He walked toward it, kicking stacks of loose paper aside like
dry leaves.

When he reached the elusive globe of light, he watched it
metamorphose slowly into a woman; from the center of the vortex,
Gretchen beckoned him with open, inviting arms.

Derek reached to embrace her. As he did, the light metamor-
phosed again; the blond hair and long lines transformed to dark

hair and full-bodied voluptuousness as he clutched at the whirling shape. Pulling back to look, he discovered that he was now holding Lisa. Then the light whirled again and in another instant he was holding both women simultaneously, moving with them in a slow, circling dance. As he kissed their transparent shadows, they slowly merged into one.

Awakening from the dream, Derek opened his eyes to bright sunlight. He was in his apartment's tiny bedroom, lying on his back in the middle of his own bed. Lisa was gone. The sun was beaming through the window from the courtyard in back, so it must be late. The clock radio blasted an old Beach Boys song from the top of the vanity. He wondered how he managed to sleep through the racket so long. It was almost ten o'clock; the alarm must have been blaring at him for over two hours after Lisa reset it on rising for school.

He threw back the sheets and reached to shut off the radio. Then, still naked, he walked to the bathroom to shave and shower again before heading out late for school.

Thirty, my ass, he thought, admiring the handsome face that stared back from the mirror. More like nineteen. He felt fresh as a colt, this morning, bold and virile as a ram.

He decided to skip his morning class and stay home to start a new poem. Words, rhythms, surged inside him, burning for an outlet. He'd write until noon, then after his second class settle down in one of his favorite cafes to revise the morning's production. Gretchen might be looking for him this afternoon: better not alter his routine too much. He didn't want to risk the chance of missing her if she came into town.

Once seated on the underground train, Derek pulled out his notebook and began to compose his second poem of the day. By the time he looked up—just in time to avoid missing his Berkeley stop—he'd composed an entire lyric even better than the one he'd written at home.

The first poem was addressed to Gretchen, the second to Lisa. Comparing them now, Derek was pleased by how easily he'd shifted from one lyric mode to another. He decided not to think about the moral ambiguities of loving two women. His present state seemed perfect and complete. For the first time in his life he was living a life worthy of a poet, a life as unrestrained and aspiring as that of a Byron, a Shelley, a Keats. No wonder the poems came so readily.

He remembered Keats's famous definition. Negative capability: To be capable of being in uncertainties, mysteries, doubts, without any irritable reaching after fact and reason.

Derek understood now what he meant.

Unbidden, a line from Shelley's "Alastor" echoed in his head.

Her voice was like the voice of his own soul

Didn't the line perfectly describe his own sweet Gretchen?

Yes, he thought, but I've succeeded where Shelley himself failed: I've met my dream maiden in the flesh, not in the wish-fulfillment of a poem. Like Shelley's imaginary maiden, his own Gretchen inspired

Thoughts the most dear to him, and poesy,
Herself a poet

Herself a poet.

Derek picked up his satchel and stepped out the sliding door onto the Berkeley platform just as the train began to slide away. He was surprised at the way Shelley's poem came so readily to mind. He'd never really liked the piece. Odd how its words stuck so firmly in memory. Maybe it was all the reading he'd done for his upcoming seminar talk.

What was it Julian had told him last night at the party?

Something about emerging from a chrysalis. That's what it was: he was beginning to spread his wings at last, a caterpillar transformed miraculously to a butterfly.

Gretchen said that Julian was about to take him up, to involve himself in Derek's stalled career. She herself was including his poems in an important anthology. All Julian wanted in return, if Derek understood his hints last night, was the lost Shelley letters he'd found. And why shouldn't he have them for his wonderful collection? Already he'd opened his library to Berkeley's ablest scholars; soon new books and studies on some of England's greatest poets would emerge. To play a small part in the drama, all Derek would have to do would be to turn the letters over to a man who'd recognize and value them for what they really were.

He'd take one last look at the letters in his safety deposit box downtown and then pass them along to Julian. Out of gratitude, the Englishman would help launch his poetry career on a scale worthy of his sacrifice and talent. Before long, he'd have a reputation that rivalled Gretchen's.

Derek smiled as he climbed the hill toward campus. The future was full of possibility and hope. He was still smiling when he hit Telegraph and turned down the busy avenue to start looking for a place to work.

It was going on one o'clock. He'd buy some lunch and wait for Gretchen to come and find him, he decided. If she didn't show, he'd still have work to show for his time spent waiting.

A half block from his destination, he smelled the familiar coffee-scented air wafting from the open doors of the Cafe Med.

Suddenly Derek was startled out of his reverie by a glimpse of a tall blond figure in a blue dress. He turned to see, and as he did, it disappeared suddenly into a record store several doors down the busy sidewalk.

Gretchen, he thought, grinning. Then he stopped grinning and started walking faster. He should have gotten here sooner. She might have come looking for him and already given up. He'd better catch her now before she went home.

He broke into an awkward jogging trot, clutching his satchel against his hip to keep it from bouncing free. At the shop's entrance, he stood panting in the doorway, scanning the racks for another glimpse of the blond. The store was full of shoppers fingering stacks of cassettes and CD's, but Gretchen was nowhere in sight. Derek swept his eyes across the room again to be sure, then noticed a door against a side wall leading to another part of the store.

He hurried to the door, passed into the adjoining wing of the shop, and quickly surveyed the room. His eyes must have been playing tricks on him. There was no blond here, either.

Then he noticed the glass door leading from the shop to an adjacent street. He dashed toward it and peered through its blue-tinted glass to the street beyond. Across two lanes of traffic, approaching the shaded entrance of a shop, was the blue dress. Derek watched grinning as he saw Gretchen enter the bookstore. He knew the layout of the place. That door was the only exit.

He stepped outside to the sidewalk and tried to dash across the street, but a surge of car traffic suddenly blocked his way. He waited for a lull, then strolled across more slowly. No need to rush. He'd see her when she came out.

Once he reached the entrance, however, Derek decided to pursue Gretchen inside and surprise her there. He strode in past the register and surveyed the ground floor, looking down the aisles between bookshelves.

He covered the ground floor with a few quick passes, then mounted the stairs to the second level, peering over the banister as he rose to double-check the floor below.

She wasn't on the second floor either. Derek climbed to the third, where the older used books were stored in ramshackle disorder. Now he had her trapped. She had to pass him on her way back down.

He stood for ten minutes at the top of the stairs before deciding to check down the aisles. The shelves were packed close together up here, and footstools and piles of old magazines cluttered the aisles. He'd have to search systematically, keeping the stairs in view whenever he could. He thought for a moment of simply going back down to the door and waiting outside on the sidewalk, but that would destroy the pleasure of surprising Gretchen here amidst this clutter of old and decaying books.

Derek checked the central aisle, then started down the path between two high shelves filled with ancient history texts. He turned the corner and searched the next row, then the next. Still no Gretchen. Finally, he walked back toward the stairs to the wide window overlooking the street and searched the ground below.

Back on the other side of the street, Gretchen stood in a bright patch of sunshine, three floors down. Derek started to shout to her; he drew back a fist to pound on the glass, but a city bus pulled up to the sidewalk in front of her, blocking his view. He resisted the impulse to tear down the steps and run after her. He wanted first to see which way she went.

Then the bus pulled away from the stop and Gretchen was gone. The sidewalk was empty. Derek looked down at the vacant patch of sunshine where she'd stood, angry at having missed his chance.

22

Four and a half hours later, Derek saw Gretchen again when she entered from the street, still wearing the same blue dress. As she stepped into the warm noisy atmosphere of the cafe, she took off her dark glasses and looked around the room.

Derek sat taller and raised his hand, signalling. Gretchen returned his smile and started toward his table.

"Sit down," he said when she breezed up a few seconds later. "I'll get us some coffee." He wanted desperately to kiss her, but something in her manner warned him off. Instead, he pulled back her chair, breathed in her perfume, and went to get their drinks.

On his way back, Derek was determined to reestablish their intimacy of last night. Already it seemed to have occurred an epoch ago.

"I've been waiting for you all afternoon," he said. "I'm glad you came."

"I was sure I'd find you here," Gretchen replied airily. "I've got good news."

Whatever it was, it wasn't what Derek wanted to hear. He'd hoped for a little more passion after last night. He waited impatiently for Gretchen to deliver her news.

"It's the anthology," she said cheerfully. "They've given me the all-clear. You'll have six poems in it. That's as much as Bradley Singleton or Daphne von Fleck. I express-mailed your poems as soon as you gave me permission and the board went along. You're in.

"And that's not all," Gretchen added, leaning closer across the table. "You know that dramatic monologue of yours about the old woman—the title always slips my mind. Well, I have a friend at the *New Albion Review* who thinks he can publish it there.

"From the workshop," she explained, seeing Derek's look of confusion. "Diane showed it to us. Julian fell in love with it. Said it was worthy of Robert Browning. He wants me to send it off for you . . . if you'll accept our intervention on your behalf."

This was good news, indeed. The *New Albion Review* was a major international journal. The best poets and critics on both sides of the Atlantic published there—Larkin, Lowell, Heaney, Plath . . . the list of famous contributors went on and on. An appearance there would mark his debut into poetry's highest circle. Derek looked at Gretchen with wonder and gratitude.

"They pay two pounds per line," she said. "You'll make close to four hundred dollars for the piece. If you're interested," she added, smiling.

"Of course I am. It's wonderful news."

Derek started to add something, hesitated, then asked the question anyway.

"I just wonder," he asked, "why you can't simply say you liked the poem and leave it at that. You said the editor was your friend. You've published there a few times already yourself. Why bring Julian into everything? You did the same thing when you first told me about the anthology. You did it last night, too, arranging our tryst."

Immediately, he was sorry he'd raised the question. It seemed ungracious, to say the least. He saw Gretchen frown slightly, registering disapproval. Then she recovered her self-possession and answered with cool precision.

"It's simply pro forma. That's one thing about Julian: if you accept his help, he insists that you remain perpetually aware of the balance sheet." Gretchen hesitated, sighed. "It's one of his less endearing qualities. Such patronage, I'm afraid, comes with a price."

"You don't seem entirely happy with your arrangement. Do I detect a note of rebellion?" Derek asked. "You seem to have done pretty well by him so far."

"Don't be facetious, Derek. It doesn't become you. I prefer you dewy-eyed and green as grass. Don't ruin it by trying to be a cynic. I never expected what's happened between us to break in on my—" Gretchen paused, searching for a word "—my quiet resolution. Please," she added more softly, "just be nice for a little while."

Gretchen looked so vulnerable and girlish that Derek felt sorry for her suddenly.

She smiled weakly. "Sorry. I don't mean to sulk. It's just that I was born a hundred years old and never had the chance to be like you—angry and defiant, beating back the world's indifference through the force of my outraged talent. I was groomed to be a writer from childhood. I published my first poem in *The New Yorker* when I was twenty years old. Sometimes I wish I hadn't been so lucky and been recognized quite so soon.

"But then," Gretchen added, reassuming her normal cool composure, "I look at the muck that passes for poetry in this country and I'm glad I met Julian. I'd do anything to stay out of that quagmire. Anything. You'll make your pact with the devil, too, if you want to keep from getting dragged down."

Gretchen dropped her eyes and fumbled at her coffee cup, which till now she hadn't touched.

"Let me ask you something," she said, still looking down at her long slender fingers.

"Have you ever come close to death? Or imagined dying? If you have, I'm curious what your first thought was, your very first thought." She looked up and levelled a stare across the narrow table.

"Well," Derek said, stalling, "I thought I was going to buy it that night Robert Best rode me home on his motorcycle from your party." He laughed self-consciously. "I wasn't sure if I was ever going to make it home."

"All right," Gretchen said, "be honest, then. What scared you the most about dying? Wasn't it that you'd never get to write all the great poems you were destined to? It wasn't love, it wasn't losing your friends and family—it was that, wasn't it—your blighted career as a poet that made you want to beat back death's shadowed hand." Gretchen's eyes bore into his, searching for her answer.

"Yeah," Derek conceded after an instant's reflection. "That's what I thought about. What's so terrible about that?"

"Nothing. Unless of course you care about the state of your immortal soul."

"I don't believe in souls. And I don't believe you do either."

"No," Gretchen replied, "You're right. But remember what Yeats said. We have to choose between perfection of the life and of the work. We've both already made our choice, haven't we? Don't you ever wonder, though, if you've made the right one?

"Let me ask you another question," Gretchen said, brightening a bit. "I'm full of them tonight, aren't I? I don't mean to be morbid—sometimes I just can't stop myself from hammering at the edges of things. I guess the old Romantic spirit's still alive in us, despite our supposed post-modern sophistication. The truth is, we're all sons and daughters of Romanticism. Some monsters won't be whisked away by talk."

"All right," Derek laughed. "Ask your question."

"It's only this," she said, the brightness suddenly dimming from her face.

"Describe what you want to happen to a reader who picks up one of your poems. I mean, one of your absolute best, written or still waiting to be born. What do you hope for, exactly, when someone reads your best work?"

"That's a good one. Let me think a minute." Derek picked up his cup and breathed into it, letting the hot steam warm his face.

"All right. What I want is this," he said, setting the cup down. "I want to occupy the reader's mind so totally, to imprint my words on his memory so completely, that whenever he hears them echoing in his head he's possessed by something of me. That's why I use meter and rhyme most of the time. They create a synthesis of rhythm and sound that locks itself perfectly into memory. A great poem is like a computer program designed to stay fixed in the brain. No, that sounds too mechanical. I'll rephrase it slightly. What I want is to capture the rhythms of my thoughts and feelings so skillfully that someone reading my poems a hundred years from now will catch some vibration of my spirit. I'll live again inside him. Since you mentioned Yeats, I'll refer to him myself. Think of all the great poems that man wrote. Right now, in you and me, in people in England, Ireland, Canada, Australia—wherever English is spoken—there are lines of his, whole poems, stored in memory. What did Auden say in his elegy? When Yeats died, he became his readers. It might be more accurate to say that we temporarily become him every time we hear his words. That's what I want. Not just fame—the last infirmity of noble minds—but immortality. Nothing less."

Derek leaned back in his chair, pleased, and a little surprised, by his answer. Gretchen grew agitated again.

"A good answer," she said. "You may be closer to realizing your wish than you ever dreamed."

"What's that supposed to mean?"

"Only that you've answered my question perfectly. You're the real thing: a man dedicated body and soul to poetry, a twenty-four carat bard. Since that's the case, you may find Julian to be of immeasurable service. I don't know if you've noticed, but he's taken quite a shine to you. I think he sees a little of himself in you, though you may find that hard to believe." Gretchen stopped suddenly, as if to measure Derek's reaction, then gathered speed, talking with uncharacteristic nervous excitement.

"You have no idea how lucky you are, Derek. You've crossed paths with Julian at a very fortunate moment, fortunate for both of you, I mean. We've both of us been very lucky, you and I. Julian's grown tired of his solitude in recent years; he's really a very lonely man. You'll find that hard to believe, the way he charms and captivates people, but you've met him at a rare moment in his life. He wants now to pass something on. Something that takes a single-minded intensity to grasp—no, to attain. The kind of thing real poets take for granted—an over-reaching ambition, a passion for immortality such as few people in this sordid little world ever even imagine, much less achieve. Julian wants to help you now in the way he's been helping me. You'd be terribly flattered if you knew what a rare opportunity this is. You'd be staggered, actually."

Gretchen's pale skin began to glow with an uncharacteristic flush, her eyes flashed as she peered across the table into Derek's face.

"Haven't you already begun to notice a change in yourself—a sense that anything is possible, that you could write a *Don Juan* or a *Prometheus Unbound* almost without effort? That you can grasp the most difficult poetic language and remember long passages without the slightest effort of will? Surely you've noticed a change, you've felt a ripeness waiting to be born, an impending sense of greatness like nothing you've ever known before?

"You have, haven't you?" Gretchen declared. "I can see it in your face.

"It's Julian," she said. "He's a sort of catalyst. There's no other way I can explain it. Don't look so abashed and confused. You have to have the talent and ambition, of course, or it wouldn't take.

"And don't pretend these thoughts haven't crossed your mind already. Remember what Pound said: poets are the antennae of the race. Your antennae have been picking up Julian's vibrations, just as he's honed in on yours. There's no rational way to talk about things like this. Either you understand me or you don't. I think you do. I think you're ready to let your talent and ambition soar to the last stratum and beyond into the unknown. If you're interested, all you have to do is open yourself to it. And stop looking at me as if you were some wide-eyed innocent. We're on the same wavelength, you and I. So let's be honest with each other. I won't say a chance like this doesn't come without a price. For starters, you have to let Julian know you're ready to put yourself under his tutelage. You can do it any way you like. And to seal the agreement, you have to give him some important token. He says you'll know what it is. Personally, I don't know and I don't want to. But apparently you've managed to lay hold of something he wants. He admires you for your resourcefulness, actually. He wants you to know you've gained his eternal respect. But now he wants you to send him a token of your friendship and cooperation.

"I don't know how to say this without sounding awful, Derek, but Julian isn't a man you want to disappoint. Be nice to him, please, for your own sake as well as mine. You're not the one to challenge Julian on a matter of this importance. He's amused by the whole thing now, but he's beginning to get a wee bit impatient. And you have your own interests to keep in mind. The clock is ticking, and you're already on borrowed time.

"There," she concluded, eyes looking away. "I've said what I came to say. You can understand it, or pretend that I've simply gone mad. That we've both gone mad. See, look at us—we look like we're having an ordinary conversation. Isn't this coffee delicious? You look very handsome today. Is this how you'd rather I talked?" Gretchen smiled, lifting her cup to her mouth as if to drink.

"You've been writing today, haven't you? You have that delicious afterglow that makes me want to cuddle up and bask in your light. See, it takes another poet to really understand a poet, doesn't it? We don't mix well with the common ruck. Remember what Byron told Lady Blessington? It's as if a being from another sphere, an immortal, came down to pass its time with a creature of another race. Something like that. That's you and me—we're from another sphere. We could never find happiness with someone less than ourselves. That's what I've learned from Julian. Before I met him I was just a talented girl with stars in her eyes. Now I'm a star myself. I won't be thirty until next month, and I've got people publishing articles about my work in international journals. It's time you did something for yourself, too. Left to chance, these things have a way of coming to nothing. There are a lot of mute inglorious Miltons moldering away in their graves. Don't let yourself be one of them, my sweet."

Derek felt light-headed in the buzz of conversation whirling about them. Gretchen's talk both enchanted and appalled him; his nerves vibrated like over-tightened strings. He understood every word she'd said, yet balked at understanding.

"You're such a virgin, Derek," she concluded smiling. "But you were writing today, weren't you? I've spent all day writing myself. I only stopped to come and see you again."

Derek was puzzled.

"What were you doing in town earlier today?" he asked. "I saw you about one o'clock going into New Harmony Records but couldn't catch up. You vanished into thin air right outside of Titan Books."

Gretchen's face went ashen.

"You saw me in town today? Are you sure? I didn't leave home till an hour ago. I had an idea where to find you and came straight here. I was at my desk all day, writing like a fiend. What was I wearing?"

"Just what you've got on now. Only you didn't have sunglasses. The same blue dress—which, by the way, looks stunning."

Gretchen's face suddenly looked drawn and severe. Her eyes darted nervously overhead.

"It's started then. There won't be much time now. Ten days at the most—probably less. Only I wanted to have a little more time with you first." Gretchen reached across the table and closed his hand in hers. Her grip felt weak and bloodless as she squeezed his fingers between icy palms.

"Sorry, Derek. I knew we didn't have long, but I thought we could have a few more nights together like last night before the bill collector came.

"Well," she sighed, letting go of his hand again, "I'm ready. I guess I'll have to put the seal to my career and be an authentic modern saint. I've been writing poems to the tune of two or three a day now for four months. A bright light comes before the end. Saint Sylvia set the pattern for all of us, I guess. Dying is an art like anything else, remember, so who am I to complain? I've already published two books and have two more in manuscript to shore against my ruin. Sorry to turn morbid again. I'm just a little nervous, is all. It doesn't change what I told you. So speak to Julian, darling, as soon as you get the chance."

Gretchen rose from her chair, as if to go.

Derek refused to follow her lead and stand.

"You can't just drop a bomb like that on me and leave. It sounds like you're going to put an end to yourself. Do you think I'm just going to let you go now?"

"Not an end," Gretchen replied, "a beginning."

"And stop quoting poetry at me. For Christ's sake, talk sense. A minute ago it was Sylvia Plath. You're no Lady Lazarus, so quit this silly talk."

"Aren't I?" Gretchen replied. "We'll see.

"I'm terribly sorry, Derek. The timing just wasn't right for us. I've got to go—my car is parked outside. No, don't try to follow me." She held out her hand as he rose, to fend off his advance. "Or I may vanish into thin air again just to see the look on your silly face.

"Talk to Julian, darling," she added. "And never trust another poet's love; you'll be hurt or betrayed every time. The only face Narcissus can love is on the other side of the mirror."

With that, she turned on her heel and stepped away. "Bye now, love," she called over her shoulder.

Derek watched the back of her blue dress as Gretchen swept through the door to the sidewalk and passed beyond window range. Then his resolve weakened and he ran to the window to look after her. She was already sitting in her red Triumph convertible, looking blond and beautiful as ever. As he watched, she turned the ignition key and veered away from the curb into the street. He watched her taillights shining as she sped into the distance, his face pressed against the glass as she vanished for the second time that day.

23

Derek arrived home still shaken by his encounter with Gretchen. Her words—which possessed a weird logic when he was with her—now seemed baffling, ominous. It appalled him that he'd let her drive away after the dark hints she'd strewn in his path. He'd call her tomorrow, he decided, first chance. He'd go to her now if he had an excuse for not coming home. If she didn't live in Julian's nightmare mansion, Derek realized guiltily, he'd probably already be on his way.

When Derek entered his apartment, Lisa was at the kitchen counter putting the final touches on the chicken she was about to bake for their late meal. He kissed her on the side of the mouth, then sat down at the round glass-topped table where they ate.

"You're not much for formalities lately," Lisa said, turning from the counter. Then after a meaningful pause, "These midnight raids of yours are getting to be something of a habit. I'm beginning to think there's a touch of necrophilia in your blood. I was sound asleep last night when you came in."

"You were like hell."

"Well, I was half asleep. You've never heard of foreplay?"

"When do we ever see each other except in the wee hours of the morning? Anyway, I didn't hear you complaining last night."

Lisa stopped her preparations to turn and size him up. She gave him a look that penetrated like X-rays. Derek dropped his eyes and studied the table top, afraid the flush stealing over his face would give him away.

Lisa hesitated another instant, then turned back to the counter, but the damage was done. Derek remembered how he came home last night after making love to Gretchen and found Lisa lying naked in their bed. Without waking her, he'd slipped under the covers and climbed over her, then gently entered her sleeping body. When she did wake, they made love with a fierce tenderness that astonished him. He could see now that he was only trying to erase his earlier encounter with Gretchen, that the tenderness was seasoned by remorse. He hated himself for betraying her. Hated himself still more for betraying his own best instincts.

He remembered the night in his Stanford apartment almost a year ago when he knew he'd marry Lisa. He'd just awakened from a nightmare and was sitting in bed in the dark, crying. He'd been dreaming about his infant brother—Jason, his parents had named the boy—who'd died, a victim of sudden infant death syndrome, in the middle of his third month, the day after Derek turned six. Derek sat in bed remembering with the clarity of childhood the little smiling wrinkled face that peeped from its swaddling blankets and for the first time in his life cried over the little lost stranger and the life that died with him that cold winter afternoon. Then as the dream images paled and his grief subsided, Derek thought of Lisa and the future that lay ahead. Her face appeared before him with the force and clarity of a hallucination. He spoke her name aloud to the empty room.

The next day, before he told her what had happened, Lisa startled him with the news that she'd been awakened in her dormitory in the middle of the night by the sound of him calling her name. It was the most uncanny experience of his life. Derek took it for a sign that they were meant to be together, that the two of them were bound by something deeper than words or flesh or friendship or formal vows. Now he'd betrayed that night, that touch of the miraculous; he lay torn and twisting in the lion claws of guilt. By some miracle, Lisa failed to read his silence and see the change.

"You're in a pleasant mood this evening," she said over her shoulder. "I have some news that ought to cheer you up. I didn't tell you last night, but your Mom called. She said she got a call from your cousin Billy a couple of days ago. He was in Reno. She gave him our address and phone number in case he decides to drop in."

"Oh, Christ," Derek muttered. The last thing he needed now was a visit from his cousin. "Is she sure he's coming this way? What exactly did she say?"

"She didn't know for sure what his plans were. In fact, she said not to count on Billy showing up. She said you'd understand."

"Do I ever," Derek sighed. "But one thing, just in case he does: don't call him Billy. He hates that name. Call him Gino. The only people who call him Billy are his mom and mine."

Lisa turned back to the counter. "Why Gino?" she asked. "Is he part Italian?"

"Only in his dreams. His stepfather was Italian. After his dad died, Gino lived with his mom and stepdad in Little Italy in east Baltimore for a few years. His stepdad started calling him Gino when he played on his high school football team.

"After Gino Marchetti," Derek explained, seeing Lisa's look of incomprehension, "a legendary player on the old Baltimore

Colts. I used to hang out at my aunt's house sometimes. Gino was the older brother I never had. Back in the neighborhood, he was something of a living legend." Derek laughed. "You'll see what I mean if he shows up."

Lisa bent to put the chicken in the oven, then stood, facing Derek again.

"What's he doing now?"

"God knows. Last I heard, he was working as a maître d' at some toney restaurant in Baltimore. That's another thing. Don't call him a waiter, or you'll lose points fast."

As Derek thought about his cousin again, he felt the weight of old grievances settle around his heart, the pang of disappointment and love. He was surprised by the intensity of his feelings. Maybe it wouldn't be so bad to see Gino again, he thought, remembering the times they shared together as boys. It'd been nearly two years since he'd last seen his cousin. Maybe he'd changed.

After their meal, Derek brought up the subject again. Old memories had begun to edge their way back. If Gino did show up, Derek decided he'd better prepare Lisa for the experience of living with him for heaven-knew-how-long in their cramped little apartment.

He told Lisa about his cousin's boyhood dreams of playing ball, his disappointment when he failed to get a college football scholarship.

"After he realized he'd be too small to play professionally, anyway," Derek said, "he took up boxing. Golden Gloves. Just when he made the finals in the city championship, he quit and decided to play football again—for a community college. That lasted a year, then he went back to boxing. He quit that again when he got married—which lasted all of eight months—and then he just disappeared for two years. He'd enlisted in the army without telling anyone. Even that didn't quite work out. He got a dishonorable discharge for roughing up an officer his last month of service." Derek paused for a moment to see how

Lisa was taking all this.

"Nothing sounds so terrible, yet," she said. "So what's his big crime?"

"There's no big crime. It's just that . . . " Derek hesitated, searching for the right words ". . . he's a throwback—a cave man, in a lot of ways. A male chauvinist of the first stripe—and a homophobe. I'm just warning you in case we're out somewhere with him. He might say something. It could be embarrassing. Or worse."

Derek sighed. He suddenly remembered what it felt like to be a teenager trying to live up to his cousin's misguided ideal of manhood. The half-forgotten story came out of its own accord.

"The only street fight I ever got into in my life happened one night when I was out with Gino on The Block," Derek began. "After we'd had a few drinks at a couple of strip joints, Gino decided we had to have another beer in a bar down the block. I think the whole excursion was his attempt to make a real man out of me. Well, at this last bar, three Japanese sailors sitting near us managed to spill some of Gino's beer. Like five drops. Gino started hassling them—they spoke just enough English to figure out they were being challenged—and the next thing I knew we were all out in the alley beside the bar.

"My part in the whole thing was pretty inglorious. All I wanted to do was get the hell out of there. I wound up grappling with the littlest one while Gino knocked the absolute shit out of the other two in like a minute and a half. Then he yanked the one off me and punched his face so hard it must have hurt the guy's whole family back in Tokyo or wherever the hell he was from. I was afraid Gino'd killed him. I waited long enough to see if he moved, then got the hell out of there and went home. I could tell you a few other stories, but that about sums the guy up."

Later, preparing for bed, Derek grew more apprehensive. The timing for a visit from Gino couldn't be worse. His seminar report was due on Thursday, he wanted to take a last look at the letters before handing them over to Julian, and Gretchen was hinting at suicide. The thought of coping with all that while entertaining his cousin made Derek's head ache. Closing his eyes, he forced himself to think of other things, but the image of his cousin's face continued to haunt him even after he fell asleep and began dreaming of his boyhood back in Maryland.

It took several seconds of studying the face hanging over him— the blue-black unshaven jaw, the straight black hair, the dark shining eyes—before Derek realized that he was awake and that the strangely familiar face he was blinking up at belonged to his cousin Gino.

"Come on, Rip van Winkle," said the familiar voice, "I been here six hours already and you haven't even said hello. Now get the fuck out of bed and say something."

Derek pulled back the covers and sat up blinking.

"Christ," he mumbled, "when did you get in?" He stood up, cleared his head, and smiled. Then he leaned forward and embraced the lean muscular form of his cousin, slapping his back as they gripped each other in the middle of the floor. Lisa stood beside them, smiling, as the two men embraced.

Gino looked back at Derek, eyes shining. "Boxer shorts?" he asked, with a soft punch to Derek's midsection. "Very sexy." Then turning to Lisa, he added, "I don't get what you see in this guy."

Lisa took Gino back to the living room while Derek put on some clothes. After a minute, he rejoined them in the kitchen, where Lisa was handing out sandwiches for lunch.

As he entered from the hall, Derek spotted a blue nylon backpack on an aluminum frame leaning against the couch. He aimed a thumb. "What have you done, join the Boy Scouts? I thought you said you liked to travel light."

"I got that in Aspen, smartass. Look here," Gino said, opening his brown leather jacket. He reached into an inside breast pocket and pulled out a toothbrush and a disposable Bic razor.

"This is all I need to travel, okay? I can buy clothes anywhere. The only reason I got the knapsack was to impress a chick. Every asshole in Aspen has one of those things.

"Anyway, I got to get rid of the thing now," Gino explained, grinning. "Every time I put it on I feel like eatin' trail mix."

"Hey," he added with sudden inspiration, as if to regain face, "look at this." Standing now, Gino pulled a thick wallet out of his back pocket and opened it so both Derek and Lisa could see.

"Twenty-one hundred bucks." He opened the wallet wide, like a book.

"I hit Reno with nothing but twenty-six bucks and a splitting headache and left with this." He riffled the wad of hundred dollar bills. "I think when I leave here I'm going to rent a car and drive down to sunny Mexico for a little visit." He gave *Mexico* an exaggerated Spanish lilt. "If you want," he added, slipping the wallet back in his pants, "you guys can come along."

Later, as Derek and Lisa dressed for dinner, Lisa explained that Gino had arrived on their doorstep at six in the morning, ringing the buzzer till she got up to let him in.

"I couldn't wake you up," she explained. "You looked so exhausted we decided to let you sleep. It gave us a chance to get acquainted a little. Thank God it's Saturday. You owe me one morning in, though. I'll collect as soon as your cousin leaves."

Gino insisted on taking them out for dinner that night at the expensive Italian restaurant on Columbus Avenue across from the square. The three of them walked from the apartment in the cool night air. Throughout the evening, Gino gave them his professional appraisal of the place, from the valet parking outside to the waiters and food within.

"Not half bad," he said finally, over dessert. "A little slow, but the food is nice. A lot of classy restaurants in this town. I read an article in the paper back home that said if everybody in San Francisco went out to dinner at the same time, there'd be enough tables to serve the entire city. I could live in a town like that."

On the way home, Lisa suggested that Derek show his cousin around town the next day.

"It's Sunday. The museum will be open," she explained. "You could go out to Golden Gate Park. I've got a test on Monday or I'd go with you. The weather's supposed to be perfect. Why don't you go, just the two of you?"

Gino wanted to see the park, so Derek acceded to the idea. When they got back to the apartment, Lisa went to bed early and Derek found himself in front of the television beside his cousin watching horror movies until after two.

He woke on the couch, a blanket clutched in his hand between shoulder and cushion. Someone was shaking his shoulder and rasping in his ear.

"Come on, Derek, for Christ's sake, wake up. I'm going to pour this ice water on your head if you don't open those eyes but quick."

Derek heard the rattle of ice against glass and opened his eyes with a start. Gino was already dressed, standing over him with a tall glass of water in his hand. "Damn. Waking you up is like trying to raise the dead.

"Here," his cousin said, handing him a wad of tangled clothing. "I already got your clothes. Lisa's still asleep. Now get the fuck up and let's eat and get out of here. I'm about starved."

The morning was cool and sunny with only a hint of fog when they stepped outside to the street. At Gino's insistence, they took the bus instead of borrowing Lisa's car. At the bus stop a short walk up Stockton, they stood in a crowd of shoppers and tourists waiting for the bus to appear. Gino spoke loudly, reviewing last night's movies.

"That Nasty Kinski has got one sweet ass," he said. "I'll bet I've watched that movie a dozen times. When she takes off her clothes and runs around on all fours . . . Ooooh." He shivered. "I get a hard-on just thinking about it."

Most of the people in the crowd were Chinese or foreign tourists, but one woman standing near them overheard the remark and turned away. Derek realized he could be in for a long afternoon. He craned his neck toward the corner, looking for the next bus. The crowd at the stop was beginning to get pushy as everyone edged toward the curb.

Suddenly, as a bus pulled around the corner, Derek spotted an unwelcome addition to the crowd: Stony, the silent stalker, wearing his usual leather suit. Somehow, without Derek's noticing, he'd forced his way to the front till he was close enough to follow them onto the bus when they got on.

The bus swung around the corner and hissed to a stop, followed immediately by two others. Once aboard, Derek found it hard to concentrate on conversation, knowing that Stony was eight rows behind them staring at the back of their heads. Recently, while hiking to campus in Berkeley, he'd seen the stranger again, loping up the sidewalk behind him like a hunting dog. He'd followed Derek all the way to Wheeler Hall, turning away only after Derek had entered the building on his way to class.

"What do you keep looking at back there?" Gino asked, finally, turning to peer over his shoulder. "You've been twitching around like you've got a bug up your ass ever since we got on the bus. What's the deal?"

Derek whispered his suspicions about the man sitting behind them. After receiving the intelligence, Gino turned around again, rising high in his seat to get a good look behind.

"Let me get this straight," he said, turning back to Derek. "This asshole has been following you around for weeks and you're just gonna sit there whispering about it like some nervous little old lady? I'll show you how to take care of this right here and now."

Then Gino leaned back in his seat, smiling at the ceiling. "It's that asshole in the leather cowboy hat, right?"

Derek waited to see what his cousin would do. After several more stops, the passengers on the bus became sparser; those remaining were people like themselves heading out for a day in the park. Derek began to hope that his cousin would let his offer slide.

"Jesus, look at that," Gino said suddenly; he pointed to a pair of men holding hands on the sidewalk beside the bus. "If I lived in this city my whole life I'd never get used to that. Somebody ought to talk to those two perverts and tell them the facts of life."

After another stop, Gino turned to look behind them again. Derek looked, too. The passenger beside Stony had gotten off, leaving his place empty. Gino stood up and swaggered down the aisle. When he came to the empty seat beside the stranger, he sat down. Derek watched with a growing sense of anxiety as his cousin addressed the man.

"Howdy, there, Tex," Gino said, grinning with malevolent charm. "You looking for some cows to punch, or what?"

The stranger continued to stare straight ahead. His impassivity only spurred Gino to new efforts at intimidation.

"Hey, fuckface, I'm talking to you." Gino gripped the man's chin with the fingers of his left hand and turned the stranger's face toward his, a barber guiding the head of a reluctant customer.

"I mean you, asshole—look at me when I'm talking to you."

Gino spied Derek watching and gave him an impish wink.

He turned back to the face in his grip and spoke with exaggerated politeness, "My cousin and I don't want you breathing down our necks all day, okay? So when we get off this bus, I don't want to see your ugly face anywhere in sight. You got that straight?"

Without raising a hand in his defense, the stranger jerked his head loose and turned back to stare straight ahead. Derek began to wonder if the man was all there.

Gino slapped the stranger on the shoulder and rose to stand in the aisle. "I'm glad we understand each other. Don't disappoint me now."

With that, Gino strutted back down the aisle and plopped down next to Derek again, smiling broadly.

"If that dipshit gets off with us, he's got more balls than brains. Twenty bucks says you never see the prick again. Twenty bucks."

But when the bus pulled up at its stop next to the park, Stony got off after them, descending from the bus's middle door just as they hopped off the last step in front.

"Son of a bitch," Gino swore, looking back. "Looks like we're going to have another little talk with our friend."

Across the street to their left, giant eucalyptus trees rose toward the sky. Vendors sold ice cream and balloons from pushcarts and vans; roller skaters dodged down the walkway in bright shorts and tee shirts, spinning and dipping to the music on their headphones. Beyond the first line of trees, a few short yards and a galaxy away, stretched Golden Gate Park.

"Forget about it, Gino. Let it go," Derek urged, loosely gripping his cousin's arm.

His cousin shook him loose as the passengers from the bus dissipated.

"Look at that cocksucker," Gino said. "He's just standing there looking at us like a goddamn scarecrow. We're definitely going to have to have another talk." He broke away and walked up to face the slouched figure eyeing them.

"I thought I told you not to get off with us," he said, approaching. "Are you deaf or something? Goddamnit, look at me when I'm talking to you."

Gino stood an arm's length away; the stranger rose an inch taller than Gino, who was exactly a quarter inch shy of six feet. When Gino reached to seize his chin again, the man clubbed at him with a wildly swung right arm.

The blow glanced off Gino's shoulder and grazed the top of his head as he ducked, warding it off. He answered with a quick jab to the stranger's left eye, then landed two vicious rights to the belly. The stranger doubled over and dropped to his knees.

Gino started to walk away, but Stony lurched to his feet and came at him again, head down, like a charging bull. Gino stepped aside and in an eyeblink smashed three hard punches to his opponent's face. The stranger grunted and reeled sideways onto the sidewalk. His face hit the ground with a sickening smack. This time he didn't get up.

Gino looked once to see that his man was down for good and

walked quickly away. Pulling even with Derek, he grabbed his elbow and dragged him toward the park across the street.

Once away from the scene, Gino pointed to a lone vendor's cart. "Get me the biggest fucking soda they got," he said, still edging toward cover. "And make sure it's got plenty of ice."

Derek looked over his shoulder across the street at the figure on the sidewalk. Two tourists were standing over the fallen man in some confusion as to what to do to help.

Derek bought the soda. He walked back to his cousin and handed it over mechanically, hardly surprised at the queerness of the request. Gino took the large collapsing cup and plunged his right hand into it, spilling the drink down its sides.

"Never go to the head in a street fight," he said philosophically. "At least not if you can help it."

Gino pulled a face, drawing his hand from the cup. Testing it, he bent his fingers; smiled.

"Nothing broken." Then grinning, "That guy had a brick for a chin." He jabbed Derek in the shoulder with his other hand. Then after tossing the soggy cup into a trash bin, he steered him away toward the park's center.

"Now aren't you glad I came?" Gino asked as they descended a grassy slope, picking up speed. "You see what I do for you?"

"It was pointless, Gino. And you know it."

It was evening. Derek was still trying to convince Gino of the wrong-headedness of what he'd done. Derek was no longer sure that Stony had been following him these last few weeks. Maybe their meetings had been coincidental. With the wisdom of hindsight, he realized he'd probably had the guy beaten up by mistake. Worse, the whole incident might have been construed by witnesses as a simple case of gay-bashing. Derek felt ashamed of his own conduct in the affair. With a little more effort, he might have prevented the whole thing.

"What if the guy pulled out a knife?" Derek asked, trying a

different tack.

Gino laughed. "I'd have knocked the shit out of him and shoved the thing up his ass."

There was no arguing with such logic. "All right, what if he'd had a gun?"

"Don't worry about me," his cousin replied, grinning. "I can take care of myself."

Later as they got ready for bed, Derek tried to persuade Lisa how impossible it would be to let his cousin come to Berkeley with him in the morning when he went to school. Gino was watching a late movie in the other room, so there was no chance of him overhearing.

"I can't have him tagging along with me on campus," Derek whispered. "I just can't. I'd feel like that guy in the Conrad story—the one where the captain has a double hidden away below deck. What's it called?"

"*The Secret Sharer.*"

"Yeah, that's the one. It'd be like walking around with a caricature of myself all day."

"You're just ashamed of your plebeian origins," Lisa said with a yawn. "Gino's okay. Forget what your friends think. He won't be here that long."

Derek turned off the light, uncomforted. As he turned over in bed, he decided he'd look for Gretchen tomorrow even if Gino ignored his excuses and came along. He could shake his cousin for an hour or two if he put his mind to it.

24

The next morning went better than Derek had dared to hope. After agreeing to meet at three-thirty at a nearby cafe, he and Gino parted amicably at the edge of campus. Gino wanted to spend the intervening hours playing pinball and pool.

"Maybe I can take some money off some dumb-ass college kid," he joked. "I've been practicing up. If I win anything, I'll spot you for lunch."

Derek attended both of his Monday classes. He spent the two hours between them in the library working on a long poem he'd been composing sporadically over the last few months. Counting up the finished pages at his carrel afterward, he was surprised at how much he'd written—nearly enough for a slender book. The poem promised to shape up into a work of some significance when it was done.

After his second class, Derek searched a few of the coffee shops around campus, looking for Gretchen. No one knew where she was or had any idea when she might be coming to town. He decided to try one last cafe down the block where Diane Gregor often hung out. She'd be the person most likely to know where Gretchen could be found.

As he scouted through the crowd at the Cafe Med, Derek bumped into Sidney Frieze. Sidney was smoking a slender brown cigarette as he held court with members of his own set.

"Did you hear about the reception tomorrow night at the Houstons' house?" Sidney asked, looking up from his chair. "We're all invited."

"No," Derek replied. "What's it for?"

Sidney grinned. "To introduce the department's selection to fill Dick Fuller's chair. You'll never guess who." He gave Derek a second to ponder the possibilities. "That tired old whore Mark Blotski."

Derek was surprised at the news. Blotski seemed the least likely of the three candidates to be chosen for the job.

"As if Galloway and St. John weren't bad enough," Sidney added with a look of disgust. "St. John, at least, is a committed feminist. But as usual we were a dollar short and a day late. Stanford made her a better offer.

"The less said about Kenneth Galloway the better. But Blotski, Blotski—" Sidney broke off, unable to continue. "He's the worst sort of rear-guard reactionary, an enemy of innovation and experiment. So naturally the department picked him. He was the only candidate with a doctorate. What more can I say?"

Derek asked about Gretchen, but Sidney, too, proved to be of no help. Derek thanked him for the news of the invitation, then left the cafe and started back toward campus. It was already after three, so he decided to wait for Gino at their prearranged meeting place.

He was surprised on entering the cafe to see that his cousin was already there ahead of him, sipping a cup of espresso.

"So how did it go with the pool?" Derek asked, sitting at an empty chair.

"Don't ask," Gino replied, looking doleful. "I lost almost eighty bucks."

"Some dumb-ass college kid take your money?"

"Fuck you, too," his cousin replied. "Worst thing was," he added, "it was a chick. And don't look so surprised. You never heard of a woman playing pool before?"

Derek decided not to rub his cousin's nose in it. He looked crestfallen enough as it was. Then Gino's face brightened suddenly.

"It wasn't a total loss, though. I got a date with her tomorrow night. A redhead. Actually, more like a strawberry blond. A very foxy babe. Nice tits."

As he commiserated with his cousin over coffee, Derek looked up from the table and spotted a group of students from his seminar coming into the cafe through the main door. Mary Abrams led the group. After a quick look around, she spied Derek, and, still talking animatedly to the man beside her, led the others toward his table.

They were about to join him. Derek shook off a moment of panic and resigned himself to making the best of it. As the group sat down, he introduced them to his cousin. Fortunately, they were so preoccupied with their discussion, they barely seemed to notice Gino's presence. Derek listened distractedly, wondering what Gino was making of it all.

The discussion was about one of Shelley's most famous poems, written during his long stay in Italy: *Julian and Maddalo.*

"You're missing the point, Mary," David Townsend said, glancing around the table to gauge his audience's reaction. "Julian's position in the poem isn't the whole story—it's only one side of a dialectic. Byron's character, Maddalo, counters Julian's optimism with a more pessimistic view. Read Vincent Newey's essay. It's too simple to say that Julian merely represents Shelley. Shelley's actual position lies in his measured balancing of the two views.

"In fact," Townsend added with a patronizing smile, "of the two characters, Maddalo's position is by far the most convincing. And don't forget the madman and his speech. That's what I admire about the poem—its openness to several readings. I think it's one of Shelley's very best."

Townsend sat back in his chair. It looked as if the subject of the poem was closed at last when, to Derek's dismay, his cousin leaned forward to venture an opinion of his own.

"I don't blame Shelley for changing his name to Julian," Gino offered. "I always felt kind of sorry for the guy, myself, having a name like that. Percy. Sounds like some kind of fag to me. Even his last name is sissy-sounding. Shelley. The poor guy was a three-time loser."

Gino leaned back in his chair. "That's why I was so surprised that he had that shootout at that house of his in Wales. Tannyrault was the name of the place . . . something like that. A bullet went right through Shelley's nightgown. Bam! Missed hitting him just like that."

Derek couldn't have been more surprised if his cousin had suddenly sprouted wings and risen bodily through the ceiling into the sky.

"How'd you know about that?" he asked with undisguised astonishment.

Gino smiled cockily. "What else have I had to do the last couple of mornings while you were sawing wood? Don't look so surprised. I read a lot of stuff you don't know about.

"You ought to see this guy," Gino added, turning to the others and aiming a thumb across the table at Derek. "He must have twenty books on Shelley at home on his desk. I'll bet he knows everything about that son of a bitch there is to know."

Derek decided to cut his losses. He rose suddenly from his chair and announced that they had to be getting back to the city. After a little urging, Gino rose to follow him toward the exit.

On the way out the door, they encountered Diane Gregor. Derek greeted her with a nod. Gino smiled broadly and winked as they passed in the doorway. He turned to Derek once they reached the sidewalk and asked, "Well, what did you think?"

"Think of what?" Derek asked. Three days with Gino was starting to take its toll on his nerves.

"What do you mean, think of what?" Gino asked indignantly. "Think of her, that chick. Diane. The girl I told you about."

"That's the strawberry blond? She's a classmate of mine. Diane Gregor."

Derek remembered the party at the Houstons' house tomorrow night and suddenly feared Gino's date with Diane might take him there.

"You aren't going to a party with her, are you?" he asked, failing to disguise the panic in his voice.

"Party? Hell no. I'm taking her out to dinner."

Then grinning, Gino added, "We might have a little party of our own, though. The chick is hot for me. Couldn't keep her hands off me while we were playing pool."

In the last several weeks Derek had often thought of revisiting the letters at the bank but was afraid of leading someone to their hiding place. Now, with Stony seemingly out of commission and Gino to guard his back, a visit at last seemed feasible. After Lisa went to bed, Derek stayed in the living room to tell Gino his plans for visiting the bank in the morning.

"All I want you to do," he explained, "is to watch my back and make sure no one follows me in."

"No problem," Gino said, grinning approval. "It'll be just like old times. Remember those Japanese sailors?"

In the morning, Gino shook Derek awake. Lisa had already left for school when Derek sat up in his bed, blinking. "Shit," he muttered, glancing toward the clock, "we should have left an hour ago."

"No alarm clock, compadre," Gino answered. "You're the one sleeping through the morning news in here. You were supposed to get me up, remember?"

They skipped breakfast to save time. As they stepped out into the late rush-hour traffic, Derek checked his watch again. If he was going to get to his seminar on time, they'd have to speed things up.

"Let's take the cable car," Gino suggested when they reached its tracks a few houses down the hill. "If we see anybody suspicious, we jump off when it slows down. If they jump off too, well," he smiled, "then we consider our options."

Taking the cable car would trim several more minutes off the time he had in the vault, but Derek saw some logic in the idea. They waited a block up the hill, then got on when the antiquated old carriage rattled up the slope to stop and let them on.

The trip over the hills to Market Street was infuriatingly slow. Derek kept eyeing his watch nervously while his cousin played lookout. When they finally reached the turn-around on Market, they jumped off and jogged for several blocks till Derek signalled that they were nearing the bank. No one seemed to be following them. Two blocks short of his destination, Derek posted his cousin on a street corner and gave him instructions.

"Wait here and make sure I'm not followed. I don't want you even to see where I go in. The less you know about what I'm doing, the better for you, the better for everybody."

Gino complained about being kept in the dark, but manned his post on the corner with only a mild show of resistance. Derek left him and walked to the bank alone.

Inside, he signed in and followed his escort to the vault. Once alone in the vault's brightly lit interior, he pulled out the box and opened it to examine the letters.

Thirty minutes later, he checked his watch and quickly reclosed the box, sliding it back into the slot behind its shining steel door and locking it in. He'd over-stayed his time allowance by fifteen minutes; now he'd have to find his cousin again outside and race across the bay to school. He could think about what he'd read on the way there.

When he stepped back onto the street, he was greeted by Gino, waving from the open door of a yellow cab.

"All right, so I looked," his cousin called with a grin. "If you want to get to class on time, come on and get in."

Gino paid for the cab when they got out on the edge of campus in Berkeley.

"Don't say I never did nothing for you," Gino said to Derek as he handed the driver a large tip.

When the cab drove off, they made their plans for later that evening. They decided to meet at a coffee shop at five before Derek headed out alone for the party and Gino left to make his date with Diane in town. Afterward, no later than ten, they'd meet back at the coffee shop again to go home.

"By the way," Gino said as they prepared to separate, "I didn't say anything to Lisa about the party. So what's the story—you got another girl there or what? Who do you think you're fooling? I can read you like a book—am I right?"

Derek laughed in spite of himself. "I don't know," he said. "Maybe she won't even show up tonight. How the hell'd you figure all that out?"

"Diane told me," his cousin explained, grinning.

"What about you," Derek asked. "How are we going to meet back here tonight if you get lucky?"

"No luck involved." Gino smiled. "Why don't you just plan on going home without me? If I'm not here by ten, take off. I can find my way back without you holding my hand."

After his seminar, Derek hiked to the library to follow up his session that morning with the letters at the bank. In the short time he'd spent in the vault, he'd managed to read through several and skim the contents of a fair number of the others. Though no major revelations appeared to be hidden in the barely decipherable script, they did suggest some startling conclusions. The letters appeared to be written in Percy Shelley's hand. Though no expert, Derek had carefully studied the poet's handwriting in facsimile reproductions in the Berkeley library, and the letters he now possessed looked identical to them. That fact, however, raised more questions than it answered, for in a number of the letters, Shelley mentioned events which he couldn't possibly have known about for the simple reason that they occurred years after his death in the Gulf of Spezia. The letters also mentioned events in the lives of Shelley's closest friends and relations—Hogg, Peacock, Claire Clairmont, even the poet's own adult son, Percy Florence—which took place years after their author's death.

So logic said that the letters had to be fakes. The overriding theme of the correspondence seemed to be how to present an expurgated version of the poet's life to the Victorian public. Times had changed since the days of Percy and Mary's youth, and the reading public—little enamored even then of the poet's atheistic principles and odd conduct—had grown even more censorious in the years after his death.

Other letters dealt with the logistics of getting Shelley's work favorably reviewed by the leading writers and critics of the new age. Though the idea was mad, Derek couldn't help remembering Julian Ginotti's comments about how advantageous it would be for a poet to achieve the immortality of a vampire in order to further his own posthumous career. Ron Pruitt, in his last interview, had all but told Derek the identity of the man who had forced him to commit his murder. "The blithe spirit of his own self-created legend." The phrase was lifted from the opening lines of one of Shelley's most famous poems, *To a Sky-lark*.

Hail to thee, blithe Spirit! Bird thou never wert—

Ron had also spoken bitterly about how his persecutor had wanted future readers to look into his Caliban face and see an Ariel. Andre Maurois had entitled his biography of Percy Shelley *Ariel*, letting the name's aura of suggestion linger around his subject like a cloud.

Derek's dream of several days ago tipped him to the final clue in the bizarre web that had been forming in his brain.

Before leaving his apartment this morning with his cousin, he searched the pockets of his old Air Force jacket for Ron's last note, the one given to him by Ron's mother the afternoon he took the letters from her house.

Without specifying which one he meant, Ron had told Derek to look up a word from their final conversation in the OED. The first time Derek read the note, he attributed the cryptic suggestion to his classmate's supposed madness. Now, sitting in the reference section of Berkeley's main library, he pulled the Oxford English Dictionary from its shelf and looked up a word that started with the letter V.

Vampire.

He read the fine print of the entry.

One of the earliest recorded appearances of the word in written English was in a letter by Percy Shelley's first wife, Harriet Westbrook—the woman he'd abandoned to elope with Mary. The dictionary's editors placed it second in their chronological list of sentences that used the word metaphorically.

Writing of her estranged husband in one of the last letters before her suicide, Harriet put it with notable brevity:

In short, the man I once loved is dead. This is a vampire.

25

As planned, Derek met Gino at a pool hall and the two of them played together for an hour before taking off for their respective engagements. Gino hiked down the street to the Italian restaurant he'd selected for his date. Derek rode to the Houstons' party with several other grad students in the back seat of Mary Abrams's car, staring out the window, his thoughts preoccupied by Gretchen. He hoped she'd appear at tonight's party just as she had at the earlier ones where they'd met and gotten acquainted. He also hoped that Julian would attend; he wanted to have a talk with the Englishman. In a white business envelope in his inside jacket pocket, Derek had stashed a letter from his cache at the bank. He'd chosen the one from the top of the pile—the very one he'd tried to read that afternoon in the Pruitt's garage. Its reference to its author's reputation and its injunction to burn the missive along with all other "p.m. letters" (post mortem, the initials clearly meant) might make it of particular interest to Julian if there was any truth to the crazy theory Derek had begun to entertain.

Smiling to himself, Derek watched out the window as the car pulled up to the Houstons' house. Soon he'd see Gretchen. As he stepped out onto the driveway with the others, his thoughts took a less happy turn. He remembered Gino and Diane. Whatever happened between them tonight, he'd have to live with the results for the remainder of his studies at Berkeley. He hoped Gino wouldn't do anything to embarrass him.

Once in the Houstons' sprawling three-story house, Derek mingled with the now-familiar crowd, keeping an eye out for Gretchen. He spotted Julian immediately on entering the living room with its familiar couch and Persian rug, so Derek assumed Gretchen was in attendance, too. His old friend Sidney delivered the bad news when they bumped into each other near the bar.

"Looking for Gretchen?" Sidney asked with the slightest trace of a smirk. "I'm afraid she didn't come. Julian said she wasn't feeling up to a party tonight, so I guess you're out of luck, old man."

When Sidney turned back to his companions, Derek decided to seek out Julian without delay. He still had the letter in his pocket. If he had to play a game of cat and mouse to find out Gretchen's whereabouts, he'd at least play the cat tonight. Derek steered his way back to the living room to look for Julian again, armed with his letter.

He found Julian encircled by a group of Berkeley scholars. For several seconds, Derek stood simply admiring the man. Though the idea defied reason and logic, though everything Derek believed told him it couldn't be true, he couldn't stop thinking that there in the middle of the floor charming a circle of the university's brightest stars stood one of the immortals of English literature. Immortal in every sense. The only way for Derek to find out would be to keep his wits about him and try to test Julian tonight. Derek watched from a short distance behind Julian's back as the Englishman entertained his listeners. After several minutes, Julian looked over his shoulder, caught Derek's eye, and smiled. Reflexively, Derek returned the greeting, surprised once again by the man's uncanny prescience and poise.

Derek wanted to talk to Julian alone, so he waited for the group to break up. After nearly an hour, he began to despair of ever talking with the Englishman. No sooner did one or two guests edge away than a new set took their place. The group was in fact growing larger and more animated as the evening progressed.

Derek watched as an old man with a blotched pink scalp and thick glasses was led to the edge of the circle by a matronly, gray-haired woman and introduced. He overheard the old man's name, Winston Daryush, a professor emeritus of the university and a renowned scholar of Greek.

On being introduced to Julian, the old man peered up, squinting through thick lenses into the younger man's face.

"And this is Julian Ginotti," the old man's companion said. The professor eyed the Englishman curiously.

"Yes, I believe we've met," he said. "Julian, you say? No, no, I met you before once in . . . " The voice faded as the old man's mind seemed to wander off course . . . . "London, I believe it was. Yes," he nodded, "London. We met at a conference on . . . Plato in English translation. What year would that have been? Ah, nineteen thirty-three, before the war. I remember it now." The wrinkled, reptilian face smiled with satisfaction. "We had a nice talk on . . . *The Symposium*. An illuminating talk."

Then the old professor looked more closely at Julian's youthful smiling face and grew confused. The others in the circle began to shuffle their feet, embarrassed by the old man's lapse of memory.

Daryush seemed to shrink as the humiliation of his failure sank in. Julian smiled politely, bowed. The conversation turned back to its former course. With a surly push, Daryush rejected the arm of his escort and walked away, wandering quietly out of the room and into the adjoining library, head still bowed.

Derek followed him, pleased to catch the old professor alone. Here was a chance to test his theory now.

"Professor Daryush," he said, approaching the old man from the rear and gently gripping his elbow. Daryush slowly turned to face him, still downcast and confused.

"My name is Derek Hill. If you don't mind, I'd like to show you something that might be of interest."

Derek left Daryush's side and quickly scanned the surrounding shelves. After a brief survey of Houston's Shelley collection, he lifted a book from the shelf, thumbed its pages rapidly, and walked back to the side of the old professor.

"Ah, here it is," Derek exclaimed, offering the open book. He pointed out Aemilia Curran's portrait of Percy Shelley on one of the book's color plates, but carefully kept his fingers over the identifying inscription.

"Now who does that look like?" Derek asked.

Daryush studied the portrait thoughtfully. Derek watched anxiously till the old man smiled with recognition.

The professor looked up from the print to Derek's face.

"It looks like you," he exclaimed triumphantly.

Derek closed the book in disgust. The old fool was obviously senile. Except for the long hair, Derek could see no resemblance between himself and the portrait. The picture bore only a crude resemblance to Julian Ginotti, anyway. Or for that matter, to Percy Shelley. The painter herself had almost burned it, she was so dissatisfied with its likeness. Derek's experiment had failed.

After a quickly mumbled thanks, Derek turned away from Daryush and stepped toward the living room again. As he did, Mark Blotski entered the library and smiled recognition, a tall clear drink in his hand.

"Well, hello again," Blotski said loudly, ignoring the presence of the old man. "Last time we talked, I didn't think I'd be seeing you again so soon."

Blotski ambled closer and reached to shake Derek's hand. The poet's forehead was moist and beaded with perspiration.

"I guess there's a little more pull in the old Pulitzer than I thought, after all these years." The bearded man chuckled. Then grinning at Derek, he said, "I hear you've been doing well for yourself. My friend Julian says great things about you. If you play your cards right, you'll find a great ally in him. When his driver dropped me off at the airport the day I left, I told him the same thing I'm telling you now. If you want to get ahead in this world, you stay close to men like Julian Ginotti. Since you're a poet, the advice applies doubly to you."

Derek politely excused himself. Lifting his empty glass, he said, "I'd better go get a refill," then started toward the door.

As he passed, he felt the poet seize his arm.

"Maybe I misjudged you," Blotski said without a trace of his usual jocular cynicism. "I thought you were too clever to snub an old man." He looked up into Derek's face, eyes glazed, panting. "You don't really think much of me, do you?"

The poet's breath smelled of whiskey; his speech was thick and slurred.

"Look at me, my little bardling," he drawled loudly. "I'm talking to you. I said you don't think much of me, do you? Answer my question."

"I like you well enough," Derek replied. "I still read your criticism sometimes. I was a big fan of your poetry once."

"Ah, once, *once*. I see. Of course you're a better man than I," the poet rasped. "You're so goddamned superior, aren't you. Well, I'll tell you what it is you don't like about me, I'll tell you, you little pup." Blotski reeled on his heels, leaning closer to emphasize the remark.

"You look at me and see yourself in twenty years. Because twenty years is the most you'll get, riding our winged Pegasus, my friend. Remember what Wordsworth said? Poets begin in gladness and end in despondency and madness. Wait and see, if you don't believe me."

Derek pried himself free of the drunken man's grip and brushed past him. It'd be a cold day, he thought, before he let himself slip that far. He strode quickly from the library and entered the living room again.

"Upstart," Blotski roared after him, his voice loud even over the buzz in the crowded room. Derek crossed the rug to get further away from the poet's drunken taunts. Julian's group had broken up; the Englishman was no longer anywhere in sight. As Derek turned another corner to look for him, he heard a final shout from the library.

"Twenty years!"

"Did you bring a token?" Julian asked when Derek finally cornered him. They were standing alone in the Houstons' kitchen near the table where Derek had once eaten breakfast. Derek was still sipping at a tall glass of whiskey he'd been nursing since encountering Mark Blotski an hour ago. Julian stood with arms lightly folded across his chest.

"You don't waste time with small talk, do you." Derek replied.

"You didn't answer my question. Did you bring a token? I know Gretchen spoke to you about the matter."

"Where is Gretchen tonight, anyway? I was hoping to see her." Derek felt bold tonight facing Julian, though it might have been partly the drink.

"First, the token," Julian said softly.

Derek decided to wait a bit before committing himself about the letters. In the meantime, he'd buy time with hints and suggestions.

"As a matter of fact, I do have something that might be of interest to you," he said. "But I want to talk a little first. When can I see Gretchen again?"

Julian laughed quietly. "You're very direct. But I'm afraid I can't allow you to see her."

Derek stared at the Englishman. "What do you mean, can't allow? Why don't we let Gretchen decide what she wants to do."

"I don't know what Gretchen told you, but I'm afraid you don't understand the nature of our relationship. Gretchen is very special to me. Very dear. I've already allowed too much; I won't allow anything more. Gretchen is mine. I'll have to ask you not to bother her again.

"But let's talk of other, more pleasant things," the Englishman said in a friendlier tone. "I wanted to tell you that I've made a few inquiries and I think I might have interested an editor in a volume of your poetry. It's high time you published a book. Poetry, after all, is a communal art; it withers when deprived of audience. Journals are so ephemeral. One really needs a book to be taken seriously."

Derek wasn't ready yet to drop the subject of Gretchen, but he felt his pulse quicken a bit at Julian's suggestion.

"If you'd like," Julian added, "I'll be happy to act as intermediary and send your manuscript to the editor myself. As you know, it's almost impossible to publish a first collection with a good press these days without some sort of connection. It's a subject not often mentioned, but nevertheless one must recognize the reality. Left to yourself, I'm afraid, you'd face many years of obscurity and neglect. Poets are a competitive lot, as our friend Ed Houston once suggested, and I hate to think of the bitterness and gall you'd have to swallow seeing your less-talented brethren stealing the bays. Please accept my help. I ask only for a friendly token of your esteem."

Julian smiled at Derek with brotherly affection. "We understand each other, you and I. You know what I am. You knew before we even met. I ask only that you help me regain what is mine. You say you've brought a token with you. That reassures me more than you can know. I'm very touched. I was afraid you might prove difficult. This is a most welcome offering, and I accept it in the true spirit of fraternity in which it's given. Now please give me the token. Our time, I'm afraid, is getting rather near the quick."

"No," Derek answered. "I don't think I'm ready to give it to you quite yet. And you can spare me your speeches about how my time is running out. I don't buy the myth that a poet has to burn out early to give off a beautiful flame. That idea's killed and crippled more young poets than poverty and neglect combined."

Derek patted his chest above the pocket where the letter was hidden. He'd kept his jacket on, though unzipped and partially open, since arriving at the party. "Why don't we just wait a little while before I let you see this. I'd at least like to talk to Gretchen first."

Julian's countenance darkened.

"I was afraid you'd act the fool. You forget that you've passed your thirtieth birthday. You don't understand what I'm offering you. So let me give you this warning. Within the next twenty-four hours, I'll show you a manifestation of my power. You'll learn that it's mine from a dream. The process of your own transformation has already begun. I bestow the gift on you freely out of my own regard for your talent and the blind recklessness of your ambition. You've brought the token with you. I'll take the thought for the deed. Your success in making the transition is now up to you, but every day that you delay in recognizing it, every hour you spend in nervous vacillation, will weaken your chances of surviving the ordeal. Your life and work will then be subject to all the vagaries of time and chance; your name, like that of many another who dreamed of immortality but chafed at paying the price, will be inscribed on water among a thousand competing ripples. I'll ask you just one last time. Give me the letter in your pocket."

Although somewhat rattled by Julian's seeming clairvoyance, Derek struck back with a volley of his own.

"All right, maybe I am a fool. But I like to think I can emulate Yeats. There's a man who was writing great poems in his sixties and seventies. There's never been a greater lyric poet in the language before or since. Compared to him, the Romantics were just what Yeats called John Keats—a bunch of schoolboys with their faces pressed against a shop window looking at sweets.

"Yeats," Derek concluded with a note of defiance, "shows what a poet can achieve without selling himself to the likes of you or that old sot Mark Blotski. I'll take my cue from him, thanks. You can keep your talk of tokens and transformations. I don't need you to be a poet."

Derek's speech had just the opposite effect on Julian that he'd expected. The Englishman smiled contemptuously, drawing his words out slowly to let them sink in.

"Ah, yes, Yeats," he said, with an insinuating leer. "A member of the Order of the Golden Dawn for most of his adult life. Now there was as quaint a group of dabblers in the occult as ever put pen to paper. One wonders just what purpose brought those odd Irish scribblers together to practice their black arts.

"And what is perhaps even more curious, if you care to consider it," Julian added, "is the source of the elder poet's inspiration. Yeats's wife was a medium, as I recall. He got the great mythological system that informed the late great poetry you mentioned from automatic writing and summoning up spirits from beyond, if my literary history is correct."

Derek's heart sank. He'd forgotten about Yeats's crazy spiritualism. Julian was right.

Julian looked into Derek's unsteady gaze.

"A great Shelleyan, Yeats," Julian added with a smile. "His

essays on the poet kept a great reputation afloat earlier this century when a few short-sighted critics thought they'd finally sunk that storm-worthy little bark.

"Yes, keep the example of Yeats before you, by all means," Julian said, grinning. "There's much to be learned from him, my young friend."

26

Derek stood on the corner where he'd agreed to meet Gino after the party, looking down at his watch. It was eight minutes after ten and the street was almost deserted except for an occasional passing car. The only people on the sidewalk now were street crazies and a few scattered students.

He wished Gino'd hurry. He'd been waiting in the cold night air for twenty minutes and was anxious to put as much distance between himself and Julian as he could after their conversation at the Houstons' house. The man's ability to see into his motives and anticipate his moves was disconcerting. Two centuries of study had no doubt given him keen insight into the workings of the human heart. Maybe he really was clairvoyant. Tomorrow, Derek decided, he'd find the evidence that proved his theory about Julian's identity. For now, it was enough to know the truth himself. Julian's demand for the letters' return confirmed it.

Suddenly Derek looked up from his musings and saw the road and sidewalk reflecting the unearthly yellow street lights, the faded tints of distant neon signs, and nearly staggered. The dirty pavement, the deserted shop windows, the road signs and scattered trees all bloomed into three-dimensionality—as if he'd just stepped out of a theater after two hours in the flatland of moving film.

I'm going mad, he thought; I've lost my reason. This is how it must have started with Ron.

Vampires, Percy Shelley, Julian Ginotti. All madness, night-mare, delusion. What's happening to me, Derek wondered, how did I step into this dream?

It was Julian, surely. He must be a hypnotist, Derek thought. Or some sort of brilliant conman playing a sinister high-stakes game. Like a fool I've taken on the role for which he's fitted me; I'm a game piece, a playing card, a token.

Derek stood panting under the streetlight, eyes blinking against the sudden collapse of order, till he finally got hold of himself and quelled his spiralling panic.

At last, by controlling his breathing and focusing his eyes on a single image—the base of the metal signpost he was standing beside—he began to regain a sense of reason. He forced himself to ignore the sinister web closing around him and concentrate on the most mundane details at hand.

Derek checked his watch again. Ten-twenty. Gino had obviously gotten lucky tonight with Diane. There was no sense in waiting any longer, he decided. He'd go home alone.

Derek peered up the street one last time, then turned down the hill to walk to the BART station to catch the last train to the city. Each passing minute brought him a little closer to normality. The swift pace of his walking soothed his mind and settled his breathing. Once he got home, he'd start to sort things out. No more panic tonight—for once, no more wild speculation. He'd put a lid on it for now and think about things later when he had himself under control.

Three blocks down the hill in a dark stretch of closed shops, Derek heard the roar of motorcycles approaching from the rear. As they drew closer, they seemed to slow down. He continued to walk down the sidewalk, eyes focused straight ahead, as the thundering engines rolled up beside him and hovered there, a few yards away in the street, matching his pace. From the corner of his eye, he counted three bikes.

"Hey, sissy," a gruff voice called out over the stuttering engines, "what you got there in your purse?"

Derek was still lugging his satchel. He ignored the remark, but cast a quick glimpse to his right to get a better look at the bikers. All three were husky and bearded, crouched over their handlebars, leering at him. He couldn't see the back of their jackets, but they looked like Hell's Angels. The closest one, who'd just addressed him, wore a threatening, gap-toothed grin.

"Hey, faggot, I asked you a question. What you got in your purse?"

Derek calculated his options and decided to keep on walking.

Suddenly, with an exploding engine, one of the motorcycles jumped the curb at his rear and shot by him down the sidewalk. Derek felt the satchel wrenched from his shoulder as the bike raced past. At the same instant, a second bike jumped the curb and pulled up behind him, dogging his heels with its front tire.

The bag now dangling from his hand, the thief planted a heel on the pavement ahead, braked, and spun around to block Derek's way.

"Son of bitch," Derek exclaimed. He stopped and turned to face his tormentors. He wanted the bag. If they were only playing with him, he'd wait them out and get it back. If they meant business, he'd write the bag off and look for a chance to run.

His range of choices narrowed when the third bike suddenly jumped the curb and pulled beside him, cutting off his last avenue of escape. The apparent leader of the group parked his huge chopper crosswise on the pavement ahead. Still holding the bag up to taunt him, he stood straddling the pavement, grinning.

"What do you want?" Derek asked. He could hear the rider behind him dismounting and propping up his bike, too. Not a good sign.

Now the third rider was dismounting to Derek's right. When Derek saw him approach and reach toward him, he turned to face his adversary, hands balled into fists. Before he could mount a defense, the biker behind seized his neck with a burly forearm and locked him in a choke-hold, nearly lifting Derek off his feet.

"Check the bag," the leader said, striding up. He tossed the bag to a companion.

Derek could hear his books hitting the sidewalk as one of the men behind him emptied the satchel's contents onto the pavement and began to rummage through his notebooks and loose papers.

"Nothing here but shit," the voice said. "Check his wallet."

Derek was almost relieved now, thinking it was a robbery. They wouldn't find much money. He hoped it satisfied them.

He felt the one choking him reach into his back pocket with his free hand and lift out the wallet, then a slight jerk as he tossed it to the leader.

Sneering, the leader rifled the wallet's contents and threw it to the ground after pocketing its contents.

"Check his pockets."

Derek started to struggle again. He didn't want them grubbing through his clothes.

"You've got my money, now why don't you let me go?"

The leader answered with a swift punch to his belly. Derek doubled over, gasped for air. A second punch crashed against his chest, knocking the last bit of breath from his lungs. His knees buckled. He no longer cared when he felt four hands fumbling through his pockets.

The leader wrenched Derek's jacket aside and lifted the hidden letter from the pocket. Through watering eyes, Derek saw the white envelope in a thick, blunt-fingered hand.

"Well, well, what's this?" The leader peered into the envelope. Then he tucked it away inside a pocket in his own leather jacket and zipped up.

"I hope that's your will."

Derek felt the grip from behind tighten as the man in front pulled back to deliver another blow.

The fist crashed against Derek's ribs as he twisted out of the way in time to avoid another belly shot. Angered, the leader swung back his arm to try again. Before he could deliver the punch, a shout echoed from up the hill.

"Hey . . . HEY!" it called. Then Derek heard the slap slap slap of leather soles racing down the sidewalk toward him.

Thank God, he thought, help at last.

The grip loosened from around his throat. The feet of one of the riders scuffled toward his motorcycle, then an engine roared to life.

The man holding Derek suddenly jerked him backward to the ground and shuffled away. The only one left was the leader, who was preparing to deliver a final kick to Derek's ribs. A gunshot sent him diving toward his chopper.

The leader revved his engine and squealed away, roaring down the hill.

The scraping of leather soles next to his ear made Derek look up at his rescuer.

"Gino!"

The familiar face smiled down.

"Jesus, I leave you alone for five minutes . . . Are you okay?"

Derek rose to his feet, clutching Gino's arm, air flowing at last into his lungs. Ribs throbbing, he saw his books and papers littering the sidewalk.

"I was never happier to see you in my whole life." He watched as Gino tucked a nickel-plated .38 revolver back into a small holster hidden inside his jacket under his belt.

"Where the hell did you get the gun?"

"Your dad gave it to me." Gino grinned. "He made me take it when I said I was coming out here. I always said Uncle Ray was a cool guy. You should have listened when he tried to give it to you." Gino laughed. "You look like you could use it a hell of a lot more than me."

Derek took another deep breath and smiled. Nothing seemed broken or seriously damaged. He bent to the pavement to gather up his scattered things.

"If you hadn't shot over those bastards' heads, I'd have caught another good one in the ribs," he said. "Thanks."

"What are you talking about, shot over their heads? I fucking missed." Gino grinned sheepishly. "I never fired the goddamn thing before. I wish that fat fuck would come back here again."

Together they gathered up Derek's scattered books and papers and stuffed them back into his satchel. "Let's get going,"
Derek said. "We can still make the last train if we hurry."

They started down the hill again, gathering speed. Derek found
walking easier after the first hundred yards. By the time they
reached the bottom of the hill, he was practically running ahead,
it felt so good to be alive and free. As they neared the entrance
to the underground platform, he asked Gino about the date.

"What happened with Diane? I figured I wouldn't see you till
sometime tomorrow morning. I'm glad things didn't work out."

Gino frowned. "Don't even fucking ask. That woman is one
crazy bitch. You wouldn't believe what I been through tonight."

Derek was so glad to see his cousin, he didn't even care what
had happened. "Too bad," he said, "you're too good for her
anyway. I can't stand the woman myself."

Gino walked beside him in silence for several paces, then cleared
his throat. He was going to tell Derek what happened, after all.

"We have a nice dinner, right?" Gino began, waving a hand
in the air. "Then she gives me this look and asks if I want to
take her home. Naturally, I'm completely in favor of the idea.
We get in her car and she drives me to this great big house in
the middle of nowhere and we go up to her room. So far, so
good, right?

"Wrong," Gino answered. "The night was a fucking disaster.
When we get to her room, you know what the crazy bitch wants?
She wants to tie me to the fucking bed. She's got these leather
cords sitting on the night stand all ready to go. Hell, I don't
know this chick from Adam and I'm going to let her tie me up?
No fucking way." Gino dropped his hand, his shoulders slumped
in exasperation.

"So now she starts trying to flatter me, telling me how hot I
make her and how she wants to fuck my brains out. Words
coming out of this girl's mouth like you wouldn't believe. This
is like the second time she's laid eyes on me. A real classy babe.
The whole thing is starting to really turn me off in a serious
way, so I start backing off.

"Then she starts licking and slobbering all over my chest, still begging me to let her tie me up. I get up off the bed and tell her *adios*, so she grabs my arm and begs for me to stay. The bitch won't let go. When I tell her to cut it out, she starts moaning and nipping at me like some kind of animal.

"By now I've had it, right?" Gino grew more agitated. He stepped away from Derek to dramatize his words with body language. "I grab her by the arms and tell her to cut the crap. She holds on tighter and starts biting like a monkey. I push her away and she just comes back at me again, so I give her one last good shove and she falls down and hits her head on the corner of the bed. Christ, I never hit a woman in my life, and now I'm knocking this crazy bitch across the room. All I wanted to do was get the hell out of there.

"Next thing I know, she's screaming her goddamn head off. 'Reggie, Reggie, Reggie,' she shouts. Then this red-headed clown with pointy hair comes busting into the room. I'm standing there with my dick hanging out, Diane's screaming like a fucking maniac, and now this dipshit Reggie's coming at me like fucking Bruce Lee."

In spite of himself, Gino chuckled at the recollection.

"Old Reggie is one of these karate assholes," he added, grinning. "He's crouching down, trying to land a kick to my nuts, I'm standing there all naked and confused, and Diane's screaming for him to kick the shit out of me." Gino chuckled again. "You should've been there," he said, "it must've looked comical as hell."

"So what happened?" Derek asked, alarmed now. He could only imagine what Diane would think after being knocked down.

"What do you think happened?" Gino asked disgustedly. "I punched the guy's lights out, grabbed my clothes, and got the fuck out of there. I had a hell of a time finding my way back downtown. Lucky for you I made it back when I did."

Derek looked at Gino; smiled. "Don't worry about it," he said. He patted Gino's shoulder. After his escape from the bikers, Derek felt generous tonight. Gino had saved him from a severe beating, or worse.

"Diane had it coming. And as far as Reggie goes," he added with a laugh, "it couldn't have happened to a nicer guy."

A block from the station, they walked past a long-haired street crazy strumming a guitar in the dark recesses of a shop's doorway. Derek had passed the stranger before on other late night walks; tonight he felt impervious to his feverish stare and solitary shuffling dance.

"Hey, Gino," Derek said, eyeing his cousin's handsome profile as they entered the stairway to the platform. "It's really great having you here. I'm glad as hell you came." He gripped Gino's shoulders in a rush of admiration and love. They tapped down the stairs together, then stepped out onto the brightly-lit tile. As they neared the platform, Derek tightened his one-armed embrace.

Gino stepped toward the tracks, looked down at Derek's arm. "Any other place, I wouldn't mind," he said, stepping toward a scattering of late-night commuters. "But how about letting go of my shoulder before people start thinking we're a couple of queers."

27

Derek missed his first class Wednesday morning and commuted to Berkeley by himself after his cousin woke him with the news that he was going to spend the day sight-seeing in San Francisco alone. "Unless you plan on taking on the Hell's Angels all by yourself again," Gino added with a laugh. "Hey, now I see why they call this the Wild West."

Gino strode to the door, then turned back to Derek, still smiling. "Hey, why don't you blow off school today and drive down to L.A. with me. Meet a couple of cute senoritas. Have a few beers. What do you say?" Then he was out the door, whirling a ring of keys on his finger.

As the door closed, Derek felt a wave of relief.

He decided now to skip his second class after all and spend the day in the library researching Shelley's life. The letters in the bank were probably forgeries, and Julian, with all his talk about magical transformations and tokens and clairvoyance, was most likely a conman playing an elaborate game. The Englishman was obviously jealous of what was happening between Derek and Gretchen; all of his hints about helping Derek with his writing career were only so much smoke.

The name Julian was not uncommon, Derek reasoned; maybe it was only a coincidence that Ginotti shared it with the alterego in Shelley's poem. Or Julian might simply have adopted it to capitalize on his resemblance to the poet. Anyone who collected a writer's manuscripts with such fanatical zeal might well be a monomaniac. Derek decided to keep an eye to his back.

He also decided that the attack on him last night was no accident, coming as it did almost immediately after his refusal to give Julian the letter. He remembered that first party at Julian's house and the row of motorcycles parked outside at the edge of the driveway. Those bikers last night knew just what they were looking for when they mugged him on that Berkeley sidewalk. He'd been a fool to take the letter with him to the Houstons' house. Julian obviously didn't know that the letters' contents were proof of their forgery.

Derek wasn't happy about the prospect of leaving Berkeley by himself this evening. Once on campus, he tried to work fast; he hoped to finish in time to make it home by dark. After several hours in the library, he broke for a quick lunch at the student center, then returned to his investigation in the stacks.

What he wanted now was to find the source of Julian's surname. If it appeared in Shelley's work, it proved that the name was a pseudonym and Julian Ginotti himself some sort of sadistic lunatic. With a thick bibliography and a copy of the collected poems in his hand, Derek began his search.

He found the name at last in an unexpected place—an obscure youthful novel published while Shelley was still an undergraduate at Oxford. It leapt out at once from the text and danced before Derek's weary eyes: Ginotti.

The novel's title was *St. Irvyne; Or, The Rosicrucian*, a lurid Gothic romance about a man named Wolfstein and his nemesis, a mysterious villain named Ginotti. One of the odd things about the story, and what was perhaps most revealing of its author, was that its hero and villain seemed to be dual reflections of a single being. A less happy discovery was the number of curious parallels between the author and the villain of his book.

In a speech to Wolfstein in Chapter Ten, Ginotti described his youthful fear of death and later studies in the occult. Percy Shelley's own dabbling in the black arts was well-documented, nowhere better than in his poem *Hymn to Intellectual Beauty*. Derek reread the poem's familiar lines in the light of Shelley's story.

> While yet a boy I sought for ghosts, and sped
>   Through many a listening chamber, cave and ruin,
>   And starlight wood, with fearful steps pursuing
> Hopes of high talk with the departed dead.
> I called on poisonous names with which our youth
>   is fed . . .
>
> I call the phantoms of a thousand hours
> Each from his voiceless grave . . .

There were other parallels between author and villain, too. In the novel, Ginotti denied the existence of God in his youth; Shelley was expelled from Oxford for his pamphlet on atheism. Ginotti described how he'd won immortality after a dream about a demonic being; Shelley spent his life writing poems about spiritual possession and ghostly pursuit.

Once again, Derek remembered Ron Pruitt telling him to read Montague Summers. Summers had dispelled the vampire lore Derek had absorbed through popular books and movies. According to Summers, one way a person became a vampire was by first becoming a magus, or magician. Another was by committing suicide. Not only was Shelley a raiser of devils, but his biographies contained hints that the poet's drowning in the Gulf of Spezia might have been planned. At the very least, Shelley foresaw his death in a number of chilling visions in the days before his last voyage and failed to heed their warning.

That suicide was on Shelley's mind was clear. In a letter to Edward Trelawny, he asked his friend to procure him a lethal dose of prussic acid. Jane Williams, the common-law wife of the man who drowned with him, reported that when she was out boating one day with the poet, a sudden storm overtook them; when it appeared their little skiff was about to sink, Shelley tried to convince her to let the boat go down with them aboard. Shelley couldn't swim. On the night before he and Edward Williams planned their final journey, Shelley dreamed that Williams and Jane appeared in his room covered with blood to tell him the sea was flooding the house and all was coming down. After the actual disaster, the captain of an Italian vessel reported coming across the floundering *Don Juan* and offering to take its passengers aboard. In answer, a high-pitched voice, presumably Shelley's, refused his help. When Williams attempted to follow the captain's advice and take in their sails, Shelley was seen to grab his friend's arm, preventing a last attempt to save their lives.

Days later, when the poet's body washed up on the beach, it was unrecognizable: the face and one arm had been eaten away. Byron and Trelawny recognized the poet by his clothing and by the book found shoved in one pocket: Keats's *Lamia*. They buried Shelley's body in the sand. Later, they returned to dig it up and burn the remains in an iron furnace. Trelawny conducted the bizarre final rites. After anointing the burning body with wine, he threw oil and spices onto the flames, uttering incantations. Byron, who witnessed the affair, joked that though he knew Trelawny was a pagan, he had no idea he was a pagan priest. Unexplainably, Shelley's heart wasn't consumed by the flames. Snatching it from the fire, Trelawny preserved it, later presenting it to Shelley's friend Leigh Hunt, who passed it on to the poet's wife, Mary. When he later buried the poet's ashes, Trelawny added an inscription to Shelley's stone from one of the poet's favorite plays, *The Tempest*.

> Nothing of him that doth fade,
> But doth suffer a sea change
> Into something rich and strange.

Even Andre Maurois in his worshipful biography *Ariel* recorded that when Shelley's ashes were removed from the fire, the Italian children on the beach whispered that when the bones were returned to England the poet would come back to life.

And then there was *Frankenstein*.

In her author's introduction, Mary told how she got the idea for her tale one night in Geneva when they were discussing the "principal of life"—in particular, how a corpse might be reanimated and the dead restored to life.

Modern critics agreed that Mary's husband Percy provided the model for both the mad scientist, Victor Frankenstein, and his famous monster. Shelley titled the book he'd written with his sister Elizabeth *Original Poetry by Victor and Cazire*. Mary's use of the name Victor for the protagonist of her book was therefore not an accident. As with Percy Shelley's own novel, the hero of Mary's story spent his youth studying occult texts and trying to raise devils.

But the passage that caught Derek's eye in his own paperback copy of the book was startling in its implications. In Chapter Seven, Victor Frankenstein described his monstrous creation in words that froze Derek's blood.

> I considered the being whom I cast among mankind
> and endowed with the will and power to effect pur-
> poses of horror, such as the deed which he had now
> done, nearly in the light of my own vampire, my own
> spirit let loose from the grave and forced to destroy
> all that was dear to me.

The monster was the shadow-half of Victor, whom Mary'd modelled after her own husband; she described its behavior in words that recalled Byron's famous vampire passage in *The Giaour*. In effect, both of Percy Shelley's wives had called him a vampire.

Shelley's last poem, *The Triumph of Life*, expressed the poet's final judgement about life and death. Though left unfinished, it provided a chilling testament. Derek reread the poem now, pausing at the haunting terza rima lines that described the phantoms peopling this infernal world.

> The earth was grey with phantoms, & the air
> Was peopled with dim forms, as when there hovers
>
> A flock of vampire-bats before the glare
> Of the tropic sun, bringing ere evening
> Strange night upon some Indian isle,—thus were
>
> Phantoms diffused around, & some did fling
> Shadows of shadows, yet unlike themselves,
> Behind them . . .

Derek pushed the book aside. He'd found what he was looking for and more. The letters might not be fakes. Perhaps Julian was having a little joke on them all and, after retrieving the letters, would simply vanish back into obscurity to burnish the luster of his literary reputation. It wouldn't do to have another incident like the one last night with Winston Daryush. In another generation or two, Ed Houston and Gloria Fiedler would be pushing up daisies, Derek would be doddering into senility, while Julian—or whatever he called himself then—would remain eternally young, enjoying the adoration of poetry lovers of each new age. For a moment, Derek almost envied the man.

He closed his notebook and shoved aside the volumes which had piled up in front of him, then laid his head down on his arm to give his eyes and pounding head a rest. In a moment he'd pack his satchel with the few books he hadn't yet gone

over and return the others to the shelves. He didn't want anyone to come nosing around his carrel while he was gone and
discover the exact nature of his research.

Once Derek's eyes were closed, the fatigue of several hours of
reading began to ebb away. He began to breathe a little more
easily. He thought how good it would feel to be back home
tonight with Lisa and Gino when a familiar whisper startled
him to attention.

"Derek," it hissed. "I thought I'd find you here."

Derek sat up and saw Gretchen standing a few yards away at
the end of the nearest shelf. In a flash, he took in her gray skirt
and sweater, the odd dullness of her golden hair, the unfamiliar snakeskin boots. When their eyes met, Gretchen smiled seductively.

Too seductively.

"How'd you find me?" Derek asked nervously. "I've been want-
ing to talk to you for days."

In answer, Gretchen began to unbutton her sweater, starting
with the round pearl at her neck. After loosening the first three
stays, she let the sweater fall open to reveal the round tops of
her breasts. Derek realized she wasn't going to stop.

His eyes darted down the row of carrels to see if the woman
studying four desks down was still there.

She wasn't.

When he looked back, Gretchen was beginning to open her
sweater slowly in a satirical, seductive tease. Derek swallowed
hard, hypnotized by the daring public display.

With a flick of her hands, Gretchen slipped the sweater over
her shoulders and let it fall behind her, eyes shining now with
barely restrained mirth.

Derek's heart stopped when he looked at Gretchen's breasts.

Round and full and uptilted, they now seemed to stare back
at him. Instead of nipples, each breast was tipped by a single
large brown eye.

How did she do it? Derek wondered. With make-up? What
kind of game was she playing?

Then the eyes blinked and rolled toward him, two white-rimmed orbs locking him in their gaze.

Derek opened his mouth to scream.

This isn't really happening, he thought, *it's only a dream.*

His eyes fluttered open. He was still at his carrel, staring at the top of his desk, forehead pressed against a forearm.

Derek looked up and found the spot where Gretchen had been leaning. Seeing the place now empty, he sighed relief.

His heart slowed as he looked around, reorienting himself. He'd fallen asleep over his books again. All this reading and commuting was beginning to wear him down. No more rest periods in the library, he told himself. From now on, he'd wait till he got home to do his napping.

The nightmare now past, Derek laughed at himself for conjuring up the vision. Even his dream was inspired by one of Shelley's hallucinations. Derek had just read about it moments before falling asleep. During one of their nightly conversations in Geneva, Byron had read part of Coleridge's *Christabel* aloud to Shelley and the others. As Byron recited the lines describing the lamia's breasts, Shelley let out a shriek and ran from the room. When questioned by the others later, he said he'd been looking at Mary when he suddenly remembered the story of a woman who had eyeballs instead of nipples on her breasts.

Once again, Derek noted with a smile, a lamia had played a role in Shelley's life. As Ron Pruitt had once reminded him, another word for lamia was vampire.

Derek stuffed his books into his satchel and picked up the rest to reshelve before he left the stacks for home. It was already dark outside, so there was no point hurrying now.

He shelved a heavy red volume of Shelley's letters, then picked up the last slender book to return to its place. Checking its call number against those posted at the end of the aisle, he at last found the row where the book was housed.

As he slid the book back in its slot, he heard a rustle of cloth on the other side of the shelf, caught a flash of movement through a space where several books had been removed. He leaned toward the opening to get a better look. As he did, a face appeared suddenly across the narrow space of shelf. Startled, Derek took a half step back.

Julian Ginotti smiled through the open square.

"I hope I didn't startle you, coming across you so suddenly like this."

"No," Derek lied. "I was just finishing up a little research." He wished now he'd finished an hour ago.

"You display uncommon curiosity," Julian answered, still showing teeth. "Not everyone reads *St. Irvyne* these days. I wonder what drew you to the little tale. It's not very good, is it?"

"No, not very," Derek replied. "I wanted to see a little more of Shelley's Gothic side—for a paper I'm working on." He quelled the tremor in his voice, steadied his nerves. The worst was over now. Julian wouldn't dare harm him till he had the letters safely in his possession.

"So here we are together, just we two," Julian said. "Or are we? Alone, I mean. I almost forgot. I promised to give you a little demonstration of my power.

"Gretchen," he called suddenly, turning his face. "Bring your friend over here where Derek can see." Julian reached across the shelf, then cleared it with a sudden sweep of his arm. After the last book thumped to the floor, Derek heard shuffling footsteps from the next aisle. Then he saw Gretchen and another woman leaning together a few feet away in the newly cleared space. He blinked his eyes when he saw whom Gretchen had locked in her embrace.

"Lisa!"

White and drawn, Lisa stared past Derek without recognition, her eyes fixed in a trance-like gaze.

Gretchen looked at him and smiled. A pair of long ivory canines protruded downward across the open pink lily of her mouth.

Derek's own horrified shriek startled him awake.

He heard his shout reverberating among the stacks as he leapt up from his chair and looked around, heart hammering.

No one. He was all alone.

He'd been dreaming again. A dream within a horrifying dream.

Derek wondered if he was really awake this time, or if, like a series of Chinese boxes, this was merely another dream enclosed by yet another in an infinite regress. He looked at his hands, checked his watch, saw the books sprawled across his desk in disarray. He hadn't returned any of them. He must have fallen asleep right after pulling his notes together.

This is what comes of believing in spooks and goblins, Derek thought with a wry grimace. This is what I get for indulging in fantasies.

He shoved the books to the back of his desk and stood up, snorting disgust.

As he stepped away from his carrel toward the exit, he remembered Julian's statement last night at the party. The Englishman said he was going to warn him in a dream before showing him a manifestation of his power.

More hypnotism, Derek thought, more tricks and mind games: Julian planted the suggestion and let my own imagination fill in its outlines in my dream. The man was a master of suggestion and innuendo.

Still, Derek thought, Lisa was probably home alone tonight in their apartment. It wouldn't hurt to get home early for a change.

He reached into his pocket and pulled out a fistful of loose coins, then noticed that his hands were shaking. There was a telephone in the lobby. He'd go downstairs and call her right away.

28

Jo Waniak reached toward the cigarette pack beside her on the table and absent-mindedly groped inside. Empty. She felt a moment of panic then looked up from her notebook to scan the surrounding table tops and shelves for a stray pack. It was too late to ask Lisa to pick up another pack at the deli; she'd just left the apartment a minute ago and wouldn't be back for another twenty or thirty minutes.

Jo tugged at her hair. She needed the nicotine to stoke her brain tonight if she was going to ace that test on criminal law tomorrow, and she'd probably have to drag her partner up the long slope of another all-nighter to do it.

Wearily, Jo stretched and rose to her feet. Her hands fluttered over her blouse and slacks, searching, searching. Maybe she had another pack upstairs on her dresser or in her spare purse on the closet doorknob.

In her bedroom, Jo glanced at the dark window and noticed that the fog was rolling in so thickly now that it nearly blotted the light from the houses across the street. It was dark outside, but even so she should be able to see more than the mist swirling against the windowpane like a gray tide. She stared into the dimensionless haze and watched as little paisley patterns danced in the air outside. Then she turned back to her search. Nothing on her dresser but scattered change and an open package of Life Savers.

She turned on the stereo to scatter the silence that filled the apartment in Lisa's absence. After a second of electronic hiss, Randy Travis began crooning about honky tonks and autumn moons, whiskey and wilting roses in that dreamy hound dog baritone that made her wish she had more to fill her nights with than law books and second-hand heartbreak. Jo was still a Georgia girl, deep down. Six years of living in The City hadn't dimmed her love of country music, though now she kept her passion to herself like a guilty secret. If only she could meet some bright, soft-spoken Southern boy. All the men she met in the city were either gay or gadget-mad yuppies with erection problems.

Jo paused for a minute to look at herself in the wall mirror. She needed to do something with her hair. Dye it, maybe. She'd look racier as a blond, not so mousy-plain. Her short, wash-and-wear haircut made her look too prim and practical. And her figure . . . well, she had pretty, well-shaped breasts, even if they weren't big.

She twisted around to view her buttocks in the mirror, but caught a glimpse of movement in the window and turned to get a better look. For a second, she thought she saw a face in the fog outside. Her heart gave a little start.

No, it was only the fog whirling in the light from the streetlamps below. Jo peered into the depthless gray and thought how if she looked hard enough she'd eventually see the face forming again out of whirling amoebas of fog.

"Wish I had a fucking cigarette," she muttered, turning back to the mirror. Night fog made her uneasy. She still wasn't used to the stuff. And out here near the ocean it was especially thick, rolling down through the trees and invading the neighborhoods like a silent gray army.

Jo turned around and tensed her legs to study her ass in the mirror again.

Flat as a boy's, hopeless. She dropped her pose with a sigh.

She'd have to settle for Randy Travis for a little while longer. What a waste.

She turned from the mirror. With her first step, she bumped into the solid black bulk of a man.

Her cry was smothered by a gloved hand over her mouth, a boa constrictor embrace around her waist. She jerked and twisted against the intruder but it was like trying to break the grip of a panther.

Eyes wide, heart pumping, Jo saw herself in the mirror struggling with empty air. There was no one there beside her; no one. She looked like a puppet in the grip of a giant invisible hand.

She tried to scream again. Then a dark shadow bloomed in her peripheral vision; she twisted to face the terrible thing that held her in its grip.

A white face with burning red eyes. Its open red mouth came toward her behind a blast of cold, fetid breath.

Derek bolted upright on the couch, awakened by the key rattling in the front door. In a flash he remembered where he was and what he'd been waiting for when he fell asleep beside the telephone on the couch. The dream images scattered like a flock of birds.

He heard soft steps on the stairs, saw a glimpse of gray business suit, auburn hair.

Lisa.

"Where have you been all night?" he asked after she'd climbed the three stairs from the narrow hall and entered the kitchen. "I've been calling all over the goddamn city."

Lisa's face looked haggard. She paused under the kitchen's bright fluorescent light, set her briefcase down next to the counter, and sighed wearily.

"I was at Jo's. I meant to call but never got the chance. Sorry. You wouldn't believe the night I've had."

"I called Jo's six times. Why didn't someone answer if you were there?"

Derek was relieved to see Lisa safe again behind locked doors. He dropped the querulous tone from his voice and added more softly, "Thank God you're all right."

"Did the police call?" she asked, brow furrowing. "How'd you find out what happened?

"Sit back down," Lisa said, kicking off her shoes, "and I'll tell you about my night." She began to pace the living floor like a nervous cat.

"It was Jo. She's had some kind of breakdown. That's why I wasn't in when you called. We must have been at the clinic. Or maybe I was at the deli. That's when it happened. When I got back to the apartment, I couldn't find her anywhere. I figured she must have gone out behind me after cigarettes."

Lisa paced back across the room, then stood uneasily next to the counter.

"All right," Derek said, after a slow breath, "you couldn't find Jo. So where was she?"

Lisa finally settled across from Derek in a big wing chair. Once seated, she seemed to grow calmer.

"I found her in the bedroom closet, curled up on top of her shoes. I heard a noise, checked inside, and there she was. Jo didn't even look up at me. She just lay there in a fetal position, trembling like a child.

"I asked her what was wrong, but all she could do was sob. Finally, I got it out of her: she'd seen a man's face at the window while I was gone. I figured that wasn't enough to cause such a violent reaction, so I questioned her some more, but that's all she'd say: there was a man in the window, an awful man.

"By now I figured something terrible had happened. Jo still had all her clothes on, but she was pale as death and I thought she might have been raped, so I called 911 and got the police to come over to check things out. By then I was scared half out of my wits myself.

"The police couldn't do anything with her either. They checked the house while I called for an ambulance. They said there was no way a man could have gotten in through that second-story window. It was still locked from inside and there wasn't so much as a ledge outside for someone to stand on.

"The paramedics said it looked to them like Jo'd had a nervous breakdown. I spent the rest of the night at the health clinic trying to call her family. I didn't want to leave till someone came to take over for me. Finally, her sister from Half Moon Bay showed up. When I left, Jo was still knocked out from the drugs they gave her to calm her down."

Derek tried to comfort Lisa but was far too upset himself to exert much calming influence. He couldn't help guessing whose face appeared outside Jo's window. Hell, he knew who it was. Only a lucky chance prevented Lisa from being in the apartment. Unless Julian had only meant to send him another signal;

unless it was just another move in their twisted little game.

"Look," Derek said after Lisa calmed down a bit, "if someone ever wants in here when you're home by yourself, don't answer the door on the first ring, okay? Wait till they ring again. Just as a safety measure. You can't be too careful these days."

Lisa looked at him quizzically. "What's the point of waiting? You're being very mysterious. What if I look through the peep-hole and the person looks okay? Am I supposed to stand there while they ring that horrible buzzer?"

"If you have to. Just don't open the first time they ask."

Derek was hoping to avoid an explanation but could see by the look on her face that he might as well go ahead and commit himself now.

"I have an idea who Jo might have seen tonight," he said. "If I'm right, there's a chance he can't come into the house unless he's invited in on his first request."

"You've got to be joking." Lisa's face was drained and ex-pressionless. "Why can't he come in?"

Derek swallowed hard, trying to get the next words out.

"He could be a man I know named Julian Ginotti. There's something strange about him; it's hard to say exactly." Derek's voice began to fail. "He's not normal. He could be a dangerous madman. Or a vampire."

After a first hurried explanation, Derek noticed Lisa's wor-ried look and got a firmer grip on himself. The change helped to allay her fears about the state of his mental health; still, she continued to eye him skeptically, worry lines furrowing her brow. He didn't mention Gretchen or the cache of letters he had tucked away downtown. There was more than enough to worry about without that. As he finished, Lisa continued to eye him with a mixture of skepticism and alarm.

"I thought you told me Byron was the vampire," she said. "Isn't that what you said the night of Simon Macbeth's reading at the Art Institute?"

"I misunderstood Ron Pruitt, at first. Anyway, I was only toying with the idea then. Maybe Byron was a vampire, too; I don't know. The whole thing's so crazy. Ron even hinted that poor John Keats was involved, so how was I supposed to take any of it seriously?"

"So Byron and Shelley were both vampires."

"Maybe," Derek answered. "Who knows? Look, you remember the guy that was following us that night? The one dressed in brown leather at the coffee shop?"

"If you recall, you told me not to look at him."

"All right, forget the guy; he's not important. What's important is that we have to be careful. This Julian character is dangerous."

"Because he's really Percy Shelley."

"Come on, I already explained all that. You ought to see the way the bastard operates. He's got half the English faculty at Berkeley doing Shelley research. It makes a weird kind of sense, if you look at it in a certain way. Shelley never got the recognition he deserved when he was alive, so maybe he found a way to stick around after his supposed death to rewrite literary history. You should read about how Mary Shelley and her daughter-in-law created the Shelley legend. There's a great little book about it by a guy named Robert Smith, who's documented the whole thing. It was absolutely sinister what they did."

"All right, Derek," Lisa conceded, "it's been a while since I've had a course in Romantic Lit., but even granting that all the stuff you say is true, don't you still think it's just a wee bit preposterous to infer from it that Shelley is a vampire? A vampire? Jesus, it sounds psychotic."

"Look," Derek said in a level voice, "I'll give you one key example, just one. Shelley left his first wife Harriet and their two children to run off with Mary Godwin. Harriet was pregnant at the time, so naturally it didn't look real good to English society. Then Harriet killed herself. Well, the facts of the case were a little inconvenient, so what did Mary do? She destroyed the relevant diaries and notebooks and letters and then had a forger operating under the name of Major Byron cook up some fake letters that exonerated Shelley; he made it look like Harriet wanted to end the marriage—they even invented a love affair for her. Hell, in one version they implied she'd become a prostitute. All to keep Shelley's image safe in its holy shrine.

"And look at Shelley's critical reception over the last century and a half. No sooner does someone like Matthew Arnold or T.S. Eliot knock it down, then it bounces right back up again. The guy's had more lives than a cat. You can't kill him off. It's insidious."

"Just look at yourself for a minute," Lisa said, her face showing undisguised concern. "You sleep half the morning, you're tired from overwork. Haven't you considered a more logical explanation for these wild theories of yours?"

"Like what?" Derek asked. "You haven't listened to a single thing I've said."

"Be reasonable, Derek. How long has it been since Professor Watson was murdered? A few months. Have you really come to terms with it so soon? His death must have been a terrible shock. I don't think you realize how much stress and grief have been affecting you lately. It's not just me. Gino noticed the change in you, too."

"The stuff I've been talking about has got nothing to do with grief over Watson's death. This is something else entirely. What about Jo's man in the window? How do you explain that?"

"You know as well as I do Jo's been nothing but a bundle of nerves for the last several months. She's had a breakdown. Sometimes I wonder why I haven't had one myself," Lisa added with a sigh. "And that visit to Ron Pruitt was really ill-advised. You're starting to talk like him now. You ought to hear yourself. It's like a classic case of paranoia: you're being followed; Julian is a vampire; don't open doors on the first knock. Seriously, Derek, if you aren't just indulging in one of your elaborate poetic fantasies, you need help. I'd be even more worried if I didn't think you really knew better. There's a logical explanation for the way you're acting, but I know if I say anything you'll just get mad."

"All right, out with it. You're in too deep to stop now."

"I've read a couple of those vampire books of yours. Girls sucking girls, boys sucking boys—isn't it obvious? Everybody these days knows the real psychology behind vampire stories: it's all just sex disguised. Be honest with yourself. Since you've been living in San Francisco, haven't you felt a little funny seeing gay men around you everywhere? The guy in the brown leather suit? Isn't it obvious what's really been bothering you?"

"Look, I know what you're implying. This is not just a case of raging homophobia. I've had gay friends since I was an undergraduate. I don't have a problem with that."

"Right. You're a good liberal who's never had the slightest twinge of anxiety. That's why you wouldn't be caught in the Castro district if they were giving away free money down there. Don't tell me you've been an understudy to your cousin Gino all these years and not absorbed just a little macho prejudice against gays."

"Look, Gino's Gino and I'm me, all right? Why don't we just drop the subject," Derek said, rising, "and quit while we're ahead. I'm going to turn in now, if you don't mind. It's getting late; I've got class tomorrow.

"Where is Gino, anyway?" he asked on his way across the room. "He told me he was going sight-seeing today. He ought to be back by now."

"Maybe he's out knocking the hell out of some poor fairy again."

"That's a low blow and you know it. The guy Gino hit was no little fairy. He was a big lanky bastard, and he wouldn't quit following us when we asked.

"Anyway," Derek added, heading toward the bathroom, "I'll get up to let him in if he comes in late. I doubt we'll see him till tomorrow. If I know him, he's off humping some strange girl."

29

Derek reached across the bed to the night stand and picked up the phone, eyes shut against the light pouring in through the bedroom window.

"Hello?"

Derek's voice was hoarse and gravelly from sleep. The two syllables of his greeting sounded odd as they echoed in the receiver at his ear.

"Speak up, please," he heard himself say to the buzzing on the other end of the line. "There's a radio on and I can hardly hear you." To silence the noise, he reached toward the radio and slapped the snooze alarm. "There," he added, "I've shut it off. Go ahead, I can hear you now."

At the first words, Derek jolted to attention.

"It's Gretchen, Derek. Don't interrupt me because I haven't got much time.

"I can't leave the house and this is the first chance I've had to call you. I'm being watched, so we don't have a minute to spare. I just wanted to tell you that Julian will be out this Saturday night. If you want, you can come to the house. I'm dying to see you again. Reggie and Diane are going with him over to the city, so we'll have all night to ourselves. Please tell me you're going to come or I'll go mad."

"Of course I'll come. What time will it be safe?"

"Anytime after seven. I've got to go now," she said in a final burst of breath. "Sorry I can't say more."

The line went dead with a click. Derek sat cradling the silent receiver like a wounded bird in his hand.

When he looked up, he saw the digital clock on the radio and threw off his remaining covers leaping out of bed. His seminar was due to start in twenty minutes. It was Thursday, so his talk on Shelley was set for today. He was going to be late now even if he were already up and dressed and running. He grabbed a pair of jeans from a chair, reached into the closet and pulled out the first clean shirt that came to hand, then danced across the room trying to put them both on simultaneously. Four minutes later as he ran out the door with his satchel swinging wildly in his hand, he was still fastening up the top button on his shirt.

He arrived in class thirty-seven minutes late. Luckily, Mary Abrams also had a talk today, so he sneaked into the little seminar room with a hasty apology and sat down in the nearest chair to listen to the last few minutes of discussion. By the time it was his turn to speak, he'd caught his breath. Even without looking over his notes beforehand, he felt the right words would come. He could extemporize now on a half dozen aspects of Shelley's work without preparation. In the actual event, his talk went surprisingly well.

After the seminar, the group regathered off campus at the Renaissance Cafe. Classes were sparse on Thursdays, so the class members sometimes continued their discussions after the seminar, often engaging in the most impassioned debate in these unofficial sessions over coffee. Derek wanted to skip the extracurricular talk today but felt his attendance might help erase the embarrassment of his late arrival. As the other members of the class left Wheeler, he lingered behind, arriving at the cafe minutes later in the middle of an argument.

As he approached their table, Derek noticed what he'd been too rushed to notice earlier: the haggard, bloodless look of Professor Fiedler and the similar gray pallor Diane Gregor tried to hide behind her make-up and horn-rimmed prescription sunglasses. Both women looked as if they hadn't slept for days. Diane was nevertheless expounding on the genius of Percy Shelley's political views while her mentor nodded silent approval.

After pulling up a chair, Derek took advantage of a lull in the talk to offer a dissenting view.

"I get very tired of hearing what a great political thinker Shelley was," he said. "If you ask me, the man was nothing more than a hypocritical clown."

His bluntness caught the others by surprise, but Diane quickly climbed the ramparts to mount a defense.

"Even ignoring the wonderful material Gloria is assembling for her new book," she began coldly, "you can't tell me Shelley wasn't the most politically advanced thinker of his day. What about his essay on political reform? When our new book comes out, we'll put a number of things about Shelley in a new perspective. His politics is just one of them. It's time the man got his due."

Gloria Fiedler cleared her throat, then weighed into the discussion behind her protégé.

"It's irresponsible to use terms like those," she said, addressing Derek. "Shelley's views on social reform were visionary in their scope. And his own personal benevolence and philanthropy were legendary."

"You're right," Derek replied. "Clown isn't the right word to describe Shelley. Fiend is much more appropriate, but I'll stick by hypocritical. Every time I hear Shelley describe himself as a philanthropist and benefactor of mankind I get a little bit sick to my stomach."

Diane interrupted. "Shelley gave up his inheritance to live out his egalitarian principles." She took off her glasses and glared at Derek with angry, reddened eyes. "The man gave money to every cause and needy acquaintance that came his way. Money he could ill afford to lose. It's slanderous to say he didn't love humanity. You're simply being mean-spirited. He did more good for the common people than anyone else of his time."

Derek laughed. "By putting pamphlets in bottles and throwing them out to sea? By cheating practically every shopkeeper or tradesman who had the bad sense to give him credit? The guy spent money like a potentate and left a trail of screaming creditors and bailiffs behind him everywhere he went. Of course he gave away loads of family money. He didn't earn it. He figured it was nobler to cheat tradespeople out of their goods than condescend to do an honest day's work. The guy spent his whole life writing poems and travelling—where did he suppose the money for that would come from if his political ideas were ever put into action and he had to pay his own way?

"And as far as his *personal* life was concerned," Derek added with a smile, "there's as pretty a piece of work as you'll ever see. I've been reading Richard Holmes's biography. After abandoning Harriet and his children, the great lover and benefactor of mankind you admire so much dragged his next brood of kids across Europe till he'd killed a couple of them off through indifference and neglect. Then he knocked-up Mary's stepsister Claire and, according to Holmes, maybe their Swiss servant Elise in the bargain—the whole time criticizing his friend Byron for being a dissolute sensualist. It didn't matter to him if he fathered a few more brats. He'd just pay the mothers off with a little Shelley money and go his merry way. After all, he was heir to a baronetcy; he was allowed a few bastards. Only he liked to call it by a prettier name.

"I'll take Byron over Shelley every time," Derek said. "He didn't have to justify his fucking around with a lot of Platonic horseshit about free love.

"And don't try to tell me what a great feminist Shelley was," he added with mocking smile. "I heard you beating that drum the other night at the Houstons' party. Shelley conned and manipulated women so badly it's a wonder they didn't run from the sight of him. The guy was more like Charles Manson than you'd probably care to hear me explain."

With that, Derek stood up. "Don't talk to me about Percy Shelley," he said picking up his books. "I'll take my poets with a little less hypocrisy and pretense, if you don't mind."

As he sat up in bed the next morning, Derek felt groggy and confused. He opened his eyes but couldn't seem to focus his attention or see the clear edges of things. His head was pounding and the muscles in his neck were sore and stiff.

"You look terrible," Lisa said from beside the bed. She leaned to touch his forehead with a cool palm.

"You feel hot. Why don't you sleep in this morning and get a little rest."

"The other night you said I was sleeping in too much."

"Yes, but you're obviously sick. Enough's enough, Derek, give it a rest. Taking your mind off work for a day or two might knock some of this vampire nonsense out of your head."

"I can't," he said, rising dizzily. "I've been writing like crazy the last few weeks. I'll compromise with you. I'll skip classes and work on a poem in the library instead."

"Do what you want. You're going to, anyway."

Derek staggered into the bathroom to shower. The hot water and steam helped revive him a little.

Still dripping, he stood before the mirror to shave. As he lathered up his face, he called to Lisa in the other room.

"Gino didn't come in last night, did he? I'm starting to get worried."

"No," she answered. "His pack is still here, so he couldn't have gone far. Don't worry, he'll turn up soon."

Derek wasn't so sure. It'd be just like Gino to take off without so much as a goodbye—especially now that Derek needed him.

"The last thing he said to me was that we should drive down to L.A.," Derek called. "Hell, maybe the crazy son of a bitch reenlisted in the army again."

As he dried his face, a more alarming explanation for Gino's disappearance occurred. Maybe he'd simply been gotten out of the way. Julian might have found Gino inconvenient now that he'd begun to use strong-arm tactics to pry the letters out of Derek's control.

Derek's hand trembled as he put the razor back in the cabinet. His whole life seemed to be coming apart. Except for his writing, which seemed to thrive on the chaos and danger, his normal concerns and habits were drifting away on swirls of mist and sand.

Yesterday, after storming out of the discussion with his classmates, he'd run into Dave Knight on the sidewalk walking back to school. Dave greeted him with a friendly nudge, chiding him for not answering his call an hour earlier when he claimed they'd met in town.

"I saw you coming out of Titan Books," Dave said. "I called you three times and you walked right by me on the other side of the street. You must have really been spaced-out."

"I was in class an hour ago, giving my report," Derek answered. "It must have been somebody who looked like me."

"No, I was right across the street. You had on that jacket and you were sticking a book into your satchel. It couldn't have been more than an hour ago."

"It must have been my cousin Gino, then. We look a little bit alike."

"I've seen your cousin," Dave said. "This wasn't him. You seriously weren't there?"

Now, staring at his own pale face in the bathroom mirror, Derek remembered the ashen color Gretchen turned when he told her he'd seen her that afternoon outside the bookstore. She was so upset, she cut their conversation short and walked out of the coffee shop. He hadn't seen her since.

Derek arrived in Berkeley earlier than usual and hiked to the nearest coffee shop to fortify himself against another relapse into sleep. He searched a few of the pool halls around campus in the hope of finding Gino, then walked to the university library to work on his poem. He wrote all day till hunger would no longer be denied. At dusk he decided to grab a bite to eat at the student center then head home. It was time to take a night off from work.

As he descended from the stacks to the lobby, the exhilaration that had sustained him suddenly wafted away like fog. The morning's fever returned, draining his last reserves of strength. Bobbing down the last few steps, Derek's knees wobbled. He left the stairway to cross the reference room and make his exit down the wide front stairs outside.

Halfway across the lobby, Derek spotted Julian Ginotti a few steps away, coming toward him. The Englishman was flanked by two distinguished-looking men in dark business suits.

Derek resisted the desire to turn and run. He set his face and prepared himself for the confrontation. There was no getting around it now. As he drew near, Julian turned from the tall hunched man on his left and met Derek's eye with a confident smile.

"Hello, Julian," Derek said. The two men eyed each other across the short space of tiled floor.

Derek recognized the tall, bespectacled man on Julian's left from photographs in the campus newspaper—Edmund Wilkes, the president of the university. The shorter man on Julian's right, who was peering suspiciously at Derek through round-rimmed glasses, also looked familiar; Derek had seen him on numerous occasions in the library.

A librarian, he decided, glancing at the soft chubby figure. Then he looked back at Julian, who was addressing Wilkes.

"A young friend of mine. Derek Hill."

"Pleased to meet you," said the president with barely a glance in Derek's direction. He turned back to Julian. "The photographer will meet us here in five minutes."

As Derek blocked their path, the librarian briefly addressed him.

"Mr. Ginotti has very kindly donated a number of rare books and manuscripts to the library." Then, feeling he'd perhaps said more than was proper, he smiled nervously at Julian.

"Really," Derek said, "let me see if I can guess what they were." He paused for an instant, smiling at Julian. "All right, I'd say a volume or two of Blake's and maybe a few rare first editions by Percy Shelley. How's that?"

The librarian glowed. "I see you're acquainted with Mr. Ginotti's excellent collection."

Derek saw what Julian was up to: extending his dark influence again. He decided to test the Englishman's look of benevolent calm by tossing a few pebbles his way.

"I might have a few manuscripts you'd be interested in, myself," he said. "Maybe I'll let you have a look at them someday."

Julian remained unruffled. Addressing his two companions, he deflected Derek's challenge with a smile.

"Mr. Hill is a very talented poet. His work might well be worth preserving—if he persists in the difficult course he's set for himself." He cast a meaningful glance Derek's way.

"You're very kind," Derek replied. "But I didn't mean my own manuscripts. I may have something of far more interest. Some Shelley papers . . . perhaps something like your own."

Both Wilkes and the librarian appeared to be embarrassed by the offer. It was clear they thought Derek was either making a bad joke or was a little touched in the head. Julian, mastered the situation at once.

"It's true Shelley papers have often appeared in embarrassing abundance over the years, but the great majority of them are simply forgeries, I'm afraid. One has to be very careful," he said, smiling facetiously. "In their exuberance, the poet's devotees have fobbed off every sort of facsimile and fake, even to the propagation of Shelley relics. The safest course in dealing with the letters of a dead poet is to assume fraud until their provenance has been verified."

Julian gazed at Derek, light dancing in his eyes.

"As you may know, there were two great waves of Shelley forgeries. The first was during the brief career of the forger known as Major Byron. The second occurred between 1916 and 1926 in London. I would wager," he added, "that these manuscripts you've alluded to were produced during one of those periods. Authentic Shelley material is very rare. Experts themselves are often hard-pressed to distinguish between true and false coin. I would advise you against making judgements on your own."

Julian appeared to have finished his lecture, but at the last moment added with seeming irrelevance, "Have you read *The Aspern Papers* by Henry James? A most amusing book. Its story is based on an actual incident." Julian smiled briefly at the two men at his sides.

"It seems an American sea captain by the name of Silsbee was such a fanatical Shelleyan that he determined to win some of the poet's love letters from Claire Clairmont, the author's former lover—"

"And his wife's sister," Derek interjected.

"Indeed. Stepsister. Well, the intrepid captain did partially succeed in getting a few trifles from the old woman. But he's had to pay the price of being portrayed for all time in James's book as an avaricious old fool. One can't help wondering if the game was worth the candle," Julian chuckled.

"No," he said, "the best course is to make no assumptions, to proceed calmly, and to rely on the advice of experts. Otherwise, one may founder on the rocks. I'd be very careful about making claims concerning putative Shelley material, if I were you."

Derek decided to try another tack.

"If these gentlemen don't mind, I'd like to have a moment with you alone. Can you spare a few seconds?"

President Wilkes glanced uneasily at his watch. "Well," he said uncertainly, "the photographer won't be here for another minute. Perhaps we could meet upstairs."

The librarian looked disappointed as Julian took a few steps to the side to confer with Derek. Then the two officials wandered toward the door to some first-floor offices and lingered there until Julian could conclude his errand with the importunate student.

Derek didn't waste time with formalities. Once they were by themselves, he leaned toward Julian and said, "Look, I've got something I think you want. Maybe we could work something out that would benefit both of us."

"I've already told you," Julian replied, "I'm bestowing my

gift on you with or without your cooperation. Why don't you just give me the letters as a gesture of conciliation. They're of no earthly use to you and they mean very much to me. You brought me one, why not make a clean sweep of it? After all, the reward for your diligence has already been put into motion."

"What I was thinking," Derek said, ignoring the drift of Julian's reply, "was that I could maybe give you some of the letters in exchange for something."

He tried to lend his voice a note of authority. "I want you to let Gretchen go. If you'll do that, I might be able to see my way clear to giving you what you want."

Julian's laugh echoed across the wide room.

"I'm afraid that's impossible."

"Why?" Derek asked.

"Because," the Englishman replied, no longer smiling, "it's too late. Gretchen has seen her double. There's nothing you can do for her now."

"What's that supposed to mean?"

"You'll find out soon enough. Your suggestion is impertinent. Gretchen is mine. Why do you want only what you can't possibly have? How dare you make such a suggestion to me."

Julian took a step back, rising haughtily as if to go.

"I'll have the letters soon enough. You have no idea what pressures I can bring to bear. You'll soon be twisting like a weasel in a hole. Now if you'll excuse me, I have a more pressing engagement."

Julian turned away and strode toward the door. Derek watched as the Englishman wrapped the two officials once again in his invincible cloak of charm and prepared to leave.

Derek remembered his appointment with Gretchen tomorrow night in Nightmare Abbey with a spiteful smile. It was time to reduce their lovers' triangle to a single corner. He still had the letters to bargain with, despite Julian's pretended unwillingness to negotiate. Let Gretchen herself decide which man she wanted. For once in his life, Julian might get a little surprise.

30

Derek waited till Lisa left the apartment for some Saturday afternoon shopping before he sat down at his desk. Opening Richard Holmes's biography, he turned to the last chapter of the now-familiar text to reread its account of Shelley's last days. The facts, as Holmes recounted them, did nothing to dispel Derek's fears. Shelley's final hours were wracked by a number of haunting visions and visitations. The ones that interested Derek were those in which Shelley himself appeared. Unfortunately, there were several; their occurrence lent plausibility to the notion Derek had begun to entertain since speaking with Julian last night at the library. The worst of it was, the witnesses not only appeared reliable, they seemed genuinely appalled by what they'd seen.

Jane Williams said she saw Shelley twice walking on the terrace outside the house while he was supposedly aboard his boat. On the night before his final journey, Shelley reported seeing his own specter in Mary's room. According to Mary, Shelley ran into her bedroom that night, screaming uncontrollably. Thinking he was only sleep-walking, as he'd been on similar occasions, she tried to awaken him. When that failed, she ran from her room to Jane's across the hall. Edward Williams then went to see the poet. In response to his questions, Shelley told him that he hadn't been asleep at all, that what had frightened him was a waking vision. When he ran into Mary's room, he said, he saw a double of himself already there, bent over Mary, strangling his sleeping wife in bed.

The following morning after things settled down a bit, Shelley described an earlier meeting with his double. One afternoon while strolling on the terrace, he'd met his doppelgänger walking in the garden. When he confronted it, the specter posed a question that might have been lifted out of *Faust*: "How long do you mean to be content?"

The encounter reminded Derek of a passage he'd read recently for his seminar. He opened Shelley's *Prometheus Unbound* and found it right away in Act One.

> Ere Babylon was dust,
> The Magus Zoroaster, my dead child,
> Met his own image walking in the garden.
> That apparition, sole of men, he saw.
> For know there are two worlds of life and death:
> One that which thou beholdest; but the other
> Is underneath the grave, where do inhabit
> The shadows of all forms that think and live
> Till death unite them and they part no more . . .

Derek looked up from the page, unable to read further. It was all there in the poem, recorded years before the poet encountered his own doppelgänger in the garden outside his house in Italy. Shelley, with his lifelong study of the occult, had become a magus, like Zoroaster, capable of conjuring up his double from the other side of the grave.

Fear clutched Derek's heart like a bony hand. He remembered Julian's comments last night in the library. The Englishman had said it plainly enough: Gretchen had seen her double. Derek had chased it himself over a half block in Berkeley. The only question now was whether it was too late to save her from an afterlife of unliving horror. He'd warn her tonight when he saw her at Julian's house.

Then Derek had another chilling thought: his own double had been seen by Dave Knight on a Berkeley sidewalk less than forty-eight hours ago. Dave was adamant about seeing him, despite Derek's insistent denials. So whatever had happened to Shelley at the end, might now be happening to him, as well as to Gretchen. Julian had said he'd reward him for preserving the letters—despite his refusal to return them—as a gift. It was a reward Derek preferred now to forgo. He recognized Julian at last for what he was. The thought that a similar fate might now await him sent a shudder of horror down Derek's spine.

No, he thought, closing the book, I won't rush to conclusions this time. There must be something else to check before accepting these crazy theories, something to corroborate the accounts of Shelley's final days, Julian's vampirism, this business of the double—something, somewhere, somehow . . . .

Then he remembered Byron. If Byron had made a similar attempt to transcend mortality, as Ron had hinted and as Derek himself once jokingly suggested at Julian's party; if Byron had become—or attempted to become—a vampire, then there might be some trace left in the historical record that would substantiate Derek's theory.

It took two more hours of reading before he found the evidence in the footnote of a book about Byron's first trip to the Middle East. According to the note, Byron's double was seen on more than one occasion during the period immediately following his adventure with the Greek girl outside Athens—the period that produced *The Giaour*; the period whose central incident inspired the poet's first mention of vampirism. Once again, the witnesses seemed disinterested; the incidents they recorded, objective fact.

Byron's friend Robert Peel insisted he'd passed the poet on two separate occasions during the fall of 1810, while Byron was far away in Greece. Other friends reported that Byron had been seen writing his name among the list of visitors inquiring after the health of the ailing king. After hearing the accounts of his appearances back in England, Byron joked that they'd have made good ghost stories if he'd died, for he was suffering at the time from a bad fever in Patras in the marshes near Olympia. As all the biographies of the poet faithfully recorded, Byron went to Patras immediately after his encounter with the Greek girl.

As far as Derek was able to determine, however, the poet never encountered his double himself. But then, unlike Shelley, Byron had never studied the occult, had never become a magus—prerequisites, it seemed, for achieving immortality as a vampire.

Gazing absently at the page of the open book, Derek felt his vision begin to blur. No wonder Byron had failed to achieve his goal, while Shelley—with less success as a poet and more acquaintance with the black arts—had the motivation and knowledge to succeed. It was only after death that Shelley equalled his friend in readership and stature. Apparently his gamble had paid off.

"My God," said a voice behind Derek's back, "you look white as a sheet. What on earth are you reading?"

Derek closed the book and turned to face Lisa, who was still studying him from the doorway, plastic shopping bag in hand.

"Something for class," he lied. "Boy, you gave me quite a scare."

Lisa eyed him another minute and then said, "You look like hell. Just sit there till I get the thermometer." She left the doorway for the bathroom. Derek heard her rummaging through the medicine cabinet down the hall.

When she returned, she shook the mercury down with a few quick flicks of her hand.

"Open your mouth," she said. "I don't know what you'd do if you had to take care of yourself. How did you survive when you lived alone?"

She placed the silver knob of the thermometer under his tongue. Derek tasted the glass rod, felt the temperature measurements etched on its rounded side.

After five minutes of awkward sucking, he felt her pull the instrument from his mouth. She squinted at its tiny gauge and declared the results of her reading.

"A hundred and two point seven. Just what I thought. You've got a fever."

"No wonder I feel so bad. I thought it was just overwork. You were right, I've got to take a break."

Lisa stood shaking the thermometer again. "Did you know there was a police car outside? I saw it pull up as I was locking the gate."

Before Derek could reply, the front buzzer rang.

"I'll bet that's them," Lisa said, heading toward the door. "You'd better put on a shirt."

Derek walked to the closet as Lisa went to answer the buzzer. As he pulled on the shirt, he heard deep voices, the shuffle of bodies in the other room. Lisa was answering their questions as he entered.

Derek recognized one of the policemen as Lieutenant Graves, the officer who came after the break-in. This time, though, the cop was accompanied by another plain-clothed detective, a sandy-haired man in his late twenties. Graves looked dour and cynical. The younger man seemed more personable, smiling amiably at Lisa from the middle of the room. Both cops wore cheap blue suits under their overcoats.

"Mr. Hill, you might remember me. I'm Lieutenant Graves. This is Sergeant McNeil." The silver-haired detective made no move to shake hands. He simply met Derek's eyes for an instant before seating himself with some difficulty in the chair on the opposite side of the room. Lisa walked from the living room to the kitchen, where she leaned behind the counter to watch.

"We won't keep you long, Mr. Hill. Sergeant McNeil and I just have a couple of quick questions we hoped you could help us with." At the mention of his name, the young officer grinned at Derek.

"Sure, go ahead. What's this about?"

Graves ignored Derek's question to ask one of his own. "Did you know an Emma Pruitt of San Jose?" The old cop watched Derek the way a fox watches a chicken coop.

"No," Derek answered. "I knew a Ron Pruitt at Stanford—as you might remember. You asked me about him last time you were here."

"But not his mother?" Graves asked. "Emma."

"No. I never met her."

Both cops regarded Derek coolly.

"The reason I ask," continued Graves, "is this. There's a young man who lives across the street from her who says he saw someone who looked like you in front of her house a few weeks back."

"No. I've never been there. He must be mistaken."

"Well," said the old cop, rising to his feet with a huff, "that's all we wanted to ask. Thank you very much for your assistance."

"Sorry I couldn't be more help," Derek said, stepping closer to the two men. "What's this all about?"

"It's not important," Graves said. "Strictly routine. Sorry to bother you." He walked toward the front door with his colleague in tow, nodding at Lisa as they passed.

"Thank you, M'am. We can find our way out."

Derek waited till he heard them slam the metal gate outside before he sat down on the couch. Lisa was staring at him from the kitchen.

"Are you going to tell me what that was all about?"

"Ron Pruitt's mother was killed in a house fire a few weeks back. They must be trying to check out something about that."

"Of course the guy across the street who said he saw you was wrong. Right?"

"There's no way he could have identified me from there. The cops were on a fishing expedition."

"So you *were* there?"

"Yes," Derek answered, "but not the day of the fire. I was there the day before. I didn't know anything about the fire until I read about it in the paper the morning after it happened."

"Are you going to make me drag the whole thing out of you a piece at a time, or are you going to tell me what the hell is going on? I can't believe my ears. You astound me sometimes, you know, you really do."

Derek figured the best course now was honesty. He told Lisa about the taped conversation and how the cassette was stolen from their apartment while he was sleeping off a drunk at the Houstons' house. Then he told her about going to see Ron Pruitt's mother in San Jose. He wasn't ready yet to tell her he'd found the letters or what terrifying possibilities they suggested.

"Do you have any idea what kind of trouble you're in?" Lisa asked when he'd finished his story.

"What trouble? I told you—there's no way that guy can tie me to the fire. I was home that day."

"By yourself, in this apartment."

Derek saw her point.

"Anyway," he insisted, "there's no way he could have recognized me. That Lieutenant Graves is full of shit."

"All right," Derek admitted after a pause, "there is something I didn't tell you. Those letters Ron told me about? I found them in his mother's garage. I've got them safely tucked away in a safety deposit box downtown. Nobody knows where they are but me. Nobody else even knows I have them. Except maybe Julian." Derek faltered. "He might be the one who took the tape. But even if someone did know where they were, there's no way they could get to them. I think they're the reason Professor Watson was murdered. From what I can tell, they were written by Percy Shelley. And there's something else about them you wouldn't believe."

"At this moment, I'd believe anything." Lisa walked from around the counter and stood before Derek, her blue eyes flaring like gas jets.

"You really don't know how deep you're into this, do you? The fire at Ron's mother's house is the least of your worries. If the cops find that tape, they've got a record of you and Ron talking about those letters. Jesus Christ, Derek, you could go up on a murder rap.

"Don't you see? You've got the letters Ron stole from Watson. The letters he murdered him for. You look like an accomplice. Think for a minute: you visit Ron in prison, you discuss the letters he stole on the night of the murder, then you go to his mother's house to recover them for yourself. As far as a court of law is concerned, you're an accessory to murder. Hell, for that matter, where were you on the night Professor Watson was killed? A few hundred yards away, alone in your Stanford apartment. Do you think a jury would believe you if you told them you were lying there asleep? There's a death penalty in this state. Your whole life is twisting in the wind and you're still trying to prove to the world that Percy Shelley was a vampire. Jesus, Derek, I half think you've lost your mind."

Derek felt nausea sweeping over him like a tidal wave.

"At least nobody can get the letters to prove I was involved," he said. "They're in the bank."

Lisa gave a bitter hacking laugh. "Of course they can get the letters. What do you think, that you've got them safely buried thirty thousand fathoms below the sea? All the police need is a court order. One piece of paper from a judge and the next thing you know you're promising to tell the truth, the whole truth, and nothing but the truth, so help you God.

"Get rid of them, Derek. Get rid of those letters as fast as you can. You're one court order away from making the headlines in tomorrow's paper."

"I can't," Derek said, "it's the weekend. I'll have to wait till Monday. And it's not going to be all that easy. Those letters are the only reason Julian hasn't already gotten to me. There's something else I didn't tell you." Derek stalled for an instant. "Julian threatened me last night. He said he'd bring all kinds of terrific pressures to bear. So now this morning these two cops show up to question me about the fire. What a coincidence. Just like the last time they showed up after the break-in, asking me about my visit to Vacaville. Somebody put them on to me. Don't you see? He's trying to squeeze the letters out of me right now. I didn't tell you before, but the bastard had me attacked a few nights ago by a bunch of Hell's Angels in Berkeley. If Gino hadn't shown up, I'd probably still be recovering in the hospital."

Lisa looked alarmed. Derek hurried to reassure her.

"I'll get rid of the letters," he said. "I promise. As soon as I figure out how to do it right.

"In the meantime, I want you to do something for me. Go to your parents' house. Please. Go to Sacramento right now.

"Better yet," he added, rising to pace the room, "take your whole family to Reno. Your mom has been bugging your dad to take her there for weeks. Go away for a while. I'll call you when I've got everything under control back here. Promise me you'll go," he pleaded. "I can't even think about something happening to you."

31

It was dark when the cab dropped Derek off at the entrance to a long gravel driveway in the Berkeley hills. The narrow lane was set in a gloomy alcove overhung by vine-tangled branches a few hundred yards downhill from Nightmare Abbey. The cabby, sensing that his passenger had chosen the spot at random, kept a safe distance as Derek counted out the money for the fare and tip. Quickly pocketing the cash, he sped away downhill, casting one last furtive glance over his shoulder as if to judge the mischief he'd escaped.

Once alone, Derek checked his watch. Ten minutes after seven. According to Gretchen's instructions, it would now be safe to hike the remaining distance to the house. If her estimate were wrong, Julian would spy him as they passed on the hill. Derek waited five more minutes before starting, then checked both directions for traffic as he stepped out of the driveway onto the narrow, shoulderless road. A full moon, partially hidden by low-flying clouds, cast just enough light onto the street for him to see his way.

Despite the awful stakes involved, an air of fantasy and excitement clung to the adventure. Though he hadn't yet formulated the ghost of a plan, he was determined to spring Gretchen from her nightmare prison before it was too late. Even if he were successful, though, he faced a host of further difficulties. Eventually he'd have to make a choice between Lisa and Gretchen.

He couldn't imagine a future in which either woman was absent. To keep from being paralyzed by indecision, Derek decided this wasn't the time to reach after fact or reason; it was time to act. He could sort things out later when his fever wasn't making it impossible to think. Lisa was safe in Sacramento; Gretchen needed him now.

As he rounded the last curve, Derek saw a half dozen bright windows beaming in the giant bulk of the house and nearly broke into a run. The sight of a black Mercedes coming down the hill brought him quickly to his senses.

He dived into the underbrush at road side and held his breath till the car rushed past.

He didn't think they'd seen him. The headlights were still sweeping the underbrush on the other side of the road when he'd darted for cover. It probably wasn't even Julian; every second car in this area was a Mercedes. Derek stepped out of the bushes, dusted off his knees, and stepped back onto the road to finish the last leg of his journey.

A minute later, he stood at Gretchen's front door, wondering what to do next. What if a servant answered his ring? Gretchen said that Reggie would accompany Julian and Diane to the city, but what about that woman, Maria—was she a regular maid, or had she only been employed the night of the last party? Surely with a place this big, Julian would have more than just Reggie and the one servant.

He decided to knock rather than ring the buzzer. He rapped at the solid oak panel three times, then leaned toward the door and listened for a response from inside. After a short wait, the lock clicked and the door slowly creaked open.

"I forgot to tell you not to ring the bell," Gretchen whispered, peering around the door. "Come in. Maria is in the kitchen. Otherwise, we've got the place all to ourselves."

Derek was shocked at the change in Gretchen's appearance. She had lost at least ten pounds. The skin of her face had visibly tightened over the soft swell of her cheekbones, which now jutted like ankles. Her skin's normal pallor had bleached to white translucency. She looked as if she'd had the life sucked right out of her.

She took Derek's hand in her icy grip. "Follow me," she whispered. "I want to show you something."

Derek let himself be led by the hand as they tiptoed through several carpeted rooms. At last they arrived at the entrance to a narrow corridor.

"Maria's in the kitchen, so we'll have to go the back way," Gretchen said, stepping into the dark hall.

After several turnings, they arrived at a large room at the rear of the house. Windows along one wall looked out onto a stand of trees. The room itself appeared to be a large pantry; long unfinished wooden shelves ran along the walls, filled with cans of vegetables, ketchup, lard. Gretchen pointed to a large, rough-hewn wooden door with a large brass handle a few feet away. The thing looked formidable, with its sturdy iron lock and iron hasp.

"We're going down to the basement."

Gretchen lifted the iron rod, then turned the skeleton key in the lock till its large workings fell into place with a rusty creak.

"What?" Derek asked with mock disappointment, "no secret entrance? no sliding walls or vanishing book shelves?"

Gretchen shushed him with a finger to her lips. Nudging him toward the dark stairway, she closed the door softly behind them. Until she flicked on her flashlight, they stood in total darkness. Derek was relieved when the light's yellow beam disclosed an ordinary flight of wooden steps.

"There's no electricity down here," Gretchen explained, her face half hidden in shadow.

They descended the stairs together, hand in hand. As they neared the stone foundation, Derek wanted to embrace Gretchen on the last step and have her right there on the dusty floor.

Gretchen flashed her beacon across the room; the light revealed a plain, if rather dank and forbidding, stone cellar.

"I wonder who's bricked up in that wall," Derek asked. Fear tickled his brain like a dirty joke. Every sensation seemed spiced by the slapstick of unknown danger. He wanted to laugh out loud, to fill the house with peals of roaring appreciative laughter.

"Did you know that Poe said the most beautiful combination of words in the English language was *cellar door*?" Derek asked. "He sure would have loved this place."

Derek looked around again at the gloomy stone interior.

"I'll say one thing for Julian. He certainly knows how to create an effect. This house is a scream."

Gretchen guided him across the floor past four squat stone pillars to a wide door that led to a second chamber somewhere near the middle of the house.

Halfway across this second room, she suddenly turned to Derek and asked an odd question. Odd at least for the circumstances.

"Have you ever been so enthralled by a poet that you wanted to write poems just like his?" Gretchen aimed the flashlight at their feet. "I don't mean just the style," she added hastily, "I mean everything: the pet words, the tone, the stance toward reality, the sense of irony—so that when you're finished the poems seem less your own work than a collaboration between you and the dead poet's spirit."

Derek wasn't sure what she was getting at. He studied her shadowed face for a clue.

"Of course," he said, "every poet goes through an apprenticeship. That's how you find your voice."

"Yes, but what if you're a sorcerer's apprentice, and the voice doesn't ever let go and you're held in thrall by a superior magic till it's too late to find your way back. What then?" The tremor in her voice brought back all of Derek's fear.

"You conduct an exorcism to get the voice out of your head. An apprenticeship is one thing, ventriloquism's another."

"What if I told you something extraordinary?" Gretchen asked, glancing nervously at the dark shadows beyond the reach of her light. "About Julian. I should have warned you earlier, but I was afraid to. I . . . I thought you already knew, so I didn't think it needed saying. Because what I was just describing has already happened—to me. I lost something—my soul, maybe, for lack of a better word—and now I'm afraid it's too late to get it back. I've let you in for more trouble than you deserve, I'm afraid." She turned her face away. "I hope someday you'll forgive me for bringing you here tonight."

"Don't worry, you're not alone," Derek assured her. "Julian's hinted that he's going to use his magic to bless me, too. Apparently, whether I want him to or not."

"Is that what you think it is," Gretchen asked, "a blessing?"

She laughed bitterly, one sharp cry of disbelief.

"Haven't you ever read about the Wandering Jew—or wondered why Shelley and Byron were so obsessed by the myth? To be unable to die . . . ." Gretchen stopped with a shudder.

"For heaven's sake, Derek, don't you see? Julian is accursed. Do you know where he is tonight? Over in the city, looking for some poor soul to suck the life out of . . . that's how the man lives. He's a predator. He'll hole up in one of his apartments over there with some poor bastard desperate enough to be taken in by all that fatal charm of his. That's why I brought you here tonight."

Gretchen looked at Derek with an expression he was unable to decipher. In it were hints of challenge, embarrassment, silent appeal.

"The worst of it," she muttered almost to herself, "is that afterward you can't write poems anymore. No soul. All you can do is caretake the little orphans of your happier days."

Her tone suddenly changed; her expression hardened. "Come here. I'll show you what has to be done."

Gretchen aimed her flashlight toward a corner, then followed it toward the web-strung alcove pierced by its feeble beam.

Derek trailed her across the uneven floor. In the corner where she finally stopped sat a tall pile of dirty white linen. Old curtains, drapes, bedspreads. Gretchen tossed the ones on top aside till she uncovered the large wooden trunk on which they'd been sitting.

She aimed her light at the lock. A short metal key was already in place. With a quick twist, she unhooked the latch, lifted the heavy lid, and shone her light into the open trunk. Inside, Derek saw a strange assortment of items: an ax, a can of gasoline, two ax-sharpened two-by-fours.

"Here," she said. "I want you to help me do it with this." She drew out one of the pointed wooden stakes. "I got the stuff ready last week, but I haven't had the nerve to use it. I was hoping you'd help. You're stronger than I am, and I don't know if I have the will to go through with it by myself."

Derek stared at the open trunk. Gretchen continued to describe her gruesome plan.

"They won't come back tonight till almost dawn. We'll wait until sunup, then sneak down here the way we came tonight. Julian's coffin is in there." Derek followed her pointing finger, which was fixed on a blank space of brick wall twenty feet away.

"If Reggie or Diane gives you any trouble," she added, "use this." Gretchen slipped something hard and metallic into Derek's hand. Even without the light, he could feel what it was. The cold metal grip rested firmly in his palm. A .45 automatic, just like his father's back home.

"I'll try to distract them if they wake up before we're finished," she added. "But as a last resort . . ." Her voice trailed off again as Derek grasped the full implications of what she was saying.

"That's another reason I need you. I figured you might know how to load and shoot the damn thing. I'm hopeless with anything mechanical."

"Wait a minute," Derek objected. "You're asking me to commit murder. I'm in a bad enough situation as it is."

"Consider it self-defense. Keep in mind what Julian has in store for you. You'll wish you weren't so damned talented and clever before he's finished with you.

"Here," she added, "I'll show you what I'm talking about."

Suddenly Gretchen paced toward the brick wall she'd pointed to a moment before. A foot or two in front of it, she paused to search its surface with her light. Then after inspecting its brickwork, she stepped forward, selected a spot at eye-level, and pressed hard with the fingers of one hand. A scraping rumble vibrated the floor under Derek's feet as an eight-foot section of the wall rolled back on hidden tracks, leaking darkness around its edges.

"Are you coming?" Gretchen stepped into the gap. "Leave the trunk. We'll close it up on our way out."

She disappeared into the murk behind the wall, leaving Derek alone in darkness. He saw the trace of light peeping from the entrance and hurried toward it, then followed the shuffling steps ahead of him into the next room.

Once through the gap, he saw the secret chamber inside.

The air here was heavy and damp, spiced with the unmistakable odor of decay. He nearly choked. Gretchen's light illuminated the polished mahogany of a large, ornate coffin sitting in the middle of the floor. The lid was open, revealing red satin lining inside. Derek pulled beside Gretchen to peer in. The bottom of the box was covered by a layer of dirt.

"From England," Gretchen explained, tracing an index finger through a foot of the dank soil. "From an estate called Field Place. That name should certainly ring a bell."

Shelley's beloved ancestral home, Derek remembered, hearing the familiar name. His worst suspicion was confirmed.

"You understand what I'm telling you, don't you?" Gretchen asked. Her face looked agitated, grim.

"This is crazy. What are you trying to say?" Derek wanted to hear the words from her.

"No," she said. "I want you to tell me. Do you know who Julian really is? If you do, tell me right now. I don't want you to think I've lost my mind."

Derek saw the desperation in Gretchen's eyes as she waited for his answer.

"He's Percy Shelley."

Once Derek said the words out loud, a wave of relief swept over him. He wasn't insane. Gretchen knew, too.

"Bravo. Now I'll show you what we're up against."

Suddenly she turned and marched off again toward another dark corner. Derek didn't see the entrance this time till she pierced it with her dimming sword of light. When she disappeared again, he hurried after her into the darkness beyond.

This room was larger, more forbidding. Gretchen crossed it swiftly, stopping to light a pair of candles on a table before the opposite wall. Derek followed her, then stood staring at what the flickering light revealed. Two naked men—apparently dead or unconscious—lay shackled to a pair of iron cots; the cots, in turn, were bolted to the floor.

"What's the IV for?" Derek asked, eyeing the metal rack beside the nearest bunk. "And what the hell is this guy doing down here, anyway?"

"Don't you recognize him?"

Derek studied the gaunt, bloodless face; the white fleshless figure; the mottled bald head.

"It's Robert Best," Gretchen said, "the performance artist. Julian's drugged him to keep him under control. He's been down here over a week now."

"Why, for Christ's sake?"

"I'm not sure. I think he refused to do something Julian asked. Does it really matter why? Look at the man."

Derek remembered the swarthy daredevil he met on New Year's Eve. This pale skeleton couldn't pass for a distant relation.

"Brace yourself," Gretchen said grimly. "Look at this."

She turned her flashlight to the body on the second cot. Derek followed its beam down the length of the figure curled on the dingy gray sheet.

At first Derek thought it was the body of a ten or eleven year old boy. Then he looked again. Though the corpse weighed no more than seventy or eighty pounds, its face sported a light growth of beard. A few strands of gray threaded the hair at the temple. The man was perhaps thirty-five, though his features were so shrivelled, his skin so speckled and splotched, he might have passed for seventy.

"Jesus, what happened to him?"

Gretchen opened her mouth, then froze. She cocked her head as if to listen. Then her hands closed on Derek's arm.

"Oh, Christ," she whispered, pulling him close, "I think they're back."

Derek's heart stopped. He heard the scrape of feet overhead, a man's voice calling out.

"Bad luck," Gretchen muttered. "They must have brought them home tonight. We've got to get you out of here. There's a tenspeed bike in the back of the garage if I can get you out there.

It's got a headlight. It would at least get you safely downtown."

"The trunk," Derek whispered. "And the coffin. They're still open."

A voice called in the distance. "Gretchen, are you down there?"

Derek's stomach sank. It was Julian. He must be calling down from the top of the cellar stairs.

"Don't worry, love," Gretchen consoled. "I know another way out. Just follow me."

Derek was more than worried; he was terrified. In another moment Julian would be breathing down their necks.

"Come on," he said. "Let's get the hell out of here."

Gretchen started toward a dark recess further down the wall. On her third step, she fumbled the flashlight, dropping it in a dizzy whirl of light.

It hit the floor with a crack and went out. The darkness ahead threatened to swallow them.

"The candles," she hissed. "Get the candles."

Derek turned to the table they'd just left and seized a candlestick in each hand; then he leapt after Gretchen again. In his haste, the rush of air nearly blew out his candles. He stood holding his breath as one of the flames rose flickering back to life. Cupping his hand around it, he shuffled after Gretchen in an awkward bow-legged crouch. Behind him, closer this time, he heard Julian's voice echoing through the basement.

"Darling, what are you doing in there?"

Gretchen fled down the dark passageway ahead of Derek, candlelight flashing off her golden hair. He wished she'd slow down, wished the pistol he'd dropped a moment ago was loaded and cocked in his hand. He could see the low stone ceiling of the narrow tunnel just inches above his head; it appeared to be getting lower; the tunnel itself seemed narrower and crookeder the further he ran.

Suddenly Derek came to a fork and realized he'd lost sight of Gretchen. He looked down both branches with the candle held before him but both shafts ended in pools of ink. He chose the tunnel on the right, prayed he guessed right, and ran shuffling down its narrow winding length, still guarding the flickering light in a cupped palm.

From behind, the voice called again. "Gretchen!" From the sound of it, Julian was closing in.

Derek picked up the pace, nearly running now. The sudden burst of speed blew out the candle. He was running blind. He threw the thing down and groped down the stone passageway, one hand reading the wall, the other flailing the darkness ahead.

A moment later his feet hit an obstruction and he lost balance. He landed against a set of sharp angles, bruising cheek, elbow, rib, shin, knee.

Stairs, he realized suddenly, running his hands over a rough plank. He scrambled to all fours and mounted them three at a time.

After twenty or thirty steps, he stumbled onto a landing and felt his way, crawling, toward the next upward flight. From below he heard the voice again, but this time it uttered only a low, guttural growl, like a cornered dog. Derek leapt stumbling up the stairs, desperate now to reach their top.

Fumbling, clawing, he scrambled up the stairs, then fell forward on a landing and slammed face-first into a wall.

Trapped, he thought, an instant after impact. His hands clawed at the wood as if to dig their way through.

Not a wall; a door. He grasped the knob and twisted. Unlocked. The door swung open. On the other side was a long dim length of hall.

Derek leapt into the corridor, looked both ways. No exit. Blind walls sealed the hall off at both ends. Closed doors were spaced at intervals down both sides; the only light emanated from a sliver in one that had been left a hair's breadth open.

Heavy footsteps pounded the steps behind him. Derek slammed and locked the door against whatever had snarled at him on the other side. Then he fled down the hall toward the light fanning from the cracked door. As he approached it, he heard the thump of a shoulder meeting the locked cellar door behind him.

Derek seized the handle and swung the bedroom door wide.

A bizarre scene greeted him. On the wide double bed twenty feet away lay two naked women, white in the lamplight. One, a dark-haired beauty, was tied spreadeagle to the bedposts, struggling against her bonds. A pale-skinned redhead crouched over her, buttocks raised toward the door where Derek stood frozen. When she heard him enter the room behind her, she paused in her descent toward her victim's neck and turned to face him over her shoulder.

Her smile revealed two long canine fangs. Derek recognized the horribly transformed face of Diane Gregor. The muffled cries of her victim suddenly grew louder as, wide-eyed, the girl spied Derek, too.

Derek turned and fled into the hallway again, leaving the girl to her fate, then ran stumbling toward the wall at the end of the corridor.

"Well, well," a voice said behind him. "Look who's come to visit."

The voice might have been Julian's, but Derek didn't turn to see. He was almost cornered now. He reached the end of the hall and, to his delight, saw that it was intersected on the right by a short corridor leading to a pair of double doors. Derek turned into the branch corridor and grasped both handles. He yanked the doors open, then threw himself forward into the large room they opened to, falling face down onto its carpet inside.

As soon as his face hit the floor, he kicked the doors behind him to slam them shut. Then he looked up, searching for an avenue of escape.

It took several seconds to take in the scene before him. The only light in the room issued from a set of large television screens set in the opposite wall. Below them sat several rows of heads, rising over the backs of chairs and sofas.

Derek scrambled to his feet, and as he did, he saw that the image on the largest screen showed a young man gaining his feet, too—a mirror image of himself.

He looked up to stare at the big center screen, still crouched to run. His own face appeared to be staring down at him. Derek blinked up at it, too dumfounded to move. The face blinked back. It took several more seconds before he realized he was being shot by a hidden camera.

Then bright lights blinked on in the ceiling, and the heads of the spectators in front of him turned from his screen image to face him, squinting against the sudden increase of light.

Derek glanced at the blinking faces, then turned back to the television screens, hypnotized. Though the large middle screen continued to show his image, he saw now that the others showed different scenes. One revealed the entrance to the cellar; the next revealed the first basement room with the hidden door; others, the trunk where Gretchen had stored her weapons, the room with the coffin, the two men chained to their cots. Two showed dim, red-tinted pictures of the tunnels he'd just raced through. Derek realized in a flash that they were being shot through infra-red lenses. A final screen showed the doorway of the room where he'd seen the two naked women.

The women could still be viewed there, in fact, though both were now hunched together on the edge of the bed in white terry cloth robes, smiling toward the camera.

Suddenly the screens went black. Then a single image filled them all: the bald head and smiling face of Robert Best. The big screen in the center magnified him to billboard size.

"Hello, Derek," the face said, grinning down. "I call this piece *Walpurgis Night*—hoped you enjoyed it. Thanks for coming. Happy Halloween."

Then the screens went black. An instant later, the room was filled with the hand-slapping of applause.

Derek stood staring at the faces of thirty smiling strangers, paralyzed by shock and anger. Then Julian Ginotti's smiling countenance turned to face him from the high-backed chair behind which he'd been screened.

"Let me introduce you to your audience," Julian said, rising to his feet.

He pointed at a thin man in a gray suit to his left. "This is

Donald Nordquist, art reviewer for the *San Francisco Examiner*. And that lovely woman over there in the red dress is Maggie Schwertlein, of *Art International*." Julian pointed to a stout woman with bright red lips. She looked like the proprietor of a brothel.

"And there of course is the creative genius behind tonight's little drama, your friend Robert Best."

Derek stopped listening as he realized at last what had happened. The artist's face on the screen a moment ago had been taped. Robert Best stood before him now healthy and smiling, having washed off his make-up and escaped his supposed imprisonment downstairs in the basement. Julian's voice in the basement and tunnels must have been recorded, too. The whole night had been a cruel hoax, a performance art piece enacted without his permission or knowledge. Worse, the whole thing had been observed by a hand-picked crowd of art critics and patrons on these giant television screens—and no doubt taped, as well.

He'd been had.

"Where's Gretchen?" Derek demanded, interrupting Julian's introductions. A cold fury mounted inside him. He wanted to talk to Gretchen to see how she was taking all this.

"Sorry, lad," Robert Best said, approaching with outstretched hands. "She's unavailable right now. Why don't you come on in and have a drink. You were quite a hit tonight. Bask in the limelight a bit. It's a little rough at first, but wait till it starts to sink in. I know, I've been there. You've just had the experience of your life, if you'll only give yourself a chance to realize it."

"I'm going to give you a gift right in the middle of your fat face if you say one more word," Derek spat. "Now get the fuck out of my way."

He pushed past the artist, who tried to restrain him with a grip on his elbow. Derek shook off the hand and opened the double doors he'd burst through a moment ago and stepped through to the hall.

Reggie, the spike-haired servant, met him as he turned into the main corridor, grinning with silent mockery as Derek drew close.

Derek realized at once that the redhead must have provided the footsteps and the shoulder against the door in tonight's drama. He looked the servant in the eye, radiating silent fury.

"Where's Gretchen?"

"Well, well, our little lover is angry," laughed the redhead. "Isn't that too fucking bad."

Derek tried to brazen his way past, but Reggie put out a stiff arm to block his way.

"I said, where is Gretchen?" Derek demanded through clenched teeth. "I'm not going anywhere till I talk to her."

"Sorry, sport. You're not allowed down here." Reggie continued to sneer as he reached a second arm around to hold Derek back.

When Derek felt the hand on his shoulder, he swung a fist at the servant's head. The blow caught Reggie by surprise and sent him staggering to the floor.

The servant's eyes glazed over for an instant; then he looked up at Derek and the familiar sneer reappeared.

"Don't let it go to your head," he said, pulling himself up. "I took that one for good old art's sake. Now I owe you one."

Derek ignored the threat and continued down the hall.

"She won't see you, you know," Reggie called, laughing. "Christ, you're thick. She was in on the whole thing, Gretchen was. She's laughing at you, mate. Why don't you wise the fuck up."

Derek stopped in midstride. Of course, he thought: she had to be in on it. The whole thing depended on Gretchen to get him here and string him along. The only question was how long ago her playacting had begun.

Derek stood for a moment in the middle of the hall seething with murderous rage. Then he turned back toward the room with the televisions, determined to find his way out.

Robert Best approached him again when Derek reentered the room full of milling spectators. Members of the little audience were gathering now in loud clusters to share reflections on the night's events.

"Get the fuck away from me, you bald son of a bitch." Derek's fury frightened away a spectator who was coming up behind the artist to congratulate the star of tonight's performance.

"All right, I admit it was a bit rough," the artist said, trying to mollify Derek now, a hand on his arm. "But, look, you've made fucking art history. You just lived through a real vampire story, man. You may not realize it yet, but Julian's given you one hell of a gift. Hey, I lost twenty-two pounds for tonight."

"There's a dead man down in that basement. How about explaining that one for me?"

"Simple," replied Best, grinning. "That's Linden Morris. You know, Simon Macbeth's friend. He died yesterday morning. Simon let us use his body for our piece."

"You're a fucking liar." Derek bulled his way toward the exit. "He'd never consent to let you use his body like that. He loved the man. You've manipulated the poor old bastard into giving him up, you lousy son of a bitch. I'd just like to know how the pair of you did it."

"There you're wrong, pal," Best replied, no longer smiling. "If Simon's one thing, he's an artist. You're the only sore-headed bastard around here too small-minded to appreciate great art."

Derek shoved the man aside and walked through the door for reply. He kept walking till he recognized at last where he was in a second-floor corridor. Another hallway and a flight of stairs later, he found the foyer that led to the front door.

He opened it and stepped out into the cool night air, breathing fast and hard. He started down the driveway, relieved to have finally escaped. As he stepped out into the moonlit road that ran past the house, a charter bus turned into the driveway.

So that's how they got here tonight, Derek thought, looking back. That's why there weren't any cars. That's how they arranged their little spectacle tonight, the clever bastards.

The thought made Derek angrier still. He strode down the hill toward campus, heels hammering the surface of the dark road. He wished destruction on the house and painful lingering deaths on everyone laughing inside. He remembered Gretchen, but the thought of her betrayal was for the moment too painful to bear. He blanked out his mind, gave himself to the rhythm of his walking, watched as the full moon slipped out beaming from behind a cloud.

32

For several seconds after he awoke to stare at the gray ceiling, Derek didn't recognize where he was. He propped himself on an elbow and saw he was lying on a mattress without headboard or footboard in a sunny room lined with books. Seeing the room from only a foot or so above floor-level gave him a confusing sense of perspective. From the open door, he could hear a man's low voice murmuring in another room. It was only with effort, after resisting the urge to fall back to sleep, that Derek remembered walking to Dave Knight's apartment last night after hiking all the way from Julian Ginotti's house to the Berkeley campus in town. The fever plaguing him had by then made him faint and dizzy after his volcano of anger finally sputtered out. Derek dimly recalled deciding not to commute back to his empty apartment, then hiking instead to Dave's a mile or so away, where he sat on the steps outside for almost an hour till Dave returned to let him in.

Derek remembered the drama last night at Julian's now with alternating waves of disgust and anger. The memory of Gretchen's betrayal filled him with dumb rage. He wanted to strangle her; no, he thought, better to drive one of her own carefully prepared wooden stakes right through that lovely pale chest and into her heart . . . if she had a heart.

He closed his eyes, unwilling to think. Sleep seduced him with its promise of forgetfulness and peace. It was with considerable irritation that he greeted the face of his host minutes later as Dave shook him back to consciousness.

"Sorry to wake you up," Dave said. "You looked so wasted I

wanted to let you sleep, but I thought you'd better hear the news."

Derek was wide awake now, brushing his hair back from his face, sitting up.

"It's bad, I'm afraid," Dave said, looking waxen and grim. "I don't know how to say it. Gretchen Nordhaus is dead." He paused for a couple of heartbeats to let the news sink in. "Apparently she killed herself last night. Mary just called a while ago to tell me."

Derek could barely grasp the words. A question rose to his lips of its own accord.

"How," he asked, "how'd she do it?" In the face of her suicide his question struck him as pointless, absurd. What did it matter now?

"She cut her wrists in the library. Apparently sometime after nine, Gretchen hid in the women's restroom on the third floor till the library closed, then slashed her wrists with a knife. They found her a little while ago. That's all I know."

Dave stood up from the bed. "I'll wait for you in the kitchen. Take your time. I've already put on some coffee." He walked out of the room, leaving Derek to puzzle over and mourn Gretchen's death alone.

Derek sat for a moment in silence before allowing the chaos of his emotions to coalesce into thought. Gretchen must have done it right after last evening's Walpurgis Night. But why then, of all times—after her convincing performance in the night's melodrama? She must have slipped away from the audience immediately afterward, perhaps evading even the watchful eyes of Julian and Reggie—only to slit her wrists in the sterile loneliness of a library toilet. The act confounded all sense of logic and reason.

Derek's head began to spin again with fever. He stood up from the bed, woozy and weak-kneed, and looked at his watch. Two o'clock; Sunday. Then he remembered the letters in his safety deposit box, the police, Lisa's departing advice. Everything was happening too fast. Gretchen's suicide, the sadistic performance at Julian's last night. He had to talk to someone about it all, to make them see. Something told him that his time was running out.

He hastily buttoned up his wrinkled shirt and bent to slip on his shoes. Once dressed, Derek walked to the kitchen and sat down opposite Dave at the little table there.

"A friend is picking me up here in about fifteen minutes," Dave said, looking up from his coffee. "We're going to a Grateful Dead concert. But if you want me to stay and keep you company for a bit . . . ."

"No," Derek answered, "go to the concert. But first I have to tell you something. Something you're going to find very hard to believe. But listen, anyway; indulge me."

Derek swallowed, gripped the edge of the table, and began.

"Julian Ginotti is a vampire." He watched Dave's face for a reaction. "I'm not speaking metaphorically. The man is a fucking vampire. He sucks people's blood. Take his house, for instance: Nightmare Abbey. Where do you think he got the name? From a book by Thomas Love Peacock. And who was Peacock writing about? His friend Percy Shelley. So what does that tell you? Right, Julian Ginotti's true identity. Peacock called him Scythrop in his book, but it was Shelley just the same. The secret doors, the hidden rooms, it's all there in the story. Look it up.

"Now here's another thing," Derek added, picking up speed. "The fire balloons. Guess who was always sending up fire balloons? Shelley again. And what do you suppose Shelley was translating at the end of his life? Goethe's *Faust.* So what does that tell you? Talk about a pact with the devil." Derek laughed at the irony.

"All right, listen," Derek continued. Dave was beginning to look confused. "At the end of his life, Shelley was translating Faust for Byron. He was obsessed with the thing. Then Byron showed him his new play, *The Deformed Transformed.* Guess what? It was about a deformed man who switched bodies, then his old body was taken over by someone else. So there's your doppelgänger theme all over again. Shelley read the play and saw how

Byron had stolen his idea—as if he wasn't jealous enough of his success already. Hell, you know what it's like being jealous of another poet's fame. Okay, maybe you don't. You're a goddamn saint, I'm the first to admit it." Derek forgot what point he was trying to make, then picked up the lost thread of his talk and continued, speaking more loudly. "Anyway, Shelley tells Byron he hates the play and Byron throws it in the fire. But the main thing was, it had Shelley's idea in it. Byron was giving away their game!"

Derek paused, dry-mouthed. He realized how incoherent his talk must sound to Dave. Nothing seemed to be coming out quite right.

"You understand what I'm telling you, don't you? I know it sounds crazy, but I've been working on this thing for months."

"You ought to see yourself," Dave said, finally, with a concerned look. "You're perspiring like crazy. You're not making a hell of a lot of sense, either. Why don't you go and lie down again for a while. You don't look so good."

"You haven't heard a single thing I've said. I'm trying to tell you something, for Christ's sake. Julian is a vampire. He's out to get me because I've got something he wants. Some letters. Come over to my place tomorrow and I'll show them to you, if you don't believe me."

Dave stood up from his chair.

"Look, I'm sorry, but I can't listen anymore. I dropped some acid before you got up and it's starting to really hit me. The phone call about Gretchen was hard enough to take stoned, but this paranoid rambling of yours is about to flip me over the edge. I'm going to wait outside for my friend. I think you'd be better off going home and pulling yourself together a bit. If I weren't so wrecked myself, I'd help you out, but right now I've got to get outside and walk this off a little. You can stay here if you don't think you can make it home."

"I'll be all right," Derek replied. "I'll leave right after I make a phone call. Is it okay if I use your phone?"

Derek left Dave standing in the kitchen and walked down the

hall to where the apartment's single phone sat on its three-legged stand. Once there, he pulled out the Berkeley phone book to locate Professor Houston's number. He decided the time had come to bring someone with more authority in on the affair. Houston was the most unimpeachable scholar Derek could think of and would make a formidable ally. There was something about the big man's presence that inspired confidence.

The phone rang four times, then Derek heard Houston's voice on the other end of the line. Without telling him what he wanted to talk about, Derek finally got him to agree to meet on campus. They decided it would be most convenient to meet in Houston's office in a half hour. The building would be deserted on a Sunday afternoon, but that would give them the freedom to talk with complete candor.

When Derek walked down the wide hall to Ed Houston's office, the open door told him the old man had already arrived. He walked to the entrance, tapped on the doorjamb, and stepped into the room. The big man sat leaning over the empty surface of his desk, wearing an open-collared plaid shirt.

"Come in," sounded the familiar deep voice. "Come in and sit down."

Derek mumbled a hello and sat in a heavy wooden chair across the desk. On the opposite wall, over Houston's head, the gray-bearded face of Walt Whitman stared down from a poster. To his left was a picture of Baudelaire.

"I'm glad to have this chance to talk to you," Houston said. "I've been meaning to take you aside for a few days now but just never found the chance."

Houston looked over Derek's head, cleared his throat, then spoke again, avoiding Derek's eyes.

"It's about your academic progress," he said. "It's been less than satisfactory; and since you hold a university fellowship, I'm afraid you're held to a higher standard than most."

"What's been unsatisfactory?" Derek asked impatiently. "I've gotten nothing but A's in my novel course, and Dick Fuller told me I've turned in the best poems in the workshop all quarter. I was late for a seminar report a few days ago, but I'm getting good grades in the course."

"Well," Houston said, "not according to Gloria Fiedler. She says you're doing C-minus work at best."

Derek stared at Houston in disbelief. "What are you talking about? I got an A-minus on the only paper we've turned in so far."

"It was your seminar report. On that, you received an F."

"What? Gloria told me she gave me an A-minus. I admit it wasn't the best thing I've ever done, but it sure as hell wasn't an F."

"Her record book shows an F. And," Houston added, to counter Derek's next objection, "there's the question of missing classes. You've missed a fair number already, according to my count."

"Okay," Derek conceded, "I did miss a few classes, but not enough to warrant talk about my unsatisfactory academic progress.

"This isn't all coming from Gloria Fiedler, is it?" Derek eyed the bearded man coldly. The way Houston averted his gaze told Derek he was right. "It's that son of a bitch Julian, right? He's had Gloria Fiedler eating out of his hand ever since he showed her that goddamn book collection of his. Come on, Ed," Derek implored, "you don't really believe I'm not cutting it in her class, do you? It's Julian behind all of this—and you know it."

The big man rose from his chair and began to pace back and forth on the office's worn rug like a caged bear.

"Maybe you're right," he conceded with a frown. Then Houston stopped his nervous pacing and looked down from his great height. "Derek, I'll tell you something. There are people in this world it just doesn't do to cross. Julian is one of them. Now I'm going to ask you to do something you'll probably object to. You're young and you don't know how hard things can go. I want you to appease Julian. Whatever it is that he wants, give it to him without delay."

The look he gave Derek while delivering this advice showed that the words had been wrung out of him. There was obviously something going on between Houston and the Englishman that was putting great strain on the scholar's nerves.

"So what does he have on you?" Derek asked in a flash of inspiration. "I see you talking, but I hear Julian's voice coming out."

The big man slumped suddenly into his chair and hid his face behind his hands.

"I . . . I've committed an indiscretion," the old man sobbed in a sudden burst of candor. "That son of a bitch is using it against me. I fought him as long as I could, but the man is heartless, relentless. You have no idea." The great head shook silently behind the shielding hands.

"You'd be surprised," Derek replied. "So why don't you just deny whatever he's got on you. After all, it's only his word against yours."

Houston suddenly regained some self-control and looked at Derek across the desk, tears of rage and frustration welling in his eyes.

"I can't," he said, now shaking with anger. "He's got it on videotape, the heartless son of a bitch. Thirty-seven years I've taught, and now it's all in jeopardy because of one thoughtless indiscretion."

On videotape, Derek thought; yes, that would be Julian's style. He wondered for an instant what could be so bad that the suggestion of someone seeing it could reduce Ed Houston to tears.

"Give him the letters," Houston implored, dropping all pretense. "Give them to Julian right away, before you drag everyone down."

The big man averted his face to hide his embarrassment. "Please. If that tape is ever seen, I'm ruined. Simply ruined."

Derek rose from his chair and turned toward the door, then stalked quietly out of the room and out of hearing range.

Derek sat alone on a middle seat on the half-empty bus, staring wearily out the blue-tinted window as the slums of Oakland rolled past. There was nothing to do now, he thought drowsily, but to go home and think and wait for tomorrow. He could deal with the letters then.

For now, Derek studied the faces of the other passengers, wondering which might be the agent of Julian's revenge. The pair of stoned and snickering teenagers two rows behind him seemed promising candidates—or maybe it was the wild-eyed, bearded man sitting directly behind the driver. Any one of them could pull the trigger or thrust the knife that would relieve Julian of his chief source of embarrassment, though now, after last night's performance, such extreme measures were probably unnecessary. All Julian would have to do to discredit Derek would be to play the videotape. Its scenes of coffins, wooden stakes, and guns would make Derek look like a crank or a lunatic—a murderer, even. He'd be laughed out of hearing if he stood up in public now to proclaim Julian Ginotti a vampire, even with the missing letters in hand.

No, the charge of vampirism wouldn't stick, even if true. Julian's long-promised gift turned out to be nothing but smoke and mirrors and secret doors, a night of bitter humiliation and public shame. Julian's real talent, Derek now saw, was far deadlier. Gretchen, Professor Watson, Ron Pruitt and his mother, his own cousin Gino—all were either missing or dead. As Derek counted up the bodies and assessed his own dismal chances of survival, he abandoned any hope of either justice or revenge.

Instead, he stared out the window to let the panorama of images blot out thought. Shutting off his brain, he for once became all eye. It became a kind of spiritual exercise to observe the passing scenes of urban blight without aesthetic reaction or moral judgement. Negative capability, he might have called it at another time.

He watched the bus halt at a corner and pick up a drunken Chinese man with a drooping mustache, who staggered down the aisle to the rear toilet and never reemerged. Derek saw the bus pull away, round a corner, pass a row of dilapidated town houses, a blank wall, the boarded windows of a public housing project, an empty laundromat, a tireless burned-out car.

At the next stop, two young black men sat on the bench, flanking a giant boom-box. Tapping their feet and shouting insults at a friend, they ignored the bus when it pulled up to let them on. After a five-second wait, engine grumbling, the driver released his brakes with a hiss and pulled away.

The next street was illuminated by yellow street lamps. Neon signs glowed over the dark entrances of the half dozen neighborhood bars scattered down the block.

Two middle-aged white men with bulging bellies staggered from the door of the nearest bar, sat down at the curb at the edge of the street. To their right, twenty feet down the sidewalk, a young prostitute lolled against the wall, chatting with a small boy, her body a rainbow of bright primary colors: bleached yellow hair, red lipstick, purple blouse, white plastic boots and shorts.

The bus pulled up to the corner, hissed to a stop. Derek heard feet mounting the bus's front steps as he watched the scene outside. Across the street two young men in leather jackets emerged laughing from the doorway of a seedy-looking pool hall. Derek watched as they strode down the opposite sidewalk, drawing closer.

Suddenly Derek sat up straight in his seat. One of the men was swaggering down the sidewalk in a way that struck Derek as familiar—hauntingly so.

Derek stood up out of his seat as the men approached the bus.

"Gino!"

The shape of his face, the set of his jaw, the fit of his slacks—

"Gino!" Derek shouted, pounding on the glass. The other passengers stared at his back as Derek hammered the window with both fists. Gino was less than twenty-five feet away. Derek watched gratefully as Gino abandoned his tall companion and walked slowly across the street, peering toward the bus as if attracted by the noise. His face was in better light now. As he drew closer, he stared up toward the window against which Derek's face and hands were pressed.

With a shock, Derek recognized his mistake.

Not Gino. The face of the man looking up at him was even more familiar than that. Derek looked in horror as his own face squinted back at him from the street below. As the bus roared away from the curb, Derek caught his breath to keep from crying out.

He'd seen his double.

Derek's knees gave out; he collapsed back onto his seat. As the bus drove away, he turned to look through the back window and saw the specter still staring after him, one hand held up as if to shade his eyes.

Derek took small comfort in the fact that the bus was now putting distance between them. Already his double had met his stare and reached out as if to touch him. Two populous cities and a wide bay seemed little protection against the possibility of meeting it again.

33

Released at last from nightmares of pursuit, Derek awoke late Monday morning with an exhilarating sense of lightness and freedom. Gone were the narrow winding corridors, the endless flights of rickety spiraling stairs that had haunted his sleep for the last several months. Instead, he swooped and dived past the gargoyled escarpments of giant cathedrals, glided among the glass-walled canyons of skyscrapers, dipped low over dew-tipped spears of grass with a heart as light as an owl's.

He lifted his head from the downy softness of his pillow, stretched his arms, and yawned. Today was the day he could at last strike back at Julian. Though still a bit woozy from fever, Derek shaved quickly, ate a large breakfast, and then sat down at his desk to put his plan into effect. He pulled three large yellow envelopes from a drawer and began to cover them with bold black lettering with a few quick strokes of his pen.

He addressed the first to the Pforzheimer Library in New York, directing it to the attention of its chief archivist, Henrietta Blunt; the second, he addressed to the director of the Bodleian Library at Oxford. The third envelope cost Derek a moment of thought.

He decided at last to make it out to Geoffrey Windgate of Harvard. Windgate was a world-famous scholar in the field of English Romantic poetry; more importantly, he'd published several articles in recent years devoted to Percy Shelley, all of which tended to denigrate his subject's achievement as a poet. Derek smiled at his inspiration in making the final choice. His chief fear in releasing his hold on the letters was that the objectivity of the people to whom he sent them might have been compromised by a past association with the man now calling himself Julian Ginotti. All three of the scholars Derek chose appeared to be beyond reproach.

The rest of Derek's plan was simple. After he picked up the letters from the bank, he'd divide the stack into three piles and place each in one of his pre-addressed envelopes. Then, travelling at random through the city, he'd mail them from separate locations to keep them from being traced back to him. The purpose of sending out three packets was to ensure that at least some of the letters got through. Even if Julian got wind of his plan and tracked one set down, there'd still be two others in capable hands. Not even a vampire could be in three places at once.

After he finished with the envelopes, Derek decided to type up an explanatory letter to accompany the packets, informing each recipient that the manuscripts enclosed had been discovered among the effects of the late Sean Watson of Stanford. The letter would of course be anonymous. He'd make no mention of himself and provide no explanation of how the letters had been obtained.

The more difficult decision Derek faced was how much of his suspicions concerning Shelley's vampirism to include. The new owners would naturally be puzzled by their references to events occurring after their supposed author's death. To keep them from being dismissed immediately as fakes, Derek would at least have to hint at an explanation.

After several attempts at a first draft, he at last composed a letter that seemed to meet the circumstances. In it, he hinted of Shelley's vampirism and briefly outlined the research that led him to such a belief. In his final paragraphs, he interpreted Shelley's haunting last days in the light of his own doppelgänger theory. Though his explanation might at first appear mad, Derek hoped his suggestions might eventually take root in the minds of the people who received his anonymous gifts. Backed by a cache of letters in Shelley's own hand, the explanation might at last begin to seem plausible. If all three packets got through, who knew? In a few years Percy Shelley might have to kiss his precious reputation goodbye.

Derek reread his finished letter, then walked it across Washington Square Park to run off two copies at a local print shop. The day was sunny and cool, the sidewalks busy with tourists and idling neighborhood women as he strolled across the square, his face splashed by a salty breeze off the bay. He returned to his apartment minutes later, pleased that his mission had successfully begun.

Once back, Derek sat for a moment daydreaming at his desk, elbows propped on the scarred wooden surface, head resting on the heel of one hand. A dreamy lassitude stole over him as he idly scanned the contents of the desk top. His eye caught on the much scrawled-over page of an open notebook he'd pushed aside earlier to write his letter. The handwriting was barely legible, but after reading a few lines, he recognized them as part of the long poem he'd been working on for the last few months. He slid the notebook toward him to read more.

Pleased by what he encountered, Derek couldn't resist turning to the notebook's first page and reading back all ten of the poem's finished sections. He read quickly, with a growing sense of pleasure and excitement, slowing gradually as the writing became more crabbed in the roughly-sketched penultimate section where he began.

To fill his ear with the sound of their lilt and cadence, he repeated the last lines aloud, then picked up his pen and began to dabble at notes for a conclusion before setting off for his date with the bank downtown.

Within seconds, Derek found himself writing frenetically, his hand barely able to keep pace with the surge of sound and images erupting from his brain. Without pausing to read back a single sentence, he wrote till he'd filled the last dozen pages of the notebook. Then, after a brilliant final flourish, he slammed the notebook shut with a cry of triumph that echoed across the room.

It was done. An entire book-length poem, in a style he'd invented to suit the fantastic nature of his subject. A bona fide masterpiece. One of the handful of major poems he was born to write.

Derek stood up from his chair to pace off the electricity still coursing through his body. He knew he wouldn't have to revise a line. Once or twice in a poet's lifetime, the muse granted such a gift. He was happy to have been the rod when lightning struck this time.

He walked again from the hallway to the bedroom where his pacing finally stalled, then stared beaming at his happy reflection in the bedroom mirror.

"You brilliant son of bitch," he said to the pale ecstatic face. Then he glanced at the dial of the radio clock and froze.

It was nearly four o'clock. Though his bank closed at five, Derek remembered suddenly that he didn't yet have postage for the letters. The post office closed in thirty-four minutes. A court order could seize the letters at any minute. If he withdrew them from the bank without mailing them, he'd be vulnerable to Julian. The spirits of Lieutenant Graves and Julian Ginotti hovered over his head like bat-winged avenging angels.

Derek snatched his wallet and keys off the dresser, then ran to the kitchen to pick up his satchel and leave. As he leapt down the three short steps to the foyer, he stumbled and fell against the door. When he got up, he fumbled at the doorknob for several seconds before unlocking it. At the front gate's electric lock, he mistimed his push and walked face-first into the iron grating, cutting the bridge of his nose. On his second try, he got the timing right.

At the bus stop he had better luck. He bulled his way to the curb, ignoring the vengeful elbows and outraged cries that assailed him. When the bus pulled up a moment later, he leapt up the stairs, pushed past the passengers blocking the aisles to a position next to the exit, then gripped the pole overhead as the bus surged away from the curb to begin its stop-and-go passage through Chinatown.

Since it was still a few minutes before the official start of rush hour, the bus made reasonably good time. Derek resisted the temptation to look at his watch until he descended from the bus on Market, where he glanced despairingly at his wrist.

Nineteen minutes after four. Eleven minutes till the post office closed its doors.

He ran the two blocks to the bank, dodging suits on the sidewalk like a halfback evading tacklers. Once inside, he quickly cornered a bank official, then followed him impatiently to the vault where the letters were stored.

As his escort left the room, Derek pulled out the letters and, after a glimpse at them, divided them into three piles; then he slid each into an envelope and stuffed the three fattened containers into his satchel. On his way out of the bank, he asked a woman at a counter to direct him to the nearest post office. After several seconds of brow-knitted pondering, the woman at last gave him directions.

Derek ran from the bank, nearly knocking over an old man at its revolving door entrance. After several more blocks of open-field running, he at last reached the post office's set of double glass doors.

Too late, he saw, reaching a second set of locked doors inside. The counter was already closed. Derek stood in the building's lobby among the walls of numbered post boxes, wondering how to make his next move. The letters weighed in his pouch like uranium.

He checked his pockets and wallet. In addition to two useless tens, he had three one dollar bills and four quarters he'd fished from his pants. By using the lobby's automated dispenser, he could buy enough postage here to mail one envelope, at least.

With trembling hands, Derek fed money into the slot till he'd purchased enough stamps to ensure delivery. Then he pulled the packet addressed to Geoffrey Windgate from his bag and gummed three dollars' worth of stamps to its upper right-hand corner. At the slot in the lobby wall labelled Out-of-City mail, he dropped the thick packet through.

As the envelope vanished into the dark receiving bin inside, Derek grew giddy.

I've won, he thought; I've beaten that bastard Julian at his own game.

As Derek celebrated this first stage in his victory, the next step in his plan became suddenly clear. He'd go back to North Beach where he knew the layout of things, break one of his large bills at the grocery store where he shopped, then either there or in the lobby of the North Beach post office buy more stamps and mail another of the remaining envelopes. Afterward, he'd catch a bus to the Marina District and mail the last packet there.

As he strode back up Market to the crowded bus stop, Derek felt triumphant. He decided to walk back through Chinatown instead of fooling with the overloaded city buses. This was an evening to savor. After a quick walk among emptying skyscrapers, he reached Stockton, revelling in the colorful tumult. In a few more minutes, he'd mail off the last packet across town.

The precious letters clutched now to his side, Derek passed a knot of shoppers haggling over a sidewalk bin, glided past a row of Chinese men reading on wooden crates, then slowed before the doorway of a restaurant to savor the pungent aroma of roast duck. Chinatown never seemed more exotic or beautiful. Even the cloud of diesel fumes from a truck's tailpipe added its pinch of spice to the brew.

Foot traffic stalled at a bus stop where the overflow of passengers blocked the sidewalk. Derek realized how much more efficiently he might have managed this affair if he'd had steadier nerves. Since he wasn't going to be precise about the amount of postage anyway, he could have bought stamps in North Beach before going downtown; then he could have slapped a few dollars' worth on each envelope in the vault and mailed them from anywhere he chose after leaving the bank. He wouldn't have had to double back like this.

Oh, well, he thought, a few more blocks and he'd be back at Washington Square Park again. If he hurried, he'd get there before dark. Streetlights held back the dusk now; in another hour it would be full dark in the quiet recesses under bridges and in the vacant alleys between buildings, though elsewhere an eternal city twilight would prevail.

Derek slowed his pace again. Another roadblock slowed pedestrian traffic ahead. Someone had left a wagon full of fruit parked in a narrow alleyway where it intersected the sidewalk. To get around it, most people were stepping into the street and dodging cars to avoid the logjam.

Just as Derek approached, the wagon was pushed into the street by its aged owner and the logjam broke. Nothing, it seemed, could impede Derek's passage through the city tonight.

Derek stepped through the gap to cross the alley and was met by a pair of stone-faced Chinese boys in orange headbands coming from the opposite side. When he saw them coming toward him, Derek tried to step out of their way, but as he did, each boy suddenly reached to seize one of his arms.

They grabbed him just above the elbows. Derek tried to shake them off with a sudden convulsion of his body, digging in his heels suddenly and jerking back both arms. His right arm broke free, but something cold and hard slipped over his neck from behind. He lashed out at the boys with his wildly swinging free hand.

Even as he thrashed and struggled, there was an island of cool reason inside Derek's head that kept thinking what bad luck it all was. Tonight of all nights. He'd walked this section of Chinatown hundreds of times and never seen the slightest hint of trouble. Now he was faced with a Chinese street gang. The oldest of the two kids facing him—Derek couldn't see the one choking him from behind—looked to be no more than sixteen or seventeen. He'd like to tell their parents; that'd teach the little snot-nosed brats a lesson.

The thing around his neck was the chain of a nunchuk. Derek could feel the metal links, hear the grating of wooden handles as he raised his free hand to take some of the pressure off his throat. As he fought off strangulation, Derek could feel himself being dragged slowly into the alley by the first two boys, who'd latched onto his arms again and were grimly pulling, like bulldogs.

Derek could see pedestrians passing several feet away on the sidewalk. One old Chinese woman looked down the alley and saw his plight but quickly dropped her eyes and hurried away out of view. The chain held his throat so tightly Derek couldn't suck air to scream for help.

Three more boys waited in the shadows in the alley. When they saw their victim resisting, one of the newcomers landed a sidekick to Derek's ribs that knocked the last bit of breath from his lungs.

He thought for an instant he was going to pass out.

But just as his head began to swim, the chain loosened from around his neck and another kick, this time from behind, sent him flying forward to the alley's damp pavement.

Derek rose to his hands and knees to survey the situation. There were three boys still in front of him and three boys behind, all wearing the same orange headbands. The boy behind him with the nunchuk was loosely swinging it by one handle. As Derek attempted to rise to his feet, two of the boys in front suddenly whipped out switchblades and advanced till they were standing directly above him.

"Get up," one of them said in unaccented English. "And give me your bag."

To his amazement, Derek discovered the leather strap of his bag still draped over his shoulder, the bag still at his side.

"Sure, why not," Derek answered. "You can have it. There's nothing of value inside. I've got a little money, though."

Derek reached for his wallet, but a foot suddenly lashed out and kicked his arm away.

"Keep your fucking money. Now stand up and follow me."

Derek stood up.

"Look, take the money," he pleaded, "and keep the bag, too. I'll empty the goddamn thing out and you can have it. But I'm not going down this alley. No fucking way."

The second boy with the knife—a stocky kid of no more than fifteen—suddenly slashed at Derek's left arm. A stab of pain. Derek looked down at its source and saw that the leather sleeve of his jacket was slit open halfway between elbow and wrist.

A second later, red blood welled up from the slit and dripped to the alley. Derek could feel warmth soaking his shirt sleeve and the lining of his jacket inside. Within seconds blood was pouring down over his wrist and streaming from his fingertips to a widening puddle on the pavement below.

A bad cut. He'd better cooperate. That slash would need treatment soon.

Then a contradictory impulse stirred in him. He decided to make a run for the street.

He turned and bolted toward the three boys behind. Better them than the knives. Charging the smallest boy with a lowered shoulder, he clutched the precious satchel to his side and barrelled forward.

To his surprise, the boy immediately gave ground and neatly sidestepped his charge like a matador. A split second later Derek felt the clout of the nunchuk as it thumped the back of his head.

Derek awoke in a pool of vomit an uncertain time later. It was full night overhead, but lights from tall buildings lit the alleyway with a sinister yellow glow. He squinted, trying to focus his eyes, then lifted his cheek a few inches off the sticky pavement with a wobbly turn of his neck. His vision was blurry, but he could see that he'd been dragged to a second alley behind the shops.

"Well, well, Sleeping Beauty is finally awake," said a voice overhead. Derek knew it right away. He refocussed his eyes on the pair of black leather shoes a foot from his head. Two pairs of white sneakers flanked them. Before he could look up to see their owners' faces, hands seized him under the armpits and lifted him to his knees.

Crouched as if in prayer, Derek looked up into the face of Julian's spike-haired servant, Reggie. The two Chinese gang members who lifted him off the pavement gripped his arms to steady his weight between them.

"We thought you must have a guardian angel the way you slipped us going downtown," Reggie said with a chuckle. "One of our boys was unhappily hit by a bus. Lucky for us, you're the stupid bloody bastard you are and came back like a dog to his vomit, or Julian would have been very annoyed.

"If you'll excuse my bad joke," he added, glancing down at the puddle at their feet.

Reggie was in unusually high spirits.

"I believe we'll relieve you of these now," the redhead added, holding up the two thick envelopes they'd taken from his bag. "They're no use to you. Not where you're going."

Derek felt too faint and weak to resist now, even with verbal taunts. His arm was still damp and heavy, he still felt the thick oozy flow of blood dripping from the open vein in his arm. He wondered how long it took to bleed to death.

"An old friend of yours is here, just to thank you for your thoughtful care of his possessions," Reggie added with another attempt at a laugh. The servant stepped back, turning sideways so Derek could watch the approach of the caped figure advancing toward them from the shining black Mercedes parked down the alley.

"This is a lovely reunion, but I'll have to return these envelopes to the car for a minute while you two have your little chat." With that, Reggie turned his back and walked toward the car.

Derek pulled feebly, but the two boys holding him barely had to tighten their grips to restrain him. The one on Derek's left barked a short clattering command in Chinese.

Derek sagged, letting his guards support some of his weight. He watched helplessly as Julian approached to stand over him.

The pale aristocratic face hovered silently for several seconds before the thin-lipped mouth opened to speak. When it did, the voice that emerged was precise and grim.

"The time has come, my friend. Our little game is over. You played your hand well, but I'm afraid the cards that fell your way made a very poor show."

The black cloud darkening the face lifted for an instant and a glimmer of light seeped through. Derek thought for a moment he heard the Englishman chuckle.

"You're a devilish little rogue," his tormentor said with a grin. "It's your rare combination of qualities that enables me to grant the gift I'm about to bestow."

Derek opened his mouth to object, but his words issued so faintly he was afraid Julian wouldn't hear them.

"No," he whispered hoarsely. "Please, no."

"Don't be absurd, my friend. You've earned your reward, now accept it graciously." Julian continued to look down from his superior vantage point, his face a white blur.

"Don't make me a vampire," Derek pleaded, putting all pretense aside. "Don't do it. Please."

"Making you a vampire would hardly require magic. I'm afraid you've taken the infection already. You're a poet. What I'm about to offer you is much, much greater. I only hope you have what it takes to survive into a second life. A successful result is by no means assured. It's a very perilous business we're about to transact, you and I. I pray I've judged right and you're up to it."

"You can't," Derek objected. "I'm not willing. I never gave you the token."

"Not willing?" Julian snorted. "When knowing full well what I am you came to me; you entered my house; you accepted my offers of help—quite eagerly, I must remind you; when you made love to the companion of my heart under my very roof; brought me the letter I asked you for, bargained with me, contested with me, dreamed endlessly of this final intimate embrace.

"No," the voice concluded, grim again, "after such faithful, fateful intimacy, I'll not deny you the consummation you've longed for, despite these unmanly denials."

Julian barked an order in Chinese to one of the boys holding Derek's arm. The young hoodlum responded by jerking Derek's unwounded arm forward and pulling back the sleeve to expose the pale flesh beneath.

Derek could see what was coming but didn't have the strength to pull free. He watched as the boy grasped his arm more tightly and steadied it to meet the descending blade.

Julian drew the razor-sharp steel across Derek's wrist in one quick slash. An instant later, blood flowed from the severed arteries and arced weakly above his arm.

Julian's eyes twinkled.

"I've already performed the preparatory rites. I was rather delighted, in fact, to discover that you already had friends on the other side. It was heartening to see my instinct confirmed. You are ripe, quite ripe. All it required from you, aside from the personal qualities I've mentioned, was a bit of hair and vital fluid, which you happily provided on a recent visit to my house."

Julian saw Derek's look of puzzlement and dumb pain and smiled again.

"Not blood. Semen. I'm sorry I had to acquire it by proxy, but one learns to make do." His smile turned coyly sinister.

"Gretchen was only too happy to assist. I wish the three of us could have met under different circumstances. But I'm afraid that as long as you possessed the letters, my own instincts were to err on the side of safety. But that's all under the bridge."

Julian turned to eye Derek's oozing wrist.

"A magical elixir, blood. You can't imagine how difficult it was for me to realize its importance. Please don't look so distressed. It's for your own benefit that I'm telling you this. Because I discovered the secret only just in time to save myself. Summoning up my double from the other side of the grave was an achievement virtually without precedent; so imagine my horror when not long after my rebirth I discovered myself losing corporeality and vital strength. At one point I found I was barely able to cast a reflection in a mirror. To die a second time would have been extinction indeed. In my panic, I consulted Paracelsus, Cornelius Agrippa, Albertus Magnus and other ancient writers, but those authors offered no help. My supposed immortality was about to expire along with any hope of divine justice or mercy.

"I had almost given up hope when, to distract myself from my plight, I began to read Greek again—a Homeric hymn, to be precise. The solution was so obvious it nearly killed me with laughter. How does one give substantiality to shades in the nether world? Recall your Homer, my boy, recall your Homer." Julian laughed like a child.

"The benefits of a classical education are incalculable. You must undertake to improve your Latin and begin the serious study of Greek. For in the midst of my travail, I suddenly remembered how Odysseus enabled the ghosts of his fallen comrades to appear before him on his journey to the underworld. Remember? He fed them blood! That was the solution to my dilemma. To give permanent substance to my newly acquired form, I saw I would have periodically to drink blood. Human blood, I discovered after a little experimentation. So there is some truth to the old wives' tales, after all. You, too, my friend, will have to draw your sustenance from the veins of your fellows, but think of the inestimable prize: a life everlasting, uncounted centuries of glory as a poet and fame never to be denied."

Julian leaned toward Derek's outstretched wrist, eyes shining. His lips parted eagerly to receive the ablution as he drew the limp arm toward his face.

"Such divine ichor. The blood of a poet. A repast fit for Jove."

But instead of merely drinking, the open mouth fastened on Derek's arm like a trap. Derek's muscles contracted as if they'd been touched by a high voltage wire. Lightning shot up his arm to his chest. He writhed in helpless agony as his heart paused, stunned by the bolt.

When Derek opened his eyes, Julian was gone. He lay facedown on the damp concrete of the alley, listening to the approach of tapping leather heels. Looking up, Derek saw that the boys were gone. The face standing over his weak and paralyzed body now belonged to Reggie, who'd approached from the distantly rumbling car.

"Didn't think I'd forget, did you?" the redhead asked, grinning.

Without warning, he lashed out at Derek's ribs with the tip of his pointed shoe, digging in hard a few inches beneath the armpit. Derek grunted with pain.

"There's that one I owe you.

"And here's another, just to show you I'm a very sporting guy."

The second kick caught Derek under the chin and lifted his head off the pavement. The last thing he felt before blacking out was the second impact as his face bounced against the alley falling back to earth, drawn by gravity's unrelenting embrace.

34

He could sense the color and texture of his surroundings even before opening his eyes. The walls were pale green, lightly rippled by overlapping strips of vinyl wallpaper; the floor was tiled, alternating squares of dark green and black. Suspended from a stainless steel pole above his bed, a drawn white curtain. The squeak and squelch of rubber-soled shoes from the floor. Outside the unshaded window, a city street; dusk.

Derek opened his eyes and saw a middle-aged woman in white blouse and pants, hair pulled tight in a bun at the back of her head. As she crossed the floor on white sneakers, she studied the wooden clipboard in her hand. The pads of extra fat on her waist and hips sat heavily on her thin-boned frame so that she panted slightly gliding toward the foot of Derek's bed.

Looking up from her notes, she saw Derek's eyes on her and stopped.

"My, my," she said. "You're back among the living. I'd better go tell your doctor."

Her round face split into a smile as she clutched the board to her bosom. A second chin appeared below her first as her mouth contracted.

"How do you feel?"

"Fine," Derek answered. His eyes swept the room. "How long have I been here?"

"Better ask your doctor," the nurse replied. She stepped forward and stood beside his bed. Her face looked like a dumpling in which two brown nuts had been pressed. A small brown mole beside her nose sprouted twin bristles.

Derek suddenly realized he couldn't move his arms. He looked down and saw both forearms wrapped in layers of white bandages. Each hand was bound by a cloth rope to a stainless steel pole running parallel to his bed. A plastic IV line rose from his left arm to a clear bag overhead. From his right arm trailed a set of electrical wires.

"Why am I tied up like this?"

"Restraints," explained the nurse. "You kept thrashing around once we'd got you back. Doctors never could figure out how you had the strength to do it."

"What do you mean, once you'd got me back?"

The nurse glanced toward the door. "I'd better go tell your doctor." She edged toward the exit. "Don't worry, I'll be back in a few minutes." She pointed to the name tag above her left breast. "Name's Irene." Then she turned and walked out the door, leaving Derek alone.

True to her word, the nurse was back within minutes, this time accompanied by a young Chinese doctor and a second nurse. The doctor wore wire-rimmed glasses and a thin mustache. The pretty nurse, when she stood towering above Derek's bed, turned out to be a doctor, too. Three inches taller than her male colleague, she was the first to speak.

"This is Doctor Chang. I'm Doctor Qualls. How are you feeling?"

A bolt of auburn hair fell over her white jacket to her shoulders. Derek could see she was proud of its thickness and color, the way she wore it so long. He assessed her face as he looked to meet her eyes.

Too angular; her nose was pinched and thin; her chin, too sharp and fleshless. Up close, she didn't look nearly as pretty.

Derek waited for someone to take his pulse or listen to his chest, but the three visitors only looked up to study the gauges of the machines he was hooked to. He could hear one of the instruments behind him registering the beat of his heart with a steady blip blip blip.

"How long have I been here? What hospital is this?"

"San Francisco General," volunteered the nurse.

Peremptorily, Doctor Qualls cut in. "Six days," she said, turning back to Derek. Her mouth twisted into a grin. "You're a very lucky man."

After a pause in which the two doctors mumbled to each other over their notes, the nurse addressed Derek again.

"There's a very pretty young woman outside who's been waiting to see you." She gave Derek a conspiratorial smile. "If your doctors think it's all right . . ." She left the clause hanging in the air. After a short delay, Chang looked up from his chart.

"I don't see why not," said the doctor, glancing toward Derek. "We're finished here. But," he added, turning to address the nurse, "only for a few minutes. Mr. Hill needs his rest."

After the doctors left, Irene backed through the door. "Don't go anywhere," she admonished Derek, smiling. "She'll be here in a wink." The closing door put a period to her sentence. Derek watched the spot till the door opened again.

Pale and distraught, Lisa stood a moment in the shadowed alcove inside the door and peeked across the room toward the bed. When she saw Derek sitting up, her face brightened, she took a hesitant first step, one hand outstretched as if to touch the apparition.

"I forgot to tell them to untie me before they left," Derek said with a quick glance at his arms. "I feel like I'm about to do something kinky, tied down like this." He caught Lisa's eye and smiled.

Lisa stepped across the room to the bed, then leaned closer to cover his hand with hers. "You look great," she said. "Really. I thought you'd be groggy and weak. Do you want me to have the nurse come and undo your arms?"

"It can wait. The doctor said I was out for six days. Have you been waiting here long?"

Derek strained at the cord on his right hand, then added, "Christ, I can't even touch you like this."

Lisa passed the back of a hand beneath one eye, brushed back a wisp of hair that had drifted across her forehead.

"They found you in an alley in Chinatown. Some Chinese lady saw you when she went out to throw away some trash. Thank God. The doctors said it's a miracle you're alive."

"That's what they tell me. I wonder when they'll let me out of here."

Lisa didn't venture a guess. "Your parents are here," she said, half in warning. "They went out for supper a little while ago, but they should be back anytime now. When I called to tell them what happened, they flew out right away."

Another brief silence as Derek and Lisa observed each other. Derek noticed her pale blue sweater, the tiny worry lines around her eyes. Lisa started to speak, paused, then started again.

"I . . . I'd better warn you," she said. "About the doctors. Don't say a word about anything . . . odd. You know what I mean—about vampires, or Percy Shelley, or anything like that. The way they found you, with your wrists slashed and all—there was a little worry you might have done it to yourself."

Derek stared at her for a moment. "You're kidding. How could they possibly figure that? I was found in an alley, for Christ's sake. Beaten and stabbed."

Lisa avoided his eyes. "You still had your money, for one thing. And it was only a few blocks from the apartment where it happened. Some old man told the police he saw you walk back to the alley by yourself. And the knife was found lying near you on the ground."

Lisa released the pressure on his hand.

"And there was something else—a word scratched on the back of your arm, in Latin. The cops didn't figure it was done by some Chinese kid. They thought you might have done it. When they questioned me, I told them you'd had a little Latin in school. I had no idea what they were asking for."

"What about my bruises? Did they think I kicked the shit out of myself before I cut my wrists, or what?"

"The bruises are what got you here instead of in the psycho ward. You can thank the guy that knocked you on the chin for that. Except for that one, the bruises were hardly noticeable. They said you could have gotten them falling down."

"What do you think?" he asked.

"That you were attacked. That's what the police think now. Lieutenant Graves came by the apartment again to question me. The emergency room must have called them. I think I successfully dodged the tricky questions. I did hint at a few things, though, to explain the attack. I told him about Julian."

"What did you say? Exactly."

"Nothing about him being Percy Shelley, that's for sure. I said he'd threatened you. That's all. And I described what you'd told me about him and his house. A few days later Graves called to tell me they'd investigated my lead."

"And?"

"And Julian's gone. The house had been vacated."

"What about all the furniture, the art work, the books?"

"Most of the stuff was still there. It came with the house, apparently. Except for the books—they were gone, too. The police are trying to get hold of the owner in Italy, but they haven't reached him yet."

Lisa tugged at Derek's arm to test the restraint. "Do you want me to untie you? I don't see what it could hurt now."

Lisa tested the knot over his right wrist. After a few seconds of fumbling, the cord loosened and she pulled it away. "There, that should feel a little better." She dropped the wad of knotted fabric onto the bed.

Derek lifted his arm, flexed his fingers; then he tightened his hand into a fist. The flow of blood made his flesh tingle, his fingertips pulse and throb.

"Here's something that will make you feel a little better," Lisa said, turning away to dig inside her purse. She fumbled over car keys and wallet, groping toward bottom.

"There," she said, grinning. She handed Derek a picture post-card.

Superimposed on a stretch of golden sand and green sea was a banner emblazoned "Greetings from Acapulco."

Derek flipped over the idealized seascape to read the message inked on the back.

Hey amigos—

Thanks for putting me up. As you can see, I made it. Another week in the sun and I'll be brown as a nigger. Why don't you two catch a plane and come down?

Gino

"Looks like Gino did a little sightseeing, after all," Lisa said, grinning. "I told you not to worry." Then straight-faced: "You think we ought to go?"

The nurse glided back into the room through the half open door before Derek answered.

"His parents are outside now," Irene announced. She looked inquiringly toward Derek. "Do you want me to tell them it's okay to come in?"

"I'm going now," Lisa told the nurse. She kissed Derek quickly on the lips, then reached for her purse. "Is there anything you want from home before I go?"

"Yeah," Derek replied. "My mail. And something decent to read.

"And," he added after a second's pause, "my notebooks. One's on my desk. The others are on the wooden shelf right beside it. I want to see how much I've got to show for the past few months. Beside my scars."

Lisa passed in front of the nurse, then turned to wave before exiting through the door. Irene followed her into the hall to fetch Derek's parents. A moment later, two shadows appeared at the foot of his bed. Derek looked up after gazing a moment at his sheet to see his mother and father standing before him holding hands.

"Sit down," he said. "Mom, Dad. It's good to see you. Lisa said you came right out after my attack."

Derek noticed how much grayer and heavier his parents had grown in the two years since he'd left home. His father's chest and belly strained at his old checked sports jacket; his mother looked round and puffy in her cardigan, her hair permed into a tight gray helmet around her head. The strong new prescriptions in her glasses magnified her red-rimmed eyes. After shuffling toward his bedside, she touched Derek's shoulder with an almost weightless palm. His dad remained standing at the foot of the bed, looking for a chair.

"We came out the day after they found you," his mom said. "We're staying in a hotel a couple of blocks down the street.

Your apartment was so small . . ." Her voice trailed away as she studied Derek's unshaven face, gently massaging his shoulder.

"How are you feeling?" she asked. "We came every day. The doctors didn't know when you'd come to."

"Or if," his father added. "What were you doing walking through Chinatown by yourself at night, anyway?"

"It was during rush hour," Derek answered. "And Chinatown's not exactly a high crime area."

"Sure, I can see that. It's a regular Disneyland. But next time you decide to go for a little walk there," his father advised, "take a gun."

For the next few minutes, Derek described his cousin Gino's brief visit. He showed them the postcard, told how surprised he and Lisa were when Gino disappeared. His parents commiserated; all three ended by shaking their heads.

"One thing about Gino, though," his dad added, handing back the card. "At least he knows how to take care of himself. Your Aunt Betty never had to worry about that."

His father rose from the chair and moved closer to stand beside the bed. He shifted awkwardly next to his wife, one hand gently patting her shoulder.

"Your mother has a funny story to tell you," he said, slipping his arm around the invisible waist. "Go on, Honey, tell Derek about your ghost."

His mother started to open her mouth, but Derek saw that his father, the better storyteller, had already appropriated the tale and was about to tell it himself.

"Last Monday night," his dad began, "I was in the den reading, and all of a sudden I heard your mother calling your name out the back door. I thought for a minute she'd slipped a little something extra in her Sanka. I got up and followed her out to the patio, but when I got there, she was looking across the lawn at the garden like she'd just seen a ghost. Eyes big as saucers. Said she saw you standing at the back door on the patio, so she got up to let you in; when she did, you disappeared.

"Well, we looked around a little, but it was so cold we gave up after a minute or two and went back in. A few minutes later, your mom's at it again. This time she's looking out the door.

"'It's Derek,' she says. 'I saw him again in the garden.' So I look again but still don't see anything where she's pointing.

"We didn't think anymore about it. Then Lisa called on Tuesday to tell us what happened. When we got out here, we figured from what the doctors said that you must've been in the ambulance about the same time your mom saw her ghost. We're three hours later, don't forget. It must have been right after your attack.

"So don't ever tell me there's no such thing as a mother's intuition," his dad concluded with a knowing grin. "There's a lot of stuff we don't know about, but not knowing doesn't mean it's not so."

Derek smiled at the conclusion of his father's story.

"Well, look," said his dad, glancing down at his watch. "You're on the mend now. Your mother and I have just about had it, so why don't we go and let you get a little rest. We're just down the block at the Sheraton. We'll come by tomorrow morning first thing to see how you're doing. Give us a call if you need anything."

Derek thanked his parents for their visit and urged them to get back to their hotel to rest. After they left, he pushed the button beside his bed to summon a nurse. Instead of Irene, an attractive young woman appeared beside his bed.

"I thought Irene would come."

The nurse answered with a display of even white teeth.

Pretty. Derek admired the girl's smile and olive complexion. Her waist looked narrow and inviting between the swell of her breasts and the guitar-shaped curve of her hips.

"Irene's shift is over. I'm Carmen. Can I help you with anything?"

"You can start by getting me a razor and shaving me."

"Sorry," she answered, smiling. "I'm not allowed. Hospital policy."

"Close the door then. It'll only take a minute. Who's going to know?"

The dark plum lips parted a moment to laugh. The nurse looked at him, a hint of smile at the corners of her mouth. "Well . . . "

Derek looked in her eyes and smiled. "You could use a washcloth and a cup of hot water from the bathroom. Shut the door," he said, "and sit next to me here on the bed. I'd do it myself, but as you can see, these wires have me all tangled up."

Derek didn't wake again until the next night at seven. Opening his eyes, he noticed the small stack of mail beside him on the metal roll-away stand by the bed; on the lower shelf, the black spines of his writing notebooks. Lisa must have delivered both items while he slept.

He sat up, alert and hungry, then propped his back against two pillows to survey the room. A vase full of flowers had been placed on a shelf near his feet. The shades were drawn on the window, the television screen on the wall was black. He waited a minute to come fully awake, then pushed the button to summon Carmen, the nurse.

She appeared beside his bed a moment later. "What do you want?" she asked, one hand unconsciously rising to pat her hair.

"I want you to help me read my mail."

"What," she laughed, "you can't read it by yourself?"

"No, I want you to look at it with me."

She placed her fists on her hips and gave him an exasperated grin. "Why don't you ask that pretty girlfriend of yours to help you then?"

"Because I'm asking you. Here," he said, handing her the stack of unopened letters, "just sit down here beside me on the bed."

"What am I going to do with you? I've still got rounds."

"It'll only take a minute." Derek reached out to take Carmen's hand and pull her to him. She let herself be drawn to a spot next to him on the bed.

"I don't know why I listen to you," she said, smiling. "You're a real charmer. All right," she conceded with a sigh. "Let's take a look." Her buttocks pressed invitingly against Derek's thigh as they settled onto the mattress.

She tore open the first envelope, glanced up to show her exasperation, then pulled out the letter and began to read aloud.

"After carefully considering your manuscript, we have regretfully decided to . . . "

"A rejection slip," Derek said, interrupting. "Throw it away. Throw that next one away, too. I can see what it is already."

Carmen tossed the two letters aside, then picked up a thinner envelope with a university letterhead impressed on its corner. She opened it with her thumbnail, unfolded it, began to read.

"Dear Derek," her voice sang, giving the conventional salutation an extra note of meaning.

"I am pleased to inform you that we would like to publish your—as yet untitled—poetry manuscript in our new Discovery Series. This will no doubt come as a bit of a surprise, since our mutual friend Julian Ginotti made the selection from poems he'd found in journals and forwarded the manuscript to me without your knowledge. Nevertheless, I urge you to let us print the book. Its publication will provide you with a brilliant debut and inaugurate our series on a level we're unlikely to match again for many years. A contract is enclosed. Julian also informed me that you have quite a bit of unpublished material, much of it quite recent, which will also be needing a publisher before long—"

"Wait a minute," Derek interrupted, placing a hand on Carmen's wrist. "Who's it from?"

The nurse glanced at the bottom of the page.

"Mark Blotski, Editor, Discovery Series. Hey," she said, placing her hand on his, "does this mean you're going to publish a book?"

"Apparently. Let me see that for a minute."

Derek took the letter and examined the stationery: Harvard University Press. The letter was dated over a week ago. Then he read the handwritten postscript beneath the signature: in it, Mark Blotski apologized for his behavior at the reception and begged Derek's forgiveness.

"Are you going to make a lot of money now?"

"Not likely," Derek mumbled. "It's only poetry."

"Still," Carmen sighed, "your own book. You don't seem very excited about it."

Derek smiled. The girl's face was only a foot away from his. He reached toward her and brushed back a strand of hair with his bandaged right hand.

As his hand drew near, Carmen closed her eyes and held up her chin to receive the touch of his fingertips.

"I dreamed about you last night," she murmured, "just like you said I would. Want me to tell you about it?"

Derek lowered his hand to let it gently graze the girl's side. Then he reached up and cupped her breast, gently caressing it through its film of blouse and bra.

Carmen's face grew distant and dreamy. Derek slowly massaged her breast. As he did, Carmen placed her hand on his thigh and kneaded the flesh through its thin covering sheet.

"You want me to do something nice for you?" she asked, breathing more heavily and leaning toward his ear.

"Not yet," Derek replied. "Later. I want you to tell me something first."

Her hand was no longer coy about its destination. She stroked his stiffness skillfully through the thin fabric.

"These marks on my chest," he said. "What are they from? You must have seen them when you were checking me."

The girl waited an instant before replying, hand still in silent communion with his flesh, then reluctantly breathed an answer.

"They lost you twelve blocks from the hospital. You were DOA. They brought you back in E.R. a few minutes after you got here."

"That's what I thought." Derek released his grip on her breast. "Here's one more letter. Read it, then check outside to see if the coast is clear."

As if called from the verge of sleep, Carmen's eyes fluttered open. She smiled shyly, lifting her hand from his lap.

"You sure you want to do this now?" She lifted the final envelope off the pile.

Derek nodded. She discarded two pieces of junk mail, then tore open the last envelope and looked at its contents for an instant before passing the note to him.

"It's only one sentence," she said. "It doesn't make sense."

She handed him the torn envelope along with the letter, as if in verification of her statement.

Derek read the sentence scrawled across the center of the page above the name.

See you on the other side of the mirror

Carmen leaned over his shoulder to see the message again. "Who's Gretchen?"

Derek looked at the date on the envelope's Berkeley postmark. The letter must have been mailed a few hours before her death.

"I'm not sure," he replied, crumpling the fistful of paper. "A poet, I think."

"What?" the girl asked. "You don't know her and she writes you a funny letter like that?"

"Yeah," Derek answered. "I don't know why she wrote. Maybe I knew her in an earlier life."

Carmen smiled, nose wrinkling. "What's that thing about the mirror supposed to mean then?"

"Here," Derek smiled. "I'll show you."

He patted the girl's thigh, then reached to the metal stand beside the bed to pick up his shaving mirror.

Derek held the mirror at arm's length and gazed into its polished silver surface for an instant, then he angled it so he could see the girl's eyes and forehead.

"See," he said. "No reflection. It's like I'm not even here."

"You're holding it wrong," Carmen replied, reaching. "Here, let me have it a minute."

"No. I'm holding it fine. See? You need a soul to cast a reflection. I don't have one."

Carmen's eyes smiled at him in the little square in his hand. "Everybody has a soul," she said. "So how do you make it do that?"

"No, they don't," Derek said. He turned the mirror back now to his own face. "A soul is a little useless organ like an appendix. I've had mine out. The only way I can cast a reflection now is by taking a little bit of someone else's."

Derek put the mirror down and turned to face the girl again.

Leaning closer, he whispered into the hair above her ear.

"Take off your blouse. It's quiet outside. No one will miss you."

Carmen closed her eyes and sat frozen as Derek touched her hair. He breathed in its rich animal scent, then fingered the top button of her blouse while she sat, breath suspended, against him.

"It'll be just like your dream," he said, hand working down toward her waist. "There." He undid the last button and slipped his hand inside against her cool ribs.

As he leaned toward her, he could smell the perspiration beading the swell above her gently rising breasts.

Clarence Hall

ABOUT THE AUTHOR

Paul Lake is Professor of English and Creative Writing at Arkansas Tech University. A graduate of Towson State and Stanford, his poems and essays have appeared in such journals as *Paris Review*, *New Republic*, and *American Scholar*. His poetry book, *Another Kind of Travel*, received the Porter Fund Award for the best book by an Arkansas writer published in 1988. He lives in Arkansas outside of Little Rock with his wife, artist Tina Selanders Lake, and their two children.

THE TYPE IS PALATINO

BOOK DESIGN BY LYSA MCDOWELL

PRINTING BY DATA REPRODUCTIONS CORPORATION